"Steve Alten has again entered the genre of 'Man vs. Nature as personified by a large animal' and has excelled at it. The story is an excellent read, with plot and characterization exceeding all expectations. As to the biology behind the story, although sensational, it is more credible then many so-called non-fiction books about the loch."

—Robert McCord Ph.D., Chief Curator of Natural History, Curator of Paleontology, Mesa Southwest Museum

"*The Loch* is a fast-paced horror-thriller. Alten has done his research, but not enough to slow the action down. Don't have nightmares—Nessie much prefers eating Americans to us locals."

—Calum Macleod, Inverness Courier

"At last a novel about Loch Ness you can actually believe! Using commendable research and excellent writing skills Steve Alten has written a book that comes startlingly close to the truth. Reading *The Loch* I was shocked that his work of fiction tallied almost exactly with my research into the Loch Ness Monster and what it really is. Forget prehistoric monsters, here is a horror novel rooted firmly in biological possibility."

—Richard Freeman, Cryptozoologist, The Centre for Fortean Zoology

"*The Loch* is a compelling page-turner. I couldn't put it down. Steve Alten has once again proven to be a literary master of the abyss."

—Owl Goingback, Bram Stoker Award-Winning author of *CROTA*

"*The Loch* is at once spellbinding and enchanting, zoologically engaging and mysteriously alluring. Steve Alten has woven pieces of breaking new cryptozoology discoveries into the best work of fiction since *King Kong* and *The Lost World*! Take it along on your next expedition to Drumnadrochit or to that armchair where you read your favorites. This is the kind of mix of real facts about cryptids like Nessie and thought-provoking speculation that I love to see in the novels I read."

—Loren Coleman, world's leading cryptozoologist, and author of *The Field Guide to Lake Monsters, Sea Serpents and Other Mystery Denizens of the Deep*, and *Cryptozoology A to Z*

"A fast-paced thriller . . . Alten gives a scientific twist to an old, enduring myth . . . Michael Crichton meets Dan Brown beneath the waves of Loch Ness."

—Dennis Palumbo, author of *Writing from the Inside Out*

"Good old-fashioned storytelling, built on a bedrock of cutting-edge science. Steve Alten brings the famous legend to life with this deeply researched, inspired interfusion of Scottish history, marine biology, environmental science, and post-trauma psychology. An exhilarating, mind-expanding voyage into the deep."

—David Angsten, Author of *Day of the Dead*

"I couldn't put *The Loch* down. It grabbed me from the first page with its rich setting, all-too-human characters, and a storyline that moves along at a breakneck pace. I like learning something new and exciting when I read fiction and Alten delivers big time, packing lots of science and history into this terrific book. Nobody writes these tales better than Steve Alten, and *The Loch* is his best yet.

–April Christofferson, Author of *Buffalo Medicine* and *Patent to Kill*

"In his latest release, *The Loch*, Steve Alten again mixes history and mystery to dazzling effect, tackling not only the myth in which the Loch Ness Monster is shrouded but also the science that promises at last to shine a light on the creature's secret identity. Moreover, he has delivered to us a bona fide page-burner, perhaps the most engrossing beach read since . . . well, his own *MEG*."

–Ben Katner, *TV Guide* Online

"As a teenager growing up on the legend of Loch Ness and its mysterious inhabitant, I dreamed of going to Scotland to help hunt for the creature. Reading Steve Alten's *The Loch* makes me glad that I never got the chance. You don't want to meet Nessie except in the suspense-filled pages of this book!"

–Michael E. Newman, *Washington Examiner*

"Sometimes you devour a book and sometimes it devours you. *The Loch* voraciously shoved all of my other reading aside and became a fixture in my hands until the last page."

–Nick Nunziata, Cinematic Happenings Under Development (CHUD.com)

"With *The Loch* Steve Alten combines meticulous research with riveting storytelling to craft a new genre—the historical science fiction thriller."

–*Washington Daily News*

"Steve Alten remains at the top of his game. *The Loch* is a fascinating blend of science and history brimming with suspense and mystery. Psychologically deft characterization melds with thorough research and nearly perfect plot and pacing to create a thinking man's thriller a cut above standard beach reading. Ye'll no' want to miss this book . . . it's friggin' great!"

–Garrett Peck, reviewer, *Cemetery Dance*

"*The Loch* is both a gripping underwater thriller and a poignant family drama, sure to delight—and at times terrify—those who brave its depths."

–Andrew Furman, *Miami Herald* reviewer, author of *Alligators May Be Present*

HEY, SHARK BAIT!

Register on-line at www.MEGsite.com and you may be one of 50 characters immortalized in the upcoming Steve Alten thriller:

MEG 4: Hell's Aquarium

ALL PARTICIPANTS RECEIVE:

- Special "back-stage" access to MEG movie previews.
- Opportunities to win tickets to major concert events.
- Free monthly newsletters updating contests and events.
- Sneak peeks at future Steve Alten thrillers.
- Free images, bonus features . . . and much more!

To register go to www.MEGsite.com and click on the SHARK BAIT link.

All e-mail addresses remain confidential.

THE LOCH

STEVE ALTEN

TSUNAMI

Copyright ©2005 Steve Alten
ISBN: 0-9761659-2-9; 978-0-9761659-2-7

Library of Congress Control Number: 2006901111

Published in the United States by Tsunami Books, Mayfield Heights, Ohio

Cover Design by Erik Hollander: www.erikART.com
Map by Bill McDonald: AlienUFOart.com
Layout by Greenleaf Book Group

To personally contact the author or learn
more about his novels, click on
w w w . S t e v e A l t e n . c o m

The Loch is part of Adopt-An-Author,
a free nationwide program
for secondary school students and teachers.

For more information, click on
w w w . A d o p t A n A u t h o r . c o m

Printed in the United States of America

10 9 8 7 6 5 4 3 2   08 07 06

This novel is dedicated to Ed and Tonja Davidson,
for their support, guidance, and friendship . . .
and
to my
grandmother, Miriam Rosen,
my godparents, Edie and Is Axler,
and
to Ann Roof,
for always pushing me to write "that big one."

ACKNOWLEDGMENTS

It is with great pride and appreciation that I acknowledge those who contributed to the completion of *The LOCH*.

First and foremost, to my friend and partner, Ed Davidson, and the rest of the great people at Cooperative Entertainment Services and Tsunami Books: Leisa Coffman, Pat O'Brien, Neil Schneider, David Spero, Evan Davidson, Carbery O'Brien, Mike Houston, Chris Pakis, and Marilyn Miller. Heartfelt thanks to my terrific publicist, Lissy Peace at Blanco & Peace and to Clint Greenleaf and his staff at Greenleaf Book Group, as well as Joel McKuin of Colden, McKuin & Frankel.

My sincerest appreciation to Hollywood producer David Foster at David Foster Productions and his associate, Ryan Heppe, for taking on the dramatic rights of *The Loch,* along with producer/screenwriter Shane Salerno. I am honored.

With pride, I acknowledge the invaluable contribution of "Nessie Hunter" Bill McDonald of Argonaut-Greywolf.com for sharing his insight regarding the "real" inhabitants of Loch Ness.

Thanks also to Calum Forrest, Bill Raby, and story board artist Rikin Parekh for their contributions, as well as George Noory at Coast to Coast Radio, Ken Ashe and Kreg Lauterbach at Matchframe Productions, and Brandon Kihl at Kihl Studios.

Special thanks to Leisa Coffman for her talent and expertise in updating the **www.SteveAlten.com** website as well as all her work in the *Adopt-An-Author* program, and to Erik Hollander, for his tremendous cover design and graphic artistry. Thanks also to Michelle Pryzstas at Southeastern Business Solutions, my computer wizard and friend.

Last, to my wife and partner, Kim, for all her support, to my parents for always being there, and to my readers: Thank you for your correspondence and contributions. Your comments are always a welcome treat, your input means so much, and you remain this author's greatest asset.

—Steve Alten, Ed.D.

To personally contact the author or learn more about his novels,
Click on www.SteveAlten.com
The LOCH is part of ADOPT-AN-AUTHOR,
a free nationwide program
for Secondary School students and teachers.
For more information, click on www.AdoptAnAuthor.com

Loch Ness holds secrets that date back to A.D. 565 and the time of St. Columba. But does a creature really inhabit its depths? After hundreds of years, thousands of reported sightings, and dozens of scientific expeditions, we have theories, but still no definite answer.

When I began the task of researching this novel, I found it imperative to separate the legend of the Loch Ness monster from the body of real science. Then, after concluding the first edit on the manuscript, I was confronted with a new theory from a cryptozoologist and fan of my MEG series who had spent years investigating the Loch. His research, combined with rumors surrounding a recent discovery, were not only credible, but go far in identifying the species of Loch Ness's famous inhabitant. His evidence also helped to explain the lack of photographic proof. Convinced that these theories were both cutting edge and credible, I re-edited my manuscript to include this important new information.

The Loch remains fiction, however, the science behind the story is quite real.

—Steve Alten, Ed.D.

To receive updates regarding ongoing developments at Loch Ness, go to www.TheLoch.com.

Nature is often obscure or impenetrable,
but she is not, like Man, deceitful.
—C.G. Jung

Shadows walk.
What is . . . isn't.
What isn't . . . may be.
—Gay Malin

It was July 13, the summer of 2000. My husband
and I were on holiday in Scotland, on the shores
of Loch Ness. We'd stopped to take a picture of
the lake, just to have something to show my friends.
I was using my little Kodak with a 23mm lens.
The shot I snapped was taken near Boleskin House,
by one of the deepest parts of the lake. The Loch
was glassy calm, and there were no boats around.
When we saw the developed photo, well . . .
we were shocked.
—Melissa Bavister, Tourist

The object is definitely on the film,
it's not a mark on the negative.
—Alistair Bowie, Inverness Photo Lab Technician

Moray Firth
Scottish Highlands
25 September 1330

THE DEEP BLUE WATERS of the Moray Firth crashed violently against the jagged shoreline below. William Calder, second Thane of Cawdor, stood on an outcropping of rock just beyond the point where the boiling North Sea met the mouth of the River Ness. Looking to the south, he could just make out the single-sheeted Spanish galley. The tall ship had been in port since dawn, its crew exchanging silver pieces for wool and cod.

Calder's daughter, Helen, joined him on the lookout. "Ye're needed. A wounded man's come ashore, a soldier. He's demandin' tae see a Templar."

*   *   *

The young man had been left on a grassy knoll. His face was pale and unshaven, his blue-gray eyes glassy with fever. His battle dress, composed of chain mail, was stained crimson along the left quadrant of his stomach. A long sword lay by his side, its blade smeared in blood. A silver casket, the size of a small melon, hung from his unshaven neck by a gold chain.

William Calder stood over the soldier, joined by two more of his clan. "Who are ye, laddie?"

"I need tae speak wi' a Templar."

"Ye'll speak tae no one 'til ye've dealt wi' me. In whit battle did ye receive yer wounds?"

"Tebas de Ardales."

"An' who did ye fight under?"

"Sir James the Good."

"The Black Douglas?" Calder turned to his men. "Fetch a physician and be quick. Tell him we may need a chirurgeon as well."

"Yes, m'lord." The two men hurried off.

"Why dae ye seek the Templar, laddie?"

The soldier forced his eyes open against the fever. "Only the Templar can be trusted tae guard my keep."

"Is that so?" Calder bent to remove the prized object resting upon the man's chest piece—the soldier's sword raising quickly to kiss Calder's throat. "I'm sorry, m'lord, but I wis instructed tae relinquish this only tae a Templar."

*   *   *

The sun was late in the summer sky by the time Thomas MacDonald arrived at William Calder's home. More Viking than Celt, the burly elder possessed thick auburn-red hair and a matted matching beard. Draped across his broad shoulders was a white tunic, emblazoned with four scarlet equilateral triangles, their points meeting in the center to form a cross.

MacDonald entered without knocking. "A'right, William Calder, why have ye summoned me frae Morayshire?"

Calder pointed to the young soldier, whose wounded left side was being bandaged by a physician. "The laddie claims tae have fought under the Black Douglas. Says he traveled frae Spain tae seek the Templar."

MacDonald approached. "I'm o' the Order, laddie. Who are ye?"

"Adam Wallace. My faither wis Sir Richard Wallace o' Riccarton."

Both men's eyebrows raised. "Ye're kin tae Sir William?"

"He wis my first cousin, my faither his uncle. I still carry William's sword in battle."

Calder examined the offered blade, sixty-six inches from point to pommel. "I dinnae see any markings on the hilt that designate this tae be Sir William's."

MacDonald nodded. "William aye kept it clean. A fine sword it is, fit for an Archangel tae wield, yet light in his terrible hand." He pointed to the silver casket. "Tell me how ye came by this?"

"I served under Sir William Keith for jist under a year, ever since the Bruce fell tae leprosy. Oor king had aye wished tae take part in the crusades against the Saracens, but kent he wis dyin'. He asked for the contents o' this casket tae be buried in the Church o' the Holy Sepulchre in Jerusalem. The Black Douglas wis tae lead the mission, joined by Sir William Sinclair, Sir Keith, an' mysel'."

"Go on."

"When we arrived in Spain, Alfonso XI of Castile and Leon . . . he convinced Sir James tae join his vanguard against Osmyn, the Moorish governor of Grenada. The Black Douglas agreed, an' we set off on the twenty-fifth of March, that is, all but Sir William Keith, who had injured his arm frae a fa' an' couldnae fight."

"Whit happened?"

"The battle went badly. The Black Douglas wis deceived by a feint, an' the Moors' cavalry broke through oor ranks. It happened so fast, bodies an' blood everywhere, that I could scarcely react. I saw Sir William Sinclair fa' doon, followed by the Black Douglas. An' then a sword caught my flank, an' I fell.

"When next I awoke, it wis dark. My nostrils were fu' o' blood, an' my left side burned. It wis a' I could dae tae regain my feet beneath the bodies. I wanted tae flee, but first I had tae find the Black Douglas. By the half-moon's light, I searched one corpse tae the next 'till I located his body, guardin' the Bruce's casket even in death. By then, the dawn had arrived an' Sir Keith wi' it. He dressed my wounds, but fearful o' another Islamic attack, suggested we separate. I wis tae return tae Scotland, then make my way to Threave Castle, stronghold o' Archibald the Grim, Sir James's son. Sir Keith wis tae return tae the Lowlands an' Melrose Abbey wi' the casket."

"But yer plans changed, I see."

"Aye. On the eve o' oor sail, Sir Keith took sick wi' dropsy. Fearful o' his condition, I decided it best if the casket remained wi' me and too' it frae him."

Calder pulled MacDonald aside. "Do ye believe him?"

"Aye."

"But why does he seek a Templar?"

"Bruce wis a Mason, born intae the Order. The contents o' the casket belong tae Scotland. It represents nothin' less than oor freedom."

MacDonald turned back toward Adam. "Ye were right tae come here, laddie. Whit lies within that silver container's far ower important tae leave in any abbey. There's a cave, a day's walk frae here, known only tae the Templar. If Cooncil agrees, then I'll take the casket there and—"

"No ye willnae!" Adam interrupted. "The coven's between the Bruce an' the Wallace Clan. Direct me, an' I shall take it there mysel'."

"Dinnae be a fool, ye dinnae ken whit ye're sayin'. The cave I've in mind leads tae Hell, guarded by the De'il's ain minions."

"I'm no' feart."

"Aye, but ye will be, Adam Wallace. An' it's a fear ye'll carry wi' ye 'til the end o' yer days."

CHAPTER 1

Sargasso Sea, Atlantic Ocean
887 miles due east of Miami Beach

THE SARGASSO SEA is a two-million-square-mile expanse of warm water, adrift in the middle of the Atlantic Ocean. An oasis of calm that borders no coastline, the sea is littered with sargassum, a thick seaweed that once fooled Christopher Columbus into believing he was close to land.

The Sargasso is constantly moving, its location determined by the North Equatorial and Gulf Stream currents, as well as those of the Antilles, Canary, and Caribbean. These interlocking forces stabilize the sea like the eye of a great hurricane, while causing its waters to rotate clockwise. As a result, things that enter the Sargasso are gradually drawn toward its center like a giant shower drain, where they eventually sink to the bottom, or, in the case of oil, form thick tar balls and float. There is a great deal of oil in the Sargasso, and with each new spill the problem grows worse, affecting all the sea creatures that inhabit the region.

The Sargasso marks the beginning of my tale and its end, and perhaps that is fitting, for all things birthed in this mysterious body of water eventually return here to die, or so I have learned.

If each of us has his or her own Sargasso, then mine was the Highlands of Scotland. I was born in the village of Drumnadrochit, seven months and twenty-five years ago, give or take a few days. My mother, Andrea, was American, a quiet soul who came to the United Kingdom on holiday and stayed nine years in a bad marriage. My father, Angus Wallace, the cause of its termination, was a brute of a man, possessing jet-black hair and the piercing blue eyes of the Gael, the wile of a Scot, and the temperament of a Viking. An only child, I took my father's looks and, thankfully, my mother's disposition.

Angus's claim to fame was that his paternal ancestors were descendants of the great William Wallace himself, a name I doubt most non-Britons would have recognized until Mel Gibson portrayed him in the movie, *Braveheart*. As a child, I often asked Angus to prove we were kin of the great Sir William Wallace, but he'd merely tap his chest and say, "Listen, runt, some things ye jist feel. When ye become a real man, ye'll ken whit I mean."

I grew to calling my father Angus and he called me his "runt" and neither was meant as an endearing term. Born with a mild case of hypotonia, my muscles were too weak to allow for normal development, and it would be two years (to my father's embarrassment) before I had the strength to walk. By the time I was five I could run like a deer, but being smaller than my burly, big-boned Highland peers, I was always picked on. Weekly contests between hamlets on the football pitch (rugby field) were nightmares. Being fleet of foot meant I had to carry the ball, and I'd often find myself in a scrum beneath boys twice my size. While I lay bleeding and broken on the battlefield, my inebriated father would prance about the sidelines, howling with the rest of his drunken cronies, wondering why the gods had cursed him with such a runt for a son.

According to the child-rearing philosophy of Angus Wallace, tough love was always best in raising a boy. Life was hard, and so childhood had to be hard, or the seedling would rot before it grew. It was the way Angus's father had raised him, and his father's father before that. And if the seedling was a runt, then the soil had to be tilled twice as hard.

But the line between tough love and abuse is often blurred by alcohol, and it was when Angus was inebriated that I feared him most.

His final lesson of my childhood left a lasting impression.

It happened a week before my ninth birthday. Angus, sporting a whisky buzz, led me to the banks of Aldourie Castle, a three-century-old chateau that loomed over the misty black waters of Loch Ness.

"Now pay attention, runt, for it's time I telt ye o' the Wallace curse. My faither, yer grandfaither, Logan Wallace, he died in these very waters when I wis aboot yer age. An awfy gale hit the Glen, an' his boat flipped. Everyone says he drooned, but I ken better, see. 'Twis the monster that got him, an' ye best be warned, for—"

"Monster? Are ye talkin' aboot Nessie?" I asked, pie-eyed.

"Nessie? Nessie's folklore. I'm speakin' o' a curse wrought by nature, a curse that's haunted the Wallace men since the passin' o' Robert the Bruce."

"I dinnae understand."

Growing angry, he dragged me awkwardly to the edge of Aldourie Pier. "Look doon, laddie. Look doon intae the Loch an' tell me whit ye see?"

I leaned out carefully over the edge, my heart pattering in my bony chest. "I dinnae see anythin', the water's too black."

"Aye, but if yer eyes could penetrate the depths, ye'd see intae the dragon's lair. The de'il lurks doon there, but it can sense oor presence, it can smell the fear in oor blood. By day the Loch's ours, for the beast prefers the depths, but God help ye at night when she rises tae feed."

"If the monster's real, then I'll rig a lure an' bring her up."

"Is that so? An' who be ye? Wiser men have tried an' failed, an' looked foolish in their efforts, whilst a bigger price wis paid by those drowned who ventured out oot night."

"Ye're jist tryin' tae scare me. I'm no' feart o' a myth."

"Tough words. Very well, runt, show me how brave ye are. Dive in. Go on, laddie, go for a swim and let her get a good whiff o' ye."

He pushed me toward the edge and I gagged at his breath, but held tight to his belt buckle.

"Jist as I thought."

Frightened, I pried myself loose and ran from the pier, the tears streaming down my cheeks.

"Ye think I'm hard on ye, laddie? Well, life's hard, an' I'm nothin' compared tae that monster. Ye best pay attention, for the curse skips every other generation, which means ye're marked. That dragon lurks in the shadow o' yer soul, and one day ye'll cross paths. Then what will ye dae? Will ye stand and fight like a warrior, like brave Sir William an' his kin, or will ye cower an' run, lettin' the dragon haunt ye for the rest o' yer days?"

*   *   *

Leaning out over the starboard rail, I searched for my reflection in the Sargasso's glassy surface.

Seventeen years had passed since my father's "dragon" lecture, seventeen long years since my mother had divorced him and moved us to New York. In that time I had lost my accent and learned that my father was right, that I was indeed haunted by a dragon, only his name was Angus Wallace.

Arriving in a foreign land is never easy for a boy, and the physical and psychological baggage I carried from my childhood left me fodder for the bullies of my new school. At least in Drumnadrochit I had allies like my pal, True MacDonald, but here I was all alone, a fish out of water, and there were many a dark day that I seriously considered ending my life.

And then I met Mr. Tkalec.

Joe Tkalec was our middle school's science teacher, a kind Croatian man with rectangular glasses, a quick wit, and a love for poetry. Seeing that the "Scottish weirdo" was being picked on unmercifully, Mr. Tkalec took me under his wing, allowing me special classroom privileges like caring for his lab animals, small deeds that helped nurture my self-image. After school, I'd ride my bike over to Mr. Tkalec's home, which contained a vast collection of books.

"Zachary, the human mind is the instrument that determines how far we'll go in life. There's only one way to develop the mind and that's to read. My library's yours, select any book and take it home, but return only after you've finished it."

The first volume I chose was the oldest book in his collection, *The Origins of an Evolutionist*, my eyes drawn by the author's name, Alfred Russel Wallace.

Born in 1823, Alfred Wallace was a brilliant British evolutionist, geographer, anthropologist, and theorist, often referred to as Charles Darwin's right-hand man, though their ideas were not always in step. In his biography, Alfred mentioned that he too was a direct descendant of William Wallace, making us kin, and that he also suffered childhood scars brought about by an overbearing father.

The thought of being related to Alfred Wallace instantly changed the way I perceived myself, and his words regarding adaptation and survival put wind in my fallen sails.

"... we have here an acting cause to account for that balance so often observed in Nature—a deficiency in one set of organs always being compensated by an increased development of some others ..."

My own obstinate father, a man who had never finished grammar school, had labeled me weak, his incessant badgering (I need tae make ye a man, Zachary) fostering a negative self-image. Yet here was my great-uncle Alfred, a brilliant man of science, telling me that if my physique made me vulnerable, then another attribute could be trained to compensate.

That attribute would be my intellect.

My appetite for academics and the sciences became voracious. Within months I established myself as the top student in my class, by the end of the school year, I was offered the chance to skip the next grade. Mr. Tkalec continued feeding me information, while his roommate, a retired semipro football player named Troy, taught me to hone my body into something more formidable to my growing list of oppressors.

For the first time in my life, I felt a sense of pride. At Troy's urging, I tried out for freshman football. Aided by my tutor's coaching and a talent for eluding defenders (acquired, no doubt, on the pitch back in Drumnadrochit) I rose quickly through the ranks, and by the end of my sophomore year, I found myself the starting tailback for our varsity football team.

Born under the shadow of a Neanderthal, I had evolved into *Homo sapiens*, and I refused to look back.

Mr. Tkalec remained my mentor until I graduated, helping me secure an academic scholarship at Princeton. Respecting my privacy, he seldom broached subjects concerning my father, though he once told me that Angus's dragon story was simply a metaphor for the challenges that each of us must face in life. "Let your anger go, Zack, you're not hurting anyone but yourself."

Gradually I did release my contempt for Angus, but unbeknownst to both Mr. Tkalec and myself, there was still a part of my childhood that remained buried in the shadows of my soul, something my subconscious mind refused to acknowledge.

Angus had labeled it a dragon.

If so, the Sargasso was about to set it free.

*   *   *

The afternoon haze seemed endless, the air lifeless, the Sargasso as calm as the Dead Sea. It was my third day aboard the *Manhattanville*, a 162-foot research vessel designed for deep-sea diving operations. The forward half of the boat, four decks high, held working laboratories and accommodations for a dozen crew members, six technicians, and twenty-four scientists. The aft deck, flat and open, was equipped with a twenty-one-ton A-frame PVS crane system, capable of launching and retrieving the boat's small fleet of remotely operated vehicles (ROVs) and its primary piece of exploration equipment, the *Massett-6*, a vessel designed specifically for bathymetric and bottom profiling.

It was aboard the *Massett-6* in this dreadful sea that I hoped to set my own reputation beside that of my great Uncle Alfred.

Our three-day voyage had delivered us to the approximate center of the Sargasso. Clumps of golden brown seaweed mixed with black tar balls washed gently against our boat, staining its gleaming white hull a chewing tobacco brown as we waited for sunset, our first scheduled dive.

Were there dragons waiting for me in the depths? Ancient mariners once swore as much. The Sargasso was considered treacherous, filled with sea serpents and killer weeds that could entwine a ship's keel and drag it under. Superstition? No doubt, but as in all legend, there runs a vein of truth. Embellishments of eye-witnessed accounts become lore over time, and the myth surrounding the Sargasso was no different.

The real danger lies in the sea's unusual weather. The area is almost devoid of wind, and many a sailor who once entered these waters in tall sailing ships never found their way out.

As our vessel was steel, powered by twin diesel engines and a 465-horsepower bow thruster, I had little reason to worry.

Ah, how the seeds of cockiness blossom when soiled in ignorance.

While fate's clouds gathered ominously on my horizon, all my metallic-blue eyes perceived were fair skies. Still young at twenty-five, I had already earned a bachelor's and master's degree from Princeton and a doctorate from the University of California at San Deigo, and three of my papers on cetacean communication had recently been published in *Nature* and *Science*. I had been invited to sit on the boards of several prominent oceanographic councils, and, while teaching at Florida Atlantic University, I had invented an underwater acoustics device—a device responsible for this very voyage of discovery, accompanied by a film crew shooting a documentary sponsored by none other than *National Geographic Explorer*.

By society's definition, I was a success, always planning my work, working my plan, my career the only life I ever wanted. Was I happy? Admittedly, my emotional barometer may have been a bit off-kilter. I was pursuing my dreams, and that made me happy, yet it always seemed like there was a dark cloud hanging over head. My fiancée, Lisa, a "sunny" undergrad at FAU, claimed I had a "restless soul," attributing my demeanor to being too tightly wound.

"Loosen up, Zack. You think way too much, it's why you get so many migraines. Cut loose once in a while, get high on life instead of always analyzing it. All this left-brain thinking is a turnoff."

I tried "turning off," but found myself too much of a control freak to let myself go.

One person whose left brain had stopped functioning long ago was David James Caldwell II. As I quickly learned, the head of FAU's oceanography department was a self-promoting hack who had maneuvered his way into a position of tenure based solely on his ability to market the achievements of his staff. Six years my superior, with four years less schooling, David nevertheless presented himself to our sponsors as if he were my mentor, me, *his* protégé. "Gentlemen, members of the board, with my help, Zachary Wallace could become this generation's Jacques Cousteau."

David had arranged our journey, but it was my invention that made it all possible—a cephalopod lure, designed to attract the ocean's most elusive predator, *Architeuthis dux,* the giant squid.

Our first dive was scheduled for nine o'clock that night, still a good three hours away. The sun was just beginning to set as I stood alone in the bow, staring at endless sea, when my solitude was shattered by David, Cody Saults, our documentary's director, his cameraman and wife, and the team's sound person.

"There's my boy," David announced. "Hey, Zack, we've been looking all over the ship for you. Since we still have light, Cody and I thought we'd get some of the background stuff out of the way. Okay by you?"

Cody and I? Now he was executive producer?

"Whatever you'd like, Mr. Saults."

The cameraman, a good-natured soul named Hank Griffeth, set up his tripod while his wife, Cindy, miked me for sound. Cindy wore a leopard bikini that accentuated her cleavage, and it was all I could do to keep from sneaking a peek.

Just using the right side of my brain, Lisa . . .

Cody chirped on endlessly, forcing me to refocus. ". . . anyway, I'll ask you and David a few questions off-camera. Back in the studio, our editors will dub in Patrick Stewart's voice over mine. Got it?"

"I like Patrick Stewart. Will I get to meet him?"

"No, now pay attention. Viewers want to know what makes young Einsteins like you and David tick. So when I ask you about—"

"Please don't call me that."

Cody smiled his Hollywood grin. "Listen kid, humble's great, but you and Dr. Caldwell are the reason we're floating in this festering, godforsaken swamp. So if I tell you you're a young Einstein, you're a young Einstein, got it?"

David, a man sporting an IQ seventy points lower than the deceased Princeton professor, slapped me playfully across the shoulder blades. "Just roll with it, kid."

"We're ready here," Hank announced, looking through his rubber eyepiece. "You've got about fifteen minutes of good light left."

"Okay boys, keep looking out to sea, nice and casual . . . and we're rolling. So Zack, let's start with you. Tell us what led you to invent this acoustic thingamajiggy."

I focused on the horizon as instructed, the sun splashing gold on my tanned complexion. "Well, I've spent most of the last two years studying cetacean echolocation. Echolocation is created by an acoustic organ, unique in dolphins and whales, that provides them with an ultrasonic vision of their environment. For example, when a sperm whale clicks, or echolocates, the sound waves bounce off objects, sending back audio frequency pictures of the mammal's surroundings."

"Like sonar?"

"Yes, only far more advanced. For instance, when a dolphin echolocates a shark, it not only sees its environment, but it can actually peer into the shark's belly to determine if it's hungry. Sort of like having a built-in ultrasound. These clicks also function as a form of communication among other members of the cetacean species, who can tap into the audio transmission spectrum, using it as a form of language.

"Using underwater microphones, I've been able to create a library of echolocation clicks. By chance, I discovered that certain sperm whale recordings, taken during deep hunting dives, stimulated our resident squid population to feed."

"That's right," David blurted out, interrupting me. "Squid, intelligent creatures in their own right, often feed on the scraps left behind by sperm whales. By using the sperm whales' feeding frequency, we were able to entice squid to the microphone, creating, in essence, a cephalopod lure."

"Amazing," Cody replied. "But fellows, gaining the attention of a four-foot squid is one thing, how do you think this device will work in attracting a giant squid? I mean, you're talking about a deep-sea creature, sixty feet in length, that's never been seen alive."

"They're still cephalopods," David answered, intent on taking over the interview. "While it's true we've never seen a living specimen, we know from carcasses that have washed ashore and by remains found in the bellies of sperm whales that the animals' anatomies are similar to those of their smaller cousins."

"Fantastic. David, why don't you give us a quick rundown of this first dive."

I held my tongue, my wounded ego seething.

"Our cephalopod lure's been attached to the retractable arm of the submersible. Our goal is to descend to thirty-three hundred feet, entice a giant squid up from the abyss, then capture it on film. Because *Architeuthis* prefers the very deep waters, deeper than our submersible can go, we're waiting until dark to begin our expedition, hoping the creatures will ascend with nightfall, following the food chain's nocturnal migration into the shallows."

"Explain that last bit. What do you mean by nocturnal migration?"

"Why don't I let Dr. Wallace take over," David offered, bailing out before he had to tax his left brain.

I inhaled a few temper-reducing breaths. "Giant squids inhabit an area known as the mid-water realm, by definition, the largest continuous living space on Earth. While photosynthesis initiates food chains among the surface layers of the ocean, in the mid-water realm, the primary source of nutrients come from phytoplankton, microscopic plants. Mid-water creatures live in absolute darkness, but once the sun sets, they rise en masse to graze on the phytoplankton, a nightly event that's been described as the largest single migration of living organisms on the planet."

"Great stuff, great stuff. Hank, how's the light?"

"Fifteen minutes, give or take."

"Let's keep moving, getting more into the personal. Zack, tell us about yourself. Dr. Caldwell tells me you're an American citizen, originally from Scotland."

"Yes. I grew up in the Scottish Highlands, in a small village called Drumnadrochit."

"That's at the head of Urquhart Bay, on Loch Ness," David chimed in. "Really?"

"My mother's American," I said, the red flags waving in my brain. "My parents met while she was on holiday. We moved to New York when I was nine."

With a brazen leer, David leaned forward, mimicking a Scots accent, "Dr. Wallace is neglecting the time he spent as a wee laddie, hangin' oot wi' visitin' teams o' Nessie hunters, aren't ye, Dr. Wallace?"

I shot David a look that would boil flesh.

The director naturally jumped on his lead. "So it was actually the legend of the Loch Ness Monster that stoked your love of science. Fascinating."

And there it was, the dreaded "M" word. Loch Ness was synonymous with Monster, and Monster meant Nessie, a cryptozoologist's dream, a marine biologist's nightmare. Nessie was "fringe" science, an industry of folklore, created by tourism and fast-talkers like my father.

Being associated with Nessie had destroyed many a scientist's career, most notably Dr. Denys Tucker, of the British Museum of Natural History. Dr. Tucker had held his post for eleven years, and, at one time, had been considered the foremost authority on eels . . . until he hinted to the press that he was interested in launching an investigation into the Loch Ness Monster.

A short time later he was dismissed, his career as a scientist all but over.

Being linked to Loch Ness on a *National Geographic* special could destroy my reputation as a serious scientist, but it was already too late.

David had led me to the dogshit, and, as my mother would say, I had "stepped in it." Now the goal was to keep from dragging it all over the carpet.

"Let me be clear here," I proclaimed, my booming voice threatening Hank's wife's microphone, "I was never actually one of those 'Nessie' hunters."

"Ah, but you've always had an interest in Loch Ness, haven't you?" David crowed, still pushing the angle.

He was like a horny high school boy, refusing to give up after his date said she wasn't in the mood. I turned to face him, catching the full rays of the setting sun square in my eyes—a fatal mistake for a migraine sufferer.

"Loch Ness is a unique place, Dr. Caldwell," I retorted, "but not everyone who visits comes looking for monsters. As a boy, I met many serious environmentalists who were there strictly to investigate the Loch's algae content, or its peat, or its incredible depths. They were naturalists, like my great ancestor, Alfred Russel Wallace. You see, despite all this nonsense about legendary water beasts, the Loch remains a magnificent body of water, unique in its—"

"But most of these teams came searching for Nessie, am I right?"

I glanced in the direction of David's boyish face, with its bleached-blond mustache and matching Moe Howard bangs, but all I could see were spots, purple demons that blinded my vision.

Migraine . . .

My skin tingled at the thought. I knew I needed to pop a *Zomig* before the brain storm moved into its more painful stages, yet on I babbled, trying desperately to salvage the interview and possibly, my career.

"Well, David, it's not like you can escape it. They've turned Nessie into an industry over there, haven't they?"

"And have you ever spotted the monster?"

I wanted to choke him right on-camera. I wanted to rip the shell necklace from his paisley Hawaiian shirt and crush his puny neck in my bare hands, but my left brain, stubborn as always, refused to relinquish control. "Excuse me, Dr. Caldwell, I thought we were here to discuss giant squids?"

David pushed on. "Stay with me, kid, I'm going somewhere with this. Have you ever spotted the monster?"

I forced a laugh, my right eye beginning to throb. "Look, I don't know about you, *Dr. Caldwell*, but I'm a marine biologist. We're supposed to leave the myth chasing to the crypto guys."

"Ah, but you see, that's exactly my point. It wasn't long ago that these giant squids were considered more myth than science. The legend of the Scylla in the *Odyssey*, the monster in Tennyson's poem, 'The Kraken.' As a young boy growing up so close to Loch Ness, surely you must have been influenced by the greatest legend of them all?"

Cody Saults was loving it, while tropical storm David, located in the latitude of my right eye, was increasing into a hurricane.

". . . maybe hunting for Nessie as a child became the foundation for your research into locating the elusive giant squid. I'm not trying to put words in your mouth, but—"

"Butts are for crapping, Dr. Caldwell, and so's everything that follows! Nessie's crap, too. It's nothing but a nonsensical legend embellished to increase Highland tourism. I'm not a travel agent, I'm a scientist in search of a real sea creature, not some Scottish fabrication. Now if you two will excuse me, I need to use the head."

Without waiting, I pushed past David and the director and entered the ship's infrastructure, in desperate search of the nearest bathroom. The purple spots were gone, the eye pain already intensifying. The next phase would be vomiting—brain-rattling, vein-popping vomiting. This would be followed by weakness and pain and more vomiting, and eventually, if I didn't put a bullet through my skull, I'd mercifully pass out.

It was misery, which is why, like all migraine sufferers, I tried to avoid things that set me off: direct lighting, excessive caffeine, and the stress that, to me, revolved around the taboo subject of my childhood.

My stomach was already gurgling, the pain in my eye crippling as I hurried past lab doors and staterooms. Ducking inside the nearest bathroom, I locked the door, knelt by the toilet, shoved a sacrificial digit down my throat, and puked.

The intestinal tremor released my lunch, threatening to implode the blood vessels leading to my brain. It continued on, until my stomach was empty, my will to live sapped.

For several moments I remained there, my head balanced on the cool, bacteria-laced rim of the toilet.

Maybe Lisa was right. Maybe I did need to loosen up.

　　　　　*　　　　　　　　*　　　　　　　　*

It was dark by the time I emerged on deck, my long brown hair matted to my forehead, my blue eyes glassy and bloodshot. The migraine had left me weak and shaky, and I'd have preferred to remain in bed, but it was nearly time to descend, and I knew David would grab my spot aboard the sub in a New York minute if I waited any longer.

A blood-red patch of light revealed all that was left of the western horizon, the sweltering heat of day yielding to the coolness of night. Inhaling several deep lungfuls of fresh air, I made my way aft to the stern, now a hub of activity. The ship's lights were on, creating a theater by which four technicians and a half dozen scientists completed their final check on the *Massett-6*, the twenty-seven-foot-long submersible now suspended four feet off the deck like a giant alien insect.

Able to explore depths down to thirty-five hundred feet, the *Massett-6* was a three-man deep-sea sub that consisted of an acrylic glasslike observation bubble, mounted to a rectangular-shaped aluminum chamber, its walls five inches thick. Running beneath the submersible was an exterior platform and skid that supported flotation tanks, hoses, recording devices, gas cylinders containing oxygen and air, primary and secondary batteries, a series of collection baskets, arc lights, a hydraulic manipulator arm, and nine 100-pound thrusters.

I caught David leaning against the sub, hastily pulling on a blue and gold jumpsuit—*my* jumpsuit—when he saw me approach. "Zack? Where've you been? We, uh, we didn't think you were going to make it."

"Nice try. Now take off my jumpsuit, I'm fine."

"You look pale."

"I said I'm fine, no thanks to you. What was all that horseshit about Loch Ness? You trying to discredit me on national TV?"

"Of course not. We're a team, remember? I just thought it made for a great angle. *Discovery Channel* loves that mysterious stuff, we can pitch them next."

"Forget it. I've worked way too hard to destroy my reputation with this nonsense. Now, for the last time, get your scrawny butt outta my jumpsuit."

"We're ready here," announced Ace Futrell, our mission coordinator. "Mr. Wallace, if you'd care to grace us with your presence."

The cameras rolled. David, back to playing the dutiful mentor, animated a few last-minute instructions to me as I slid my feet into the jumpsuit. "Remember, kid, this is our big chance, it's our show. Work the audience. Relate to them. Get 'em on your side."

"Chill out, David. This isn't an infomercial."

The hatch of the *Massett-6* was located beneath the submersible's aft observation compartment behind the main battery assembly. Kneeling below the sub, I poked my head and shoulders into the opening and climbed up.

The vehicle's interior was a cross between a helicopter cockpit and an FBI surveillance van. The claustrophobic aluminum chamber was crammed with video monitors, life-support equipment, carbon dioxide scrubbers, and gas analyzers, along with myriad pipes and pressurized hoses. Conversely, the forward compartment was a two-seat acrylic bubble that offered panoramic views of the sub's surroundings.

Taking my assigned place up front in the copilot's seat, I tightened the shoulder harness, then inspected the controls of my sonic lure, which had been jury-rigged to the console on my right. Everything seemed stat. Looking above my head out of the bubble, I watched as a technician double-checked the lure's underwater speaker, now attached to the vessel's exterior tow hook.

Donald Lacombe, the sub's pilot, joined me in the cockpit, wasting little time in establishing who was boss. "All right, boy genius, here's the drill. Keep your keister in your seat and don't touch anything without being told. *Capische?*"

"Aye, aye, sir."

"And nobody likes a smart-ass. You're in my vessel now, blah blah blah blah blah." Tuning him out, I turned to watch Hank Griffeth as he climbed awkwardly into the aft compartment. A crewman handed him up his camera, then sealed the rear hatch.

The radio squawked. "Control to *Six*, prepare to launch."

Lacombe spoke into his headset, clearly in his element. "Roger that, Ace, prepare to launch."

Moments later, the A-frame's crane activated, and the submersible rose away from the deck, extending twenty feet beyond the stern. The *Manhattanville*'s keel lights illuminated, creating an azure patch in the otherwise dark, glassy surface, and we were lowered into the sea.

For the next ten minutes, divers circled our sub, detaching its harness and rechecking hoses and equipment. Lacombe kept busy, completing his checklist with Ace Futrell aboard the research ship, while Donald showed me photos of his children.

"So when will you and this fiancée of yours start having kids? Nothing like a few rug rats running around to make a house a home."

No problem havin' children, runt. The Wallace curse skips every other generation.

"Zack?"

"Huh?" I shook my head, the lingering ache of the migraine scattering my estranged father's words. "Sorry. No kids, at least not for a while. Too much work to do."

I returned my attention to the control panel, forcing my thoughts back to to our voyage. Descending thousands of feet into the ocean depths was similar to flying. One is always aware of the danger, yet comforted in the knowledge that the majority of planes land safely, just as most subs return to the surface. I had been in a submersible twice before, but this voyage was different, meant to attract one of the most dangerous, if least understood, predators in the sea.

My heart pounded with excitement, the adrenaline escorting Angus's words from my thoughts.

Ace Futrell's commands filtered over the radio. "Control to *Six*, you are clear to submerge. Bon voyage, and good hunting."

"Roger that, Control. See you in the morning."

Lacombe activated the ballast controls, allowing seawater to enter the pressurized tanks beneath the sub. Weighed down, the neutrally buoyant *Massett-6* began to sink, trailing a stream of silvery air bubbles.

The pilot checked his instruments, activated his sonar, engaged his thrusters, then turned to me. "Hey, rookie, ever been in one of these submersibles?"

"Twice, but the missions were only two hours long. Nothing like this."

"Then we'll keep it simple. Batteries and air scrubbers'll allow us to stay below up to eighteen hours, but maneuverability's the pits. Top speed's one knot, best depth's thirty-five hundred feet. We drop too far below that, and the hull will crush like a soda can. Pressure will pop your head like a grape."

I acknowledged the pilot's attempt to put me in my place, countering with my own. "Know much about giant squids? This vessel's twenty-seven feet. The creature we're after is more than twice its size—forty to fifty feet—weighing in excess of a ton. Once we make contact with one of these monsters, be sure to follow my exact instructions."

It's okay to use the "M" word when attempting to intimidate.

Lacombe shrugged it off, but I could tell he was weighing my words. "Three hundred feet," he called out to Hank, who was already filming. "Activating exterior lights."

The twin beams lanced through the black sea, turning it a Mediterranean blue.

And what a spectacle it was, like being in a giant fishbowl in the middle of the greatest aquarium on Earth. I gawked for a full ten minutes before turning to face the camera, doing my best Carl Sagan impression.

"We're leaving the surface waters now, approaching what many biologists call the 'twilight zone.' As we move deeper, we'll be able to see how the creatures that inhabit these mid-water zones have adapted to life in the constant darkness."

Lacombe pointed, refusing to be upstaged. "Looks like we've got our first visitor."

A bizarre jellylike giant with a pulsating bell-shaped head drifted past the cockpit, the creature's transparent forty-five-foot-long body set aglow in our artificial lights.

"That's a siphonophore," I stated, fully immersed in lecture mode. "Its body's made up of millions of stinger cells that trail through the sea like a net as it searches for food."

Next to arrive were a half dozen piranha-sized fish, with bulbous eyes and terrifying fangs. As they turned, their flat bodies reflected silvery-blue in the sub's beams.

"These are hatchet fish," I went on. "Their bodies contain light-producing photo-phores which countershade their silhouettes, allowing them to blend with the twilight sea. In these dark waters, it's essential to see but not be seen. As we move deeper, we'll find more creatures who rely on bioluminescence not only to camouflage themselves, but to attract prey."

Jellyfish of all sizes and shapes drifted silently past the cockpit, their transparent bodies glowing a deep red in the sub's lights. "Pilot, would you shut down the lights a moment?"

He shot me a perturbed look, then reluctantly powered off the beams.

We were surrounded by the silence of utter blackness.

"Watch," I whispered.

A sudden flash appeared in the distance, followed by a dozen more, and suddenly the sea was alive with a pyrotechnic display of bioluminescence as a thousand neon blue lightbulbs flashed randomly in the darkness.

"Amazing," Hank muttered, continuing to film. "It's like these fish are communicating."

"Communicating and hunting," I agreed. "Nature always finds a way to adapt, even in the harshest environments."

"Two thousand feet," the pilot announced.

An adult gulper eel slithered by, its mouth nearly unhinging as it engulfed an unsuspecting fish. All in all, I couldn't have asked for a better performance.

But the best was yet to come.

It was getting noticeably colder in the cabin, so I zipped up my jumpsuit, too full of pride to ask the pilot to raise the heat.

Hank repositioned his camera, then reviewed the list of prompts Cody Saults had given him. "Okay, Zack, tell us about the giant squid. I read where you think it might actually be a mutation?"

"It's just a theory."

"Sounds interesting, give us a rundown. Wait . . . give me a second to re-focus. Okay, go ahead."

"Mutations happen all the time in nature. They can be caused by radiation, or spontaneously, or sometimes by the organism itself as a form of adaptation to changes within its environment. Most mutations are neutral, meaning they have no effect upon the organism. Some, however, can be very beneficial or very harmful, depending upon the environment and circumstance.

"Mutations that affect the future of a particular species are heritable changes in particular sequences of nucleotides. Without these mutations, evolution as we know it wouldn't be possible. For instance, the accidents, errors, and lucky circumstances that caused humans to evolve from lower primates were all mutations. Some mutations lead to dead ends, or extinction of the species. Neanderthal, for instance, was a dead-end mutation. Other mutations can alter the size of a particular genus, creating a new species altogether.

"In the case of *Architeuthis dux*, here we have a cephalopod, a member of the family *teuthid*, yet this particular offshoot has evolved into the largest invertebrate on the planet. Is it a mutation? Most certainly. The question is, why did it mutate in the first place? Perhaps as a defense mechanism against huge predators like the sperm whale. Was it a successful mutation or a dead end? Since we know so little about the creatures, it's impossible to say. Then again, who's to say *Homo sapiens* will be a success?"

The pilot rolled his eyes at my philosophical whims. "We just passed twenty-three hundred feet. Isn't it time you activated that device of yours?"

"Oh, yeah." Reaching to my right, I powered up the lure, sending a series of pulsating clicks chirping through the timeless sea.

I sat back, heart pounding with excitement, waiting for my "dragon" to appear.

*   *   *

"Yo, Jacques Cousteau Junior, it's been six hours. What happened to your giant octopus?"

I looked up at the pilot from behind my copy of *Popular Science*. "I don't know. There's no telling what kind of range the lure has, or whether a squid's even in the area."

The pilot returned to his game of solitaire. "Not exactly the answer *National Geographic*'ll want to hear."

"Hey, this is science," I snapped. "Nature works on her own schedule." I looked around at the black sea. "How deep are we anyway?"

"Twenty-seven hundred feet."

"Christ, we're not deep enough! I specifically asked for thirty-three hundred feet. Giant squids prefer the cold. We need to be deeper, below the thermocline, or we're just wasting our time."

Lacombe's expression soured, knowing I had him by the short and curlies. "*Six* to Control. Ace, the kid wants me to descend to thirty-three hundred feet."

"Stand by, *Six*." A long silence, followed by the expected answer. "Permission granted."

*   *   *

A half mile to the south and eleven hundred fathoms below, the monster remained dead still in the silence and darkness. Fifty-nine feet of mantle and tentacles were condensed within a crevice of rock, its 1,900-pound body ready to uncoil like the spring on a mousetrap.

The carnivore scanned the depths with its two amber eyes, each as large as dinner plates. As intelligent as it was large, it could sense everything within its environment.

*   *   *

The female angler fish swam slowly past the outcropping of rock, dangling her own lure, a long spine tipped with a bioluminous bait. Attached to the underside of the female, wagging like a second tail were the remains of her smaller mate. In an unusual adaptation of sexual dimorphism, the male angler had ended its existence by biting into the body of the female, his mouth eventually fusing with her skin until the two bloodstreams had connected as one. Over time, the male would degenerate, losing his eyes and internal organs, becoming a permanent parasite, totally dependent upon the female for food.

Feeding for two, the female maneuvered her glowing lure closer to the outcropping of rock.

Whap!

Lashing through the darkness like a bungee cord, one of the squid's eighteen-foot feeder tentacles grasped the female angler within its leaf-shaped pad, piercing the stunned fish with an assortment of hooks protruding from its deadly rows of suckers. Drawing its prey toward its mouth, the hunter's parrotlike beak quickly crushed the meat into digestible chunks, its tongue guiding the morsels down its throat, the meat actually passing through its brain on its way to its stomach.

Architeuthis dux pushed its twelve-foot torpedo-shaped head out of its craggy habitat, then swallowed the remains of the angler fish in one gulp.

The giant squid was still hungry, its appetite having been teased over the last eight hours by the sonic lure. Though tempted to rise and feed on what it perceived as the remains of a sperm whale kill, the immense cephalopod had remained below, refusing to venture into the warmer surface waters.

Now, as it finished off the remains of its snack, it detected the enticing presence moving closer, entering the cooler depths.

Hunger overruled caution. Drawing its eight arms free of the fissure, it pushed away from the rocky bottom and rose, its anvil-shaped tail fin propelling it through the darkness, its movements alerting *another* species in the Sargasso food chain to its presence.

*   *   *

Blip.

Blip . . . blip . . . blip . . .

Donald Lacombe stared at the sonar, playing up the drama for the camera. "It's a biologic, and it's big, headed right for us. Fifteen hundred feet and closing."

"Are we in any danger?" I asked, suddenly feeling vulnerable.

"I don't know, you're the marine biologist. Nine hundred feet. Stand by, it's slowing. Maybe it's checking us out?"

"It doesn't like the bright lights," I countered. "Switch to red lights only."

The pilot adjusted the outer beams, rotating the lenses to their less-brilliant red filters. "That did it, it's coming like a demon now. Three hundred feet. Two hundred. Better hold on!"

Seconds passed, and then the *Massett-6* shuddered, rolling hard to starboard as the unseen beast latched on to our main battery and sled.

My heart pounded, then I nearly jumped out of my shoes when the padded sucker, as wide as a catcher's mitt, snaked its way across the outside of our protective bubble.

Eight more tentacles joined in the dance, each appendage as thick as a fire hose, all moving independently from its still unseen owner.

Even the pilot was impressed. "Jeez–us, you actually did it! And will you look at the size of those tentacles? He must be a monster."

"She," I corrected. "Females grow much larger than males, and this monster's definitely a female."

Ah, the "M" word again. If only I had known . . .

The pilot flicked the toggle switch on his radio. "*Six* to Control, break out the bubbly, Ace, we've made contact."

We could hear clapping coming from the control room.

"We're getting the feed. Congratulations, partner," David broke in over the radio, "we did it."

"Yeah, *we*," I mumbled.

The sound of wrenching aluminum caused me to jump. "What was—"

"Stand by." Lacombe seemed genuinely concerned, and that worried me. At three thousand feet, water pressure is a hundred times greater than at the surface, meaning even the slightest breach in our hull would kill us in a matter of seconds.

What if she tears loose a plate? What if she breaks open a seal?

The thought of drowning sent waves of panic crawling through my belly.

"Hey!" Hank aimed his camera at one of the video monitors. The grainy gray picture revealed an impossibly large tubular body and the edge of one gruesome eye, as massive as an adult human's head. Several of the squid's tentacles were tugging at the sealed lid on one of the collection baskets.

"She's only after the fish," I declared, praying I was right. The creature tore the lid off the steel basket as if it were a child's toy, releasing 200 pounds of salmon to the sea.

As we watched, one of the two longer feeding tentacles deftly corralled a fish, while the others resealed the collection basket, preventing more fish from drifting away.

The pilot shook his head, amazed. "Now that's impressive."

"Yes," I agreed, trying to mask my concern. "Her brain's large and complex, with a highly developed nervous system."

"Control to *Six*." This time it was the surface ship's radioman who sounded urgent.

Lacombe and I looked at one another. "*Six* here, go ahead, Control."

"We've detected something new on sonar. Multiple contacts, definitely biologics, not a squid, and like nothing we've ever heard. Depth's seven thousand feet, range two miles. Whatever they are, they've just adjusted their course and are ascending, heading in your direction. Feeding the acoustics to you now. Dr. Caldwell seems to think it's just a school of fish, but we're officially recommending you surface immediately, do you concur?"

Lacombe turned the volume up on his sonar so Hank and I could listen.

Blee-bloop . . . Blee-bloop . . . Blee-bloop . . . Blee-bloop . . .

The pilot looked at me, waiting for a verdict.

"Way too loud to be a school of fish," I whispered, my mind racing to identify the vaguely familiar pattern. "Sounds almost like an amphibious air cavity."

"Must be a whale," offered Hank.

"At seven thousand feet? Not even a sperm whale can dive that deep." I plugged my own headset into the console to listen privately.

Blee-bloop . . . Blee-bloop . . . Blee-bloop . . .

It was a freakish sound, almost like a water jug expelling its contents.

And suddenly my brain kicked into gear. "I don't believe it," I whispered. "It's the *Bloop*."

"What the hell's a Bloop?"

"We don't know."

"What do you mean you don't know?" the pilot shot back. "You just called it a Bloop."

"That's the name the Navy assigned it. All we know is what they're not. They're not whales, because of the extreme depths, and they're not sharks or giant squids, because neither species possesses gas-filled sacs to make noises this loud."

"Are they dangerous?" Hank asked. "Will they attack?"

"I don't know, but I sure as hell don't want to find out this deep."

Lacombe got the message. "*Six* to Control, we're out of here." Grabbing his control stick, he activated the thrusters, adjusting the submersible's fairwater planes.

We began rising, crawling at a snail's pace.

"Look!" yelled Hank. The giant squid had abandoned the catch basket and was now scampering up the bubble, its tentacles wrapping around the cockpit glass, blocking much of our view. "She knows it's out there, too."

"What scares a giant squid?" I wondered aloud, then grabbed my arm rests as the submersible was jolted beneath us and the sound of twisting metal echoed throughout the compartment.

Lacombe swore as he scanned his control panel. "It's your damn octopus. It's wedging itself beneath the manipulator arm."

"She's frightened."

"Yeah, well so am I. That sound you're hearing is our oxygen and air storage tanks being pried away from the sub's sled. We lose that and the *Massett-6* becomes an anchor." The pilot repositioned his headset as he dialed up more pressure into the ballast tanks. "*Six* to Control, we've got an emergency—"

Another jolt cut him off, followed by an explosion that rattled our bones and released an avalanche of bubbles. Thunder roared in our ears as the sea quaked around us. Red warning lights flashed across Lacombe's control panel like a Christmas display, and the once cocky pilot suddenly looked very pale. "*Six*, we just lost primary and secondary ballast tanks. Internal hydraulic system is off-line. Propulsion system's failing—"

And then, my lovelies, the *Massett-6* began falling.

It fell slowly, tail first, but it was worse than any thrill ride I'd ever been on. Metal groaned and plates shook, and my hair seemed to stand on end, rustling against the back of my chair.

The rest of me just felt numb.

The pilot glanced in my direction, his expression confirming our death sentence.

Ace Futrell's voice over the radio sent a glimmer of hope. "Control to *Six*, hang in there, guys, we're readying an ROV with a tow line. What's your depth?"

Lacombe's perspiring face glistened in the control panel's translucent light. "Three-three-six-four feet, dropping fifty feet a minute. Better get that ROV down here quick!"

I felt helpless, like a passenger aboard an airliner that had just lost its engines, accompanied by an inner voice that refused to shut up. *What are you doing here? God, don't let me die . . . not yet, please. Lisa was right, I should've lived a little. Lord, get me out of this mess, and I swear, I'll—*

The sub rolled and rattled, shattering my repentance, and I fell back in my seat, my sweaty palms gripping the armrests, my eyes watching the depth gauge as I tensed for our one final, skull-crushing implosion.

"Jesus, there's something else out there!" Hank cried, pointing between the squid's thrashing tentacles.

I leaned forward. Several long, dark figures were circling us, stalking the squid. I could see shadows of movement, but before I could focus, our bubble became enshrouded in clouds of ink.

The Bloops were launching their attack.

Through my headphones, I could hear them as they tore into the giant squid, their sickening high-pitched growls, like hungry fox terriers, gnawing upon their prey's succulent flesh.

My mind abandoned me then. Too terrified to reason, I squeezed my eyes shut—and was suddenly hit with a subliminal image from my childhood.

Underwater.

Deathly cold.

The darkness—pierced by a funnel of heavenly light!

Get to the light . . . get to the light—

"The light!" Opening my eyes, I tossed aside my shoulder harness and twisted the knob on the control station panel, changing the arc lights from red back to normal.

The sea appeared again, and we could see the torn hydraulic hoses and the sub's mangled manipulator arm dangling from its ravaged perch, along with the severed remains of lifeless tentacles, all swirling in a pool of black soup.

"Control to *Six*. The ROV's in the water. Hang in there, Don, we're coming to get you."

"Huh?" Lacombe pulled himself away from the spectacle outside to check our depth. "Control, we just passed thirty-eight hundred feet. Put the pedal to the metal, Ace, we're living on borrowed time."

I was on my feet now, looking straight up through the bubble cockpit at a lone tentacle still wrapped around the sub's tow arm. The arm's death grip was preventing the rest of the dead squid's gushing mantle and head from releasing to the sea.

Lost in the moment, I stood and watched that lifeless appendage as it slowly unfurled. The remains of the giant squid's torpedo-shaped body released, drifting up and away, away from our light.

They were upon it in seconds, long brown forms darting in and out of the shadows, each maybe twenty to thirty feet in length, ravaging the carcass like a pack of starving wolves.

They were dark and fast and were too far away for me to identify, but their size and sheer voracity intensified my fear. I was witnessing a gruesome display of Mother Nature—it was pure animal instinct—and for a brief moment I felt relieved I'd be dead long before their voracious jaws ever tore into my flesh.

Craaaaack . . .

Death danced before me once more as the hairline fracture worked its way slowly, inch by crooked inch, across the acrylic bubble. The fear in my gut seemed to suck me in like a black hole.

Lacombe grabbed desperately for his radio. "Ace, where's that goddamn ROV?!"

"She just passed twenty-two hundred feet."

"Not good enough, Control, we're in serious trouble down here!"

I fell back in my chair again, then I was up on my feet, unable to sit, unable to keep still, the pressure building inside the cabin, building inside my skull, as the crack in the acrylic bubble continued spider-webbing outward, and the depth gauge crept below 4,230 feet.

I closed my eyes, my breathing shallow, insane last thoughts creeping into my mind. I imagined David Caldwell reading my eulogy at a grave site. ". . . sure, we'll miss him, but as the Beatles said, oh blah dee, oh blah da, life goes on . . . bra—"

Just when I thought things couldn't get worse, the Grim Reaper proved me wrong. With a sizzling hiss, the sub's batteries short-circuited, casting the three of us in a sudden, suffocating, claustrophobic darkness.

Panic seized me, sitting on my chest like an elephant. I gasped for air, I couldn't breathe!

Neon blue emergency lights flashed on as the blessed backup generator took over.

I wheezed an acidic-tasting breath, then another, as I watched the blue lights begin to dim.

"Just hang on, just hang on, we'll be all right." Lacombe was hyperventilating, clearly not believing his own lie.

The aft compartment's five-inch aluminum walls buckled in retort.

All of us were losing it, waiting our turn to die, but poor Hank couldn't take any more. Limbs shaking, his eyes insane with fear, he announced, "I gotta get out of here—" then lunged for the escape hatch.

Paralyzed, I could only watch the drama unfold as Donald Lacombe leaped into the rear compartment and tackled the cameraman, pinning him to the deck. "Kid, get back here and help me! Kid?"

But I was gone, my muscles frozen, my mind mesmerized, for staring at me from beyond the cockpit's cracking acrylic windshield was a pair of round, sinister, opaque eyes . . . cold and soulless, unthinking eyes of death . . . mythic and nightmarish, eyes that burn into a man's mind to haunt him the rest of his days . . . as final as a casket being lowered into the earth and as unfeeling as the maggots that reap upon the flesh.

It was death that stared at me, brain-splattering, final as final can be death—and I screamed like I've never screamed before, a bloodcurdling howl that halted Hank Griffeth in his delirium and sent Donald Lacombe scrambling back over his seat.

The dragon can sense yer fear, Zachary, he can smell it in yer blood.
"What? What did you see?"

I gasped, fighting for air to form the words, but the creature was gone, replaced by a blinking red light, now closing in the distance.

Lacombe pointed excitedly, "It's the ROV!"

The mini torpedo-shaped remotely operated vehicle homed in on the sonic distress beacon emanating from our tow hook. Within seconds, the end of the tow-cable was attached, the line instantly going taut.

Our submersible groaned and spun, then stopped sinking.

I closed my eyes and continued hyperventilating, still frightened beyond all reason.

"Control, we're attached, but the pressure's cracked the bubble. Take us up, Ace, fast and steady!"

"Roger that, Don. Stand by."

Tears of relief poured from my two companions' eyes as the crippled *Massett-6* rose. As for me, I could only stare at the depth gauge as I trembled, counting off seconds and feet as we climbed.

4,200 feet . . . 4,150 . . . 4,100 . . .

To my horror, the cracks in the acrylic bubble continued radiating outward, racing to complete the fracture.

3,800 feet . . . 3,700 . . . 3,600 . . .

My mind switched into left-brain mode, instantly calculating our constant rate of ascent against the pattern of cracks and declining water pressure squeezing against the glass.

No good, the glass won't hold . . . we need to climb faster!

A pipe burst overhead, spewing icy water all over my back. Leaping from my seat, I attacked the shut-off valve like a madman.

"Faster, Control, she's breaking up!"

3,150 . . . 3,100 . . . 3,050 . . .

The pipe leak sealed, I curled in a ball, allowing Hank to replace me up front.

2,800 feet . . . 2,700 . . . 2,600 . . .

The first droplets of seawater appeared along the cracks in the bubble. "Come on, baby," Lacombe chanted, "hold on . . . just a little bit longer."

1,800 feet . . . 1,700 . . . 1,600 . . .

We seemed to be rising faster now, the ebony sea melding around us into shades of gray, dawn's curtains filtering into the depths.

The pilot and cameraman giggled and slapped one another on the back.

Hyperventilating, I exhaled and inhaled, preparing my lungs for the rush of sea I prayed would never come.

"Thank you, Jesus, thank you," Hank whispered, crossing himself with one hand, wiping sweat and tears from his beet-red face with the other. "Praise God, we're saved."

"Told you we'd make it," Donald said, his cockiness returning with the light.

"My kids . . . I can't wait to hug them again."

What were they talking about? Didn't they realize we were still too deep, still in danger?

"Hey, Zack, hand me my camera, we need to document our triumphant return."

Like a zombie, I reached to the deck and picked up the heavy piece of equipment, passing it forward, confused about why we were still alive.

See, you're not such a genius, you can be wrong. Now lighten up. As Lisa would say, enjoy the ride.

1,200 feet.

1,000 feet.

800 feet . . .

David's voice blared over the radio. "Dr. Wallace, you still with us?"

Hank swung his camera around, but I pushed the lens away.

"Dr. Wallace? Hello? Say something so we know you're alive."

"Fuck you."

600 feet . . . 520 feet . . . 440 feet . . .

The ocean melded from a deep purple into a royal blue as we passed the deepest depths a human had ever ventured on a single breath.

The second deepest point, only a few feet higher, had resulted in death.

365 feet . . .

Good . . . keep going, the water's weight subsiding every foot, the cracks slowing now.

310 feet.

I wiped away tears, my face breaking into a broad smile. Hank slapped me on the back and I giggled. *Maybe we were going to make it.*

"Control to *Six*, divers are in the water, standing by. Welcome back, team."

Lacombe winked at Hank. "Hey, Control, wait until you see what we've got on film."

Life is so fragile. One moment you're alive, the next, a semi-tractor trailer plows into you and it's all over, no warning, no final words or thoughts, everything gone.

At 233 feet, the bubble exploded inward, the Sargasso roaring through our sanctuary like a freight train, blinding us in its suffocating fury.

I saw the pilot's face explode like a ripe tomato as shards of acrylic glass riddled his harnessed body like machine gun fire. Hank appeared out of the corner of my eye, and then the Atlantic Ocean lifted me from my perch and bashed me sideways against the rear wall. Only the sudden change in pressure kept me conscious, squeezing my skull in its vise. Buried beneath this howling avalanche, I lashed out blindly in the darkness, my muscles lead, my hands groping . . . my mind recognizing the rear hatch even as it ordered my spent arms to turn its wheel.

I felt the surface ship's support cable *snap* beneath the weight of the sea. My hands held on desperately to the hatch as the freed submersible tumbled backward, falling once more toward the abyss.

The sudden loss of pressure tore at my eardrums.

And then, miraculously, the hatch yawned open.

My kids . . . I can't wait to hug them again . . .

Hank!

The left side of my brain screamed at me to get out, my chances of making it to the surface already less than 10 percent, but it was my right brain that took command, suddenly endowing me with the courage of Sir William Wallace himself.

I groped for Hank. Grabbed him from behind his shirt collar, then pushed his inert 195-pound body out the hatch, into the Sargasso's warm embrace.

A laborious twenty-five seconds had passed, and I was struggling to haul an unconscious man topside through 245 feet of water.

Get to the light . . .

I kicked and paddled, forcing myself into a cadence so as not to excessively burn away those precious molecules of air.

You'll never make it, not with Hank. Let him go, or you'll both drown.

But I didn't let go, not because I wanted to be a hero, not because I actually believed we would make it, but because, at that moment, I knew in my heart that his life was more important than mine.

My lungs seemed on fire, my beating heart the only sound I could hear.

Was I even making progress? My legs were lead . . . were they even kicking?

Scenes from my adolescence flashed before my eyes. My inner voice took over the play-by-play: *This should be the last play, Princeton down by four. Here's the snap, the quarterback pitching to Wallace. He escapes one tackle, then another, and he's heading for daylight.*

The light . . . so precious. Get to the light.

He's across mid-field . . . he's at the forty . . .

Get . . . to . . . the . . . light . . .

Wallace's at the thirty . . . the twenty . . .

The liiiiii . . .

He's at the ten, with just one defender to beat . . .

Shadows closed in on my peripheral vision. I saw death's dark hand reach for me . . . reach for Hank.

Oh, no! Wallace's tackled at the goal line as time expires.

Out of air, out of strength, out of heartbeats, my willpower gone, I slipped out of my body, and drowned.

Again.

It is hard to fight an enemy who has outposts in your head.

—Sally Kempton

CHAPTER 2

FLOAT.

Just float to the light . . .

Mmmmmm. So soothing, when all of life's pain and stress and fears finally wash away. In the vacuum of existence, the soul floats . . . floats along heaven's silky stream.

Merrily, merrily, merrily, life is but a dream . . .

Was my life a dream?

More like a bridled storm, its fury long overdue to be unleashed.

My winds of despair could be traced back to Loch Ness and my ninth birthday—the day of my first drowning. That's right, I'd died once before, dead as a doorknob . . . until my savior had come in the form of my best friend's father, Alban MacDonald, the only man I knew who could scare death away. Since the moment I'd been revived, my mind had harbored a dark secret, bottling it for my own protection. It was always there, following my existence like a shadow, but since my child's mind had created this false reality, how could I have known it was all a lie?

Seventeen years later, everything was about to unravel.

*   *   *

I never actually felt the jolts of electricity delivered by the medic's paddles, only the thunder that roared in my ears and throttled my nerves with an excruciating pain that welcomed me back to the living. Every cell in my body burned with pins and needles, and each breath hurt, my chest feeling as if it had caved in upon my internal organs. A fish out of water, I convulsed upon the *Manhattanville's* frigid deck, vomiting seawater, alone and insane as the medic worked me over.

He shot a clear solution into my trembling veins and once more, I recoiled into blackness.

Upon arriving in the province of the Picts, Saint Columba had to cross the River Ness. Reaching its bank, he saw a poor fellow being buried by other inhabitants, who reported that, while swimming not long before, the victim had been seized and most savagely bitten by a water beast. When Saint Columba heard this, he ordered that one of his companions should swim out and bring back to him a boat that stood on the opposite bank. Hearing this order of the holy and memorable man, Lugne mocu-Min obeyed without delay, and putting off his clothes, excepting his tunic, plunged into the water. But the monster, whose appetite had earlier been not so much sated as whetted for prey, lurked in the depths. Feeling the water above disturbed by Lugne's swimming, it suddenly swam up to the surface, and with gaping mouth and with great roaring rushed towards the man swimming in the middle of the Ness. While all that were there, barbarians and even the brothers, were struck down with extreme terror, Saint Columba raised his holy hand and drew the saving sign of the cross in the empty air; and then, invoking the name of God, he commanded the savage beast, and said: "You will go no farther. Do not touch the man; turn back speedily." Hearing this command, the beast, as if pulled back with ropes, fled terrified into Loch Ness in swift retreat. The pagan barbarians, impelled by the magnitude of this miracle, magnified the God of the Christians.

—From Saint Adamnan's biography of Saint Columba, Abbot of Iona,
A.D. 565

CHAPTER **3**

St. Mary's Hospital
West Palm Beach, Florida

PAIN AND CONFUSION greeted me that first morning
after escaping my second drowning. It was bright wherever I was,
and I forced open my eyes, then thrashed wildly, panicking, when I
discovered I couldn't move.

Several frightening moments passed before I realized I was in
a hospital room. Tubes were embedded in my veins, my wrists and
ankles strapped to the sides of the bed.

The change in vital signs must have alerted the nurses' station. A
Jamaican woman entered, her dialect like a child's nursery rhyme. "So,
you've decided to wake. I was sure we'd lost you, heaven's sake."

I tried to speak, but something was obstructing my parched
throat.

"Try not to move, Mr. Wallace. You've a badly bruised sternum
and two cracked ribs, all from the CPR. You saved that other man
you know."

Hank? Did she mean Hank?

"Don't know his name, but he's two doors down. So I guess that
makes you a hero."

"Harghra longre hag eye–" Frustrated, I gestured at the tube as
best I could with my still strapped hands.

The nurse unbuckled the leather harness. "Now don't move about,
the doctor's on his way, he'll remove the tube in a few minutes. Your
fiancée's outside. Pretty little thing. Shall I send her in?"

Lisa, my angel of mercy. I nodded an emphatic "yes," my heart
pounding with joy.

I had met Lisa Belaski during my first year at FAU, she, an undergrad struggling to make it as a biology major; me, the school's youngest associate professor. By day, we pretended not to know each other as I dazzled her and seventy-five other underclassmen at the lectern; by night, we were in bed together, her slender, tan legs wrapped around my waist, her hazel-green eyes glassy with infatuation and lust.

It wasn't long before Lisa was talking about marriage, her sorority wanting to throw her a candle-lighting ceremony or some other nonsense upon our engagement, how she wanted to start a family as soon as she graduated, and live in a gated community with good schools. I told her a family would be fine, as long as she was prepared to do most of the parenting while I worked.

Feeling pressured, I finally proposed on Thanksgiving Day, but refused to set a date until after returning from my voyage.

Now I was back, and my latest near-death experience had given me a whole new perspective on what was really important. I couldn't wait to hug Lisa, to tell her how much I needed her. I'd set aside my career, help her with the wedding plans. I'd accept the tenured position the university was offering me, just so we could stay in south Florida. Hell, I'd even start picking out baby names. *Let's see . . . how about Drew Wallace? Or Michael? Mike Wallace . . . nah, sounded too* 60 Minutes-*ish*.

"Gosh, Zack, you look awful."

Not quite the tearful greeting I had anticipated.

"They said you saved that cameraman. They also said you drowned. Did you know you were actually dead? That's got to be a bit freaky, huh? But hey, you're doing better now, right?"

Better than dead? Okay, so she wasn't the swiftest fish in the sea, but she was my fish.

I reached out for her, squeezing her hand. "Risa, rye rove roo."

She squeezed me back, then pulled away. "Maybe you shouldn't talk with that thing in your mouth. In fact, it might be better you just listen. See, while you were away, I was doing some serious thinking, and—"

Uh-oh . . .

"I realize this probably isn't a good time for you, but I'm going away tomorrow on winter break, and before I leave, I wanted to tell you that . . . well, I think we should postpone the wedding. Indefinitely."

"Rhat?"

She was breaking up now? Now! Wasn't there some kind of mandatory non-breaking-up grace period after one's fiancé came back from the dead?

"Risa, rye?"

"Face it, Zack, you don't really need me, in fact, you don't need anybody, and me . . . I'm someone who needs to feel needed."

"Risa, rye reed roo!" Sounding ridiculous, I struggled to rip out the cursed tube.

"Be honest, you were never crazy about the whole commitment thing. You have your career, and God knows nothing can stand in its way."

"Risa, rye'll range."

". . . plus you hate going out with my friends. Honestly, other than sex, I wonder if you even enjoyed spending time with me."

"Risa—"

She broke eye contact then, and even an emotional dunce like me knew what was coming next.

"The truth is, I met someone while you were gone."

While I was gone? I was gone four days! You'd think I was Ernest Shackleton, lost in Antarctica.

". . . and he's fun and he makes me laugh. You even know him, he's in our biology class."

Tell me his name! Tell me and I'll flunk the bastard.

"Anyway, I'm sorry, but the way I see it, if I'm having doubts now, it's best we just break away clean. Here's the key to your apartment. Oh, I, uh, I sort of sold the engagement ring. I know that was rotten, but Drew and I needed the money to go to Cancún on winter break."

Drew? But we were going to name our firstborn Drew!

"I'll send you a check or something next semester, promise."

She left the key on my nightstand, leaned over and kissed me on the forehead, told me to "feel better," then helped herself to the orange juice from my breakfast tray and left.

*   *   *

David Caldwell visited me later that day, his turn at "cheering me up." He told me Hank was doing better, that our pilot never made it, and that the submersible had been recovered but no body was ever found.

The thought of those creatures devouring Donald Lacombe's remains made me queasy.

David wasted little time in dropping his next "cluster bomb."

"Despite your heroics, Zack, everything's canceled. The pilot's death, combined with the loss of a $12 million submersible . . . Jesus, it's a fucking disaster. While you've been lying here sleeping, I've had to deal with one helluva mess. Plus we lost all that great squid footage Hank took—"

"Forget about giant squids, David, there's something even more fascinating down there—Bloop!"

"Bloop?"

"Don't you ever pick up a science journal? Back in '97, the navy discovered these mysterious deep-water biologics, which they named Bloop. SOSUS picked them up."

"SOSUS?"

"Come on—the Sound Underwater Surveillance System. The microphones the navy used to detect Soviet subs during the Cold War!"

"Oh, that SOSUS . . . right."

"They're animals, David. Big, nasty undiscovered predators, only they swarm, like . . . like piranha. They attacked us in the Sargasso. They were after our giant squid!"

"Zack—"

"This is big stuff, David, an undiscovered species. You have to organize another expedition and—"

"Zack, you're not listening. It's over. No more expeditions. No more grants."

"What're you talking about?"

"The pilot's family hired some hotshot attorney, a Mike Rempe out of West Palm. Talk about a piranha. The guy's already filed a wrongful death lawsuit against you and FAU. As far as the University's concerned, you're unmarketable, pal. Poison."

"A lawsuit? But it was an accident."

"Save it for the deposition. Anyway, the dean and I think it's best we sort of sever all ties with you, at least for now."

I was incredulous. "FAU's blaming me? David, what did you tell them?"

"Look, you did open that escape hatch."

"Yes, schmuck, to escape!"

"And by doing so, you may have put too much strain on the tow cable."

"You son of a bitch . . . you told them I flooded the sub!"

"No . . . I . . . I mean, look, maybe you'd better get an attorney."

"No way, David, no fucking way! I won't play the fall guy for you or FAU, you can forget it. The sub's bubble cracked, that's what killed the pilot."

"Hey, I'm just the messenger, and the message is you're no longer associated with the university. It's a visibility thing, nothing personal."

"Yeah, well, fuck you, nothing personal."

It was all I could do to keep from strangling him with one of my IVs.

*   *   *

The hospital released me two days later, only after I signed a paper agreeing to keep an appointment with a psychiatrist. Apparently, my doctors feared depression setting in.

They were right to worry.

I took a cab to my on-campus apartment, a perk FAU had used in recruiting me. Demonstrating uncharacteristic efficiency, David had already struck, ordering the university's housing authority to pack my possessions into cardboard boxes. Under the watchful eye of a security officer (what was I going to do, steal my own belongings?) I tossed everything into the back of my Jeep. Then, with nowhere else to go, I headed for my mother's place in Bal Harbour.

*   *   *

Upon returning to America with her nine-year-old son, the former Mrs. Angus Wallace had struggled for several years to earn a living as a travel agent before meeting her future husband, Mr. Charlie Mason of Long Island, New York. Charlie was a writer, spending his days penning columns for soap opera magazines, his nights pounding out screenplays. His breakthrough as a scribe came six months after marrying my mother, when a friend of hers enticed a prominent Hollywood agent to read one of his scripts, a comedy about a man trying to kill his legally wed homosexual partner so he could collect on a lottery ticket. The sale netted six figures and reaped a nice payday at the box office, and suddenly Charlie and his new bride were moving up in the world.

I liked my stepfather. He was a slight man with thinning hair, fifteen years older than my mother, but he loved her dearly and treated her with respect, and that's all that mattered in my book.

The fact that he was wealthy never bothered me in the least, though I never asked Charlie for a dime. With FAU paying my room and board, along with a decent salary, I was able to sock away enough over the years for a down payment on a house.

Having lost my job, I was now going to need those funds to survive.

Bal Harbour Island is a seaside resort located in northern Miami-Dade County. A favored hideaway of the rich and famous, it is single-family homes nestled in gardened, gated communities, and high-rise condos lining private white beaches and azure coastlines. Upscale shopping malls and restaurants run north and south along its main thoroughfares, and yachts inhabit the deep water channel of its intracoastal.

Mother and Charlie were in Manhattan for the week. We had spoken briefly on the phone, with me assuring her that I was fine, and that rest and relaxation were all I was interested in. I told her not to worry, that I'd see her soon enough.

Their apartment was a four-bedroom condo on the tenth floor, facing the ocean. It was late by the time I settled in, so I took a quick shower, slipped on my favorite boxer shorts, and crawled into bed in one of the guest rooms. I left the balcony door open, the salty breeze and pounding ocean soon guiding me into a heavy sleep.

*   *   *

It is dark.

It is dark and I am in the water. Deep, frigid water.

I am in the Loch.

I am drowning!

Kick to the surface! Gag, spit, tread water.

My capsized rowboat sinks beneath me.

Salmon everywhere, jumping, snapping. I'm swimming in a school of fish!

Look around. Search for land, but the fog is everywhere, and the sun has set. Which direction is home?

Stay calm, Zachary, don't panic . . . just tread water and wait . . . wait until the fog lifts.

Help! Can anybody hear me?

Muscles growing heavier, I'm so tired, so numb.

A powerful current swirls around me . . . is something down there?

I'm scared.

Help! Help! Ahh . . .

Gulp! Underwater! I'm underwater! Something has me, has my ankle! Sharp pain . . . what is it? What has me? Is it my rowboat? Am I entangled in the bow line?

Panic . . . struggle . . . twist . . . fight to get air . . .

"Ahh! Ahhh!"

Catapulting out of bed, still half asleep, I bellowed a bloodcurdling howl and ran blindly from the bedroom—the wrong way! Past the billowing curtains, I sprinted straight out onto the balcony, my momentum flipping me head over heels over the aluminum rail!

Hands that once plucked footballs from the air lunged one last desperate time, my left smashing uselessly against the balcony's concrete lip, the right managing to grasp the aluminum rail's divider that separated the two plastic balcony panels.

"Owwff!"

For a surreal moment I simply held on, suspended 128 feet above the pavement. The fingers of my right hand held on for dear life while my mind, soothed by the ocean's dull roar, fought to convince my nightmare-laden brain that I was indeed awake and a butterfly's flutter from dying, only this time, there'd be nothing left of me to resuscitate.

Do something, Wallace, move!

Carefully, I raised my legs, my bare toes embracing the rough concrete along the underside of the balcony. My right ankle found a perch near the outside of the rail so that I could grab hold with my left hand, and I hauled myself up and over the cracked partition. My body trembled as my feet touched down upon the warm tile, my bruised chest heaving as I looked down ten stories, staring in disbelief at what might have been.

"Hey, son, you all right?"

"Isn't that Andrea Mason's boy?"

"The guy in the newspaper? Didn't know he was *meshuga*."

The neighbors were out on their balconies, dressed in shorts and robes and nightgowns, talking about me like I was some kind of suicidal freak.

Waving them off, I retreated inside the apartment and double locked the glass door.

I was wide-awake and pumped full of adrenaline, but the dark bedroom seemed filled with demons. Feeling myself beginning to freak out, I bolted from the chamber, flipping on light after light until I reached Charlie's liquor cabinet. Tearing it open, I grabbed the first unsealed bottle I could find and swallowed two long gulps, then heaved the cursed container of cooking sherry across the Saturnia marble floor and retched.

The life of wild animals is a struggle for existence. The full exertion of all their faculties and all their energies is required to preserve their own existence and provide for that of their infant offspring. The possibility of procuring food during the least favorable seasons, and of escaping the attacks of their most dangerous enemies, are the primary conditions which determine the existence both of individuals and of entire species. These conditions will also determine the population of a species; and by a careful consideration of all the circumstances we may be enabled to comprehend, and in some degree to explain, what at first sight appears so inexplicable—the excessive abundance of some species, while others closely allied to them are very rare.

—Alfred Russel Wallace
"On the Tendency of Varieties to Depart Indefinitely From the Original Type," 1858

There are at least 10,000 known reported sightings at Loch Ness, but less than a third of these are recorded.

—Dr. Roy Mackall, Crypto-Zoologist

CHAPTER 4

South Beach

I WOKE UP THE NEXT MORNING on the den sofa, the horrors of the previous night a fading memory. Staggering to the drapes, I drew them back, revealing blue skies, a shimmering white stretch of beach, and an azure ocean.

Nirvana.

I showered and shaved, ate a quick breakfast, then headed down to the beach in my shorts and sunglasses, ready for some much needed rest and sun.

The condominium had reserved chairs on the beach. Helping myself to a chaise lounge and a handful of towels, I scanned the coastline.

Lying on her stomach close by the water's edge was a woman in her early twenties. My eyes targeted shoulder-length brown hair and a white thong that was wedged so deep into the crack of her yoga-firmed buttocks that it was nearly invisible. The bikini top that barely contained her dark, baby-oiled breasts was unhinged, preventing tan lines.

God, I love South Beach . . .

I set my chair within ten feet, spying on her from behind my tinted sunglasses. I waited until she rotated her head, then offered, "Beautiful day."

No response.

Goofball, you're coming off like Sir Alfred.

Playing it cool, I moved closer, flexing my muscles with every movement. "I'm Zack," I said, kneeling close to her basting body. "And you are?"

"Not interested."

"Right. Sorry. I just, I dated a lot of athletes back when I played football in college, so I have a thing for physically fit women."

She looked up. "Leesa Gehman."

"Hi, Lisa."

"Not Lisa, Leesa."

"You're uh . . . not a student, are you?"

"Not anymore. Why?"

"Just curious. My former fiancée was an undergrad."

"So now you're on the rebound. Good luck."

She laid her head back down, then looked up again. "Wait, did you say your name was Zack, as in Zachary Wallace?"

"Guilty as charged."

"I read about you in the paper. You drowned while saving some guy, right?"

And Wallace catches the ball in the end zone for a touchdown!

In South Beach, fame is the key that unlocks all chastity belts. In the next twenty minutes I learned Leesa was from Allentown, Pennsylvania, had worked in an architect's office in Miami, and taught aerobics part-time. She told me what schools she'd attended, her brother's name, her favorite books, the meaning of the Chinese symbols tattooed on her left ankle, and where she wanted to go to dinner that evening.

At any moment, I expected to be discussing her favorite baby names.

"Zack, do you like it in the water?"

"I'm a marine biologist. I'm always working in oceans and—"

"No, Zack, I meant sex." She rehooked her top and stood, taking my hand. "I've never done it with a dead guy. Come on."

God, I love South Beach . . .

Hand in hand, we walked into the water, the thought of what lay ahead pumping blood to my already alerted groin.

We hurried through the shallows, our feet splashing one another, my heart pounding—

—my chest suddenly hurting, my vision impaired by purple spots. The blood rushed from my face as we waded into hip-deep water.

Not now . . .

My flesh tingled then burned, as if stung by a thousand jellyfish.

I let go of Leesa's hand and stumbled blindly back to shore, the world spinning in my head. Collapsing to my knees in the wet sand, I fought to gasp a breath.

Leesa looked at me, perplexed. "Come on, the water's perfect!"

I tried to answer, but couldn't speak, unable to stop hyperventilating. A cold sweat broke out all over my body, my vision still impaired.

This wasn't a migraine, it was something else . . .

I was afraid.

Leesa moved closer, undoing the clasp on her top. "Zachary. Zach-ar-y!" The vixen smiled as she lifted her bikini, flashing the twins at me.

Torture . . .God's torturing me—

"Come on, hero, I'm horny."

The blind spots faded, the pain and cold sweat mercifully subsiding. Feeling embarrassed, I stood, wiping perspiration from my face. "Sorry."

"What happened?"

"Low blood sugar, I guess." I sucked in a few more breaths, my limbs still trembling. "Okay, I'm coming."

"Not yet, I hope." She grabbed my hand, leading me back out.

I took two strides, and was suddenly blinded by subliminal images, flashing across my mind's eye.

Dark water. Heavy fog. Salmon everywhere. Jumping. Panicking. A presence . . . circling below! Left ankle, seized with pain. Dragged underwater . . . can't breathe!

"Can't . . . breathe."

"Zack?"

"Can't breathe!" Freaking out, I turned and fled, still clutching Leesa's hand as I dragged my once sure-thing face-first through the shallows and halfway up the beach before releasing her to vomit.

Office of Dr. Douglas G. Baydo
Coral Springs, Florida

"I never felt anything like this before. You gotta help me, Doc. I'm a marine biologist, I can't be afraid of the water!"

The psychiatrist was a big man, probably a former football player, an offensive guard, I guessed. A plaque on one wall indicated he'd been in the air force.

"And you've only experienced this hydrophobia since the Sargasso Sea incident?"

"Yes."

"Zachary, phobias are created in the subconscious mind. It may eventually pass, or you might have to learn to live with it."

"Live with it? To hell with that! I can't live with not being able to go near the sea. How do you expect me to work?"

"You may have to find yourself a new line of work."

I paced his office like a madman. "You don't know what you're saying. I've spent my whole life busting my hump to get where I am, no way I'm gonna just walk away from my career."

"Stay calm and sit down. Now tell me more about these dreams."

"They're nightmares, only far more intense, and always a version of the same dream. I'm underwater when I hear these sounds, the same growling sounds I heard in the Sargasso. It's like they're whispering into my brain, and somehow I just know I'm going to die."

"And then you wake up screaming?"

"I wake up, and my eyes are wide open, only I can't speak or move. It's like part of me is still stuck in the nightmare. But the worst thing, Doc, the very worst thing is that I feel this terrible presence in the room with me. I can feel it. I can hear the echo of its whispers still growling in my head. My skin tingles from it, and my fear . . . it's so intense that I just have to get out of there."

Dr. Baydo made a few notes, then continued. "Have you ever experienced episodes like these before?"

"No. At least none I can remember."

"But you're not sure?"

"Well, when I was younger, there was a time when I was sleep-walking a lot. It got so bad, my grandmother had to add a dead bolt to her front door."

"Your grandmother?"

"My mom's mother. We moved in with her right after my parents' divorced."

"I see. Out of curiosity, what do you do for fun?"

"Fun? I don't know. Why?"

"You seem wound pretty tight."

"I almost leaped to my death last night, then tossed my cookies in front of a girl that I'd have given my right arm for. Wouldn't that stress you out?"

"I'm sensing something deeper. Let's talk more about your child-hood. You said you never got along with your father?"

"I said he enjoyed pushing my buttons. Look, I know it's a Freudian thing with you guys, but do we have to talk about my child-hood? What happened in the Sargasso has nothing to do with my father. That was seventeen years ago. I'm a totally different person."

"Maybe. But everyone handles trauma in different ways. Some people repress or block out painful childhood memories that affect us subconsciously on a daily basis throughout our adult years. The near-death experience you suffered in the Sargasso Sea could have forced these childhood memories back to the surface."

"So what do I do now?"

"Discussing your past can often help resolve these conflicts. Do you still feel hatred toward your father?"

"Hatred? Not hatred. More like disappointment. Angus wasn't much of a father. He never let up on me . . . never. Always badgering, teasing. Scared the shit out of me when he was drunk. And always play-ing his stupid mind games. I remember one time, when I was six, my mother bought me one of those Rubik's Cubes. I must have worked that damn puzzle all day and night until I was able to master it. I remember running to my father, you know, looking for his approval. You'd think he'd be slightly impressed, maybe offer me a pat on the head. Not ball-buster Angus. First he accused me of cheating, then he challenged me to a Rubik's Cube duel. Now I knew I had him. Well, I worked that puzzle like a demon, rearranging the colored panels in their proper order in only seventeen minutes, a personal record. To my amazement, it took Angus only four minutes to finish, it just blew me away. For the next several weeks he'd berate me about it, making me feel inferior, until finally I figured out how the drunken bastard did it."

"How did he do it?"

"He cheated, of course. Never moved a block, he merely peeled away the stickers and restuck them in order."

Dr. Baydo grinned.

"You think that's funny?"

"You have to admit, he's resourceful."

"Try having him as your father."

"There's no excuse for his behavior, but let's try looking at things from Angus's perspective. Here's a man who never finished high school, trying to keep pace with his precocious six-year-old son, a boy genius in the making."

"He never saw me that way. I was nothing more than his runt. And being clever doesn't justify his constant drunkenness, or his cheating on my mother."

"He committed adultery?"

"Only every chance he got. Live for the moment, deal with the consequences later, that was my father."

"You caught him doing this?"

"Several times, including . . ." I paused, realizing I'd stepped in it again.

"Go on."

"Forget it."

He sat and waited for me to continue.

"It was on my ninth birthday. Angus bought me a new fishing rod, only later I found out he'd actually won it in a dart game. Anyway, he told me to meet him at the Loch, promising me he'd take me out in our rowboat after he grabbed a cup of coffee. So I waited. An hour went by and it was getting dark, so I left the boat and went looking for him.

"There was a campsite nearby. I heard noises coming from a tent. As I came closer, I could hear someone moaning inside. So I peeked through the tent flaps."

"He was with another woman?"

"A girl, the brunette from the coffee shop, and she wasn't a day over sixteen. She was on top of him, totally naked, pumping up and down like one of those bobblehead dolls. Her back was to me, but I could see Angus lying there on the ground, a stupid grin on his face, drunk as a lord."

"What did you do?"

"I was mad. Bad enough he blew off my birthday, but to be cheating again on my mother? I pulled up the stakes and collapsed the tent, but the two of them just giggled and continued humping one another. So I left. I marched straight back down to the Loch and went fishing by myself."

"And that's the night you nearly drowned?"

"Did drown."

"What happened? What caused your boat to flip?"

"It was a tree. Bottom of the Loch's covered with them. Compressed gases build up inside the trunks. When the pressure exceeds the depths, they come shooting to the surface like missiles. I can't remember much, only that the bow suddenly flipped over and *bam*, I was in the water. When the tree re-sank, it took me with it."

"I don't understand."

"The tree trunk was wrapped in barbed wire. The wire snagged my left ankle, nearly tore my foot off. God knows how deep it dragged me before I managed to kick myself free."

"That must have been petrifying. It's amazing your friend's father managed to get to you."

"I got lucky, old man MacDonald must've been nearby. Scariest guy you'd ever want to meet. Kids around Drumnadrochit used to call him the Crabbit. Even his son, my best friend, True, was afraid of him. Still, I was under for a long time and blacked out. What probably saved me was the Loch's water temperature. It's only about forty-two degrees, close to freezing. In water that cold, your muscles turn to lead, and all your vitals slow to a crawl."

"Zachary, people don't just walk away from traumatic experiences like yours. Sure, you may block it out for a time, but the memories still linger in the subconscious . . . and so can the effects. Obviously, Angus was at fault, but all this anger you're still holding inside toward your father, it isn't healthy either. And keep in mind, he's not the one suffering, you are."

"So I've been told. But it doesn't matter. He'll never apologize, and I'll never forgive him."

"And what if—"

"Fuck what if! I didn't come here so you could reconcile me and Angus, I came because of these damn nightmares."

He closed his notepad. "For the record, they're not nightmares. What you're experiencing are classified as night terrors, a sleep disorder common among individuals suffering post-traumatic stress. It's your mind's way of dealing with what happened. I once treated a group of patients who just made it out of the Twin Towers before they collapsed. Many of them experienced these same intense dreams of death. While nightmares can occur anytime during REM sleep, night terrors take place only during stage four of sleep, which is the deepest, most difficult stage to awaken from. Patients bolt upright in bed, screaming, paralyzed in fear, their hearts beating at upwards of a 170 beats per minute. Even after awakening, many patients remain in a state of confusion for twenty minutes or more."

"Yeah, I've experienced all that."

"Hopefully, our sessions will help, but I have to warn you, it could take years."

"Years? And until then?"

"Until then, we'll do what we can." Reaching into his desk drawer, he pulled out a prescription pad. "I'm going to prescribe an anti-depressant. Take it once a day before bedtime. As for the night terrors and your sudden fear of water, sometimes the best therapy is to deal with their causes head-on."

"And how do I do that?"

"That, only you can figure out."

*   *   *

I left his office, convinced the only way to salvage my career and "re-move the Wallace curse" was to return to the Sargasso Sea and "face my dragon." That meant resolving the mystery of the Bloops, no easy task, even without my psychological condition. Returning to the Sar-gasso meant raising money to fund another expedition. David had de-serted me, and few companies would want to risk men and machinery in the wake of my recent disaster at sea.

Still, I had to try.

My mother and Charlie were returning home that afternoon. Charlie not only had money, but connections with several networks. Maybe his production company would be my sponsor?

*   *   *

"Absolutely not!" My mother stalked the living room, enraged that I'd even broach the subject. "You nearly died out there, Zachary, and now you want to go back?"

My stepfather winced. "Take it easy, Andrea—"

"Charlie Mason, you lend Zachary one silver nickel for this expe-dition, and you and I are through!"

She stormed off, the slamming door punctuating her words.

"Sorry, Charlie, I didn't mean to get you in any trouble."

Good ol' Charlie just shrugged it off. "As Will Rogers said, there are two theories to arguing with a woman, and neither of 'em works. Your mom's just worried about you. Let me work on her a while."

*   *   *

But heart-stopping screams in the middle of the night were not exactly what my mother or Charlie had in mind when they invited me to stay with them. After the third straight night of listening to my mother threaten to send me to a sanitarium, I decided it would be best if I checked into a motel.

The next several months were a blur. I applied to every school with a marine sciences department, but the on-going war in Iraq, combined with the federal government's massive tax cuts had led to deficits that were strapping the states and forcing universities to cut positions and programs. While I waited to hear something, I bounced around from job to job, painting houses, trimming landscapes, basically allowing my mind to turn to mush. The antidepressants made me nauseous, but had little effect on my night terrors. I soon found something that did: alcohol.

Being inebriated kept me from entering the deepest stages of sleep, the stages where the night terrors lay in wait. Given the choice between preserving my sanity and my liver, I chose my sanity.

I'd never been much of a drinker in college, but my tolerance rose quickly with my "cure," and it wasn't long before occasional use became abuse. Days were devoted to sleeping off hangovers, my nights reserved for binging on expensive drinks and cheap women, both of which I found in abundance in South Beach, my new favorite haunt.

Hey, everyone from my ex-fiancée to my shrink had told me to loosen up. As far as I was concerned, I was just following their advice. And it didn't get any looser than South Beach after dark.

I'd hit the clubs by ten and party past dawn. Sometimes I'd make it back to my motel room, other times waking up in strange places I had no recollection of entering. I hung out with people whose names I couldn't remember, and had sex with women who couldn't care less.

And neither could I.

Having been goal-oriented and disciplined for as long as I could remember, I quickly became a rudderless, sinking ship. I stopped working out. I quit my job and lived off my savings, which vanished as quickly as the women in my life. No longer interested in the future, I was merely biding my time in the present.

I became a social vampire, a drunk haunted by my failures.

I became my father.

*   *   *

It was a Thursday afternoon in May, five months after the Sargasso incident, when destiny came calling again. I was lying in a pile of wet towels on the bathroom floor of a motel efficiency when my brain registered a pounding on the door.

Sobriety greeted me with migrainelike symptoms. Pulling myself up by the porcelain, I spewed the prior night's toxins into the toilet bowl (is there a worse stench than Jack Daniel's over tacos?), then crawled toward the door.

The pounding awakened my escort from the previous night, a buxom rinsed-out blonde whose name never registered. Stumbling out of bed, totally naked, she unchained the door as the two of us confronted the stranger.

"Zachary Wallace? My name is Max Rael. How'd you do?"

He was a tall man in his late twenties, English, with strawberry blond hair, short and spiked, and his green eyes were highlighted by black eyeliner. Though temperatures were in the mid-eighties, he wore a heavy black trench coat and slacks, giving him a Gothic look.

In any other city he'd have been gawked at, but this was South Beach.

"What do you want? I'm paid up for the week."

"No worries, brar, I'm not with the hotel. Actually, I work for your father." He pushed past the blonde, then turned up his nose. "This room stinks of gunge. Pay off the bird and get dressed, we need to talk."

*   *   *

An hour later, I found myself facing the Englishman on a park bench, hiding behind dark sunglasses.

"If you don't mind me saying so, you look like you've come out on the wrong side of a swedge."

"A swedge?"

"A fight. So who's the battle with? Drugs? Booze? Women? Or all of the above?"

"Dragons. State your business, Mr. Rael. You said you work for my father?"

"I'm his barrister, his attorney. Your father's been arrested for murder."

"Murder?" I felt myself sober up. "Did he do it?"

"No. But it's complicated. There were witnesses."

"What happened? Who's he accused of killing?"

"John Cialino Jr. Recognize the name?"

"Cialino . . . wait, isn't there a big real estate company in Britain—"

"Cialino Ventures. One of the largest in Europe. Angus was doing business with Johnny C. himself."

"That makes no sense. What would a man as wealthy as John Cialino want with my father?"

"The company's building a fancy resort and health spa along the northwestern bank of Loch Ness, just south of Urquhart Bay. Angus held title to the land and—"

"Whoa . . . My father owns land on Loch Ness?"

"Passed down to him from his paternal ancestors."

"Funny how that never came up in my mother's divorce settlement."

"The land was unsellable for commercial use until a recent change in zoning. Anyway, Angus sold the land to Johnny C., but on the day in question, the two of 'em got into a big squabble on a bluff overlooking the Loch. Witnesses saw your father take a swing at Cialino, who fell into Loch Ness. They're still looking for the body, but with the depths and cold temperatures . . . well, the Loch's known for not giving up her dead."

"Sounds more like an accident than murder."

"Like I said, it's complicated. There's rumors that Angus and Johnny C's wife were carrying on a bit under the sheets."

And there it was. The moment Max mentioned the affair, I knew my father was guilty as charged.

"He was probably drunk," I said, ignoring my own fall from grace. "Guess the numbers finally caught up with him, not that I'm surprised. Anyway, best of luck. I hope you're a better lawyer than you are a hair stylist."

"I'm not here as a messenger, Zachary. I've come to Miami to bring you back to Scotland. Angus needs you, he needs your emotional support."

I blurted out a laugh, the sudden movement sending a fresh wave of pain through my hung over brain. "Emotional support? Since when does Angus Wallace need anyone's emotional support? Where was my emotional support? Hell, the man hasn't so much as sent me a birthday card in seventeen years. As far as I'm concerned, he can use a few years in prison. Maybe next time he'll think twice before screwing around with another man's wife."

Max shot me a stern look. "If Angus's found guilty of murder in the first, he's looking at the death penalty."

"Death penalty? I thought Europe abolished capital punishment?"

"Britain's quietly changed their view since that last series of terrorist attacks. Make no mistake, the Cialinos are a powerful, well-connected family. The murder's become our equivalent of your O.J. Simpson trial. It's in every paper, on every TV station. If Angus is found guilty, he'll hang."

I sat back and stared at the passing beach-goers, feeling a bit lost. "Max, I haven't spoken with my father since I was nine. Why would he want me with him after all this time?"

"Maybe he sees it as his last chance to make some sort of restitution."

"Toward me? You obviously don't know my father. The man's a liar and a cheat and that's on his best days. The man never gave a damn about anyone but himself."

Max stunned me with a hard slap across the top of my skull. "That'll be quite enough negativity. After all, the man is *our* father."

I balled my fists, until the Englishman's words sank in.

"That's right, little brother. Angus is my father, too. Knocked up my mum three years before leaving her and marrying yours. Maybe he did me a favor, seein' as how you turned out. But people change as they get older, and, in my book, they deserve a second chance. No doubt Angus did us both some wrong, but he's made amends with me, and now he's reachin' out to you. So now it's up to you. Will ye be there for him in his time of need, or do you prefer to take your anger with you to the grave?"

Two hours later, Max and I boarded a Continental Airlines flight out of Miami, bound for Inverness.

I was seated on a rock, above Abriachan, just watching the water
when I saw what I took to be a log coming across the Loch.
Instead of going towards the river, as I expected, it suddenly came
to life and went at great speed, wriggling and churning
towards Urquhart Castle.

—D. Mackenzie, Balnain resident, 1872

I regularly traveled on the mail steamer from Abriachan from Inverness.
During the early morning hours, just before the dawn, I'd often see a
strange, huge, salamanderlike creature frolicking along the surface.

—Alexander MacDonald, Abriachan resident, 1889

CHAPTER 5

Aboard Continental Airlines Flight 8226
Over the Atlantic Ocean

IT WAS AN EIGHT-HOUR FLIGHT to Gatwick Airport, where we would have to switch planes to fly on to Scotland. We would not arrive in Inverness until seven in the morning, local time.

I was already exhausted, but determined to stay awake, fearing sleep and the possibilities of experiencing a night terror while on the plane. With the ongoing threat of terrorist attacks still keeping most Western travelers on edge, I knew that one bloodcurdling scream at forty thousand feet might result in an intense, free-for-all beating.

With Max snoring next to me, I remained awake, sobriety forcing me to think. Avoiding all thoughts of the Sargasso, I tried focusing my mind on Scotland, a land I scarcely remembered.

My mother had barely been out of college when she traveled to Britain with two friends and first laid eyes on my father. Angus Wallace was brash and handsome and larger-than-life to twenty-six-year-old Andrea McKnown, and the fact that she had recently lost her father and Angus was twenty-seven years her senior no doubt added to her infatuation. Their courtship lasted barely six weeks before he insisted they marry. Andrea said yes, partly because there was nothing waiting for her back home, partly because she was pregnant and couldn't bear to face her mother, a strict Catholic. To this day, mom still insists I was born nine weeks prematurely instead of only three.

My mother put up with a lot during those early years, and, over time, as the glitter of her infatuation gradually faded, she began to see my father for what he truly was, an irresponsible drunk who loved to flirt as much as he liked to drink. I kept my father's affairs from my mother as long as I could, but after nearly drowning, I'd confessed everything I knew. Biding her time, my mother waited until Angus's next "business trip," then sold our cottage and its furnishings, packed our bags, and filed for divorce. By the time Angus returned from Inverness, a new family had moved into his dwelling, and Mom and I were living in her mother's home on Long Island, New York.

That was the last time I saw my father or Scotland, and I was surprised at how anxious I felt to see the Highlands again. Perhaps Angus was right when he said, "Born a Highlander, aye a Highlander, oor blood bleeds the plaid."

*   *   *

Scottish identity comes from both the land and its history, and its history, like most of Europe's, is a bloody one. Separated from continental Europe by the North Sea, Scotland forms the northern boundary of Great Britain, attached to England's northern hip, and our people have always been in conflict with our neighbor to the south—a people greater in number and wealth and more advanced, especially in the art of warfare. Coexisting with the English has been our greatest challenge, and remains so, even today.

Like other nations, Scots are descendants of every race who ever settled upon our shores. Our earliest immigrants, primitive hunters, most likely came over from Europe about eight thousand years ago, shortly after the ice from the last Ice Age finally melted. We don't know much about these ancient ones, but their island would be invaded some five thousand years later by a people known as the Celts. Hailing from parts of northwestern Europe, these conquerors referred to themselves as "Pretani," which was later misconstrued by future Celtic settlers as "Britoni."

Britons soon found themselves invaded by the Romans, the masters of Europe and the Mediterranean world who never met a land they didn't seek to conquer. The Romans quickly subdued the Celtic tribes of the south, then gradually worked their way north toward the future nation of Scotland. Unfortunately for the Romans, the farther they distanced themselves from their southern ports, the more difficult it was to maintain their supply lines.

The northern region also involved another challenge: the Highlanders.

To the Roman conquerors, these mountain barbarians were known as the Picts, a name derived from the Latin word, *Pictii*, meaning painted, perhaps referring to the tribes' body tattoos, or their written records, left in the form of pictures carved on great vertical stones. To this day, we're not sure where they came from, what language they spoke, or what they even called themselves, but one thing is clear, these Highland warriors refused to succumb to the rule of Rome, or of any other invader. Like relentless vermin, the Picts never ceased attacking the Romans, and by A.D. 409, the Romans had finally had enough, abandoning Britannia, leaving as legacy their lifestyle and the Christian religion.

It was about this time that a Gaelic-speaking tribe invaded Britain and settled along Scotland's southwest coast, establishing the kingdom of Dalriada. These were the Scots and they came from Scotia, the northeastern region of Ireland, then called Hibernia. By the seventh century, they had succeeded in moving their frontier a half day's march south of Inverness, the Pictish capital, before eventually being pushed back again toward Dalriada.

By A.D. 834, the Picts found their armies occupied to the north by the invading Vikings, to the south by the Angles, and to the west by the Scots. Seriously weakened by the Viking raids, Drust IX, the new Pict king, accepted an invitation by Kenneth MacAlpin, a Scot from the Gabhran clan, to settle the issue of Dalriada. Arriving in Scone, Drust and his nobles were plied with alcohol and became quite drunk. The Scots then pulled the bolts from the Picts' benches, trapping the king and his nobles in earthen hollows, where they impaled them on sharp blades and killed them.

Having defeated the Picts, MacAlpin claimed the Scottish crown and renamed his new kingdom, Alba, which he ruled until his death in A.D. 858. For the next three hundred years, the Scots continued to battle the Angles to the south and the Norsemen in the north. The

Viking wars would finally end in 1266 with the battle of Largs and the Treaty of Perth.

But Scotland's turbulent history was just getting started.

The accidental death of Alexander II, King of Scots, in 1286, left an empty throne. As a sign of friendship and respect, the Scottish nobles invited King Edward (Longshanks) I of England to act as judge during the selection process for their new king. Instead of choosing, Longshanks arrived in Scotland with his army, citing a dynastic marriage made a century earlier as basis for his own right to the crown. Though Longshanks's claim had no legitimacy, Scotland was forced to accept Sir John Balliol as their newly elected king as part of England's compromise.

But Longshanks was not through. Still seeking Scotland as part of his own kingdom, he imprisoned John Balliol in the Tower of London, then used state terrorism to subdue the Scottish nobles and their subjects.

The Scots finally rebelled in the spring of 1297. They were led by Sir Andrew de Moray in the north and, in the south, by my own kinsman, Sir William Wallace.

William Wallace was born sometime around 1270, most likely in Ayrshire. He had an elder brother, Malcom, an uncle Richard, and another uncle—a priest—who prepared him for life in the church. The death of William's father at the hands of English troops changed William's destiny, marking him as an outlaw. After killing several soldiers, Wallace was captured and locked up in a dungeon where he lapsed into a coma. Rumors spread that he died of fever, but when a former nanny received permission to bury him, she found he still had a pulse. She nursed him back to health, and soon he was out recruiting other patriots, organizing a guerrilla army against the English.

Longshanks had become William Wallace's dragon, and a warrior was born.

In late August 1297, Longshanks sent an enormous army into Scotland to defeat Wallace. When Moray heard, he joined forces with Wallace, and together they headed south to Stirling. Three days later, half the English cavalry crossed the narrow Stirling Bridge then paused, realizing their leader, John de Warenne was not among them (he had overslept). In the confusion, no more troops were sent across, while Wallace and Moray's army, half-naked and screaming, swept down from the hills to attack. Carpenters pulled pegs from the bridge and destroyed it, killing hundreds while cutting off the rest of the English army's retreat. As Moray continued his frontal assault, Wallace led his troops downriver, where they crossed and attacked the remaining English forces, soundly defeating them. It is said English fatalities exceeded five thousand.

Moray died from his battle wounds, leaving Wallace as sole commander. More conquests ensued, and Wallace's reputation as a charismatic leader grew. His army of followers recaptured Stirling Castle, then invaded the English shires of Cumberland and Northumberland. Later that December, he was knighted and proclaimed Guardian of Scotland, ruling in Balliol's name. Still, most of the Scottish nobles refused to support him.

On July 3, 1298, Longshanks invaded Scotland, his ninety-thousand-strong army soundly defeating Wallace at Falkirk. His military reputation ruined, Wallace resigned his guardianship and traveled to France on a diplomatic mission.

By 1303, the hostilities between England and France were over and Longshanks could again concentrate on his conquest of Scotland. Stirling was recaptured in 1304, Wallace betrayed a year later by a Scottish knight, who served Edward.

On August 23, 1305, Sir William Wallace was hanged, kept alive, then disemboweled, his entrails burned before his eyes. His body was then decapitated and quartered, his head impaled on a spike and displayed on London Bridge.

The barbarism of Wallace's execution made him a martyr to the Scots and gave Robert the Bruce the momentum he needed to lead another uprising. In 1306, the triumphant Bruce was crowned King of Scotland.

Bruce's army would defeat the English in 1314 in the battle of Bannockburn. Twice he invaded England before finally accepting a truce with Longshanks's son, King Edward II. Peace between Scotland and England lasted thirteen years before another war broke out. The Scots were again victorious, and in 1328, Bruce secured a treaty recognizing Scotland's independence. A year later, the king would die of leprosy, leaving the crown to his son, David II.

In 1390, David II died, and Bruce's nephew, John Stewart (Stuart), Earl of Carrick, was crowned King Robert II.

Thus began what is known in Scotland as the Stuart Monarchy.

The next three centuries of rule would be marred by internal strife, conflicts of commerce, and marriages manipulated between Scotland's and England's royal houses. More bloodshed followed, as brother fought brother and religion battled religion in the age-old nonsense of settling whose method of worship was holiest to our Creator, who, for all our murderous efforts, most likely despises the lot of us.

Religious differences would lead to the House of Stuart's undoing.

In 1603, King James VI of Scotland, son of Mary Stuart, Queen of Scots, cousin to Elizabeth I, Queen of England, also became King James I of England in the Union of the Crowns. By succeeding to the throne of England, he thus united Scotland and England as one kingdom—Great Britain—believing the English would accept his Scottish brethren just as they accepted him. But centuries of bloodshed are not so easily forgotten, and England's parliament quickly voted against the proposal.

The King's successor, James VII of Scotland (James II of England), openly supported Roman Catholicism, Scotland's traditional religion. England's parliament forced James VII out, and rather than fight for his crown, he went into exile in France. England offered the crown to his son-in-law, William of Orange, who became known as King William III of Great Britain.

James VII and the House of Stuart were gone, but they still had support from many Catholic Highlanders, who considered the Stuarts Scotland's true bloodline. These Stuart supporters became known as the Jacobites.

When James VII died in France in 1701, the Jacobites felt his son, James VIII, the old Pretender, was rightful heir to the crown. When King William III of Great Britain died a year later, the crown fell to his daughter, Queen Anne, who had no heirs.

Back in France, James VIII's son, Charles Edward Stuart, also known as Bonnie Prince Charlie, decided it was time to lay claim to the Scottish crown. Supported by France (or so he believed), he journeyed to Scotland's Highlands and recruited an army of Jacobite followers. The first Jacobite uprising had taken place years earlier, ending in defeat. The second uprising gained more support, and soon Bonnie Prince Charlie and his followers were marching south to Edinburgh, where his troops easily defeated Britain's opposing forces.

News spread quickly in England that, once again, an army of Highlanders was on the march. The British King, George II, sent British, Dutch, and German troops to intercept, under the command of General Wade and William Augustus, Duke of Cumberland.

Meanwhile, the French decided not to back Charlie, leaving him to fight these masses with only his Jacobite troops. The prince closed within 120 miles of London, then retreated when he heard (false) rumors that Cumberland had amassed a force of thirty thousand men and was heading his way.

Fearing a massacre, Charlie led his rebels on a long, exhausting retreat back through snow-covered hills and up through the Highlands. Upon reaching Inverness, the Jacobites learned that Cumberland's army had made camp in Nairn, fifteen miles away.

On April 16th, 1746, Bonnie Prince Charlie and his exhausted Jacobites faced Cumberland's heavily armed veteran force on Drummossie Moor, near Culloden.

The massacre took a mere thirty minutes.

Upwards of two thousand Jacobites died that day, some Highlanders losing entire clans. But the worst was yet to come.

After the fight, the Duke of Cumberland rode into Inverness, brandishing his bloody sword, shouting out orders, "No quarter given," meaning none should live. By the end of the day, the bloodied bodies of men, women, and children lined the roads into town. Hundreds of innocent Highlanders were butchered, and for months, Cumberland's forces continued to search the countryside for Jacobites, refusing to stop until the ethnic cleansing was completed.

Bonnie Prince Charlie managed to escape, but England was far from done with the Highlanders. Fearing the ancient crofting way and the fighting men it yielded, the "Highland Clearances" were put into law, intended to destroy the clans' very culture. The speaking or writing of Gaelic and the wearing of tartan were made hanging offenses. Entire communities were "encouraged" to emigrate to the New World, while other Highlanders were sold off as slaves, their land stolen and used to raise sheep.

More than two centuries have passed since the dark days of Culloden. Those Scots who fled long ago have seeded great generations that have flourished the world over. George Washington claimed Scottish ancestry, and more than thirty other American presidents bear the Scot credentials as well.

Today, a new kind of invasion is under way. Italians and Pakistanis, Asians and Africans, and many other nationals have settled in Scotland, calling it home. Though they may not share our turbulent history, they, too, are Scots, and now they are part of our heritage.

Still, there are those of pure Gael blood, those like my father, who swear they'll never forget what the English did to their ancestors on the moors of Culloden so long ago.

That John Cialino hailed from London did not surprise me in the least.

* * *

Dawn blinded me, the sun's rays striking my sleep-deprived eyes beneath the partially drawn window shade. We were circling Gatwick Airport, the long night finally over. In just a few short hours I would be back in the Highlands, reunited with my father, and though I had no inkling about what lay ahead, if history was any teacher, then I knew my stay in Scotland would be filled with turmoil.

A country having species, genera, and whole families peculiar to it, will be the necessary result of its having been isolated for a long period, sufficient for many series of species to have been created on the type of pre-existing ones, which, as well as many of the earlier-formed species, have become extinct, and thus made the groups appear isolated. If in any case the antitype had an extensive range, two or more groups of species might have been formed, each varying from it in a different manner, and thus producing several representative or analogous groups.

—Alfred Russel Wallace
"On the Law Which Has Regulated the Introduction of New Species," 1855

As I have no doubt you are aware, some animal or fish of an unusual kind has found its way into Loch Ness. I think I can say the evidence of its presence can be taken as undoubted. Far too many people have seen something abnormal to question its existence . . . I have indeed been asked to bring a Bill into Parliament for its protection.

—Excerpt from a letter to Sir Godfrey Collins, Secretary of State for Scotland, from Sir Murdoch MacDonald, M.P. for Inverness-shire, 13 November 1933

CHAPTER 6

**Inverness, Scottish Highlands
Scotland**

I STARED OUT MY WINDOW, a lump in my throat,
as we flew over the snow-covered peaks of the Grampian Mountains.
Through wisps of clouds I could see evergreen patches of pine and
the dark waters of Loch Ness, an ominous highway of water running
northeast through the Great Glen before narrowing at Tor Point into
the River Ness.

Ten minutes later, we landed at Inverness Airport.

Located at the mouth of the Ness river (*Inver* meaning "mouth
of," thus the name) the capital of the Highlands is a city of sixty-five
thousand, its architecture steeped in Scottish tradition, its land filled
with history. Inverness began as an ancient fortress on Craig Phadrig,
a hill fort with huge ramparts, which served as the capital of the
Pictish Kingdom as far back as A.D. 400. It was here that St. Columba
embarked on his quest to convert the Picts to Christianity . . . and, in so
doing, discovered a water creature that would be turned into a legend.

I walked through the terminal, dead on my feet, not having slept
for the last twenty-eight hours. Max led us to the baggage carousel,
and twenty minutes later we were in his car, motoring south along
Old Military Road, the sounds of *The Cure*'s synthesizers and guitar
blaring from the radio speakers.

"Max, I need to get some sleep. Just drop me off at my hotel, I'll
see Angus later."

"Sorry, but Angus was quite insistent on seeing you now."

"It's been seventeen years since I've seen him, he can wait another
twelve hours."

"Actually, he can't. We go to trial tomorrow." He handed me a copy of the *Inverness Courier*. The article covered most of Thursday's front page.

<u>**Inverness Prosecutors seek Death Penalty in Cialino Murder Case**</u>
Lord Neil Hannam and the High Court of Justiciary have agreed to consider the death penalty in the murder trial of Angus Wallace of Drumnadrochit. Wallace is accused of killing John Cialino, Jr., CEO of Cialino Ventures, one of Great Britain's wealthiest and most influential businessmen. Witnesses report seeing Cialino fall into Loch Ness after being stricken by Wallace on the banks of Urquhart Castle. Police are still dredging Loch Ness, searching for the victim's remains. Opening statements are scheduled to begin Friday.

"First calling was months ago," Max explained. "Judge decided to keep the old man locked up, afraid he'd skip bail. We entered a plea of not guilty back in March, been waiting ever since."

We passed Castle Stuart, heading for the A96, my pulse quickening as I took in the deep blue waters of the Moray Firth. Beaches and cliff tops lined its shoreline; dolphins, porpoises, and killer whales inhabited its North Sea waters.

Despite being part of one island, England and Scotland look nothing alike, due to the fact their geologies were actually conceived thousands of miles apart. About 550 million years ago, the planet's landmasses were all located in the Southern Hemisphere. Scotland belonged to the North American continent (part of Canada's Torngat Mountain Range) while England, Wales, and southern Ireland were united in the remains of a massive continent known as Gondwana. The two kingdoms that would one day form Great Britain were separated by a three-thousand-mile expanse of ocean, known as the Iapetus. After 75 million years of continental breakup and drift, the islands of Scotland and England collided—a million to one shot if ever there was one.

Today, Scotland's topography can be divided into two distinct regions: the Lowlands, densely populated with its industry and bustling cities, and the Highlands, a vast mountainous region rich in wildlife, surrounded by hundreds of coastal islands.

During the last ice age, which ended some ten thousand years ago, Scandinavia and the Scottish Highlands were buried beneath great expanses of glaciers. As these mountains of ice and snow moved, they deepened and rounded out the Highlands' existing river valleys, leaving behind deep lakes (lochs) and long valleys (glens).

Imagine one enormous trench splitting Scotland in two and you'd have the Great Glen. Spanning nearly seventy miles, this 400-million-year-old glacial rift is set upon a geological fault line that widened and deepened during the last ice age. When the ice finally retreated, it left behind a series of freshwater lochs that cut diagonally across the Highlands from the Atlantic to the North Sea. These four bodies of water have been connected to one another through a series of man-made locks, known collectively as the Caledonian Canal.

Completed in 1822, the Caledonian Canal spans twenty-two miles through the Great Glen, connecting the North Sea's Moray Firth to the Atlantic by way of Lochs Dochfour, Ness, Oich, and Lochy. Its most impressive feature is at Fort William, where "Neptune's Staircase" uses eight locks to raise and lower vessels seventy feet above sea level.

We were traveling along the east bank of the Ness River when Max surprised me by making a quick left, following a winding access road up to Inverness Castle.

"We're not going to Portfield Prison?"

The attorney-slash-Goth freak shook his spiked head. "Portfield's overcrowded, and the labdicks don't want to mix an accused murderer in with the rest of the remands, most of the wankers being held for nothing more than bar brawls. So the High Court plucked our father from Her Majesty's Prison and shoved him inside the bowels of the Sheriff Court."

By "Sheriff Court," Max meant Inverness Castle.

Originally built in the twelfth century, Inverness Castle was reconstructed in 1835 after nearly being razed by Bonnie Prince Charlie in 1746. Besides being a popular tourist attraction, the enormous

Victorian red sandstone, sitting majestically on a low-lying cliff over-looking River Ness, also housed the Sheriff Court.

"Sheriffdom" dates back eight centuries to when the sheriff, an officer of the king, presided over all judicial matters in his district. Today, there are six sheriffs in Scotland, each a legally qualified judge oversee-ing civil cases in his region.

Angus's case involved murder, so its jurisdiction was left to the High Court, but the castle still had ample jail space to house the accused.

Max parked and we followed a flower-lined path to the main entrance. A bronze statue of Flora MacDonald, the woman who aided the escape of Bonnie Prince Charlie, stood on a stone pedestal on the castle lawn. Entering the castle gate, we bypassed the tourist line for the "Garrison Encounter," and headed for the Sheriff Court.

After twenty minutes of paperwork and an embarrassing body cavity search using a metal detector, a prison guard led us down a century's old winding stone stairwell into the bowels of the castle. Modern lighting mixed with ancient iron fittings as we approached another officer guarding a corridor of holding cells.

"Here tae see oor Angus, I take it. That'd be the honeymoon suite, last cell."

"You go on," Max said, "I'll meet you outside. Got a few calls to make."

The guard slid open the barred door, allowing me to pass.

The first six cells on either side were empty.

The last one on the left held my father.

He was lying on a mattress, his back against the wall, reading a copy of the *Inverness Courier*. The years had turned his mane of jet-black hair to silver, and a neatly trimmed beard and mustache, more salt than pep-per, had replaced his goatee. Liver spots blotched his tan skin, crow's-feet cornering his eyes, but his gray-blue irises were still piercing and animated, his physique still imposing, though his waistline showed a slight paunch.

I stood outside his locked cell door, my body trembling from nerves and fatigue.

"Bloody daft reporters. Must've telt that coffin-dodgin' slag at least ten times aboot us bein' direct kin tae Sir William Wallace, but does he mention it? Hell no! Well, that's the last he gets oot o' me, I tell ye."

"Nice to see you, too," I managed.

He rolled off the mattress and stood, still light on his feet, but no longer a giant. "Ye sound like a Yank, but ye look like hell. Yer eyes are blood-red an' hollow, and I can smell the stench o' whisky in yer sweat."

"I haven't been sleeping well."

"Aye, since the accident. Read aboot that. That's twice ye've drooned an' been brought back. Best be careful, Nancy, I hear three times is the kicker."

Thirty seconds, and he'd already picked the scab clean off our old wounds.

"If you've got nothing else to say—"

"Now, now, dinnae get yer skirt in a ruffle. Let me have a look at ye." He reached through the bars, placing his hands on my shoulders. Powerful fingers kneaded my deltoids, working their way down to my biceps.

I clenched subconsciously.

He gave me a half grin. "Nae longer a runt, are ye? Thank Christ the Wallace men 'ave resilient genes. So tell me, whit dae ye think o' my bastard, Maxie? I ken he's half-English but—"

"He's a nutcase. Are you deliberately trying to piss off the judge?"

"Is that how we determine whae's innocent an' whae's guilty these days? By their barrister's appearance?"

"This isn't a game, Angus. Max says the Cialinos are pushing for the death penalty."

"A' men die, Zachary. Funny though, how I'm the one facin' the death penalty, an' ye're the one whae's feart. They can only hang me once, but ye'll die a thoosan' deaths afore they put me six feet under."

"I'm not afraid."

"Bollocks. I can smell the fear crawlin' in yer belly like I can smell my ain farts."

"What have I got to be afraid of?"

"I think we baith ken the answer tae that. Seventeen years is a long time tae keep somethin' tucked inside ye."

"Sorry to disappoint you, Angus, but I moved on long ago."

"Have ye? Then why have ye no' gone back tae the Sargasso?"

"Expeditions cost money, and no one's interested. I'd go back in a heartbeat, but—"

"Butts're for crappin'. Maxie's done some checkin'. The Royal Navy contacted ye six weeks ago, interested in financin' a voyage tae locate thae Bloop thing-a-mah-jingies. Word is they offered ye a research vessel an' another sub, but ye turned them doon."

I ground my teeth, confronted by the truth. The Royal Navy *had* tried to contact me, but I had refused their calls, still struggling with my hydrophobia. "Not that it's any of your business, but I'll go back to sea when I'm good and ready."

"No ye willnae. The longer ye wait, the harder it'll be. Look how long it's been since ye returned hame tae yer auld man."

"First, Scotland's not my home, at least not anymore. Second, you've never been much more to me than a sperm donor. I was always your runt, the disappointment God gave you to carry on the Wallace name. You want to give me one final lecture before they hang you, go ahead, it's your time, your dime."

"So ye think yer auld man's guilty, is that it?"

"Honestly, Angus, I don't know what you're capable of anymore."

That stung, I could see the hurt in his eyes.

"Zachary, I ken ye're ashamed o' me, but as far as these charges, I didnae dae it. Johnny C. an' me were pals. Sure, we had words, just as we aye had, but whit happened wis an accident. No matter whit ye may think o' me son, I'm no' a murderer."

Son. I couldn't ever remember him referring to me as his son.

"What is it you want?"

"Nothin' more than yer support. The morn, when I walk intae that courtroom, it'd make me proud tae have both o' my laddies by my side."

Maybe it was fatigue, but when he got choked up I lost it, too, the tears streaming down my cheeks as I embraced him through the bars. "Okay, Angus, I'll be there."

My wife and I were returning to Drumnadrochit from Inverness, driving along the old narrow road near the seven-mile stone. As we passed Aldourie Castle, she suddenly shouted at me to stop, claiming she saw an enormous black body, rolling up and down in the water. By the time I pulled over, all that was left were ripples, but you could tell something big was out there. Moments later, a huge wake became visible, caused by something moving just below the surface. The wake headed toward Aldourie Pier, then its source submerged, showing us two black humps, one after the next. It rose and sank in an undulating manner, circled sharply to port, then disappeared.

—John Mackay, March 1933
(First modern-day sighting since Saint Columba)

CHAPTER 7

Inverness, Scottish Highlands
Scotland
7:15 A.M.

I WOKE UP SCREAMING, limbs quivering, my boxer shorts and T-shirt drenched in sweat. For a terrifying moment, I wasn't sure where I was, and then the empty hotel room yawned back at me, the television still displaying BBC2 from the night before.

You're okay . . . you're okay . . . you're okay . . .

I kicked off the blankets, stripped off my soggy undergarments, and climbed into a hot shower.

A furious banging on the outside door forced me to abandon the shower prematurely. Wrapping a towel around my waist, I left the bathroom, dripping wet. "For Chrissakes, hold on—"

It was the manager, accompanied by hotel security. "Everythin' a'right here, sir?"

"Uh, fine. Is something wrong?"

The security man pushed his way in. "Some o' the guests reported hearin' an awfy scream. Said it sounded like someone wis bein' stabbed."

"Stabbed? Oh, uh, sorry, that must've been the television, you know, one of those American shows. Woke me up as well."

The manager seemed relieved.

Security continued searching for a body.

"Morning." Max entered, dressed in a gray pin-striped suit and matching tie, his spiked hair slicked back, the mascara gone. "There a problem?"

"They heard someone screaming. It was just the television."

"Course it was. Don't say another word."

"Nothin' here," the security man announced. "But if it happens again, I'll write ye up for disturbin' the peace." He shot me a look, then pushed his way out the door, followed by the manager.

"Wanker. He's not even a real bobby." Max pushed me towards the bedroom. "Get dressed, little brar, the High Court awaits."

*   *   *

The High Court of Justiciary is the supreme criminal court in Scotland. Because the only purpose-built High Courts are in Edinburgh and Glasgow, all murder trials taking place outside these cities are held in Sheriff Court buildings. Inverness Castle accommodated the High Court in Inverness, providing its own unique medieval setting to the proceedings.

There were two prosecutors: Mitchell Obrecht, a tall, stocky man with light brown hair that formed an imposing "V" shape on his forehead, and his assistant, a short-haired blonde in a navy business suit named Jennifer Shaw.

Angus was dressed in an old brown wool suit, seated in the dock, an area behind the prosecutors. Max was at another table, facing the judge's bench. Fifteen jurors were seated in the jury box, three police constables at their posts, one by my father. The rest of us—reporters, family, friends, and the nosey—were packed into rows of wooden benches at the rear of the courtroom.

Johnny C.'s widow, Theresa Cialino, an athletic-looking beauty with long, wavy auburn hair, sat three benches ahead of me, an angel tattoo exposed on her left shoulder blade. By the way her dark brown eyes kept focusing on Angus, I felt certain they'd been lovers.

At 9:03, the Clerk of the Court signaled us to rise.

"The High Court of Justiciary is now in session, Lord Neil Hannam presiding."

The judge, a short, fit-looking man with olive-tan skin and dark, slicked-back hair, took his place behind his bench, nodding to his clerk to continue.

"Case number C93-04, Angus William Wallace versus Her Majesty's Advocate in the case of murder in the first degree. The accused has entered a plea of not guilty."

"Lord Advocate, your opening remarks."

Mitchell Obrecht stood and faced the jury. "On February 15 of this year, the accused, Mr. Angus William Wallace of Drumnadrochit, met with the deceased, Mr. John Cialino Jr., of Cialino Ventures, London, on the grounds of the soon-to-be-opened Nessie's Retreat and Entertainment Center. Her Majesty's Advocate shall show that Mr. Wallace had owned some of the acreage along Loch Ness and had sold it to Mr. Cialino's real estate firm for development some eighteen months prior.

"At approximately four-thirty that evening, no less than a dozen people witnessed Mr. Wallace and Mr. Cialino engaged in a heated argument, which ended when Mr. Wallace struck Mr. Cialino directly in the face with his fist, sending him caroming seven meters into the unforgiving six-degree Celsius waters of the Loch. If Mr. Cialino was not dead when he struck the water, then he drowned minutes later. The waters surrounding Urquhart Castle are in excess of two hundred meters, and it is doubtful we'll ever find the body.

"Her Majesty's Advocate intends to prove that Mr. Wallace is not only guilty of Mr. Cialino's murder, but that the act was premeditated, murder in the first degree."

Murmurs filled the courthouse as the prosecutor returned to his seat. I watched the faces of the jury, and from what I could tell, they were buying what Obrecht was selling.

Now it was Max's turn.

"Ladies and gentlemen, my client, Angus Wallace, admits he was arguing with his friend and one-time business partner, Mr. John Cialino Jr., on that tragic 15 day of February last. He confesses that yes, he did strike his friend, much as one might strike a mate in a pub over a pint of ale. But Mr. Wallace did not kill John Cialino, neither by accident nor intention, for Mr. Cialino was quite alive after he hit the water. We intend to prove that Mr. Cialino's death was, in fact, caused by his own negligence, and not by the hand of his friend, Mr. Angus Wallace."

The judge made a few notes, then turned to his Court Macer. "You may call the first Crown witness."

"The High Court calls Mr. Paul Garrison of Las Vegas, Nevada to the stand."

A middle-aged American with light brown hair, graying at the temples, entered the witness box and was sworn in.

Jennifer Shaw questioned him from her seat. "Please state your full name and occupation for the record."

"Paul Garrison. I work for a large, high-end resort casino located in Las Vegas, Nevada."

"What brought you to Scotland last February, Mr. Garrison?"

"Vacation mostly. Nice of you to fly me back like this."

"Were you at Urquhart's Castle on the evening of February 15?"

"Uh, yes . . . yes, I was."

"And what did you see?"

"Well, it was winter, so it grew dark pretty fast. Looking over from the ruins, I saw that big silver-bearded guy—"

"Let the record show Mr. Garrison has identified the accused."

"Right, that's him. Anyway, I saw that guy with the silver beard punch the other little guy—"

"Mr. Cialino?"

"Right, Mr. Cialino, right in the face. Anyway, this Cialino guy stumbled, then took a nosedive right into the Loch."

"No further questions."

The judge turned to Max. "Mr. Rael, your witness."

Max looked up from his notes. "Mr. Garrison, from your vantage, were you able to see Mr. Cialino as he fell?"

"Yes."

"Did you actually see him hit the water?"

"I saw the splash, but the drop's too steep."

"So you never actually saw him in the water?"

"No. Like I said, the angle was wrong, me being close to the castle tower. With that drop, you'd have to be right near the edge to see straight down into the water."

"So then, you had no way of knowing if Mr. Cialino was still alive after he fell into Loch Ness?"

"Yeah, I mean no, there's no way I could see him."

"Thank you, Mr. Garrison. No further questions."

And that's the way it continued for the entire first day. The prosecution would present its eyewitnesses, and Max would establish that none of them actually saw John Cialino in the water after Angus had hit him.

At 4:22 that afternoon, the prosecution rested. Max would present his defense on Monday.

Reporters hustled to transmit their stories.

The best was yet to come.

The Diary of Sir Adam Wallace
Translated by Logan W. Wallace

Entry: 17 October 1330

Three weeks have passed since J came upon the care o' the Chivalric Military Order o' the Temple o' Jerusalem, the Templar name havin' been discarded, so J'm telt, since the massacre under Phillip the Fair. The Priest Knight, MacDonald, claims bloodlines goin' back tae Saint Columba himsel', an' his healin' ways offer me little doubt. The fever is gone, an' J am beginnin' tae feel like mysel' again. Guid news, J'm telt, as J will need my strength against whit lies ahead.

Entry: 22 October 1330

A long day has come an' gone, the night settlin' in ower oor arbor. A tempest wind whips the flames o' oor fire, causin' it tae dance, makin' it difficult tae write, but J am determined tae complete the entry.

We had set oot on foot frae the Moray Firth jist afore the dawn, eight Templars, mysel', an' the Bruce's sacred casket, hung safely roond my neck. For hours we followed the River Ness as it wove its way south, but by midday, the mountains had risen along either side o' us. The goin' got awfy rough, but ne'er had J seen such a bonnie sight. Hills once emerald were dyin' intae golds an' reds an' purples, an' J could smell the winter in the air. The river thickened along a bend an' MacDonald pointed out the very spot where Saint Columba wis said tae have saved a Pict warrior frae one o' the beasts we noo sought.

J remained a disbeliever.

By last light we completed oor day's march, comin' tae the banks o' a narrow channel that widened along the mooth of Loch Ness. 'Twis the first time my eyes gazed upon its dark waters, which ran tae the horizon as far as J could see. The sky was heavy an' grey noo, an' thunder shook the valley roond us. Seekin' shelter, MacDonald instructed we make camp in the forest awa' frae the shore, lest the dragons surface an' become curious.

The Templar's talk o' dragons, at first jovial in nature, has begun tae unnerve me a bit in these ominous surroundings. Though I still refuse tae believe, the blade o' Sir William shall remain close by my side as I sleep.

The general proportion that (Nature) must obtain between certain groups of animals is readily seen. Large animals cannot be so abundant as small ones; the carnivora must be less numerous than the herbivora; eagles and lions can never be so plentiful as pigeons and antelopes; the wild asses of the Tartarian deserts cannot equal in numbers the horses of the more luxuriant prairies and pampas of America. The greater or less fecundity of an animal is often considered to be one of the chief causes of its abundance or scarcity; but a consideration of the facts will show us that it really has little or nothing to do with the matter. Even the least prolific of animals would increase rapidly if unchecked, whereas it is evident that the animal population of the globe must be stationary, or perhaps, through the influence of man, decreasing.

—Alfred Russel Wallace, "On the Tendency of Varieties to Depart Indefinitely From the Original Type," 1858

CHAPTER 8

**Inverness, Scottish Highlands
Scotland**

MAX DROPPED ME OFF at the hotel lobby after the first day of Angus's trial, but I was antsy, and in no mood to stay in my room. Despite being convinced of Angus's guilt, this was the first time my father had ever acknowledged me in a positive way, dissolving years of anger. A well of emotions filled my soul, sobered only by the skeptical, analytical left side of my brain, which kept screaming at me to leave Scotland immediately, warning me that allowing Angus back into my heart was like putting out fire with gasoline.

Stop thinking with your left brain. Give the man a chance to redeem himself.

I should've known better.

With a long weekend ahead, I decided to rent a car and reacquaint myself with the Highlands, hoping to track down Finlay "True" MacDonald, my boyhood friend from Drumnadrochit. The transportation plan changed slightly when I passed the motorbike rental.

I was not a biker, having ridden a motorcycle less than half a dozen times, but something about being in the Highlands on the open road tugged at me. Twenty minutes later, I was motoring out of Inverness, the twin cam engines of a Harley-Davidson Softail rumbling between my legs as I wove south through bumper-to-bumper traffic along the Caledonian Canal, heading for Loch Ness.

There are two roads that encircle the Loch. General Wade's Military Road is the less traveled, a single-lane tarmac that follows the eastern banks of the Ness. As it reaches Fort Augustus at the Loch's southernmost tip, it connects with the A82, a busier two-lane highway that completes the circle along the western shores.

As Drumnadrochit lies on the western bank, about a third of the way down, I settled on the A82.

Rush hour traffic opened as I cleared the canal's swing bridge and accelerated up the asphalt hill, heading toward mountain country. A cold wind whistled through my helmet, Lord Burton's Estate a mere blur on my left as I approached Loch Dochfour, a man-made waterway that had raised Loch Ness nine feet when the canal had first been built.

I slowed, downshifting as I rolled through the sleepy villages of Dochgarroch and Kirkton, then opened her up again as I raced past a roadside farm. The thunder of the Harley's engine scattered geese and chickens and echoed along the mouse-gray rock face that rose majestically on my right. At the foot of these mountains was the Caledonian forest, appearing to me now as a continuous wall of evergreen. Glistening below and on my left were the lead-gray waters of Loch Dochfour.

After a few minutes, the man-made waterway all but disappeared as it bent away from the A82 to the east, narrowing again into the River Ness.

I passed a car park for the Abban Water Fishery, a small stocked waterway where True MacDonald and I had often fished. My mouth watered at the thought of grilled rainbow trout, the memory fading quickly as I was forced to refocus in order to maneuver around a dump truck hauling gravel.

The Harley spewed blue exhaust as I roared past the overloaded vehicle and headed for the outskirts of Lochend, the northernmost beginning of Loch Ness.

Looming ahead, stretched out before me like a dark serpent, was the infamous waterway. I had to slow, the dark beauty of the Loch and its rising mountain walls too mesmerizing not to admire.

Beep! Be–eep . . . beep!

The dump truck was right behind me, its grille threatening to bounce my motorcycle off the side of the road.

Shifting gears, I distanced myself from the threat, then swerved off the A82 into a roadside parking area, known in the Highlands as a lay-by.

I shut off the engine and listened to the Great Glen breathe in between passing cars. I inhaled the moisture of a freshly rained-upon spruce forest and smelled the presence of Loch Ness's acidic waters in the valley below.

The ghosts of my childhood whispered in my head, beckoning me to the ancient shoreline.

Leaving the bike, I made my way down a rock-strewn path until I reached a pebbled beach.

The Loch was calm, its black surface reflecting an overcast sky. Across a half-mile stretch of water, through rolling wisps of fog I could see Aldourie Castle perched along the opposite bank—the exact spot where Angus had lectured me so long ago.

Calm yourself, Zack. There's no dragons or monsters in Loch Ness, there's only Angus, still screwing with your head.

I stared at the three hundred year old chateau. Situated on four hundred acres of forest and grassy knolls, Aldourie Castle was like a vision out of Camelot. Long abandoned, rumored to be for sale, the baronial mansion was known for its many Nessie sightings and had once hosted the premiere party for *Loch Ness*, a movie starring Ted Danson and Joely Richardson. I had enjoyed the flick, up until its fairy-tale ending, which featured Nessie as a pair of friendly plesiosaurs—exactly the kind of rubbish that kept most reputable scientists away from the Loch.

Tea-colored waters, stained brown by an overabundance of decomposing vegetable matter, lapped at the gravel beneath my hiking boots. Overhead, a slit of sun peeked through the ceiling of clouds. The view was breathtaking, the mountains rolling away to the southwest—

—as subliminal dark, underwater images flashed in my head, replaced by a sickening rush of fear that sent my stomach gurgling.

They were the same mind-flashes I had experienced in South Beach, and, unnerved, I backed away, then hurried up the path to the lay-by. It was all I could do to keep myself from retching.

Easy, Zack. It's just a lake. It can't hurt you if you don't go in.

My hydrophobia said otherwise.

I took several deep breaths, then staggered to the Harley. Climbing back on, I started the motor and gunned the engine, continuing south along the busy two-lane highway toward Drumnadrochit.

The cold mountain breeze whipped through my clothing, doing little to soothe my frayed nerves. Seventeen years may have passed, but the drowning incident of my childhood still haunted me.

I rode on for another three miles, then forced myself to steal a quick glance at the Loch as I passed Tor Point. It was here that the eastern shoreline receded, doubling the Ness's width to a full mile. It would remain that wide until the waterway reached Fort Augustus, another twenty miles to the south.

It was almost eight o'clock, yet the evening summer sky was still bright as I passed the hamlet of Abriachan.

Fifteen minutes later, the A82 curved away to the west as the Loch's shoreline opened to Urquhart Bay. Another mile and the waterway was gone, replaced by a small cemetery and the river Enrick.

Crossing the Telford bridge, I followed the road into the village green of Drumnadrochit.

I was home.

My wife and I were driving on the southeast side of the Loch, between Dores and Foyers. It was an overcast day, maybe four in the afternoon, when we spotted this huge animal, slithering across the road about 200 meters ahead of us. The body was 1.5 meters (5 feet) in height, and I estimated its length at 7–9 meters (25–30 feet). Its color could be called a dark elephant grey. We saw no tail, but later concluded that the tail must have been curled around alongside. It did not move in the usual reptilian fashion, instead, its body shot across the road in jerks. Although I accelerated towards it, it had vanished by the time we reached the spot.

—Mr. F.T.G. Spicer, London, 22 July 1933

CHAPTER 9

Drumnadrochit, Scottish Highlands
Scotland

SEVENTEEN YEARS . . . and the village hadn't aged a day.

Drumnadrochit is the first in a series of Highland communities that push west from Loch Ness's Urquhart Bay up the River Enrick and into Urquhart Glen, Glen Affric, and Glen Cannich.

To the two hundred thousand tourists who visit Drumnadrochit each year, the town is the epitome of Highland commercialism, bustling with hotels and guesthouses, European bed-and-breakfasts, tubs of colorful flowers, friendly people, restaurants and bars, quaint shops, and private mountain lodges that overlook the Loch. More important, Drumnadrochit lies near Castle Urquhart and its mysterious deepwater bay, making it the Loch Ness monster capital of the world. The village is home to two competing Loch Ness Monster exhibits, and now John Cialino's soon-to-be-open resort.

To the 813 residents who depend upon tourism to earn their wages, Drumnadrochit is six months feast and six months famine, a pattern that follows the extremes of tourism and the length of its days. Because the Highlands are located so far to the north, summer days at Loch Ness can run from three in the morning until as late as eleven at night. Conversely, midwinter days are reduced to six-hour slots, from nine-thirty in the morning to only three in the afternoon. Living in Drumnadrochit was like living in Alaska, only with more moderate temperatures and less snow, old world charm and nosey neighbors, everyone seeking a livelihood among some of Mother Nature's greatest works.

To a young Zachary Wallace, growing up in a Highland village so far from civilization meant antiquated textbooks, third-run movies, wrath-of-God sermons, and closed-minded teachers. It meant excessive schooling in farming and the ways of crofting, and hanging out at the petrol station with friends. It was stealing the gnomes from old lady Dougall's garden and living in a place few outsiders could spell, let alone pronounce, and its isolation from the rest of the world seemed to impose a ceiling on my ability to garner knowledge about the rest of the world . . . at least until I was old enough to sneak bus rides into Inverness.

Of course, Drumnadrochit would always be Angus Wallace and his mind games, and pretending not to hear Mom's tears. As a child, I couldn't wait to leave, if only to be at peace with myself.

Seventeen years later, the nightmares of my childhood had returned . . . and so had I.

I drove through the village green and past the petrol station where I used to hang out. I idled by Blarmor's Bar until I could smell the chicken and fish, then passed the Sniddles Club, my father's favorite watering hole.

I parked and stretched my legs, my groin feeling numb. The post office was nearby, and I entered, just as it was about to close.

There was one clerk on duty, an old man in his eighties who had taught me history back in grammar school. "May I help ye?"

"I'm looking for an old friend, his name is MacDonald, F. True MacDonald."

"Dae ye mean Alban MacDonald's laddie?"

"That's him. Know where I can find him?"

"Usually in the North Sea. Dives off one o' them oil rigs, but this month an' next he's back in toon. Stays wi' his faither, who works up at the lodge, I'd check there first."

"Thanks."

The old man squinted at me through a pair of copper-rimmed spectacles. "Ye look a wee bit familiar. Dae I ken ye?"

"You did. Thanks, Mr. Stewart, I gotta run."

I made it halfway out the door before he shouted, "Ye're Angus Wallace's laddie, the big-shot scientist. Had tae come hame tae look for yer monster, didn't ye?"

"The only monster I know of, Mr. Stewart, is locked up in Inverness Castle."

I hopped on the Harley and drove south, accelerating up a steep gravel path that led into the hills.

The lodges at Drumnadrochit were a series of private cottages and chalets set high above the village on a mountainside overlooking Loch Ness. I parked, then entered the main office, hoping to find True before I ran into his father.

Too late.

Alban Malcolm MacDonald, known to the bairns (children) of Drumnadrochit as "Crabbit MacDonald," looked as gruesome and bad-tempered as I ever remembered. His moon-shaped Norseman's face remained half-concealed behind a thick, graying auburn goatee and sideburns, neither doing much to hide the scars left behind from a childhood ridden with smallpox. Fog-gray eyes stared at me as I entered his dwelling, his thickly callused fingers and yellowed nails tapping the wooden check-in desk in rhythm.

"Mr. MacDonald, good to see you, sir," I lied. "Do you remember me?"

He removed a toothpick hanging from his liver lips, his crooked, yellowed teeth revealing themselves as he spat, "Zachary Wallace."

"Yes, sir. I can't believe you remembered."

"Didn't. Saw yer photo in the papers five months back."

"Oh, right. Is, uh, is True here?"

"Nah."

"No? How about Brandy? Gosh, last time I saw your daughter, she must've been five, maybe six years—"

"Go back tae the States, Zachary Wallace, there's nowt here for ye."

"My father's here. I came to lend my support."

"Since when does he ask for it? Men like yer faither cannae be trusted. They're ruinin' the Great Glen, dae ye ken whit I mean? Him, an' a' thae bastards like them that selt their namesake's land. Let them spend their money in hell, says I."

"Grrraaah!" Air wheezed from my chest as I was hoisted clear off the floor by two burly, auburn-furred arms that wrapped around me from behind.

Old man MacDonald shook his great head and went back to work.

"Zachary Wallace, returned to us from the dead!" He put me down, spun me around, and embraced me again.

The last time I had seen Finlay True MacDonald, he was a skinny runt, with freckles and wild burnt-orange hair. No one ever called True by his real first name, his middle name, passed down from his late mother's side, being far more interesting. We'd kept in touch for a while after I'd moved to the States, and always called each other on birthdays, but it had been a good ten years since I'd seen a current photo.

The imposing giant with the auburn ponytail who stood before me now was six-foot-five and heavily muscled, weighing close to 260 pounds. "Jesus, True, you're as big as a friggin' horse."

"Aye. An' listen tae *you*, wi' yer snooty American accent, ye sound like ye're talking' oot o' yer nose. Ye're no runt any mair, I see, an' by God, it's guid tae see ye."

"I hear you've been working out on the oil rigs. What happened to the career in the Royal Navy?"

"Had my fill. Her Majesty's Navy wis guid enough tae train me tae work in atmospheric dive suits, an' the pay in the private sector's a whole lot better."

"I didn't know they made dive suits large enough to fit the likes of you."

"Aye, well, it can be a squeeze, right enough! Have ye ever been doon in one?"

"I climbed inside one once. Every step was like carrying a ton of bricks."

"Probably one o' thae auld JIM suits. We use nothin' but WASPs an' the new Newt Suits on the rigs nowadays. Both have thrusters that propel ye along. Much easier on the legs. Now I spend four hours a day, nine months a year skimmin' the bottom o' the North Sea, checkin' the lines an' doin' repairs. High stress, but the pay's guid, so I cannae complain. Lots o' folk in the Highlands are barely makin' it these days."

"How long are you off for?"

"Another three an' a half weeks. Then I'm back for four months, or until the winter seas get ower rough."

"Guess you heard about my father."

"Aye, an' every pub frae Lochend tae Fort Augustus's toastin' his name. Tourism's been doon ye ken, thanks tae the whole terrorist thing. Maybe the trial'll drive some business this way. That, or the new resort."

"You think Angus meant to kill Johnny C.?"

True mulled it over. "No, but I think he meant tae teach him a lesson. You an' me both ken yer faither carries a fierce temper, especially when it comes tae money. This Johnny C. wis English, an' a big-shot developer, no less, and I'll wager he didnae get that way toein' the line for the likes of us Highlanders. Angus most likely caught him tryin' tae pull a fast one an' decked him guid. I'd have done the same, 'cept no' on the cliffs off Urquhart Bay, an' sure no' in front o' witnesses."

"They're talking about the death penalty."

"Aye, but I widnae fret much aboot that. Angus is still as slippery as an Anguilla eel, an' this is still the Highlands. We tend no' tae hang one o' oor own. Anyway, enough aboot the trial. Am I right in that ye're freed for the weekend?"

"Yes. But I have to be back in Inverness Monday morning."

"Which gi'es us plenty o' time tae poison oor livers. First things first, ye'll need a bed." He reached behind his father's desk and grabbed a room key.

"True, I really didn't plan on staying, I wasn't even sure I'd find you. I left all my clothes back in Inverness."

"So ye'll borrow. Ye're stayin', an' that's a' there is tae it. Ye seem a bit stressed. First things first, we'll blow off some steam, jist like we used tae dae when we were laddies."

Before I could respond, True had me around the shoulders and was sweeping me out the door.

*   *   *

The ruins of Castle Urquhart stand on Strone Point, a rocky promontory set along the southern shores of Urquhart Bay, one of the deepest parts of the Loch. The castle's origins can be traced back to a Pict fort built in the fifth century, and it was there that Saint Columba, Abbot of Iona, first visited the Pictish Kingdom in A.D. 565.

Eight hundred years later, the English fortified the settlement, following Longshanks's victory over the Scots at Dunbar. William Wallace and Andrew Moray eventually attacked the castle, securing it for Scotland. Years later, another bloody siege ensued, with Longshank's invading army starving the Scot occupants into submission. The castle remained under England's control until Robert the Bruce retook it in 1306.

The Scots controlled the castle for the next four centuries, until the English used explosives to demolish most of the fortress in order to keep it out of the hands of the Jacobites.

What remains today of Urquhart Castle are the upper bailey, sections of its fortifying wall, and part of its five-storey tower house. While there are certainly more impressive structures along the Loch, none are as popular as this haunting castle ruins, surrounded on three sides by deep water known for its frequent Nessie sightings.

*   *   *

It was after ten and summer's dusk was nearly upon us, the mountains fading into rolling purple shadows, the bleeding scarlet horizon graying into night. True and I wandered along the perimeter of Urquhart Castle, each of us carrying a golf club and a small bucket of practice balls. Moving south along the grass-covered knoll, I paused to look down upon the steep twenty-foot drop on our left.

Below, a foreboding black surf rolled against the rocky vertical embankment, cloaking the Ness's extreme depths.

"This is where it must've happened," I said.

"Aye. It's a survivable fa' though, dependin' upon where he goes off. 'Course, he could have hit his head on one o' thae rocks, an' that wid have been that. Come on then."

True led me to a hill that overlooked the castle parking lot. To the south was the lighted construction site of what would soon be Cialino's five-star resort. "Nice, huh? Fancy pools an' restaurants, an' a' its rooms wi' a Loch view. They're even sellin' time-shares, so I hear. Johnny C. would have made a killin' on that place if only he'd have lived tae see it."

"There's still the merry widow."

"Aye. From whit I hear, she gets everything. An' she's no' exactly hard on the eyes, yeah?" True removed a golf tee from his pocket, grabbed a ball from his bucket, then addressed the shot. "Okay, the construction fence's 220 yards, the patio's 227, the pool 235, an' if ye plunk it doon in the hot tub, ye automatically win. We'll start the pot at ten pounds an' raise it two pounds a shot."

I teed up to his left, giving those long arms of his plenty of space. "True, what did your father mean when he said those bastards are ruining the Great Glen?"

True swung, his ball soaring high over the construction fence, ricocheting off a bulldozer. "Forget my faither, he's strictly auld school. Alban MacDonald wid sooner bash a computer wi' a cricket bat than learn how tae use it. In my mind, it's plain hypocritical no tae encourage development. The auld Clans have aye held ontae the best acreage around Loch Ness, yer faither bein' among the first tae sell. More will follow, wait an' see. Go on then, take a swing."

I gripped the driver, took a few practice swings, then wound up and struck the ball, watching it rise, then curve left into Loch Ness.

"Jesus, Zack. My Auntie Griselda hits a better ball, an' she's doon tae one leg."

"Blow me." I teed another ball.

True hit his next shot, a line drive that disappeared over the bulldozer. "Ye heard they selt Aldourie Castle, aye? Word is some big firm's comin' in, convertin' the whole place intae an exclusive country club, sort o' like they did wi' Skibo. Figure one day I'll retire frae oil rig divin' an' get a job there as a golf pro."

"You'd make a better parking lot attendant." I hit another drive, this one skidding off the grass before hitting a rock and ricocheting into the water.

True grinned, then struck another ball, a moon shot that bounced twice off the brick balcony before plunking into the whirlpool. "Like I said, golf pro."

"Since when do golf pros wear ponytails?" I retorted, slicing yet another ball into the drink.

He fingered the thick lock of hair. "Dinnae knock my tail, it drives the birds right intae my bed. Go on, I'll gie ye one last shot tae tie or make it an even fourteen pounds, then we best be gettin' ower tae Sniddles. Brandy'll be waitin'."

I hit my final shot, which soared toward the heavens before banana-curving into Loch Ness. "I hate this fucking game," I said, threatening to toss my driver over the cliff.

"Temper, temper," True cooed, draping a burly arm across my shoulder. "See, when oor ancestors invented the bloody game, they understood two things. First, it takes exactly eighteen shots tae polish off a fifth o' a bottle o' Scotch, thus, a game o' golf equates tae eighteen holes. Second, yer game's ultimately a measurin' stick of how well ye deal wi' life's shits and giggles. Like yer game, yer life needs work."

"Okay, Mister Golf Pro, what's your advice?"

"That's easy. Any man who cannae keep his balls oot o' the water needs tae get laid. Come on, let's find my sister."

*   *   *

It was a Friday night and the club was packed, the tables filled with tourists, the bar four deep in regulars. There were darts and lager and music and lager and laughter . . . and did I mention lager?

True entered and the crowd was forced to part, me following in his wake. He shook a dozen hands and kissed a half dozen women, and I was thankful he didn't introduce me.

And then he waved to a raven-haired beauty who was waving back at us from a corner table, and I was smitten.

Claire MacDonald, who preferred her American middle name, Brandy (mostly to spite her father) was the kind of girl shy guys like me daydreamed about in high school and stayed up at night thinking about, but never had the nerve nor the credentials to ask out. These were girls reserved for the star quarterback and the guys who drove sports convertibles, and when they got older, they became trophy wives—arm-candy to the rich and powerful.

To me, Brandy was a swan, and I was a duck, and as a basic rule of nature, as my great uncle Alfred might have said, ducks and swans don't mate.

But in her own mind, Brandy was tarnished goods. When she was sixteen, her high school heartthrob had gotten her pregnant, right before his family abruptly relocated to Edinburgh. Old man MacDonald wasn't too keen about his daughter's obvious lack of celibacy and promptly threw her out of his house, forcing her to move into a shelter. Though she'd lost the child at the start of the second trimester and eventually returned to high school, Brandy was on her own, having never been invited back in her bitter father's home again.

At nineteen, Brandy met Jack Townson, an American stockbroker vacationing in Loch Ness. Seeing an opportunity to escape the Highlands, she returned with him to the States, and two months later they were married—more to spite her father than out of love.

Brandy enjoyed living in southern California and for a time things were fine. Then one afternoon, on a bike ride through the Hollywood Hills, she was struck by a car, and in that instant everything in her life changed.

The extent of Brandy's injuries were severe, a skull fracture and bruised brain, to go along with multiple fractures to her arms and legs, a punctured lung, a broken left eye socket, and a shattered jaw. She would undergo three major surgeries, spend weeks in intensive care and five months in physical therapy, during which time her husband had an affair.

Townson stayed with his wife through most of her recovery, waiting until she was well enough to leave the hospital before presenting her with divorce papers. Fourteen months after leaving Scotland, Brandy returned to the Highlands, divorced, lonely, and depressed.

As Darwin once said, there are exceptions throughout the natural selection process. Brandy was a swan with an injured wing, and that's how ducks like me land swans.

What I didn't know was Brandy's phobias ran as deep as my own.

"So, the son o' Angus Wallace returns. Quit starin' an' give me a hug."

We embraced, my nostrils inhaling her pheromones, my groin awakening for the first time in months.

"I'll get us some drinks," said True. "You two keep getting' reacquainted."

She smiled and sat opposite me, the light catching the burnt orange highlights in her ink-black hair. "If I know my brother the matchmaker, he'll no' be back anytime soon."

"So, how're you feeling? I mean, you look . . . amazing."

"True told ye about my wee accident, huh? I'm fine now, but it *was* bad, plus we had no insurance, leavin' the lawyers tae sue the driver's company. It was a nasty fight but we won, then in the end, my ex-husband confessed he was screwin' my private nurse."

"Geez."

"It gets better. Seein' how I wasn't yet a citizen, the ex an' his new whore helped themselves tae all the insurance money. Sixty grand they stole from me, the no-good thieves."

I leaned in, hoping to impress her with my own relationship scars. "Six months ago I was engaged. She was actually one of my students, an undergrad in biology. She waited until final grades were posted, then broke up with me while I was lying in a hospital bed. Told me she sold the engagement ring and was using the money to go to Cancún on Christmas break with her new boyfriend."

Her laugh energized my soul. "Well, are we no' two peas in a pod. So tell me, Zachary Wallace, how does it feel tae finally be a big shot scientist?"

"I don't know, am I famous or infamous?"

"Ye located a giant squid, I'd say ye're famous. Just like ye aye wanted. I can still remember you an' me dissectin' fish an' frogs an' birds in yer father's cellar."

"That's right, I forgot about that."

"No' me, I remember everythin'. Tae me, those were my good times. Did True tell ye I'm takin' a correspondence course at the local college."

"That's terrific."

"No, but it's a start. I'm learnin' all sorts o' stuff. Did ye know an ostrich's eye is bigger than its brain?"

"No, but I won't forget it."

She smiled, then became melancholy. "I read about yer sub sinkin'. One o' the men died, eh?"

"It was an accident."

"I know. I was relieved ye came out okay."

"Technically, I drowned."

"The article said ye *nearly* drowned."

"Nope, I was dead. *Pffffttt.*"

"An' exactly how does one know if one's dead? You see a heavenly light?"

"Sort of." Feeling antsy, I looked over my shoulder to see where True was with those drinks. He was at the bar, absorbed in a conversation with two scantily clad Scandinavian women who were showing him their belly-button rings.

I signaled for a waitress.

"So Zack, what does one do after one returns from the dead?"

"Get drunk, become depressed, and return to the Highlands, what else?"

We laughed and talked and drank and ate and flirted. An hour later, we slipped out of the pub and walked half-drunk through the center of town, arm in arm, and I knew then that I had never loved

Lisa, at least I had never been "in love" because what I was feeling now was like walking on air.

"Did True tell ye how I earn my wages?" she asked.

"He was vague. Something about working in Brackla."

"I run a tour boat from the docks o' the Clansman Hotel. It's a used *Sea Angler*, just over nine meters. Topside's got benches, enough tae accommodate sightseers, down below's where I live. Want tae see?"

It was the kind of line a man might wait his whole life to hear, but the thought of getting on a boat docked at night in Loch Ness sobered me up like a pot of coffee.

Still, this was love, and love (and lust) conquered all. So we climbed aboard the Harley and motored north on the A82, the howling wind in our hair, Brandy's nibbling on my earlobe driving me wild.

Brackla is a small hamlet located along the Loch's northwestern shore, approximately halfway between Drumnadrochit and Lochend. Its draw is the Clansman, the only hotel (save for Angus's new resort) situated directly on the banks of Loch Ness. The facility has twenty-eight suites, all offering panoramic views of the Loch, along with large dining rooms and halls that have hosted many a wedding and Scottish dinner dance.

Situated directly behind the Clansman Hotel was a rectangular inlet that served as a docking area for Loch Ness. Brandy's boat, the *Nessie III*, was tied off at the end of one of the piers. As we crossed over the wooden boardwalk that led to her berth, I could feel trepidation rising in my gut.

"So Zachary? What dae ye think?"

"That depends. What happened to the *Nessie I* and *II?*"

"Oh, the monster ate them," she teased, rubbing my groin.

I felt queasy. "Brandy, why don't we go back to the lodge and—"

"Come on, I'll give ye the tour." Ignoring my objections, she took my hand and dragged me aboard, reciting more obscure facts she had learned from her correspondence course. "Did ye know butterflies taste wi' their feet?"

White-washed wooden benches, set parallel to one another and nailed to the main deck, ran the length of the deck. Forward was the wheelhouse, its entry framed by a pair of doors. One guarded a sea toilet and sink, the other led below deck to Brandy's private quarters.

Fear pounded in my pulse as Brandy coaxed me below, pointing out the engine room, her galley, and the refurbished bathroom. And then she led me forward into her cabin, slipped out of her sandals, and kissed me hard on the lips.

Her Scotch-laced tongue flitted in my mouth as her hand unzipped the fly of my pants. I fumbled like an orangutan with the back of her bra, the clasps of which must have been welded shut.

"Let me." She reached behind her back and freed her breasts.

For a precious moment, my desire overcame my phobia . . . until the boat rose and dropped beneath a half-dozen wakes and the fear rose again in my gut, tossing ice water over my hard-on.

I jumped as she unbuckled my pants. "Brandy, wait, I . . . I can't do this."

"Why?" she purred. "Did yer knob perish on the Sargasso, too. Perhaps I'll have tae resuscitate it, yeah?"

"No!" My mind raced like a demon, not wanting a repeat of what had happened on South Beach. "I mean, your father . . . it's your father. He'll know I stayed with you tonight."

"Since when do *you* give a shyte what my old man thinks?"

"Since . . . since he saved my life. See, if I slept with you tonight, our first night together, I'd be disrespecting him, see? And that would ruin any chance we had with him later on."

"I don't care. I hate the bastard worse than you hate Angus, now take off yer clothes, I need tae feel you inside o' me."

The boat swayed beneath us again, and I panicked like a bear caught in a trap.

"What? Do ye no' want tae be wi' me then? Is that it?"

"No, I mean I do, I swear—"

"What's wrong then? Ye're as pale as a ghost, an' ye're tremblin'. Come on, we'll lie down."

"I . . . I need some air!" Pulling up my jeans, I tore up the steps, the main deck spinning in my head as I half leaped, half tumbled over the stern rail, landing awkwardly on the dock.

"Zachary Wallace, where do ye think ye're going?"

I looked back, the dark waters swirling on either side of me. "I'll call you! I'll come by tomorrow!"

Not waiting for a reply, I stumbled down the boardwalk until I made it back to the parking lot, then kept running until I reached a grove of trees.

Lying back against the trunk of a pine, I closed my eyes, my limbs trembling as I hyperventilated like a frightened deer.

... in the case of an island, or of a country partly surrounded by barriers, into which new and better adapted forms could not freely enter, we should then have places in the economy of nature which would assuredly be better filled up if some of the original inhabitants were in some manner modified; for, had the area been open to immigration, these same places would have been seized on by intruders. In such cases, slight modifications, which in any way favoured the individuals of any species, by better adapting them to their altered conditions, would tend to be preserved; and natural selection would have free scope for the work of improvement.

—Charles Darwin, *The Origin of Species*, 1859

CHAPTER 10

UNDERWATER . . . *can't see . . . can't breathe. Cold, scared.*
Kick with the free leg, twist and kick, don't swallow. Throat burns, ears
popping, suffocating, keep kicking . . . twist, struggle . . .
Free!
Swim, kick, my ankle hurts so bad. Gurgling growls . . . rising beneath
me! Oh, God, Zachary . . . get to the light!

I lashed and kicked, tearing the sheets from the mattress, flinging the
suffocating wool blanket from my face as I flew off the bed and barrel-
rolled out the front door of the lodge cabin as if on fire.

Breathing, shaking, quivering, the mountain air chilling my
sweat-soaked boxers and T-shirt, the cold helping me to awake.

You're okay . . . you're okay . . . you're okay.

I looked around, panting. The woods were quiet, the solitude
heavy in the predawn light. And then my eyes caught movement.

It was old man MacDonald crossing through the forest. Seeing
me, he paused, hiding behind a clump of birch trees.

"Mr. MacDonald?"

He refused to move, which was more than a little bizarre, so I
decided to approach—anything to distance myself from the night
terror.

"Get back tae yer cabin."

Ignoring his command, I moved closer.

He was dressed in an almost medieval-looking black surcoat,
marked by a crimson-colored *X* that was woven around a heart-
shaped emblem.

Splattered across the tunic was fresh blood.

"Mr. MacDonald, are you hurt?"

The old man hurried off, but I quickly overtook him. Grabbing his shoulder, I spun him around, only to be confronted with the business end of a double-edged sword, the gold-plated blade dripping with blood.

"Back off, young Wallace. My business is my ain affair, dae ye ken whit I mean?"

I was in no position to argue.

He stared at me for a long moment, then continued down the mountainous slope to his cabin.

*   *   *

Several hours later, still baffled by the surreal encounter with the Crabbit, I drove the Harley into the parking lot of the Clansman Hotel, then headed for the wharf to meet up with the old man's daughter.

I was armed with a bouquet of freshly cut flowers and a simple plan: Beg forgiveness, give her the flowers, then ask her to dinner in Inverness, hoping we'd end up in my hotel room.

I hesitated, then walked out onto the pier, the daylight easing last night's feelings of dread. As I approached the *Nessie III*, Brandy emerged from the wheelhouse, dressed in a gray cotton sweat suit. "Well, look who it is? Thanks for a helluva night, lover."

"Can I at least explain?"

"I've a better idea. Why don't ye go make nice wi' my old man, 'cause I want nothin' tae do wi' you!"

"Brandy, wait!" I climbed aboard, quickly presenting her with the flowers. "For you. I picked them myself."

"Did ye now?" She inhaled the bouquet, then tossed them overboard. "I hate flowers. Flowers are what my bastard ex used tae give me while he banged my nurse."

"That won't ever happen with us!"

"Us? There is no us, now get off my boat."

"I'm sorry. Let me make it up to you. We'll spend the day in Inverness. We'll go shopping, have some dinner—"

"I'm no goin' anywhere. I've a sold-out tour scheduled tae leave in forty minutes. Besides, ye cannae just bribe yer way back intae me heart, there's too much scar tissue." She pushed me toward the rail.

"Brandy, just hear me out. You're the first good thing that's happened to me in a long time, and I don't want to blow it."

"Should o' thought about that last night."

"Give me a second chance, I'll do anything."

She paused. "Anythin'?"

Uh-oh . . .

"Okay. Like I said, I've a full boat intae Fort Augustus. We do a good job, an' most'll book me for their return trip."

"We?"

"Ye said ye'd do anythin', now ye can play first mate. When we get back, ye'll help clean the boat, then ye can take me tae Inverness for dinner."

Before I could negotiate, she removed her hooded sweatshirt, revealing tanned curves barely concealed behind a heart-stopping black floss bikini.

My left brain rolled over as the right sealed the deal.

*   *   *

Forty minutes and a triple dose of prescription pills later, my brain was buzzing like a bee as I undid the *Nessie III*'s bowline, allowing the overcrowded vessel to push away from the dock. There were twenty-three passengers on a boat that legally held eighteen, but for all I could tell, it could have been a hundred.

Too unbalanced to stand, I wedged myself on the starboard-facing bench between an American fellow named Clay Jordan, who was with his German wife and two young sons, and a chatty woman named Bibi Zekl, a bookstore clerk on holiday with her husband, Stefan. In no time, the *Nessie III* was puttering south along the Loch, all eyes, save mine, focused on the water as we approached Urquhart Bay.

Brandy was in the wheelhouse, playing both boat captain and tour guide. Over two badly crackling loudspeakers she announced, "Welcome to the Highlands. In Scotland, we call lakes "lochs," and the biggest and deepest is Loch Ness, at over thirty-six kilometers long. That's twenty-three miles to our American guests. From Tor Point south, she averages a mile wide, with depths over one hundred and eighty meters, or six hundred feet. Amazingly, Loch Ness is deeper than even the North Sea.

"We're approaching Urquhart Bay on our starboard, or right side. Urquhart Bay is one of the deepest parts of the Loch, descending to depths of two hundred and forty meters, almost eight hundred feet.

"Loch Ness is one of four long, narrow lochs that run diagonally through the Scottish Highlands. Forty rivers and streams, what we call "burns," feed into Loch Ness, with only one, the River Ness, running out of the Loch and into the Moray Firth and the North Sea. Did ye know that Loch Ness holds more water than all the lakes and rivers in England and Wales combined? The water's extremely cold, about five degrees Celsius, and visibility's very poor. This is because of peat, which are particles of soil brought down from the rivers, giving the Loch an acidic taste. Of course, if yer gonnae drink it, we recommend addin' a shot o' cheap Scotch."

The German woman, Bibi, nudged me and laughed, wondering why I was taking the tour with my eyes squeezed shut behind my sunglasses.

"Now, who can tell me what Loch Ness is famous for?"

"The Loch Ness monster!"

"That's right. There've been thousands of sightings over the years, but the very first took place over fourteen hundred years ago, when Saint Columba traveled to the Highlands to bring Christianity to the native Picts. According to legend, a fearsome monster rose from the murky depths of Urquhart Bay and grabbed a native swimmer. The Saint raised his hand, and yelled, 'Thou shall go no further, nor touch the man,' and the monster released him, then returned to the deep."

The children oohed and ahhed, while I ground my teeth, wishing I had slept in.

"On our starboard side is the town of Drumnadrochit where the first modern-day Nessie sighting took place. Mr. and Mrs. Mackay, owners of the Drumnadrochit Hotel, were traveling along the A82 in 1933, just after it was built. From the road they saw a huge beastie rolling and plunging in the middle of the Loch. Soon, hundreds of other people reported similar sightings, and now the Loch attracts the attention of monster hunters the world over. Dozens of documentaries have been filmed on these waters, including a movie starring Ted Danson. We've also had our share of famous scientists visit the Loch, and today, ladies and gentlemen, I'm excited to say we've got us a very special treat . . ."

Oh shit!

". . . exclusively, only on board the *Nessie-III,* is one of the world's top marine biologists . . ."

No, Brandy, don't do it . . .

". . . the only man ever to witness a giant squid in its own habitat . . ."

Stupid bastard! See what happens when you think with the wrong side of your brain! You should've stayed in Inverness. You should've . . .

". . . straight from the United States, by way of the Highlands, Drumnadrochit's own Dr. Zachary Wallace."

I opened my eyes to applause, my heart pounding like a timpani.

"Raise your hand for us, Dr. Wallace. Dr. Wallace? Come on, now, don't be shy."

I raised my hand, clutching the bottom of the bench with the other.

"I'm sure Dr. Wallace would be happy to answer any questions you might have, isn't that right, Doctor?"

In the corner of my left eye I saw Clay Jordan's older boy excitedly raise his hand. "Dr. Wallace, do you believe in Nessie?"

"No."

"Why not?" This from the gabby German woman.

My clenched throat managed, "Nessie's folklore."

Brandy rescued me, if only temporarily. "Oh . . . kay, tell ye what, if you could hold yer questions for Dr. Wallace a moment, we're just drifting by Urquhart Castle, one of the most popular sites on the

Loch. Many famous photos of the monster have been taken from the shores of these castle ruins and—"

"Hey," called out a dark-haired Canadian woman, "isn't this the spot where that rich guy was murdered?"

"John Cialino, that's right," answered Wezzi Hoeymans, visiting from the Netherlands. "Maybe we'll see his body!"

Passengers followed the purple-haired youth to the starboard rail, snapping pictures of the shoreline like a bunch of ravenous paparazzi.

The dramatic redistribution of mass was too much for the over-loaded, under-ballasted craft, and it began rolling, its two-foot free-board quickly disappearing as its starboard rail dipped precariously close to the water.

Brandy fought the wheel. "Take yer seats, people . . . please, we need tae keep the boat balanced. Please, take yer seats, we don't want tae tip."

They ignored her and continued to film, oblivious of the danger.

"Sit your asses down . . . now!"

What deep recess this guttural bellow came from, I've no clue, but come it did, straight out of my mouth, and it echoed across the Loch as if Sir William himself were leading a battle charge.

The passengers froze, then hustled back to their spots on the benches, tails between their legs.

Brandy stared at me, aghast.

Clearly in trouble, I stumbled out an apology. "Sorry. I . . . uh, it's just that I don't want us to tip, not in these freezing waters . . . uh . . . not with the *monster* lurking so close."

Having crapped on deck, I voluntarily stepped in it.

"But Dr. Wallace, you just said—"

"I said I didn't believe in the *folklore* of Nessie, but there's defi-nitely something large living in Loch Ness, of that I'm certain."

The words came out of my mouth, and again I didn't recognize them.

The crowd did, and they quickly gathered around, aiming their video cameras at me as if I were Mel Gibson.

"Go on, Dr. Wallace," coaxed Brandy, "don't stop now."

With nervous perspiration flowing from every pore, and my boxer shorts hopelessly wedged up the crack of my butt, I gritted my teeth and focused on the distant shoreline. "In . . . in order to understand the mysteries of Loch Ness, first . . . well, first we have to separate the real science from all of this legend nonsense. For instance, some Highlanders speak of a Kelpie, a sort of water horse, that lives not only in Loch Ness but in other Lochs and . . . and even in lakes across the world. At Loch Lochy, they call their monster Lizzy, and at Lake Champlain, the beast is known as Champ."

A pale, blonde American woman suddenly pointed from her wheelchair, crying out, "Oh my God, look! There it is!"

Passengers stood, several searching with binoculars.

"Hey, she's right, there it is! It's the monster!"

An avalanche of flesh tripped over itself to get to the port side rail, the crowd gesturing at a series of humps that were indeed moving along the otherwise mirrorlike surface, several hundred yards away.

"Dr. Wallace, Dr. Wallace, do you see it?!"

The boat began rolling again, this time to port.

"It's not the monster," I commanded, "now take your seats."

"No, look, it's moving right . . . aww, see, it's gone."

"It was just a boat wake, people. Sit down, and I'll explain."

Reluctantly, they returned to their seats, their eyes still lingering to the east as the *Nessie III* resettled in the water.

I turned to the woman in the wheelchair. "Miss, what's your name?"

"Kate Coffey."

"Kate, do you see the mountains that form walls along either side of the Loch? Those mountains actually continue straight underwater, creating a sort of geological trowel, seven to eight hundred feet deep. Think of Loch Ness as Mother Nature's version of a giant bathtub. When you splash in your bathtub at home, you create waves, which strike the far side of the tub and reflect back again. Loch Ness sort of works the same way. When a boat like ours passes a steep shoreline like the one below Urquhart Castle, the boat's wake will strike the cliff face, then reflect back out again. Loch Ness is so big that sometimes the boat that created the wake is long gone by the time it's reflected back to the next passing boat. In calm conditions like today, a reflected wake moving at an angle toward another reflected wake will create a disturbance that looks very much like multiple humps in the water."

"And that's what I saw?"

"That's right. Don't feel bad, Kate, it fools a lot of people, though people tend to see what they want to see. Another popular illusion is created by large-keeled boats, like ferries or tugboats. As they move through Loch Ness, these powerful vessels create deep wave disturbances that travel along the bottom. When these waves eventually reach the shallows, the energy is forced up to the surface, causing a great upheaval of water that people swear is the monster breaching."

"Tell us more," said the German woman, as she snapped a picture of me with her digital phone-camera.

I continued, the diversion of the lecture, combined with the effects of my prescription pills combining to lessen my hydrophobia. "The abundant wildlife at Loch Ness has been deceiving tourists for decades. The area is home to cormorants—water birds with large necks that stick out of the water. And Merganser ducks, they can drive Nessie watchers crazy. As they move through the water, the ducks create V-shaped wakes, which resemble something large moving below the surface. From far away, a line of ducks can resemble humps in the water. Deer, otters, and seals are also found in Loch Ness, then you've got your pumas and badgers, leopards, bobcats, sheep, goats, and rats—"

"Rats?"

"Don't worry, the Anguilla eat them."

"What are Anguilla?" Kate Coffey asked.

"They're a nasty species of eel that inhabit Great Britain, with sharp teeth and—"

"I saw a moray eel once in the Sea Aquarium," said the older Jordan boy, Neil. "It was cool."

"Oh, Anguilla eels look and act nothing like morays," I said. "They're long and serpentlike, with thick bodies and two fore fins that allow them to crawl on land. They've been called the meanest, moodiest fish ever to grab a hook."

"How big do they get?"

"The males remain small, maybe reaching twenty-five pounds, but the females . . . they can grow to twelve feet, exceeding several hundred pounds."

"Geez."

"Are they born in Loch Ness?" Clay Jordan asked.

"Actually, no . . ." My voice trailed off, an acorn of thought planting itself in my subconscious, its growth instantly retarded by the squawk of Brandy's loudspeaker. "Sorry to interrupt, Dr. Wallace, but if everyone would look to starboard, you'll see Achnahannet. Back in the sixties, this small village was the location for the Loch Ness Phenomenon Investigation Bureau. It was also in these waters that the famous speedboat racer, John Cobb, died tragically in 1953 when he attempted to break the world's water speed record."

"Was it the monster that killed him, Dr. Wallace?" This from a thin American woman sporting a dozen painful-looking body piercings.

"Well, Miss—"

"Johnston. Dena Johnston. It *was* Nessie, wasn't it?"

"Tell me, Dena, which of the two is more likely, that an ancient creature rose up from the Loch and struck the boat, or that John Cobb simply lost control when his speed surpassed 240 miles an hour?"

"I don't know, the speed, I guess, but it's still possible, right? I mean, I've seen photos taken underwater, photos that clearly show the monster's flipper. How can you deny that?"

"Unfortunately, the famous photo you're talking about was not Robert Rines's original, it was an enhanced version, created by an ambitious graduate student working at NASA's Jet Propulsion Lab. It was his digital signal scanning process that fleshed-out the flipper effect, not Rines's original negative."

A heavy silence took the boat, the passengers obviously disappointed with having me shoot holes into the Loch Ness legend.

Brandy quickly attempted to lighten the mood. "Hey, folks, Invermoriston on our right, look at Invermoriston. The hamlet's surrounded by a dense forest known as the—"

"Not so fast, Dr. Wallace." An American wearing a University of Iowa T-shirt raised his hand. "James Keigan, I do a lot of freelance writing on the Internet, my blogs deal with the unexplained. After doing extensive research, I happen to agree with the experts that claim Nessie's a plesiosaur."

Nods of agreement.

"Okay, James, since you've done so much 'extensive research,' maybe you could explain to us how a plesiosaur, a prehistoric aquatic reptile that went extinct 65 million years ago, is still living in a freshwater Loch."

"First, plesiosaurs and ichthyosaurs used to live in the area of the North Sea. Do you deny that?"

"No denial here."

"And do you deny that Loch Ness was once open to the North Sea, prior to the last ice age?"

"Technically, Loch Ness still flows into the North Sea, but the depths of the River Ness are far too shallow to conceal something as large as a plesiosaur."

"I know that, but isn't it possible an undiscovered underwater passage might still exist, linking the North Sea to Loch Ness?"

"That's theory, not fact. Even so, you still haven't used your extensive research to show me how a colony of air-breathing plesiosaurs managed to escape extinction to inhabit Loch Ness without anyone actually seeing them."

"I never said it was a colony. Could just be a few survivors."

"From 65 million years ago?"

"Why not? The coelacanth was believed extinct for 300 million years, yet we discovered them to be alive, inhabiting the deep waters off the coast of Madagascar. And Loch Ness is deeper than that."

Several passengers clapped in agreement.

"Okay, but you're comparing a forty-foot reptile with a six-foot-long species of lobe-finned fish."

"What about this!" The German woman, Bibi, held up a copy of a photo she had purchased in Drumnadrochit. It was the famous "surgeon's photo," a surface shot of a long-necked animal resembling a breaching plesiosaur taken by an English gynecologist, R. K. Wilson, back in 1934.

"Sorry, Bibi, the photo's a fake. The photographer claimed the animal had been several hundred yards from shore when he shot it. An analysis of the angle of the shot and its ripples, completed decades later, proves the photographer was only about thirty yards away. The man who took it actually confessed to using a miniature model before he died."

"Attention! attention!" Brandy interrupted, "we're approaching Eileen Mhuireach, or Murdoch's Island, sometimes called Cherry Island. This island, the only one on Loch Ness, is actually a man-made structure known as a crannog. It was built back in the sixteenth century as a fortified retreat. This particular crannog is made of a raft of oak logs and heavy rocks. The whole thing's secured to the bottom using a series of wooden posts."

The passengers hardly glanced at the man-made island, their attention still focused on me.

A stocky American rose from the far end of the bench, and I recognized his wrestler's physique, which was covered in tattoos. "We met years ago, Dr. Wallace. Chris Oldham?"

"Yes. You were one of the assistant producers who worked on that NOVA special."

"That's right. 'The Beast of Loch Ness', the one that aired back in '99. Our show reunited researchers Charlie Wyckoff and Bob Rine. Anyway, if you recall, despite having access to modern sonar equipment and high-tech underwater cameras, nothing conclusive ever came out of our investigation."

"Just like all the other investigations that preceded it."

"Exactly. Now you began this little boat ride stating you felt certain something large inhabits this Loch—those were your very words. Coming from the only person ever to witness a living giant squid, well, let's just say I take your claim rather seriously. Still, everything you've said since then flies in the face of that statement."

A telltale purple spot winked at me in the corner of my right eye.

"You've eloquently told us everything the monster is not. How about telling us what you think the monster really is."

Murmurs of agreement. The passengers pushed in closer to listen.

"Maybe I should clarify my earlier statement. It was just a personal belief, nothing more."

"Based upon what body of evidence?"

Brandy stepped down from the wheelhouse. "That evidence'll be explained fully on our return trip from Fort Augustus, right Dr. Wallace? As fer now, I'll need ye all to gather your belongings as we'll be docking in just a few minutes. A two-hour break'll give ye plenty o' time tae do a little sightseein' an' shoppin'. Fort Augustus is the largest village on Loch Ness, with many fine restaurants and shops. I recommend stopping at the Abbey, and ye'll definitely want to see . . ."

But Oldham refused to be put off by Brandy's sales pitch. "Yes or no, Dr. Wallace, do you believe large, mysterious aquatic animals inhabit Loch Ness?"

The passengers waited.

Brandy returned to the wheelhouse, emphatically nodding yes.

I closed my eyes, the migraine teasing at my right eye, the ghosts of Loch Ness at my spine.

"It's a simple question, Dr. Wallace. Yes or no?"

"No."

Moans of disappointment.

"Then you lied to us earlier?"

"I didn't lie. What I should've said, what I meant to say was there *could* be something large down there, but whatever it is, it's nothing to do with the Nessie lore as we know it."

"All right then, if you actually believe that, then why not investigate the Loch yourself? Whether you realize it or not, the Sargasso incident, combined with everything that's happened to your father, has drawn huge interest from our sponsors. I'd say the timing couldn't be more perfect for a well-financed investigation of Loch Ness, headed by Dr. Zachary Wallace himself."

The passengers clapped enthusiastically.

"Is that what brought you on this boat, Mr. Oldham?"

His smile revealed his intentions. "Let's just say, we try to deliver what our viewers want to see. The Werner Herzog movie was tongue-in-cheek, the public prefers something more scientific. Just say the word, Dr. Wallace, and I can have a film crew, research vessel, and sonar equipment at your disposal in less than a week."

My heart beat like a race horse's as Brandy cut the *Nessie III*'s engine, maneuvering us into an open berth in the Fort Augustus marina. "Dr. Wallace, could ye grab the bow line for me? Hello? Zachary . . . the bow line?"

I refused to move, the pressure in my head continuing to build, the NOVA producer refusing to back down. "The public trusts you, Dr. Wallace. Why not end the controversy here and now?"

Frustrated, Brandy grabbed the line herself and jumped onto the dock. "I think Dr. Wallace would like to mull this over and discuss it on oor return trip, ain't that right, Dr. Wallace?"

Return trip? Was she insane?

"And everyone who prepays now will save an extra two pounds—"

"No," I said, interrupting her commercial. "Look, Mr. Oldham, I appreciate your offer, but I'm not a cryptozoologist, and I don't want the world to perceive me as one. All this nonsense about monsters creates an impossible environment to conduct a serious study. Fakes, phony sightings, doctored photos, childish pranks, tongue-in-cheek movies . . . is it any wonder so many reputable scientists avoid Loch Ness like the plague? You want to know if there's a large water creature inhabiting these waters? My answer is maybe, but I'm not interested in risking my reputation as a marine biologist to find out."

"That's where you and I disagree," Oldham said. "Settling the debate once and for all would actually enhance your status as a scientist."

"Tell that to Denys Tucker," I mumbled.

"Maybe he's just afraid?" Bibi surmised.

The migraine moved into its next stage as the *Nessie III* settled into an open berth.

"Are you afraid, Dr. Wallace?" Oldham accused.

"It's okay to be afraid," offered the younger Jordan boy. "I'd be afraid to go down there, too."

My insides gurgling, I patted the four-year-old on the head, then stood, pushing my way through the wall of passengers.

"Zachary, wait!"

Ignoring Brandy's calls, I jumped onto the dock, my eyeball throbbing as I frantically searched for a public bathroom in which to be sick.

It was about 3 PM on an overcast day when I saw it. Its head and neck rose from the calm surface of the Loch and moved along quite near the shore. The head was small in comparison to the thickness of the creature's neck. After about five minutes, a passing steamer sounded its siren and the creature, after turning its head in an agitated manner, plunged out of sight.

—Miss Rena MacKenzie, Invermoriston, 22 December 1935

Loch Ness was calm the day my first mate (Rich) and I took the (steam tug) *Arrow* on her maiden voyage from Leith to Manchester. Suddenly, we noticed a huge black animal, like a humpbacked whale, emerge on the surface and keep pace with the ship. At first we saw two distinct humps, one after the other, but after a brief disappearance, the beast reappeared with seven humps or coils, before tearing past the tug at a terrific speed, leaving large waves.

—Captain Brodie, 30 August 1938

CHAPTER 11

Fort Augustus, Loch Ness
Scotland

NEARLY TWO HOURS after docking in Fort Augustus, I emerged from the men's public bathroom, drained and pale, the effects of the migraine still lingering like a bad morning hangover. I was in no shape, physically or mentally, to manage a return trip up the Loch, and yet I knew I was in deep shit with Brandy.

Honesty's the best policy, Zack. Tell her about your phobia, and she'll have to forgive you.

Rehearsing my speech, I walked slowly back to the *Nessie III*. Brandy was out on deck, cleaning. Before I could get in a word edgewise, she launched her attack from the starboard rail.

"Well, look who decided tae come home. First, ye blow me off last night, then ye ruin my bloody tour."

"Ruined?"

"Do ye see anyone besides us standin' here? Ye dumb bastard, ye chased them all away! Never tell payin' customers there's no Nessie. What the hell were ye thinkin'?"

"Wait, I didn't say that."

"Tae hell ye didnae. *No, Miss Kate, that's a wave. No, Mister James, that's a duck. No, Mr. Nova-Producer,* I'd never risk my bloody Albert Einstein reputation by investigatin' a ridiculous Highland legend like Nessie. Twenty-three tourists, my best load all season, an' ye sent every one o' them off tae ride home wi' my competition."

"Brandy, I'm sorry, but see, ever since the Sargasso thing I . . ."

"Fuck yersel', Zachary Wallace! I never want tae see ye again, dae ye hear? Far as I'm concerned, ye can crawl back tae Inverness an' hang wi' yer no good faither."

Having worked herself into a good lather, she proceeded to toss things at me. First it was her bucket and sponge, then her shoes, one of which caught me across the shoulder. Still not satisfied, she hustled down to the galley, emerging moments later with a cast-iron frying pan, which barely missed my head.

When she went for the anchor, I took off running.

I left the waterfront and hailed a taxi. Forty minutes later, the driver dropped me off at the Clansman Hotel, where I picked up my motorcycle and rode back to Drumnadrochit.

True was gone, probably fishing somewhere. I considered waiting for him, but the thought of being alone at the lodge while Crabbit stalked the mountainside in his thirteenth-century pajamas and sword was clearly not an option. So I left True a note, included my contact information in Inverness, then drove off, convinced this would be my last appearance in the village of my birth.

*　　　　　*　　　　　*

There was a note waiting for me at my hotel when I returned.

Dearest Half Brar:

　　Monday's an important day for us. After being locked up for nearly four months, Angus is anxious to have his square-go at it. He thanks our Creator in heaven that his own flesh and blood will be in court to help him in this, his time of need, and requests you wear a nice suit and clean keks (boxers) so as not to put off the jury. (Ha) See you at 8:30 AM sharp.

　　—Maxie

The thought of my father, isolated from society, alone in his cell, sober and grateful to have me by his side after so many years brought tears to my eyes.

Had I known then what Angus had in store for me, I'd have been on the next plane home to Miami.

Isolation (also) is an important element in the modification of species through Natural Selection. All fresh water basins, taken together, make a small area compared with that of the sea or of the land. Consequently, the competition between fresh water productions will have been less severe than elsewhere; new forms will have been more slowly produced, and old forms more slowly exterminated. And it is in fresh water basins that we find seven genera of Ganoid fishes, remnants of a once preponderant order. These anomalous forms may be called living fossils; they have endured to the present day, from having inhabited a confined area, and from having been exposed to less varied, and therefore less severe, competition.

—Charles Darwin, *The Origin of Species*, 1859

I had no doubt that there was something abnormal in the Loch and that it must be the monster or some unusually big living object which was making one of its rare appearances.

—Mr. J.W. McKillop , 4 April 1947

CHAPTER 12

**Inverness Castle, Scottish Highlands
Scotland**

"**THE HIGH COURT OF JUSTICIARY** is now back in session, Lord Neil Hannam presiding."

The judge took his place behind his bench, wished his clerks a cheery good morning, then addressed Max. "Mr. Rael, is the defense prepared to make its case?"

"We are, my lord."

"Then you may call your first witness."

"Call to the stand, Mr. Angus William Wallace of Drumnadrochit."

Angus turned, gave me a wave, and was sworn in.

"Mr. Wallace, what is your relationship with the deceased?"

"He was a friend and one-time business associate."

"Describe your business dealings with Mr. Cialino for the High Court."

"Cialino Ventures wis interested in constructin' a five-star resort, hotel, an' holiday apartments on a parcel o' land my ancestors owned overlookin' Loch Ness. I selt him the land, which wis tae be paid in installments. He owed me for the last payment, but he'd been puttin' me off for weeks. So I went ower tae his site an' we went for a wee walk tae chat."

"And?"

"An' the lyin' bastard telt me he wis short o' cash, which wis crap, bein' that he'd jist bought his mistress a fancy new diamond necklace no' two days earlier."

I glanced at Theresa Cialino, who seemed unfazed about the mistress comment.

"Johnny didnae ken it, but I saw his tart wearin' it when they left the jewelers together. Quite a piece of ice for that piece o' ass. Ye willnae catch me payin' for—"

"Objection!" The prosecutor was standing. "My lord, the victim's personal life is not on trial here."

"Sustained," said the judge, his dour expression intended as a warning to Max.

Max signaled for Angus to ease up. "What happened after Mr. Cialino told you he was short of cash?"

"He claimed he'd pay me after the resort did some business, an' if I didnae like it, it wis too bad, that wis the price o' doin' business wi' the Cialinos. So I hit him."

"You struck Mr. Cialino?"

"Aye, square in the nose. Didnae break it, but I drew blood, an' he stumbled back a few steps, cursin' up a storm, then he twisted his ankle on a tree root an' tumbled ower the edge, right intae Loch Ness."

"What happened next?"

"I dropped tae my knees an' looked ower the slope. John had surfaced an' wis treadin' water. He wis in fair shape, though blood wis pourin' frae both nostrils. I called oot, 'and that's the price o' doin' business with a Wallace, ye cheatin' bastard.' Suddenly, the water came alive wi' salmon, must've been hundreds o' them. Some were leapin' straight oot o' the water, a few smackin' John right in the heid. Made me laugh, it did, but then . . . then the sun slid behind a cloud an' I saw *it*."

"It?"

The benches creaked in unison as the public leaned forward to listen.

"Aye. A huge animal it wis, long an' serpentlike, had tae be at least fifteen meters, an' it was circlin' John an' thae salmon like a hungry wolf. Grayish in color, or maybe broon, hard tae tell 'cause it wis stayin' jist below the surface, an' visibility in the Loch's like lookin' through a dark lager. I could jist make oot a bizarre dorsal fin runnin' the entire length o' its body, almost like a horse's mane. John couldnae see the creature, but he could feel its powerful undertow as it circled, an' he grew all panicky, callin' oot tae me for help."

"What did you do?"

"Nothin' I could dae, for whit happened next happened awfy fast. The sun appeared again an' splattered across the surface, blindin' me in its reflection, so that I lost sight o' the beast. An' then . . ." Angus paused, pinching the bridge of his nose with a quivering hand.

"Go on."

"Then John let oot a cry . . . a terrible wail it wis, the most awfy sound I ever did hear, only it ended abruptly as the creature grabbed hold an' dragged him under frae below, an' the two o' them jist disappeared."

The courtroom erupted in a hundred conversations, some people laughing hysterically, others aghast, howling and swearing like they'd seen the Holy Ghost. The widow Cialino bit her lip and covered her face in her hands, and more than a few of the older ladies fainted dead away.

Me? I just sat there, incredulous.

The judge banged his gavel for quiet, nearly breaking it in the process. "Let me remind you that this is the High Court. Another outburst and I shall order this courtroom cleared!"

The silence became deafening, no one, save me, wanting to leave.

The judge turned to Angus, a skeptical look on his face. "Mr. Wallace, are you actually testifying, under oath, that you witnessed Mr. Cialino devoured by . . . by the Loch Ness monster?"

"No' devoured, m'lord, but snatched an' dragged below, absolutely."

I closed my eyes, praying not to see any purple spots.

Angus turned to the jury, reciting a well-rehearsed speech. "I seek no alibis for my actions. It wis wrong o' me tae strike my friend an' business associate, an' I never meant him tae go ower the cliff, that wis an act of God. But I've been sworn tae tell the truth, an' this is whit I've done. No matter whit ye may think, I saw that beast, an' he saw me. Whether he intended to snatch John Cialino or did it by accident, we'll never ken, but snatch him he did, an' he took him straight under, never tae be seen again. The Polis can drag Loch Ness frae now tae my hangin' day, but they'll never find nothin', mark my words, an' I'll never change my testimony, for it's the truth, so help me God."

The judge banged his gavel again, silencing the buzz, then requested all attorneys to join him immediately at his bench for a conference.

The courtroom exhaled and the media's feeding frenzy officially commenced. Reporters typed furiously on laptop keyboards and Blackberrys as fast as their cigarette-stained fingers could move, while others frantically called their editors on cell phones, demanding front-page space in their evening editions.

The judge chastised Maxie with a hard scowl. "Mr. Rael, I warn you, if you intend on turning this trial into a three-ring circus, I shall hold you in contempt and burn your barrister's license."

"My lord, the accused has given us his account of what happened, and we intend to prove it to the jury."

"That I'd like to see," scoffed Jennifer Shaw, the assistant prosecutor.

As I watched them talk, my mind underwent sort of an out-of-body experience. Was I really here in Scotland? Had my father actually testified that the victim had been dragged below by the Loch Ness monster?

And what part was I to play in this, Angus's latest charade?

The attorneys took their seats.

It was time for Act Two to begin.

"Lord Advocate, would you care to question the witness?"

"Indeed we would, my lord." Mitchell Obrecht shot back, his voice booming through the two-hundred-year-old courtroom. "Mr. Wallace, I've been a prosecutor for twelve years and a barrister for eight before that, and in all my years, I've never heard such a ridiculous, fantastical testimony as yours. The legend of a water beast in Loch Ness has never been proven in fourteen centuries, and even if accepted as a mystery, no accounting has ever been documented of a person actually being attacked."

"Ye're forgettin' the Pict warrior Saint Columba saved. An' there's plenty more attacks that remain documented only as drownings."

"Nonsense, ridiculous. What shred of evidence do you offer to back such a claim?"

"At this juncture, only my word."

"Your word? Do you take us all for fools, Mr. Wallace, or are you merely—"

Maxie interrupted. "Objection, my lord. If the Lord Advocate has a question for the witness, he should ask it, and not use this as an opportunity to practice his closing remarks."

"Agreed. Get on with it, sir."

But the prosecutor had nothing to add, for how does one prove or disprove a legend in a court of law?

Max Rael was about to show us.

"Call to the stand, Mr. Calum Forrest of Invermoriston."

A tall, thin Scotsman in his late sixties took the stand and was sworn in.

"Mr. Forrest, what is your present occupation?"

"Head water bailiff o' Loch Ness."

"And how long have you held this position?"

"Ten years an' two months, but I wis assistant bailiff for seventeen years prior."

Max retreated to his table and removed a document from a manila folder. "Mr. Forrest, would you explain to the High Court the contents of this document."

Calum Forrest took a quick glance. "It's the accident report I supplied ye wi' several weeks ago."

"The accident report of Loch Ness?"

"Aye."

Max handed the document to the witness. "My lord, we'd like this document marked Defense Exhibit A."

"So be it."

"Mr. Forrest, how many drownings were there at Loch Ness last year, and feel free to use the report as a reference."

"Last year? Nine."

"And the year before?"

"Five."

"And the year prior?"

"Six."

"And if you were to estimate an average year of drownings at Loch Ness over the last two decades, excluding the past nine months?"

"Be aboot the same I'd say, roond aboot half a dozen."

"In your opinion as water bailiff, why do so many people drown at Loch Ness?"

"Well, the Ness is vast, o' course, an' she's cold . . . real cold. A lot o' tourists dinnae realize jist how cold she is 'til their boat tips an' in they go. Only takes aboot a minute or two of exposure before the whole body starts shuttin' doon."

"And what might cause a boat to tip?"

"Could be lots o' things. The Great Glen's like a giant wind tunnel, sometimes blowin' waves mair than two tae three meters high. If ye get in trouble oot there, there's no' many places tae dock. Plus ye get yer usual crazies overdoin' it wi' the alcohol, that makes for lots o' problems."

"Do you usually recover the victims' bodies?"

"Almost never. The extreme cold an' high peat content sink almost everythin' like a rock, an' that's a long way doon. If ye ever drained Loch Ness, ye'd probably find hundreds o' skeletons stuck in the bog."

"So, prior to this year, Loch Ness averages about a half dozen drownings each season."

"Aye."

"Now tell us how many drownings have been reported so far this calendar year."

"Seventeen."

I felt my scalp crawl as the courtroom buzzed again.

"Seventeen drownings? Seventeen you say?"

"Aye, an' tourist season's no' even in full swing."

"Why the sudden change, Bailiff Forrest?"

"Wish I kent why."

"And no bodies?"

"No, sir. As I said, the frigid water temperatures prevent bloatin'. Loch Ness . . . she disnae like tae give up her dead."

"Any other unusual happenings around the Loch?"

"Aye. We've been getting' overloaded wi' reports aboot missin' animals, by that, o' course, I mean domestic pets, dogs mostly. Golden retrievers, dachshunds, poodles, shepherds . . . name a' breed, an' I can check my list an' tell ye whit's missin'. We've posted signs aboot keepin' them chained up at night, but often, they break loose an' chase after rabbits an' squirrels."

"Thank you, Mr. Forrest. Anything else?"

"No . . . I dinnae think so."

"What about Nessie sightings?"

"Oh, we aye get them, nothin' unusual there."

"But more than usual?"

The water bailiff hesitated. "Perhaps."

"In fact, according to your own log, you've received over fifty sightings since late January through May, is that correct?"

"If it says so in my log, sure. Disnae make them real, though."

"Understood. No further questions."

"Lord Advocate?"

The two prosecutors conferred with one another. "No questions at this time, my lord."

"Very well. Any other witnesses, Mr. Rael?"

"Just one, my lord. Defense calls to the stand Dr. Zachary Wallace."

A hundred heads swivelled in my direction as my jaw muscles locked in place and my throat squeezed tight.

"Dr. Wallace?"

I looked up to see my no good bastard half-brother pointing me out to the judge and Court Macer.

"Dr. Wallace, you will proceed to the witness stand immediately."
The Court Macer was standing over me now, but I still couldn't
breathe, my lungs refusing to draw a breath.

Mitchell Obrecht was objecting, and I silently rooted him on.
"My lord, Her Majesty's Advocate has not been informed of this
defense witness, who is, in fact, directly related to the accused."

"Mr. Rael?"

"My lord, the fact that Dr. Wallace is related to the accused will
have no bearing, once we hear his testimony, which is vital, not just to
my client but to Scotland entire. The fact is, my lord, up until a few
days ago, Dr. Wallace and the accused had not seen each other nor
even spoken for seventeen years and we were not even sure he was
coming, prior to late last week. For the record, my lord, Dr. Wallace
was given no forewarning that he would be called to testify in these
proceedings, and would not have come had he known. As you can see,
he is obviously perturbed by all this, and as such, we request that the
High Court consider him a hostile witness."

*Hostile witness? Thirty seconds alone with Max and I'd be up for
murder myself.*

"I'm going to give you some latitude, Mr. Rael, but proceed with
caution, I warn you."

"Thank you, my lord."

Amid much clatter, I was escorted to the witness box, then sworn
in. Angus watched me from behind the prosecutor's table, a smug look
of satisfaction pasted on his face.

Glancing around the courtroom, I was surprised to spot True
MacDonald, dressed in his Sunday finest, watching me proudly as if
attending my graduation.

"Sir, would you state your name and current address for the
record."

"Zachary Wallace. Prior to this trip, I was living in a motel in
South Beach, Florida."

Max took over the questioning, and I stared at him, filled with a malice once reserved only for my father. "Dr. Wallace, where were you born?"

"Drumnadrochit."

"And how long did you reside in the Highlands?"

"Until I was nine."

"Why did you leave?"

"My parents divorced."

"The accused, Mr. Angus Wallace, being your father?"

"Biological father."

"What is your current occupation?"

"Technically, I'm unemployed."

"I, uh, see. And why is that?"

"Because I don't have a job, asshole."

The judge banged his gavel to stifle the laughter, much of it coming from True. "The witness will conduct himself properly or be held in contempt."

"Let me rephrase. What is your chosen occupation, Doctor? In what field did you earn your Ph.D.?"

"Marine sciences."

"And your present age?"

"I'll be twenty-six in two months."

"My lord, for the sake of time, I'm going to read the highlights of Dr. Wallace's credentials, just so the court understands why we've summoned this witness." Retreating to his table, Max removed several sheets from another manila folder and began reading aloud.

"Graduated with honors from Washington High School in New York . . . at the age of fifteen. Accepted an academic scholarship at Princeton, where he played football and graduated with honors while earning both a bachelor's and master's degree in marine biology. Received his doctoral degree from the University of California at San Diego . . . all this before the ripe old age of twenty-three. In the last four years, Dr. Wallace has authored three papers published in *Nature* and *Science* and has patented two underwater hydrophonic devices, including one that was used successfully six months ago to locate a giant squid, this in the waters of the Sargasso Sea. In 2003, Dr. Wallace was listed among the Top 100 scientific minds in the world and was on his way to earning a second doctorate from Florida Atlantic University while he taught courses and lectured. Am I leaving anything out, Dr. Wallace?"

"You forgot to mention I had a crush on my tenth-grade math teacher."

That one drew another stern look from the judge. "Last warning, Dr. Wallace. If you insist on making a mockery of my courtroom, you'll be doing it from a jail cell."

The ridiculousness of my predicament got to me then, and I started to snicker.

The judge banged his gavel and cited me for contempt.

Max jumped in before I could extend my jail sentence to two nights. "Our humblest apologies, my lord. As you can see, the witness is a bit unnerved at having to testify at his own father's murder trial."

"Get to your point, counsel, or I shall dismiss this witness and toss you in jail along with your client."

I winked at Max, enjoying a small token of revenge.

"Dr. Wallace . . . the accused claims to have witnessed John Cialino dragged below by a large water creature, a creature often referred to as the Loch Ness monster. As a doctoral candidate at Scripps, didn't you once author a scientific paper on this same species?"

"No."

"No?" Max strode back to his table, returning with a Xeroxed copy of a report. "I have it right here, *Loch Ness: A New Theory*. Written by Zachary Wallace, Scripps, 1999. You are Zachary Wallace, yeah?"

"Listen, Mr. Rael, I don't know how you managed to obtain a copy of this document, but it's essentially an unpublished dissertation."

"Why unpublished?"

"My dissertation committee rejected it."

"Rejected? On what grounds?"

"On the grounds that legitimate scientific bodies aren't interested in chasing legends, and they don't like their doctoral candidates chasing after them, either."

"Still, the report certainly makes a good case for Nessie's existence."

"The paper merely highlights Loch Ness's uniquely isolated ecosystem and—"

"Oh, I think it does a *wee* bit more than that. If I may," Max thumbed through the dissertation to a previously marked page, "And I quote, 'The true mystery of Loch Ness lies in its relationship with the North Sea and the Great Glen. The Great Glen was forged 380 million years ago when a sixty-mile fault line fractured, creating a huge trench that split the Highlands geology from southwest to northeast. From this gorge, present-day Loch Ness was created, when a massive glacier advanced through the Great Glen some twenty-thousand years ago. As the ice melted and sea levels rose, Loch Ness may have actually existed as an arm of the North Sea. This theory is backed by recent discoveries of sea urchin spines, clamshells, and other marine material made in deposits recovered from the bottom of the Loch. However, once the glacier fully retreated ten thousand years ago, the land rose in an isostatic rebound and the waterways separated, perhaps trapping a few large sea creatures in the process.' End quote."

"Yes, Mr. Rael, this is the mantra recited by most Nessie theorists, that the retreat of the glaciers from the last ice age trapped ancient sea creatures in Loch Ness. But if you had bothered to read on, I go to great lengths to shoot this theory down. Ten thousand years is far too long for a small colony of large predators to remain isolated in a Loch, and inbreeding alone would have terminated their existence some time ago."

"Ah, but then you go on to state . . . hang on, hang on . . . ah, here it is, 'A deep-dwelling sea creature repudiated to be as large as Nessie would avoid traversing the shallows that lead out of Loch Ness and the Bona Narrows to the Moray Firth. The solution to returning to the North Sea may, in fact, lie in the Loch's unique geology. While the surface of Loch Ness lies fifty-two feet above sea level, its depths remain more than seven hundred feet *below* sea level. The bottom of this trough is flat and smooth, covered in a layer of sediment, twenty-five feet deep. At its northernmost section, Loch Ness is blocked by glacial sediment, however, it is now believed its northern basin may extend beyond Inverness and all the way to the Moray Firth. It is therefore likely that the extreme depths of the Great Glen do not stop at Loch Ness, but may in fact, continue north into the sea by way of a deep underground aquifer.'" Max stopped reading. "Aquifer? That's an underground river, correct?"

"A river running through stratum . . . through rock, yes."

"And do you still stand by these words, Dr. Wallace?"

"It's just a working theory."

"A working theory from an accomplished scientist. Now let's look at your working theory about Nessie." He turned to the next marked section. "Again I quote, 'It is my opinion that the animal referred to as Nessie, if it exists, is an undiscovered species of sea creature, perhaps even a mutation. Even in this day and age, large, extinct land and water creatures are being discovered all the time, thanks to advances in technology and our ability to gain access to hostile environs. The giant Muntjac of Laos, the two hundred pound Saola, a cowlike beast, and the discovery of six new species in the Andes Mountains all being examples. Though most probably of the same species, Nessie is not, however, the same animal confronted by Saint Columba in 565 A.D., back at a time the theorized Loch Ness aquifer may have been open to the sea. In fact, our timeline suggests the modern-day Nessie is a rogue, an animal that became trapped and cut-off from the Moray Firth, not millions or even thousands of years ago, but post-Saint Columba and fairly recently at that, most likely within the last hundred years.'"

I looked around, amazed at the number of people nodding their heads in agreement.

"Dr. Wallace, could you clarify this last part for our jurors?"

"What part?"

"About the monster being less than a century old."

"Again, it's just conjecture."

"Humor us."

I took a deep breath, fighting to maintain an even temper. "The Great Glen . . . it's a seismically active area. The last major earthquake took place in 1901 and was so violent it actually cracked the bank of the Caledonian Canal. The epicenters of these earthquakes are usually around Lochend, located at the northern end of Loch Ness, precisely where a theorized aquifer running northeast into the Moray Firth might lie. It's possible debris from the 1901 tremor sealed off the aquifer's underground access into Loch Ness, theoretically trapping one or more of these creatures, assuming they even exist."

"And the other evidence you cite, Dr. Wallace, the theory regarding man-made explosions?"

I glanced at Judge Hannam, relishing the fact that he too was clearly losing patience. "Is this going somewhere, Mr. Rael?"

"Aye, my Lord, in fact this specific inquiry provides us with a clear reason the creature surfaced in February to attack John Cialino."

"Go on then, but be quick about it."

"Thank you, my lord. Again, returning to Dr. Wallace's research paper, 'Whether one or more of these seismic quakes collapsed the theorized aquifer is unknown, but another event—a man-made event— clearly coincides with the beginning of Nessie's modern-day sightings.

"'It was in the 1930s that construction work first began on the A82 highway. Massive quantities of dynamite were needed to blast through the mountainous rock. No doubt these blasts reverberated through the basin, upsetting any large creatures inhabiting Loch Ness. From this time period forward, sightings of the creature increased dramatically. In fact, while only a handful of sightings existed prior to the A82, they have numbered in the thousands since construction began.'"

Max closed the dissertation and turned to me. "Dr. Wallace, theoretically speaking, if a large predator or predators were trapped in Loch Ness, would dynamiting the Loch's basin agitate the monster, causing it to surface?"

"You just read my statement. Isn't that what I said?"

The judge eyed me a warning.

"Then, if dynamiting agitated these bottom dwellers back in the 1930s, wouldn't the same hold true for construction that occurred last winter along the banks south of Urquhart Bay?"

"Objection! My lord, this entire testimony, while entertaining to some, has no bearing on—"

"Overruled. Answer the question, Dr. Wallace."

I scratched my head, impressed at Max's logic. "I suppose if dynamite were being used, yes."

Max nodded to the jury. "The record will show that Cialino construction began using dynamite as early as last October, coinciding with numerous Nessie sightings and drownings, as confirmed by the water bailiff."

A fervor rose in the courtroom, temporarily quelled by the judge's gavel.

Max was far from through. "Dr. Wallace, hypothetically speaking, if a large water creature did prey in Loch Ness, is it possible it could have developed a taste for human flesh?"

"Objection! My lord?"

Attorneys and jury stared at the judge, the court's visitors holding their collective breath.

"No, I'll allow it," the judge said. "Answer the question, Dr. Wallace."

I felt exhausted. "A taste for flesh? Hypothetically, yes I suppose, but only if, (a) this creature or creatures of yours was a predator and not a vegetarian, and, (b) only if the species' diet had been substantially altered by some unusual break in the food chain, both of which, might I add, are highly implausible."

"And why is that?"

"Because Loch Ness has an abundance of prey. There'd have to be an unnatural ecological disaster to create such obtuse behavior. As to my unpublished theory about dynamite agitating a large predator, while the majority of sightings have occurred since the A82 went up, there have never been any documented reports of an attack on humans."

Max strolled around the witness box, preparing his next attack on my mental armor. "A personal question, Doctor, if you don't mind. If hard evidence justified your father's claims, would you then be interested in pursuing a search of the Loch?"

"No."

"No? And why not?" Max turned, playing to his audience. "Surely, you're not afraid of hypothetical theories, are you now?"

A purple flash of light blurred the vision in my left eye, the warning sign increasing my pulse. "I've no interest in Loch Ness."

"Seems like you once had great interest."

"Not anymore."

"Not even if an investigation could save your own father's life?"

I stared at Angus, meeting the intensity of his gaze with my own. "My father's never needed me before, Mr. Rael. Let him fight his own dragons."

God, that felt good.

Max only grinned.

"Let's get back to John Cialino. You state, correctly, that no attacks on humans, save back to Saint Columba, have ever been documented. However, from a practical sense, if an attack had led to a human being's demise, then would there really be any evidence, any documentation?"

"There'd be a missing person's report."

"Yes, but with no evidence, no body to collect, the report'd most likely record a drowning, yeah?"

"I . . . suppose."

"We've heard from the water bailiff. He says drownings 'ave been unusually high since construction began on—"

"'Tis the monster for sure!" cried out an old man seated close to True. "Same thing happened back in '33. For the next three years, we had dozens o' drownings! My ain cousin—"

The judge banged his gavel as two officers of the court escorted the old man out. "On the next public outburst, I will clear this courtroom, is that understood?" He turned back to Max, realizing the defense counsel had led him to step in dogshit. "I'm losing patience, Mr. Rael."

"My apologies, my lord. The subject is a sensitive one to many a Highlander, but Dr. Wallace's testimony is vital in determining what really killed John Cialino."

"Wrap it up."

Max looked over at Angus, who nodded.

"Dr. Wallace, please tell the court what happened to you on the evening of your ninth birthday."

"What?" The reference sent stabbing pains behind both eyes.

"Dr. Wallace?"

I looked at Angus, incensed that he would bring up such a black chapter in our history, and in a court of law of all places.

"Answer the question, Dr. Wallace."

"My father . . . he was supposed to take me fishing that afternoon, only the drunk was too busy cheating on my mother to be bothered with his only child."

The courtroom buzzed with opinion.

"So you decided to go fishing without him?"

"Yes."

"In a rowboat?"

"That's correct."

"Had you ever been out on the Loch in a boat alone?"

"Once or twice."

"Tell us what happened to you on this particular occasion."

"Oh, and did I mention the waitress he was with was a minor? They should've arrested your client back then. If you ask me, he's got a lot of nerve judging Mr. Cialino."

The judged banged his gavel. "Direct your replies only to counsel's question, Dr. Wallace."

"My boat flipped over, and I drowned, as in I was legally dead. Lucky for me, the water bailiff at the time, Mr. Alban MacDonald, was in the area and saw what happened. He dragged me aboard his boat and resuscitated me. Literally brought me back to life."

More murmurs filled the courtroom.

"Let's talk about what happened while you were out on the Loch. How did your rowboat happen to flip?"

"It was struck by a tree."

"A tree?"

"That's right, Mr. Rael. As most *real* Highlanders know, Loch Ness was once surrounded by great forests of Scots pine. When these one-ton trees fell into the Loch, they became waterlogged and sank to the bottom, more than seven hundred feet down. In these great depths, the pressure increases to about twenty-five atmospheres, roughly sixteen hundred pounds per square inch, enough to power a steam engine. The composition of the Scots pine is high in petrochemicals. As the trees decay, tiny gas bubbles form inside the trunk. Eventually, the bubbles reach a point where the pressure within the log is greater than that of the depths, and the tree begins to rise. The higher it rises, the less the pressure, and suddenly the log becomes a frothing projectile that literally explodes out of the water."

"And that's what struck your boat?"

"Yes."

"You're certain of that? Because according to your testimony, you drowned."

"I drowned after my boat was struck. It was a log."

"Then you saw the log as it struck the boat?"

Images suddenly blinked in my brain—subliminal images straight out of my night terrors.

Black water, fog rolling in. The sky suddenly gone topsy-turvy, the rowboat exploding upward, flipping bow over stern.

"Dr. Wallace?"

"No, I . . . I never actually saw the log, but I felt its impact."

"Perhaps then, it was something else altogether, something much larger? Something alive—"

"Objection!"

"Sustained. Stop leading the witness, Mr. Rael."

"My apologies, my lord. Dr. Wallace, what happened after your rowboat flipped? Dr. Wallace?"

Black water, paralyzing cold. Kick to the surface, limbs trembling. Tread water, so much fog. Which way to swim?

"Dr. Wallace, are you still with us?"

"Uh, yes, sorry. What was the question?"

"Your rowboat flipped and?"

"And I went under, then I surfaced. I was freezing, but I couldn't see the shoreline, it was too foggy. So I treaded water and yelled for help."

"I understand there were salmon in the water. A whole school?"

"Salmon?"

The water frothing with salmon, the fish battering my legs and buttocks.

"There were fish, yes. It's . . . it's possible they followed the tree up from the depths. Fish'll do that sometimes."

Max leaned in. "Then what happened?"

Sharp pain, like a thousand stabbing daggers . . .

"Something stabbed me . . . something below the surface. Coils of barbed wire had wrapped around the log, probably the remains of a decaying farm fence. My left ankle got snagged. As the log re-sank, its weight dragged me under with it."

"Barbed wire?"

"Yes."

"You saw the barbed wire?"

"Of course not, it was too dark and deep, but the fencing entangled me pretty good, stripped the skin clear off of me."

"That sounds positively frightening. You still have the scars?"

"Some. I had to have a skin graft."

"Would you mind showing us the scars, Dr. Wallace?"

The judge and jury leaned forward as I removed my left shoe and sock, revealing a tiny ring of scars that encircled my left ankle, the skin noticeably devoid of hair.

"The plastic surgeon did a nice job. Still, how can you be sure the wound was caused by barbed wire?"

"The physician who initially treated me certified it in his report. There were heavy traces of rust around the edges of the wound."

"I see. And is it at all possible an animal might have bitten your leg, Dr. Wallace?"

A nauseous feeling simmered in my belly as more images from my night terrors blinked in and out of my mind's eye.

Black water. Sinking faster. Struggle . . . kick . . . twist, must break free.

"Dr. Wallace?"

"No."

"No, it's not possible, or no you don't remember?"

Deeper . . . suffocating . . . ears ringing from the pressure. Suddenly free! Go, Zack . . . swim away! Get to the light!

"Dr. Wallace?"

The migraine's wave of pain was rising higher by that time, and it was going to be a tsunami. Reaching into my pants pocket, I fished out two *Zomig* and swallowed them, praying they'd shunt off the coming disaster.

"Answer the question, Dr. Wallace."

"There was no water creature, Mr. Rael," I said, my eyeballs beginning to throb.

"Let's go back a moment, Dr. Wallace. You said you took the rowboat out yourself to go fishing, is that correct?"

"Yes."

"With the new reel your father had given you?"

"Yes."

"Then why did you leave your new fishing rod on the shore?"

"I, uh . . . what did you say?" A chill ran down my spine.

"The fishing rod. Your father found it onshore after you'd been rescued. You never brought it out with you."

"He did? I . . . I don't—"

"Why were you really out on the Loch, Dr. Wallace? Were you trying to prove something to your father?"

The courtroom began tilting in my vision.

"What was it you were really searching for?"

The judge leaned over to me. "Are you all right, Dr. Wallace? You've gone quite pale."

I wiped cold sweat from my brow. "It's a migraine. I get them sometimes. This one's real bad."

"You don't like to discuss your drowning incident, do you, Dr. Wallace?" Max cooed. "It's painful for you. It causes the migraines to worsen, yeah?"

I squeezed my eyes shut and nodded.

"Still, we must discuss this frightening chapter in your childhood in order to get to the truth, in order to determine your father's guilt or innocence. Let's go back to the water creature your father described under oath. He claimed it was at least fifteen meters long. That would give it the length and bite radius of a small whale, am I right?"

I looked up at him, the spots in my eyes nearly blinding me. "It was barbed wire that snagged my ankle, Mr. Rael. Not a whale or serpent or monster. Barbed wire!"

"And was it barbed wire that nearly swallowed you in half?"

"What?"

"It rose up after you, didn't it? You managed to twist yourself free, but it rose up after you, then snagged you a second time as you fled to the surface. Only this time it took you about the waist, just like it did poor John Cialino!"

My head erupted, and so did the courtroom. The two prosecutors were on their feet, yelling their objections in order to be heard over the crowd, while the judge whacked his gavel over and over, each earsplitting *clap* sending splinters of pain shooting through my brain as he futilely attempted to regain control of the proceedings.

It was a free-for-all, and I was at the center of the storm.

Barely able to tolerate the jabbing eye pain, I laid my pounding head upon the ledge of the witness box and swallowed great gulps of air, trying my best to quell the volcano of bile gurgling in my gut as long-dormant memories from my childhood continued to burst across my mind's eye.

Free! Race for the surface, faster . . . faster . . . A presence . . .rising from the depths beneath me! Swim faster! Ignore the pain, kick harder . . . A light! Get to the light . . . get to the light!

I clutched my head, pleading to the judge for mercy, "My lord, I need a recess."

Angus stood and yelled, "Order him tae lower his troosers, Maxie! His waist'll still be scarred by Nessie's bite!"

An officer of the court shoved Angus back in his chair as the judge beat his gavel again. "Another outburst like that, Mr. Wallace, and I shall have you bound and gagged. Mr. Rael—"

Max motioned to Angus to stay calm. "My apologies, my lord."

"Mr. Rael, finish your questions now, or I shall dismiss the witness to seek medical attention."

"Yes, of course. Dr. Wallace, on or about your ninth birthday, was there any construction going on at Loch Ness? Dr. Wallace?"

"I have no idea," I muttered through the pain.

"In fact, Dr. Wallace, the record shows that a new layby was being blasted at Urquhart Castle, expanding the parking lot from twelve spaces to its present forty-seven. Did you not know that?"

I bit my tongue and swallowed, fighting to keep the bile from rising up my throat.

"Dynamite, Dr. Wallace. By your own theory, an agitator to large predators living in . . ."

Had God granted me one wish at that moment, I'd have requested a gun. My first shot would have struck Maxie between the eyes, stifling his incessant voice, the second and third bullets reserved for Angus and that pompous judge. The rest of the clip would be dedicated to my throbbing head, ending my misery, once and for all.

But I had no gun, all I had was intense pain and anger.

Judge Hannam was about to add humiliation to the list. "Dr. Wallace, we'll take a recess and get you some medical attention in just one minute, but first, I'm going to ask you to lower your trousers, just a bit, for the jury."

"What?"

The jury leaned forward, mentally salivating, the visitors hunching up in their seats.

I swallowed hard. "Your honor, this is absurd!"

"You're wearing boxers, yes?"

"Yes, but–"

"I agree it's unorthodox, but I mean to put an end to Mr. Rael's antics before this murder trial turns into a search for the Loch Ness monster."

The shadow ascends beneath me, homing in on the trail of blood. It rises higher, I can feel its presence around my knees, I can hear it growling in my ears . . . oh, Jesus, get to the light, Zachary! Get to the light!

"Clear the courtroom," said the judge, turning to his Court Macer. "Everyone but the jury, the accused, and the prosecutors."

The migraine was skewering my eyes, the Macer moving too damn slow. No one wanted to leave, and I was beyond desperate, the images and the migraine causing my entire body to tremble.

To hell with them!

Standing upon my chair on quivering legs, I unbuckled my trousers, then ceremoniously yanked my pants and boxers down six inches, allowing the High Court of Inverness to ogle my waistline, revealing to one and all, the hideous line of two-inch purple scars that encircled the fleshy upper region of my buttocks.

The Diary of Sir Adam Wallace
Translated by Logan W. Wallace

Entry: 23 October 1330

Whit have J done, whit course err'd that has led me to this evil place an' oor impossible task? J try tae write, but is it night or day, J dinnae ken . . . J canna think, my mind overcome by darkness an' the madness o' oor mission.

We had set off again at dawn, or close tae it, as the valley remained hidden in clouds. Each Knight bore a heavy pack on his back, mysel' included, though J didnae ken the contents, only enough no' tae ask. MacDonald seemed sullen, but determined, as we followed the eastern bank o' Loch Ness, movin' steadily south.

An hour later, we arrived at oor intended destination . . . or so J thought.

It wis a hillock o' rock, its location set back a bit frae the shoreline, at a place jist north o' where the waters doubled in breadth. MacDonald ordered six o' us tae roll one o' its boulders, revealin' a hole in the ground. It wis the entrance to a cave, its mooth only wide enough tae allow one man at a time tae descend intae its darkness.

Where it led tae? J wid soon find oot.

MacDonald assigned oor formation, keepin' me between himsel' an' Sir Jain Stewart. We secured oorselves in this single file by lengths o' rope, then lit oor torches an' lowered oorselves backwards, one by one, intae the darkness o' mother earth.

Havin' ne'er been in a cave, J wis quite excited, but quickly, the ground beneath my feet dropped away, becomin' a narrow crevice. 'Twis as if God had cut a jagged slice in the earth wi' his sword. Every treacherous step took us away frae the day until it finally disappeared, each o' us kent only by his tug an' the light o' his torch. J fell several times frae dizziness an' fatigue, but MacDonald an' Stewart were aye there tae catch me, assurin' me that as long as the torches remained lit, we'd be a'right.

I cannae say how long we journeyed, nor how deep, but quickly the ravine widened too far an' plunged at too harsh an angle for us tae walk, so that noo we had tae lower oorselves by rope, one by one, tae the next crags below. Fortunately, MacDonald had appointed two fine guides tae lead us, Keef Cook an' his younger brother, Alex, an' it wis obvious that baith o' them had followed oor intended route many a time.

We continued on like this for many hours, descendin' doon this jagged slope intae Hell, oor heavy satchels threatenin' tae cast us over an unseen ledge intae oblivion.

Jist when it seemed my bloodied hands couldnae grapple any mair, we dropped doon tae a level plateau . . . at the bottom o' the gorge.

We rested, MacDonald pullin' me aside. "Listen noo, Adam Wallace, can ye hear it?"

I could hear a dull roar, like distant thunder, comin' frae the darkness tae my left. "Whit is it?"

"Loch Ness's belly."

After a brief respite, the brothers led us west through the darkness until we arrived at the entrance o' a narrow tunnel, gusts o' cold air howlin' frae its mooth. One by one we entered, forced tae crawl on hands an' knees. Mair than a dozen times I banged my heid against rock, the walls o' the tunnel damp, the echo o' rushin' water growin' louder wi' each passin' minute.

An' then, finally, we arrived.

It wis a massive subterranean chamber, harborin' an underground river, black an' cold, its depths impossible tae fathom by the light o' our torches. Thoosands o' pointed rocks hung like fangs frae its vaulted ceilin', an' a steep wall along the opposite shoreline wis alive wi' bats. The hideous animals scurried over one another like winged vermin, wi' several occasionally flyin' off intae the darkness.

MacDonald offered answers afore I could organize my thoughts intae words. "The river flows frae the belly o' the Loch tae the northeast for four leagues afore emptyin' intae the sea."

"An' the cavern?"

"Forged by ice long afore men came tae these parts. This juncture marks the river's narrowest point, an' we shall use it tae complete our mission."

"MacDonald, if we can access this passage, then the English can, too. An' who among us wid remain in this hellhole tae guard the Bruce's keep?"

"Ah, but that is the beauty o' the plan. We shall use the Guivre as oor appointed minions, an' none, no' even Longshanks, shall challenge them."

An' whit are the Guivre?"

"Some folk say they're sea serpents, others describe them as dragons. Me, I call them the De'il himsel'. The head is that o' a great gargoyle, wi' teeth that can carve a man doon tae his bones. The females are feared the most as they grow the largest, as long as a belfry is high. Nasty creatures they are, but born intae darkness, they prefer the depths, away frae God-an' man's light."

"An' how are we tae use these creatures tae safeguard that which belonged tae the Bruce, an object the English King wid gie half his treasure tae capture?"

"This is the passage the young Guivre must traverse when they enter Loch Ness frae the Moray Firth. When they reach maturity, the adults must again follow the river and return tae the sea. By blockin' the passage, we'll keep the largest o' the creatures frae leavin', an' Scotland's Holy Grail shall be protected."

As he spoke, the Templar Knights began unpackin' their satchels, removin' heavy lengths o' flat irons, the kind used tae gate drawbridges.

MacDonald smiled at me, the madness aglow in his eyes.

An hour has past, an' I rest noo by the fire, my body still weary frae oor descent. As others toil, boltin' together the iron gate, I ponder the repercussions of MacDonald's plan. Assumin' these dragons even existed, whit wrath wid Nature bring doon upon our heads . . .

My husband and I had just arrived at Strone Holiday Chalet
near Urquhart Castle, overlooking the bay. We parked at the rear
of the chalet and my husband paused from unloading the car to
admire the view. That's when he saw it! It was a long, dark object,
its skin very slick. The two of us watched the object for about 30–45
seconds, until it slipped gently beneath the surface and disappeared.

Both my husband and I have seen seals and dolphins in the wild,
and this object didn't look like either. This was not a boat wake
nor wind slick or any other dark shape often mistaken for Nessie.
It was simply a very large, black animal.

—Mrs. Robert Carter, Resident, Marsden, West Yorkshire, 19 September 1998

CHAPTER **13**

**Inverness Castle, Scottish Highlands
Scotland**

KEEPING HIS WORD, Judge Hannam ordered me medicated, then held in contempt, his "official" excuse for sequestering me away from the descending hordes of media, to which I was eternally grateful. I quickly found myself in a holding cell across from my father's, the castle's dense walls isolating me from the screams and shouts of reporters demanding answers to their questions.

Within minutes, the physician's medication knocked me out.

It was dark when I finally awoke.

For several wonderful moments, I simply remained on my back, staring at the details of the ancient jail cell's stone ceiling, luxuriating in the blessed relief of having been pardoned from the pain.

"The migraine's passed, eh?"

I sat up slowly and looked across the darkened corridor into Angus's cell.

"I'd see a doctor aboot those if I wis you." Angus said, pressing his face between the iron bars. "I wis boffin a Welsh woman for a time, an' she suffered the same ailment. Said it wis brought on by her menstrual cycle. Naturally, I avoided her time o' the month after that. Ye're no' on the rag, are ye, Lassie?"

"I knew better than to come back, I knew you'd never change. You really set me up good this time, didn't you, Angus?"

"Och! Ye set yersel' up. How long were ye plannin' on livin' wi' yer wee secret anyway? Another seventeen years?"

"What secret? Wake up, old man, there never was a monster, not then, not now. Putting me on the witness stand won't change the fact that you killed a man, whether by accident or choice."

"Ye're still too feart tae remember, is that it?" He glared at me from his cell, his blue eyes aglitter in the florescent light. "These migraines are yer brain's way o' avoidin' the past. Same thing happened after the first accident. Headaches anytime ye tried tae talk aboot whit happened. 'Course, they were nothin' compared tae yer nightmares."

"Nightmares?" I sat up in bed, my heart racing. "I had night terrors back then, too?"

"Aye. Ye used tae wake up, screamin' bloody murder. Thank Jesus yer mother finally took ye tae America, it wis a' I could dae tae get a guid night's rest. When that creature bit ye—"

"Nothing bit me! These aren't teeth marks, Angus, they're puncture wounds, scars from the barbed wire. I must've swam right through its coils as I surfaced."

He shook his head sadly. "As a bairn ye could hide frae the truth, it's no' sae easy as an adult. This Sargasso drownin', it's forcin' back the memories, isn't it? Dinnae deny it, lad, I can see it in yer eyes. This time roond, ye've got tae face yer demons."

"You're one to give advice."

"Frae where I'm standin', we're baith in prison, only yours is up here," he said, tapping his head.

"As you said, I'm not a child any more, so keep playing your mind games, I'm immune. As for your doubts about the barbed wire, try reading the damn medical report. The doctor who stitched me up—"

"Doctor?" Angus bellowed a laugh. "Ye call Ryan Hornsby a doctor? Hornsby's a vet'rinarian, he worked on farm animals. Highlanders like us used him 'cause we couldnae afford tae pay real doctors."

"He was still a medical professional."

"Open yer eyes, laddie. The only reason Alban MacDonald brought ye tae Hornsby was 'cause he's kin, an', o' course, he's Templar, which means he'd take the truth tae the grave wi' him . . . or a'ready did, seein' as he croaked last year."

"Save your breath, Angus. I'm not buying into it."

"What still gets me is how ye managed tae escape. I mean, sweet Jesus, look at them scars, it's like the De'il tasted ye an' spat ye back oot."

"I saw the medical report, Angus. It said barbed wire."

"Aye. Hornsby wrote whit he was telt."

"Enough already! Even if he was a veterinarian, why would Hornsby listen to a water bailiff and risk losing his license?"

"Because, Judy, Alban MacDonald wisnae jist a water bailiff, he's also Priest Knight o' the Templar."

"I don't understand?"

"Ye've never heard o' the Knights Templar?"

"I've heard of them, sure, but what do they have to do with Loch Ness?"

Angus shook his head. "A genius when it comes tae sea creatures, but ye're lost when it comes tae yer ain folk, are ye no'?" He moved away from the bars, sitting on the edge of his mattress. "Pay attention, Gracie, an' jist maybe yer auld man'll teach ye somethin'. The Order o' the Knights wis officially founded in Jerusalem back in the early 1100s, roond the end o' the First Crusade. I say officially, 'cause they'd been roond long afore that, goin' back tae the days o' Saint Columba hi'sel'. They were part-warrior, part-monk, an' a' chivalrous, dedicated tae protecting Christians makin' the pilgrimage tae the Temple o' Solomon. King Baldwin II o' Jerusalem offered them a hame in the temple, an' livin' on alms, they became kent as the Poor Knights o' the Temple."

"What does any of this have to do with—"

"Patience, Sally, patience. Now some ten years after he formed the Knights, Hughes de Paynes traveled tae Europe, seekin' new recruits. In France, he joined forces wi' another monk, Bernard de Clairvaux, an' his Cistercian brotherhood. Vowin' tae fight in Christ's name against evil, the Knights successfully recruited thoosands intae the Order, a' donnin' the white vestments, now adorned wi' the Knighthood's red cross. Now in 1139, the Pope, Innocent II, he decides it's best if he took control o' the Templars. First thing he does is exclude them frae taxation, which allowed them tae accumulate great wealth. Bein' clever sorts, the Knights adopted the practice o' lendin' money usin' interest terms, practically inventin' modern-day bankin' in the process.

The order became rich an' quite powerful, an' their numbers swelled, neither o' which wis appreciated by France's King Phillip the Fair, an ambitious bastard if ever there wis one. Phillip coveted the Knights' accumulated wealth, an' it wis he who gave Friday the thirteenth its true infamy, for on that day in October o' 1307, he ordered a' Knights residin' in France tae be arrested for heresy. Three thoosand innocent Templars were imprisoned an' tortured, their property seized by the king. Under Phillip's pressure, the Pope then ordered the arrest o' a' Templar Knights. Fifteen thoosand mair monks were jailed an' brutally beaten, effectively dissolvin' the Order. The Knights' Grand Master, Jacques de Molay, wis coerced intae a false confession, then burned at the stake. Legend says that Molay recanted his confession as he burned, an' placed a curse on the king an' the Pope, baith o' whom died within seven months."

"And what does all this have to do with True's father?"

"I'm gettin' tae that. Fleein' France, the survivin' Templars branched oot intae two successful Orders, the Sovereign Military Order o' the Temple o' Jerusalem an' the Freemasons. Many o' the Fraternal Order came tae Scotland, which had been a stronghold for the Templars back in the day o' Hughes de Paynes, him havin' worked oot a deal wi' King David of Scotland for the lands of Ballatradoch. Robert the Bruce an' the Stewart Clan were all born into the Order, which eventually became kent as the Masonic Templar. Thus, the Scots Royal line wis established, linkin' us tae the bloodline o' King David o' Jerusalem an' his son, Solomon, who commissioned his Temple be built by a Master Mason. Remember, it wis Solomon's Temple that held the Arc of the Covenant an' its wealth o' secrets. Many believe the Knights were the ones left to guard it, and when a Templar guards somethin', it stays guarded.

"Anyway, after Bonnie Prince Charlie fell at Culloden, the Masons continued their attempts tae re-establish oor bloodlines an' adopt the Templar laws intae Scotland's crown. This movement became kent as the Scottish Rite, an' it wis very popular in the Colonies durin' the American Revolution. Fact is, both George Washington an' Benjamin

Franklin were Knights, an' they based much o' America's Declaration o' Independence on the teachings o' the Masonic Temple."

I listened intently, this, the first serious conversation I could recall ever having with my father. I was amazed at his depth of knowledge, but suspected he was again setting me up for something.

". . . the Puritans, being a narrow-minded an' superstitious lot, were aye accusin' folk o' witchcraft, while the Masons encouraged scientific discoveries; the law of gravity, the invention o' the reflectin' telescope, an' the list goes on."

"You're a Templar Knight, too, aren't you?"

He paused then, thinking it over. "Wis, Gracie, I wis, 'til that bastard, Alban MacDonald, removed me frae the Order. Can ye believe it? Me, a direct descendant frae Sir William Wallace himsel', kicked oot o' the Masonry? The Wallace clan's aye given oor all for Scotland. It wis a descendent o' Wallace that spilt blood at Bannockburn wi' the Bruce. An' when the Bruce died, a Wallace went tae the Holy Land, only tae find oor entourage outnumbered by the Moors at Teba. There, in Calavatra—"

"Yeah, yeah, I know the story, and stop exaggerating! It was there that the *Black Douglas*, Sir James the Good, flung the Bruce's heart into the Moorish lines and proclaimed, 'Go Braveheart and we, your Knights will follow,' and that's where the name, Braveheart, was really coined."

He shook his head. "Why dae I waste my time?"

"Just answer me this, Angus. If you were such a chivalrous Templar, why did Alban MacDonald expel you."

"Politics. The auld fart refuses tae change wi' the times. The Knights guard the ancient ways, see, but there are those among us who prefer tae live in the twenty-first century. Alban's a Priest-Knight o' the highest order, so what he says goes. He an' a few o' the senior cooncil members didnae like me sellin' my ancestor's land tae Johnny C., though it's okay for the hypocrites' sons tae work for Cialino Ventures, includin' one True MacDonald."

"Cialino's company owns the oil rig?"

"Six o' them, a' in the North Sea, plus part o' a new hydroelectric dam bein' built east of Fort Augustus. They've got underground pipelines runnin' through the Moray Firth intae Inverness an' throughoot the Highlands. Alban disnae like it, an' he's made a big environmental stink aboot it tae the Masonic Cooncil. The auld bampot booted me oot o' the Order the day I selt my acreage tae Johnny C., an' my life's been hell ever since."

"Angus, on Saturday morning, I caught the Crabbit hiding in the woods, dressed in Templar garments, only they weren't white, they were black, and instead of the Knight's Cross, the tunic bore a symbol, like a heart with an X across it."

My father looked away.

"What?"

"I cannae say."

"Why not? Wallace blood flows through my veins, just as it flows through yours."

"It's no' a clan thing. Blood oaths've been taken, preventin' me frae speaking o' certain things."

"You're talking in riddles."

He looked up at me with those piercing Gael eyes, but said nothing.

"Okay, you want to keep playing head games, fine. But Alban's sword was covered in blood. I don't know whether it was animal or human blood, but he had that crazed look in his eye, the one that used to scare the shit out of me when I was a kid."

"Aye. MacDonald lost his marbles long ago. He's no' fit tae run the Cooncil, if ye ask me. A disgrace he is, an' a liar—"

"You're one to talk. Do you really think the judge and jury are buying into your ridiculous little scheme? So you used my childhood scars as a means of kicking over a hornet's nest, that still doesn't make you innocent. In fact, in the end, you may have just sealed your own fate."

"How dae ye work that one oot?"

"Had you simply claimed Cialino's death was an accident, Max probably could have gotten you down to manslaughter, and you'd have served five to ten years in prison, maybe less. But now, with this whole ridiculous Loch Ness monster claim, everything changes."

"And how's that?"

"Because the monster alibi, as hokey as it is, required planning. You had to get Cialino to Urquhart Castle, you had to fly me in as a witness, you even went so far as to obtain my unpublished dissertation. Planning means Johnny C.'s murder was no accident, it was premeditated. When that jury rules you guilty, and believe me, when the smoke clears they will, you'll spend the rest of your days behind bars . . . if you're lucky. See, this isn't a Rubik's Cube you've cheated this time, Angus, it's the High Court of Scotland. You may have had fun tossing dynamite at the media, but you've overplayed your hand, pissing off that prosecutor, who's going to nail your hairy ass to the wall."

"So says *you*."

"And what says the merry widow?"

He looked up at me then, anger in his eyes. "Theresa? She had nothing tae dae wi' this."

"Sure she didn't. I saw how she was looking at you . . . playing you like a fiddle."

"Och! Ye dinnae ken anythin'!"

"Pretty face, gorgeous body, it was sweet bait, and you grabbed it, hook, line, and sinker. Only this woman, she's got her own ambitions. Tell me, how many times did you screw her behind Johnny C.'s back before she began planting the idea of killing her husband?"

"Shut up."

"I'll bet it was her idea to use Nessie as an alibi. Just think of what this publicity will do to generate business at her new resort. And then you jumped right in, telling her how you could solidify your defense by dragging me into it."

"Ye're aff yer heid!"

"*Use the Nessie story, Angus, and I'll triple the money Johnny owes you. We'll live happily ever after* . . . except, of course, she'll have all of Johnny's assets, including his new resort, while you're pledging your undying love as you dance on the end of a rope."

"Shut up! Theresa's a friend, nothin' more."

"Yeah, sure. No wonder you hired Max instead of a real attorney. Bet he's getting a piece of the action on the side, too, huh?"

"Get oot! Get the fuck oot o' here, ye wee bastard! I never want tae see ye again! Ye're no son o' mine!"

"Ah, how I wish that were true," I said, rolling over to get some sleep, congratulating myself on finally being able to push Angus's buttons. "But here's some free advice from one bastard to another. Be sure to hold your head up nice and high when they hang you, Pop. Remember, you're a Wallace."

It was late, just after one in the morning. I was on my motorcycle, approaching the Abriachan turn out of Inverness when I noticed something large in the bushes up ahead. I was almost upon it when it abruptly turned, exposing a long, hefty body, maybe 4.5–6 meters (15–20 feet). It possessed a very powerful tail, rounded at the end, and two front flippers. The head was snakelike, flat on top, and my headlight reflected an oval eye. The animal made two great bounds across the road and down into the water, followed by a big splash.

—Mr. W. Arthur Grant, Veterinary Student, 5 January 1934

I was driving on the A82, just south of Invermoriston when I saw it! It was half ashore and I had a clear view of it for nine minutes in my binoculars. It was at least 12–18 meters long (40–60 feet) but did not see its full tail as it was not quite completely out of the water. As it turned I had a clear view of its left fore flipper, which is grey in color, spade-shaped, and devoid of any markings which might indicate toes or claws. It was a clearly a flipper and not a foot. The animal eventually made sort of a U-shaped turn and flopped back into deep water. It did not reappear and left only ripples, no wake.

—Mr. Torquil MacLeod, Excerpted from a letter to Inverness author, Constance Whyte, 28 February 1960

CHAPTER 14

Invermoriston, Scottish Highlands
Scotland

WHILE I TOSSED AND TURNED on my lumpy jail cell mattress and hundreds of reporters from around the world descended upon Castle Inverness like bees to honey, the real story was unfolding twenty miles to the south on the banks of Loch Ness.

*   *   *

Two major rivers intersect Loch Ness along its western shores. Enrick River is the larger of the two, flowing west to east through the Great Glen and past Drumnadrochit until it reaches Loch Ness at Urquhart Bay. Fifteen miles farther to the south, the River Moriston passes through the Glen Moriston dam, rages into a grade-five waterfall, then rushes below the old stone Telford Bridge on its way past Invermoriston before it too releases into Loch Ness.

The hamlet of Invermoriston dates back to the early 1600s. It's home to a handful of lodgings, taverns, and quaint craft shops, and its pier was once a popular destination for steamships traveling up and down the Loch in the 1890s.

Invermoriston first found fame in 1746 when the town harbored the "Seven Men of Moriston," a loyal band who protected Bonnie Prince Charlie from the English forces following the massacre at Culloden.

Thirteen generations later, the tiny Loch Ness village was about to become popular for an entirely different reason.

*   *   *

Tiani Brueggert had been planning her family's weeklong camping trip around Loch Ness for months. Although her husband, Joel, and their two teenage daughters, Chloe and McKailey, preferred to stay in bed-and-breakfasts, Tiani would hear none of it, insisting her "average American family" rough it in tents along the legendary banks of the Loch.

Their backpacks loaded with gear, the Brueggerts set out on their walking tour in Fort Augustus, the Loch's southernmost town. An eighteen-mile trail awaited them as they hiked north past scenic Loch Ness through forests heavy in spruce and pine.

The first day's journey ended eight hours later in Invermoriston. Crossing the Telford Bridge, the Brueggerts posed in photos of the majestic Moriston Falls, then followed the river farther west, but by seven-thirty, they were back in the village, their bodies spent.

The sun was still high when they stopped for dinner at the Glenmoriston Arms Tavern and Bistro. Two hours later, the exhausted family finally made camp on the banks of Loch Ness, just southwest of the inlet. There were dozens of other campers at the site, most on holiday from Europe. A few were fishing, all were enjoying the remains of a Highland summer sunset.

By the time they had crawled into their sleeping bags, the graying skies had darkened into storm clouds, and the Glen's southeasterly breeze had intensified, whipping up whitecaps on the Loch's threatened surface.

The more experienced campers quickly battened down, anticipating a rough night.

The two Brueggert girls were in their tent, having fallen asleep within minutes of their heads hitting their pillows. Joel was lying on his side next to his wife, reading by flashlight, but Tiani was in too much pain to sleep. It was the second day of her period, the heaviest bleeding day of her menstrual cycle. Her lower back ached, and both her ankles were swollen from the day's hike. She knew another long day lie ahead, having scheduled her family to be in Drumnadrochit by the next night, and the trail would be steep one—assuming she could even get her feet back into her hiking boots by morning.

Swallowing two more aspirin, she turned to her husband. "I'll be back in a few minutes, I want to soak my ankles before it rains. Joel?"

Her husband mumbled a reply, his eyes already closed.

Tiani crawled out of the tent, pulling on her hooded navy sweat-shirt against the wind. Locating the wooded path leading to the Loch, she staggered gingerly through the forest down the sloping trail, her flashlight barely cutting the darkness.

The pain forced her to pause at a park bench situated in a small clearing littered with trash from an overflowing steel barrel, then she continued down the steepening path to the shoreline.

Gusts of wind and spray greeted her as she left the shelter of the forest. Turning right, she followed the heavily pebbled beach to the boating dock. Menacing dark waves rolled against the launch, sending a dozen aluminum canoes and wooden kayaks banging against one another as they fought their tethers.

Walking to the end of the pier, Tiani removed her unlaced boots and thick wool socks, rolled up her pant legs, then sat along the edge and plunged her throbbing ankles into the near-freezing waters.

Tiani yelped in protest, and it took several attempts and four full minutes before her skin finally numbed to the cold. Lying back, she gazed east across the Loch at an ominous outline of mountains and thunderheads, then closed her eyes, believing she was alone.

*   *   *

"Huh!" Tiani bolted upright, her heart pounding, her eyes wide as she searched her surroundings.

Something had startled her awake. *What was it?*

Raindrops pelted her, and she laughed at her foolishness. She pulled her legs from the water, but her feet were so numb she could no longer feel them. She massaged them until the circulation returned, her eyes never leaving Loch Ness's choppy surface.

Stop being stupid. Next, you'll be searching the woods for Big Foot.

Still nervous, she slipped her socks back over her feet, then gently tugged on her boots, keeping the laces loose. The swelling was down, and that was good, but now she just wanted to be back in her tent and out of the rain.

Tiani stood, then headed back down the pier, her unlaced shoes clopping on the weathered boards.

Leaving the boating area, she turned right and retraced her steps along the rocky shoreline until she came to the beginning of the wooded trail that led up to the campsite.

Tiani paused, inhaling the wind. An acrid scent lingered in the brisk air, the smell reminding her of a zoo cage that desperately needed hosing.

Whomp!

Tiani let out a half scream, startled by the sudden crash of metal somewhere up ahead. "Hello? Who's there? Joel?"

Gusts of wind whipped the rain-soaked pine needles against her arms, urging her to begin the climb.

Focusing her flashlight on the path, she started up the slope, the scent growing stronger.

She was perspiring by the time she arrived at the park bench—the halfway point to the campsite. Raindrops pelted the rusted steel trash barrel, which, strangely, was now lying on its side, garbage strewn everywhere.

The wind? Impossible. The can must weigh over two hundred pounds. She circled the small clearing with the beam of her flashlight.

Nothing.

The climb had loosened her unlaced boots to the point they were slipping off her feet. Shuffling over to the picnic table, she lifted her right boot to the bench and began pulling the laces tighter.

She jumped again as a gunshot of thunder echoed across the heavens—and something huge floundered across the path leading up to the campsite.

Tiani's heart fluttered. *What the fuck was that?* She crept to the edge of the trail, shining her light up the dark, tree-lined path. *Maybe a bear?*

There was nothing there now . . . but *something* had been there a minute ago. She caught a heavy whiff of decaying fish in the swirling wind.

And then the heavens opened up overhead, drenching her in a summer squall. "Terrific." Tiani yelled up the path as loud as she could. "Joel! Joel, help!"

The cloudburst rose into a crescendo of splattered leaves, swallowing her cries.

Wind lashed at the limbs of pine encircling the rest area, scattering the garbage at her feet.

"Joel! Hello! Can anybody hear me?"

A spiderweb of lightning answered her, igniting the heavens, revealing the shadowy figure, now poised at the edge of the clearing.

Tiani Brueggert looked up in horror . . . and screamed.

The Diary of Sir Adam Wallace
Translated by Logan W. Wallace

Entry: 24 October 1330
I can only estimate this date of entry, no' that it matters, for I fear my words will ne'er see the light o' day nor another's eyes. Still, whit mine have seen . . . scarcely can I steady my hand to record the tale.

When last I wrote, the Knights were hard at work, assemblin' an iron gate meant tae block the Guivres' exit tae the North Sea. The cavern's air had grown heavy wi' smoke frae oor torches, an' Sir Iain wis close by, busy preparin' a meal o' mince an' tatties. The scent o' the meat caused my stomach tae gurgle, when suddenly a terrible scream shattered oor calm an' I dropped my quill.

'Twis Sir Michael Bona that screamed, an' by oor torches' flickerin' light I saw him—his body raised above the edge o' the overlook, caught within the powerful jaws o' the most ungodly creature I could e'er imagine.

It had risen frae the underground river, its enormous head, ten times that o' a horse. Its fangs were sharp an' curved, the largest teeth barbed, positioned ootside its hideous mooth. Nodules covered the top o' the skull, taperin' doon a thick neck, the remains o' its body remainin' hidden in the water.

Grabbin' my sword, I lunged at the beast, inhalin' its horrid stench even as I lashed at its throat. My blade sliced its oily dark hide, but could barely penetrate against its heavy coat o' slime.

Stunned by the blow, the creature released Sir Michael and submerged, its immense tail loopin' oot frae the river an' slappin' wildly at the surface, the icy splashes drenchin' us . . . . an' oor torches.

Cast in darkness, we were at the De'il's ain mercy.

I backed carefully awa' frae the edge, drookit (wet) an' shiverin', unable tae see my ain hand afore my face. Sir Michael lay by my feet, his gurglin' cries drooned in his ain blood.

"We need a flame," MacDonald called out. I heard flints scrapin' against the cave walls behind me, an' then a spark caught fabric, an' we had light.

Sir Michael's wounds were fatal, an' even MacDonald's whisky couldnae comfort oor fallen comrade. I have seen many men die o' battle wounds, but none in so much agony. The beast had crushed Michael's internals, an' his insides were burstin' forth frae his mooth like air frae a bellows, makin' it impossible tae swallow. Blood gushed frae a half-ring of teeth holes, each as big as a man's fist.

We held him doon until he died. MacDonald offered last rites, an' then we lowered his body into the water, an' watched it swept away.

MacDonald divided us after that, three men on the gate, three at sentry, the remainin' two tae rest. Long hours have passed, an' it's noo my turn tae sleep. My body is heavy frae this terrible day, but my mind refuses rest, for noo I have seen the De'il—his brood is close, an' I am too feart tae close my eyes.

I was standing at the shore near the mouth of the Altsigh Burn, watching to see whether any trout were rising when I saw this extraordinary sight. It was the monster's head and neck, less than eight meters from me and it was without any doubt in the act of swallowing food! It opened and closed its mouth several times quite quickly and then kept tossing its head backwards in the same manner as a cormorant does after it's devoured a fish!

After two minutes, it put its head down and a hump and tail came into sight. It submerged, then surfaced again, farther away. I saw no limbs or flippers, but the skin was slick, dark in color, paling along the belly. I'd guess it was at least six meters [19.68 feet] long.

—John MacLean, Invermoriston, June 1937

CHAPTER 15

Inverness, Scottish Highlands
Scotland

TRUE MACDONALD ARRIVED EARLY the next morning, bundles of newspapers tucked under each of his burly arms. He pushed my breakfast cart away from my cell door, then shoved a stack of papers in between the iron bars. "Wake up, Zack, there's work ta be done."

I pinched sleep from my eyes, then rolled over in bed to the smell of powdered eggs and bad aftershave. "Aren't you a little old to be working a paper route?"

"No' when my best mate's the toast o' Scotland." He handed me an *Inverness Courier*. "Go on, take a' look at this."

It was hard to tell which was the more shocking, the photo of me standing on the witness chair, exposing part of my buttocks, or the story's headline.

Renowned Marine Biologist Survived Nessie Attack
Testimony expected to launch largest search of
Loch Ness in Scotland's History.

Dr. Zachary Wallace, the renowned American marine biologist and son of accused killer, Angus William Wallace of Drumnadrochit, shocked the High Court on Monday when he revealed scars left by teeth marks from a bite that nearly severed him in half seventeen years ago. Dr. Wallace, whose testimony has yet to be questioned by prosecutors, barely survived an encounter with a giant squid six months ago in the Sargasso Sea.

Dr. Wallace's testimony is sure to be challenged. The Courier has learned that the marine biologist was dismissed from his teaching position at Florida Atlantic University shortly after the Sargasso accident and has since been undergoing psychiatric treatment.

"What a load of crap! I never said I was bitten, and what's with the psychiatric bit? Yes, I saw a shrink, but that doesn't mean I'm nuts. I went one time and—"

"Whit dae ye expect? This is Nessie news. Since when dae facts count for anythin'?"

"You don't understand, True, this is exactly the kind of nonsense that'll destroy my reputation, at least whatever's left of it."

"Why? It wisnae yer fault ye got bitten."

"I wasn't bitten!"

"Sure, sure, but it's better if ye jist say ye cannae remember. Now start signin' the newspapers, I've customers waitin'."

"You're kidding, right?"

"Hey, business is business. Right now, ye're mair popular than Bonnie Prince Charlie. Strike while the iron's hot, that's what I say." He tossed me a felt-tip marker. "Sign them anywhere but across the headlines. We'll get ten pounds sterling fer each, maybe twelve."

"Unbelievable."

True removed a camera from his jacket pocket. "Now I'll be needin' ye tae drop yer pants. The *Examiner* offered me two hundred pounds for a clear close-up, but I ken I can get more."

"Forget it."

"Why? Ye mooned 'em for free yesterday."

"I said forget it! I'm sick of everyone exploiting this Nessie crap. And you . . . you're supposed to be my friend. You're as bad as your sister."

"Brandy . . . I'd almost forgot. I've a message frae her. Come closer so I don't wake Angus."

I leaned in like a dummy, thinking he was going to whisper it in my ear.

Wump! True's fist caught me flush in the breadbasket, dropping me to the concrete floor.

I sat up, fighting to catch my wind. "You big lummoxe, what the hell was that for?"

"That's for steppin' on my sister's heart. Did I no' warn ye Brandy's been havin' an awfy hard time? Last thing she needed wis mair rejection."

"I wasn't rejecting her."

"Ye led her on, then ran off is what I heard."

"Maybe he's no' man enough tae handle yer sister," Angus said, greeting the day with a burst of flatulence.

"Lovely."

"At least I fart like a man, Gertrude, whit's *your* excuse?"

"Ignore him," I said. "He's a dead man talking."

"Give it a rest, you two. Brandy's condition's nothin' tae joke aboot. Wis bad enough when Alban kicked her oot, but this last go-around in the States, I think somethin' snapped in her pretty little heid."

"What do you mean?"

"When she first got back, I had her stayin' wi' me. One day I found blood a' ower her sheets. She claimed it wis her woman's time, but I found razors tucked inside the mattress. She'd been usin' the blades tae carve up her legs."

"Jesus . . ."

True helped himself to my breakfast. "Psychiatrist fella, he called it self-mutilation. Says it's part o' Brandy's whole fear o' abandonment thing. Her mood swings like a pendulum, calm one moment, a storm the next."

"So I've noticed."

"Doctors had her on pills, but God only knows if she's still takin' them. I worry aboot her, Zack. Last thing she needs now is another guy steppin' on her heart."

Angus pressed his face between the bars. "Trust me, True, ye dinnae need yer sister hangin' oot wi' the likes o' Zachary. The laddie's battlin' his ain childhood demons, an' he's still feart tae face them."

True looked confused. "Whit's he talkin' aboot?"

"Ignore him."

"Wish I could've ignored thae bloody screams," Angus said. "A' night, yellin' like a lunatic, jist like he did after the first accident. Head doctors had a fancy name for it . . . post-traumatic somethin' somethin', but I just called it what it was—bein' feart. Waste o' time, a' that analysis, I should've jist tossed him right back in the Loch the day after it happened. That wid have nicked it in the arse, right there an' then."

I shook my head. "Growing up with a father like you, it's a wonder they haven't locked me up in a mental ward by now."

"Boo-hoo. Jist remember, Gretchen, it's you who has tae live wi' these nightmares, an' ye're the only one who can stop them."

"How's that?" asked True, finishing off my breakfast.

"By findin' the monster, o' course. Zachary may be feart, but he kens how this monster thinks. That's how he brought the De'il tae the surface the first time."

"You're insane."

"At least my memory works, as does Nessie's, an' believe you me, now that the dragon's tasted human flesh again, it'll be comin' up tae feed a lot mair."

True's eyes widened. "Nessie's a dragon?"

Angus nodded. "Maybe no' a dragon as we ken it, but these Guivres have got the blood o' a dragon in them."

"What did you call them?"

"A Guivre, Mister Marine Biologist. Accordin' tae lore, Guivres were wingless dragons, resemblin' giant sea serpents. The beasts once resided in a' the Great Glen's lochs, but in winters when food wis scarce, they'd cross countrysides, too, in search o' anythin' they could swallow. Back when I was a lad, yer grandfaither, Logan, taught me a' aboot them. Said they didnae breathe fire like other dragons, but their oily skin spewed noxious vapors, bad enough tae cause vegetation to shrivel an' rot. They're the De'il, they are, but—"

"Butts are for crapping, Angus, and your tale's a load if there ever was one, a pathetic alibi designed to use Nessie's popularity to take the spotlight away from your guilt."

"An' ye're a disgrace tae the tartan an' a' who bore the Wallace name. Since the time o' Saint Columba these De'il's have stalked oor Glen, feastin' off the flesh o' those that droon, yer ain grandfaither among them. You'd be deid, too, if no' for some miracle. Keep ignorin' the truth, but ye cannae run away frae yer fear forever."

"Whit're ye suggestin', Angus?" True asked.

"It's Zachary's callin'. He needs tae help us find this beast an' kill it."

"I'm a scientist, Angus, not a monster hunter."

"Then be a scientist an' find that creature! It's oot there, Zachary, I swear that on my faither's soul, an' ye're the only one that can find it an' prove my innocence."

"You *swear*? Your word means nothing to me. The moment that asshole judge releases me, I'm on the next plane back to Miami."

True cringed as he looked down the corridor. "Uh, Zack—"

"What?"

"The asshole's back," Judge Hannam announced, as he led Sheriff Brian Holmstrom and six brutes dressed in police uniforms toward our cells. "You may release Dr. Wallace, Sheriff, provided he cooperates."

"Cooperates? How?"

Holmstrom, a no-nonsense fellow carrying a muscular build on his smallish frame, opened the cell door, but blocked my exit. "Dr. Wallace, I'm requestin' that ye accompany these men. You will not speak o' anythin' ye see or hear tae anyone other than my inspector, or I shall be forced tae incarcerate ye until ye're as auld an' stupid a man as yer faither."

"What's this all about?"

"You'll find out when you get there."

"Do I have a choice?"

The judge nodded. "You can stay in your cell another day if you'd like. Give you and your father here more time to reminisce about old times."

"I'd rather eat haggis." I laced up my shoes, stepped out of the cell, then, nodding at True, punched him as hard as I could in his stomach, nearly breaking my fist in the process.

True grimaced but never buckled. "Well done, lad. We're even then."

"We're not even. That was for eating my breakfast."

*   *   *

Sheriff Holmstrom handed me a black nylon Inverness Police jacket. "Put this on, we need tae pull a quick bait an' switch. Castle grounds are congested wi' dozens o' news vans, television crews, an' reporters, most o' whom have been campin' out since last night. Every reporter an' his mother wants tae speak wi' ye, an' I can't have them followin' us tae the crime scene."

Crime scene?

Before I could question him, he paraded me through a mezzanine filled with media, who swarmed upon me like hungry sharks.

"Dr. Wallace, how large was the creature that bit you?"

"Could you show us those scars?"

"Dr. Wallace, are you planning to go after the monster then?"

"Dr. Wallace, how do you respond to accusations about this whole thing being a ruse?"

"Dr. Wallace . . ."

"Dr. Wallace . . ."

Holmstrom pushed me through the crowd. "Dr. Wallace is late for a meetin' in North Inverness an' has no comment at this time."

We exited the mezzanine through a side door, entering a private access way. A door to the right led outside to the police parking lot, the door to the left, an indoor garage.

"All right, doctor, if you'll give your jacket to Officer Johnston here, we'll have you on your way."

Johnston, a man about my size and weight, placed the police jacket over his head, effectively hiding his face, then was hustled out to the parking lot by the six escorts to an awaiting police van.

Sheriff Holmstrom ushered me inside the garage and an awaiting black Mercedes Benz. The vehicle's windows were tinted, meant to keep nosey reporters from seeing inside.

The driver waited ten minutes before driving off. As we rounded a bend outside the castle, we saw the last of the reporter's vehicles pulling out of the parking lot to chase after the police van.

Neither the driver nor his partner spoke to me as we followed the back roads south out of Inverness and onto the A82. Heavy gray rain clouds hung over the Great Glen, and the trees' leaves blew upward, forecasting another rainfall.

We continued south, escorted by that cursed Loch, then suddenly I was overcome by a terrible sense of dread. *Crime scene? Oh, God, it's Brandy! True said she was unstable. She must've committed suicide . . . or maybe her crazy old man wigged out and stabbed her with his sword?*

"Was it Brandy Townson? Did something happen to her? Hey goons, I'm talking to you, answer me!"

They said nothing, but I felt easier after we circled through Drumnadrochit and continued south past Urquhart Bay.

Where were they taking me? What had happened?

Another fifteen minutes passed before we entered the village of Invermoristan.

The police lights told me we had arrived.

A lay-by, camping area, and the entire southwestern tip of the Moriston Estuary into Loch Ness had been cordoned off by the police. Villagers were being lined up along the A82 and questioned. An ambulance was pulled off to the side of the highway, its driver standing on the roof of his vehicle, trying to see beyond the dense woods.

We parked in the lay-by where a half dozen witnesses were giving statements to police. I was escorted past a sobbing man in his late forties and two shocked teenage girls to a picnic table that served as a central information point.

A tall man with brown hair and athletic build looked up from his notepad as we approached. "You're Wallace? Michael Gajewski. I'm a scene o' crime officer wi' the Northern Constabulary in Inverness. Tell me, Doctor, have you had breakfast?"

"No."

"Good. Come wi' me."

I followed him through the campsite, then along a narrow wooded trail that descended towards the Loch. "What's this all about, Officer?"

"I'm hopin' you'll tell me."

We approached a small clearing where a police photographer was taking pictures. Garbage was strewn everywhere, apparently from a heavy trash barrel lying on its side.

"Oh, Jesus!"

There was little left of the victim to identify. Blood was splattered everywhere, on the ground, across the leaves, the barks of trees, the picnic table . . . it was as if a dozen gallons of scarlet paint had been set in the clearing and detonated.

The photographer aimed his camera at the lower branches of a fir tree, where the remains of a left arm, severed above the elbow, hung from its perch. More human shrapnel had been tossed into the underbrush. There were fingers, an ankle and foot, still wrapped in a wool sock, scraps of a navy sweatshirt, divots of human hair patches of torn-away flesh.

I turned away, sickened.

"A' right, Dr. Wallace, ye've seen what ye've seen. So tell me, are we dealin' wi' an animal or a lunatic?"

"God, I don't know, I'm not a forensic specialist. If it was an animal, it looks more like the work of a grizzly than anything living in Loch Ness."

"It's no' a bear. Haven't been bears in the Highlands for a thousand years."

I took a deep breath, fighting the nausea. The air held a strange raw scent, like the insides of a rotted intestine. "What is that odor?"

"Again, we were hopin' you'd know. Smells like bad anchovies."

"Or raw sewage. And what happened to the rest of the victim's body?"

"We don't know. We're still searchin' the area, an' a team's on their way tae dredge the shoreline. 'Course, if it ate her—"

"Ate her? Officer, to cause this much widespread damage to an adult human being, the animal, assuming it was an animal, would have to be huge, at least fifty feet, with a bite radius larger than a great white shark's."

"You say if it wis an animal. What else might it be?"

"I don't know." I covered my nose, looking around. "It's possible this entire gruesome scene could've simply been staged to make it look like an animal attack."

"Aye, we considered that. Perhaps, say, an ally of yer father's?"

Suddenly I felt relieved at having spent the night locked up in a cell.

The police officer who drove me to Invermoriston approached. "Sir, two film crews jist showed up. We're keepin' them back by the road, but it willnae be long before they work their way 'round on foot tae see intae the lay-by. The judge specifically said he disnae want the media knowin' Dr. Wallace wis here."

"Sorry, Doctor, that means your time's up."

"Officer, you brought me here, at least give me a few minutes to walk around the area and search for clues. If this was an animal, maybe it left behind some tracks."

"We've a'ready checked, didnae find a thing."

"How would you know what you're looking for?"

"I think we'd recognize an animal track if we saw one. Besides, nothin' as big as ye described inhabits these glens. Personally, Dr. Wallace, I think we've got us a madman on the loose."

I had just pointed out Urquhart Castle to the children when one of them asked, "Is that a rock out there?" Glancing across the water, I saw something a third of the way out and knew it was no rock. Unable to see it clearly, we hurried down to the water's edge, but by that time, it had gone. Still, it had left a terrific wash which hit the shoreline with such violence it caused one of the children to run back in horror.

—Lady Maud Baille, C.B.E. Commander of the A.T.S.,19 April 1950

It was midday and I was driving north on the A82 out of Fort Augustus. As I passed Cherry Island, I saw a great disturbance in the water, maybe 150 meters from shore. About two meters of a black object appeared along the surface, disappeared, then reappeared about 100 meters closer to shore. The speed of the movement was incredible.

—Col. Patrick Grant, 13 November 1951

CHAPTER 16

Inverness, Scottish Highlands

I WAS BACK IN THE MERCEDES, heading north on the A82, the chief constable's words echoing in my brain. *Personally, Dr. Wallace, I think we've got a madman on the loose. A madman with a sword? Or a murderer with an accomplice, blaming his escapades on a fictitious dragon?*

The thought made me ill.

Instead of being returned to Inverness Castle, I was taken to Town House for an emergency session of the Highland Council. By the time we arrived, rumors of a "new Nessie attack" were already circulating across the British airwaves.

Judge Hannam was at the meeting, having called a one-day recess of Angus's trial "to examine the validity of the defense's claims." The jury had been sequestered in a hotel, but few believed the developing events could be kept from them much longer.

The Highlands were becoming a tinderbox, and Angus and his attorney were tossing matches.

Owen James Hollifield, newly elected provost and head of the Highland Council, was a gentle man by nature, though he carried a power-lifter's physique on his squat, six-foot frame. "Chairmen an' Councillors, please . . . I'd like tae call this meetin' ta order. We'll dispense wi' the minutes an' get right at it, if that's a' right by you."

The room quieted.

"By now, ye've a' heard the rumors, so let's see if we can dispel wi' the fantasy an' get tae the facts. Sheriff?"

Sheriff Olmstead stood and read from his notepad. "At approximately four-thirty this mornin', the remains of the deceased were found by her husband along a wooded trail located at an Invermoriston campsite. The victim wis an American woman named Tiani Brueggert, identified by a weddin' ring taken from the remains o' a digit on her severed left hand. While we've found traces o' other body parts an' a large quantity o' blood, the rest o' the victim's body remains missin'. This suggests the victim's assailant either took the body with him for disposal, or tossed it intae the Loch. As we speak, two boats are dredgin' a two-kilometer area along Loch Ness's shoreline. Technically, it is possible the woman is still alive."

"Sheriff, are you suggestin' the victim was kidnapped?"

"I'm only statin' that, at this time, we have no body, only nonvital body parts. However, an' this is only a preliminary report, medical examiners have determined that the woman's left arm wis severed by an extremely sharp serrated instrument, possibly a long blade, an' yes, possibly by an animal's bite."

The room buzzed with opinion.

"Quiet please! As our guest, Dr. Wallace, has pointed out, if it wis an animal, the bite radius wid be bigger than any species inhabitin' our glen—"

"Except for Nessie!"

Murmurs filled the chamber.

"Go on an' ask him whit it wis, Olmstead, he should know!"

"Come on, Wallace, wis it Nessie or no'?"

The provost banged a thick palm against the table for quiet. "This is a Council meetin', no' a mob scene. Sheriff Olmstead's tellin' us whit he knows, no' whit *you* want tae hear."

"An' what *is* Nessie exactly?" the sheriff threw back at them. "Last I heard, legends don't kill people. If it wis an amphibious beast, does that make it Nessie? An' since when does Nessie attack humans?"

One of the council rose, pointing at me. "Whit aboot him? He wis attacked."

"Not according to the physician's report," Judge Hannam retorted. "Now all of you, I want you to listen very carefully to what I have to say, because how we react to these grave circumstances will determine how the rest of the world perceives this little community we call home. My courtroom's already been turned into theater, and unless we keep a handle on this woman's murder, this whole Nessie thing's going to blow right up in our faces, just like all the expeditions did back in the 1960s."

Lorrie Paulsen, Deputy Chairman of Tourism, stood, addressing the Council. "Before ye shut doon this story, Mr. Provost, there's another issue we need tae consider, and that's tourism. As everyone in this room kens a' too well, tourism's been way doon. But this trial, it's already havin' a positive impact on our economy. I'm receivin' reports frae a' ower the Great Glen that hotels an' bed-'n'-breakfasts are fillin' up fast, an' most o' that's jist frea the media. Jist wait until season hits. This could be the best summer we've had in thirty years . . . in fact, I spoke wi' the airlines less than an hour ago, an' flights comin' in tae Inverness are already booked solid through June. Could be the best thing that's happened tae the Highlands in a long time."

Murmurs of agreement.

"Ridiculous," said William Greene, convener of the Northern Joint Police Board. "We're no' dealin' wi' monster sightings here, this is multiple murders, at least one o' which wis most likely committed by a man whose ravings aboot a water creature are based on lies an' circumstantial evidence at best. As tae this recent death, who's tae say Angus Wallace didnae hire an accomplice tae dae the deed an' make it look like a monster? This whole thing stinks, if ye ask me."

More murmurs, with a few accusing glances aimed my way.

Jesus . . . I've got to get off this island before these lunatics lynch me.

Owen Hollifield signaled for quiet. "Go on, Sheriff."

"I don't disagree wi' Convener Green's analogy, but one way or another, we need tae dae somethin'. Whether it wis human or beast that killed that woman, tae me, a' these summer tourists flockin' tae Loch Ness jist means more potential victims. How dae we police seventy-six kilometers o' shoreline? I simply don't have the men or the means."

"Might I make a suggestion?" Judge Hannam offered.

The provost nodded. "Please do, my lord."

"By involving the monster in his defense, Angus Wallace has opened a Pandora's box on the High Court's proceedings. Like it or not—and off the record I don't—what's done is done, but it's still my job to see justice served. As such, the only way we'll ever secure a fair and just verdict is to allow the authorities the opportunity to actually search the Loch. Now I'm not suggesting that a water beast killed John Cialino or this American woman. I'm only saying that the public, and the world, must at least perceive that we're doing our due diligence to learn the truth, even concerning matters of proving, or, as the case may be, disproving a water beast exists."

"Council should offer a reward for proof demonstratin' Nessie's existence." Lorrie Paulsen called out. "I think ten thousand pounds should show we're serious."

Owen Hollifeld scoffed. "I could increase that tenfold wi' a few phone calls. *Discovery Channel* an' *National Geographic* both called this afternoon, wantin' permits tae send film crews. Turned them a' down. Told them we're considerin' offerin' exclusive rights tae the highest bidder."

Loud murmurs of agreement.

"Do as you need to do," the judge countered, "but I'm only delaying the trial for two weeks. That's about as long as I can keep this jury sequestered."

That sent the room abuzz once more.

The provost banged his hand again. "Run yer trial as ye see fit, Neil, but I can't allow dozens o' monster hunters cruisin' Loch Ness without rhyme or reason. It's counterproductive, an' it's dangerous. Seen it all before. Amateurs start playin' *Moby Dick*, comin' out wi' dynamite and home-made bombs. What we need is someone tae manage this whole affair, someone whose credentials are unquestioned."

All eyes turned toward me, and I realized that this was why the judge had insisted I be at the meeting.

"How about it, Dr. Wallace?"

"Sorry, my lord, you've got the wrong man."

"Actually, ye're perfect," William Greene declared. "Ye were born in the Highlands, yer reputation as a marine biologist precedes ye, an' ye're related tae the accused, which means ye'll dae everything in yer power, as far as the public's concerned, tae complete an efficient, yet comprehensive search. An' those scars—"

"What about them? Half the world thinks I was bitten by a beast, the rest think I doctored them in order to save my father. My reputation as a scientist is being destroyed even as we speak."

"Then prove them wrong," the provost said. "There's somethin' very real goin' on in Loch Ness, has been ever since the A82 was blasted. Your testimony an' involvement could finally separate fact from fantasy."

"Forget it. This whole affair's been humiliating enough, and besides, there's plenty of other qualified scientists out there. Kevin Gonzalez at Scripps, or that British scientist, Antony Chomley. And what about Robert Rines? Dr. Rines has far more experience than—"

"Dr. Rines has been up and down the Loch a thousand times," Judge Hannam retorted. "No, you were our first choice, Dr. Wallace. If Nessie's really out there, then we're convinced you'll find her."

"And if I refuse? What will you do? Hold me in contempt again? No, I don't think so. See, I may have been born here, but I'm an American citizen now, and my government will have a few things to say to Parliament if the High Court of Inverness jails one of its more prominent scientists just because he refused to search your lake for monsters."

From the judge's dour expression, I knew I had him.

"Now, Lord Hannam, if you don't mind, it's been a bit too real and not much fun, but I need to make some quick flight arrangements if I'm to be back home in Florida by tomorrow night. *Hasta la vista.*"

I made it halfway to the exit before Sheriff Olmstead stopped me. "Lord Hannam?"

The judge thought for a moment. "Dr. Wallace is right, of course. We certainly can't force him to organize our search. For now, we'll just have to allow the researchers to organize themselves, God knows the media attention should draw them to Loch Ness in droves. However, Doctor, bear in mind you're still a witness in a murder trial, which means you can't just leave the country either, at least not until the prosecution's had a chance to cross-examine your testimony. Confiscate his passport, Sheriff, then you can release him."

The bastard took my passport, then showed me the door.

*   *   *

"I dinnae understand," said True, slogging down his third lager in the last half hour. "Seems tae me they're offerin' ye a chance of a lifetime. Why no' jist dae it?"

I poured another shot down my throat, the burning sensation now a warm friend. "If I tell you, and you repeat this to another living soul, then you and me as best friends . . . *pffftt.*"

He leaned in with his big shaggy Viking head. "Go on, I'm listenin'."

I pointed to my temple. "Angus was right about one thing. I'm screwed up, right here in the brain. Ever since that Sargasso thing, I can't get near the damn water."

"Meanin'?"

"Meaning? Meaning I'm afraid to get near the water, ya dumb bastard, what the fuck did you think I mean?"

"Why? Whit's wrong wi' the water?"

"Nothing's wrong with the water, ya dullard, I just can't get near it. Jesus, why do ya think I didn't boff your sister Friday night? Outta respect for your whacked-out old man? Geez Louise, give me a little credit."

"Wait a minute . . . are ye sayin' ye're feart o' the water?"

"Yes, shit-for-brains, yes!" I stood upon my chair, teetering like a drunken fool. "Now hear this! I, Zachary Wallace, marine fucking biologist, son of Angus the drunken murdering bastard, distant cousin to Sir William Wallace the Braveheart, am deathly afraid of the water!"

The rest of the drunks at Sniddles rose and applauded.

I took a wobbly bow, then fell sideways into my friend's brawny arms. "Was I clear this time, True? Are you getting the whole picture?"

"Aye, lad, but dinnae ye worry, I willnae tell a soul."

* * *

Afraid to sleep, I found myself greeting the dawn at the summit of Drumnadrochit's highest peak, sobriety returning fast as I contemplated my existence.

What had happened to me? In six short months, I had gone from goal-oriented bastion of science to a sulking shell of a man, afraid of his own shadow, afraid of his own life.

A former teetotaler, I was well on the road to becoming an alcoholic. A former thinker, I was now afraid to reason, making pathetic excuses for my new-found phobia . . . and a long-lost fear that seemed to be reappearing in my dreams.

I was burnt out and exhausted. I hated myself, I hated my life, and there was no way to escape from my own head.

Except one.

Removing the vial of prescription drugs from my pocket, I stared at the pills, debating a fatal overdose.

How many times had I considered suicide since my ninth birthday? Six times? A dozen? With the help of my teachers and coaches, I had reinvented myself, but deep inside, I knew I was still Angus's runt.

What was keeping me alive? What did I have to live for?

What did I have to lose?

I had spent the last six months poisoning myself slowly with alcohol. Why not just get it over with now?

Do it, Zachary! Swallow the pills! End the pain and fear and humiliation, once and for all.

I cupped the pills in my hand, but there was still one thing preventing me from offing myself on that beautiful mountainside. This time it wasn't fear—it was anger.

I was angry at Angus for forcing me to return, for forcing me to take a harsh look at myself. And having looked, I now realized that as disgusting as my father was, he was just a convenient excuse for my pain.

In truth, I was angry at myself, because Angus was right. I had been living a lie.

With each passing night terror, fragments of long-buried memories were moving into the light. As frightening as they were, I finally realized the dreams were serving a purpose—to shake loose my false foundation of reality.

As much as I tried to fight it, I now knew that something monstrous *had* grabbed me in the Loch seventeen years earlier. Unable to cope with the truth, my child's mind had buried it. Somehow, my second drowning in the Sargasso Sea had released these long-dormant memories, and now I had a choice; take the coward's way out and kill myself, or track down the very being that was responsible for my pain.

The dragon can sense fear, he can smell it in yer blood. Will ye stand and fight the dragon like a warrior, or will ye cower and run, lettin' him haunt ye for the rest of yer days?

"No!"

The echo of my voice crackled across the Glen like gunfire.

Leaping to my feet, I tossed the vial of pills as far as I could into the bushes. "No more cowering. No more running. If I'm going to die, then let my death serve a purpose!"

Standing beneath that gray morning sky, I looked down upon the ancient waters of Loch Ness, my words growling beneath my breath, sending shivers down my spine. "Okay, beast, whatever you are, you've haunted my existence long enough. Now I'm coming, do you hear me?

"I'm coming after you!"

Police Sergeant George Mackenzie and I were standing among a group of people near Altsigh Youth Hostel watching two humps travel up the Loch doing ten knots. It was obvious these two humps were part of one animate long object, making it at least thirteen meters [42.6 feet]!"

—Police Inspector Henry Henderson, Inverness, 13 October 1971

Suddenly there was a terrific disturbance in the Loch. In the midst of this commotion, my friend (Mr. Roger Pugh) and I saw quite distinctly the neck of the beast standing out of the water at a height we later calculated to be about three meters (ten feet). It swam towards us at a slight angle, then thankfully disappeared.

—Father Gregory Brusey, Fort Augustus Abbey, 14 October 1971

CHAPTER 17

Drumnadrochlit, Loch Ness

FOR THE FIRST TIME in as long as I could remember, I felt a true sense of purpose. Feeling reborn, my long-dormant mind focused upon my mission like a laser.

As to my hydrophobia, I wasn't quite ready to rush back into the water. Still, I convinced myself that logic and reason would provide me with the courage needed when the time came . . . if it came.

First things first, I needed information.

I knew there were hordes of self-proclaimed monster hunters on the way to Loch Ness, and they'd be well equipped and financed, armed with the latest sonar buoys and remotely operated vehicles, underwater listening devices and high-speed cameras, strobe lights and depth sounders. They'd probe the Loch from dawn to dusk and dusk to dawn, just as they had for decades. They'd talk about capturing the beast in a net (though technically Nessie was still protected by Highland law) and brag about selling underwater photos to *Time* magazine and *Life* and the *Times* of London. As my stepfather, Charlie, would say, they were the embodiment of insanity, performing the same rituals over and over again, yet always expecting different results. Though each was willing to sell their souls for a fleeting glimpse of a fin or a passing signal on sonar, in the end, they'd fare no better than the rest.

Nessie hunters were like bad golfers who lose their ball out of bounds, yet always search the most advantageous rough for their shot.

Whatever lurked in Loch Ness might be a semiamphibious species, but it still preferred the deep. Locating a creature in a lake that was twenty-three miles long, a mile wide, and seven-to-eight hundred feet deep was equivalent to finding garter snakes in an Olympic-sized swimming pool filled with black ink. As history attested, it was purely hit-and-miss . . . mostly miss, especially with the public anticipating glimpses of the monster along the surface.

As a scientist, I needed to narrow those odds considerably by understanding my quarry. To do that, I had to attack the challenge from a completely different angle.

What would Alfred Wallace do?

Rather than focus on locating an elusive and quite mobile creature, I decided to analyze Loch Ness as a whole. Granted, the waterway was a unique body of fresh water, its surface waters running into the North Sea (and perhaps, at one time, its deeper recesses as well) but the Loch was still an isolated ecosystem, supporting a variety of different species. At least one of these, presumably an apex predator or predators, had suddenly changed its behavioral pattern and, as a result, its diet. To me, that meant something within the food chain itself had been disturbed.

The first task would be to figure out what was off-kilter.

The second would be to use this information in order to track down the creature. . . and find a means to lure it up from the deep.

I spent most of that morning in the village buying supplies, and everywhere I went, people were talking about the monster. Word had spread that two large fishing trawlers were already making their way south through the Moray Firth, while another research vessel was coming north up the Caledonian Canal from Fort William. Later in the day, a tractor trailer loaded with sonar buoys was expected to arrive at the Clansman Hotel, this part of an American expedition funded by AMCO Productions, out of Cleveland.

The circus had officially come to town, but I refused to play the clown.

The "strongman" was awake by the time I returned.

"Whit's a' this then?" True demanded, seeing the brown paper bags in my arms.

"I've decided to resolve this whole Nessie thing, once and for all."

"YES!" He grabbed me beneath my armpits and lifted me to the ceiling. "This is bloody brilliant, Zachary, an' I'm wi' ye every step o' the way. So we'll need a boat then, yeah? I'll ring Brandy first thing an' tell her tae cancel all her tours—"

"No boat."

"No boat?"

"Clues and info first. I want to walk as much of the shoreline of Loch Ness as I can, beginning with the Invermoriston site where that woman was killed."

"Walk the shoreline? Why?"

"Because I'm not interested in blindly searching the largest body of water in Europe, hoping to get a blip on sonar. What we need, True, is hard evidence that'll tell us what's going on down there."

"Yeah . . . sure, I guess we can walk. But I'm bringin' my binoculars an' camera, jist in case."

From my shopping bags I retrieved glass jars, rubber gloves, flashlights, plastic bags, bottled water, and some snacks, then started packing my knapsack. "We'll need sleeping bags, we'll probably have to camp out a few nights."

"Christ, Zachary, whit's the plan then? Tae drop cookies along the shoreline an' hope Nessie hops in one o' these jars like a bloody bullfrog?"

"Actually, the cookies were for you."

*   *   *

An hour later we arrived at the Invermoriston boating dock. Police had closed down the launch, and had cordoned off the campsite and trail, but when they saw who I was, they allowed us to negotiate the shoreline.

From the Moriston River inlet, we followed the Loch to the south as far as the pier, True playing the part of my impatient shadow. Like most of Loch Ness's beaches, the ground was covered in smooth, rounded stones, which served to camouflage anything but the most obvious tracks.

"So, Sherlock Holmes, whit're we lookin' for then? Nessie turds?"

"Sure, Nessie turds would be great." I took a long scan of the shoreline, then began retracing my steps back toward the river.

True shook his head. "This science stuff, it's pretty borin', yeah?"

"Well, it's not deep diving off a North Sea oil rig, but it beats aimlessly searching the Loch."

"Maybe, but I've had better times watchin' grass grow. Now whit're ye doin'?"

On hands and knees I crawled by the water, pausing occasionally to press my nose to the rocky surface.

"Zachary, please, yer embarrassin' me. Ye think ye're a bloodhound now?"

"I detected a rancid odor yesterday. I'm hoping to catch another whiff."

"Sweet Jesus. Tell ye what, how 'bout I blah blah blah blah blah . . ."

I closed my eyes and inhaled, my mind absorbed in my "zone."

". . . back wi' a few cold ones an' some lunch. Okay? I said okay? Hey, Zack?"

I stood, moving to another section of shoreline, repeating the exercise.

"Ken whit? I think ye've lost yer marbles."

We both heard the rumble and looked up as a motorboat maneuvered close to shore, blasting its horn at us. "Hah, it's Brandy, shouldae known. Hey, Brandy girl!"

The *Nessie III* was again overloaded with passengers, all aiming their cameras at the now-legendary campsite. Brandy was visible in the wheelhouse, as was her string bikini top. She waved at her brother, then, seeing me, flipped me the middle finger.

"Look's like she's still pissed at ye."

"Hell hath no fury like a Highland woman scorned."

"Amen."

I returned to my work, my mind, tainted with the vision of Brandy in her bathing suit, fighting to refocus.

"A sandwich then?"

"Huh?"

"Are ye deaf? I asked if ye wanted a sandwich? Thought I'd grab us some lunch while ye finished polishin' thae rocks wi' yer belly."

"Yeah, sure. Whatever."

He turned and walked away, then stumbled, the toe of his right boot catching the lip of a slight depression in the geography.

I stared at the spot, my heart racing.

"Whit? Dae ye see somethin' then?"

There were three of them—*S-shaped depressions*, each eight feet long, five feet wide, and three to four inches deep. They were angled from the water's edge up across the embankment and into the forest, and were so broad and sweeping that the pattern looked natural to the untrained eye.

On hands and knees, I inhaled the imprint, gagging at the lingering stench.

"Is it the monster then?" True dropped down and inhaled. "Phew, smells like a girl I once knew."

"I can't speak for your social life, but something biological was definitely here, and it left behind its slime."

"Slime?"

"At least that's what it feels like. Rain washed most of it away, but its slickness still lingers." Retrieving a glass jar from my backpack, I took a soil sample, the sudden rush of adrenaline tingling my bladder.

*   *   *

True and I continued walking south along the western shoreline, the discovery of the impressions having reinvigorated my friend's excitement. "Okay, Zack, let's say it wis an animal that left thae impressions. To crush the earth like that, how heavy wid ye say it'd have tae be?"

"I don't know, maybe ten thousand pounds or more, but that's just a rough guess."

"Whit did Angus call it then? A Guivre?"

"True, there's no such species as a Guivre. It's just folklore."

"Then how'd ye explain—"

"Easy, big guy, let's not repeat the same mistakes other explorers at Loch Ness make. They create some preconceived idea of what might be out there, then spend all their time attempting to prove they're right by only searching for their imaginary beast."

"Ye mean, like the plesiosaur guys?"

"Exactly. A dinosaur in Loch Ness is a romantic notion, but it's not science, it's just myth-building. We'll let the lab results tell us what this creature is . . . or isn't."

I stopped. Taking out an empty glass jar and my gardening shovel, I bent down and took another soil sample by the water's edge.

"Now what're ye doin?"

"Checking the worm population."

"Worms? It wisnae a worm that made thae tracks, I'll tell ye that for now."

"Your Guivre has to eat, right? Before it allegedly added humans to its diet, it must have subsisted on food from the Loch."

"Aye. Makes sense."

"Loch Ness's food chain begins with microscopic vegetation called phytoplankton. From there, it progresses to zooplankton, then worms and small fish, tadpoles, minnows, and so on and so forth. Then you've got your bigger fish, salmon, sea trout, brown trout, charr, pike, lamprey, eel, and sturgeon, some of which can weigh in at several hundred pounds. Somewhere along that food chain is a major break in one or more of its links. I want to know where it is, and what caused it."

"An' this'll tell ye where oor Guivre's hidin', aye?"

I shook my head. "You know, you really have to ease up on those deep dives. Cuts off oxygen to the brain."

"Okay, take yer jabs, Dr. Doolittle, as long as ye're no' playin' in the mud jist tae avoid gettin' yer feet wet."

Maybe he wasn't such a dumb strongman after all.

*   *   *

We walked all morning and late into the afternoon, passing Port Clair and Cherry Island until we eventually rounded the southern tip of the Loch. We passed the old pier at Bunoch, arriving finally at Fort Augustus, the largest town on the waterway.

The village was immersed in a carnival atmosphere, overflowing with locals and tourists and scores of media. True headed off to the nearest pub for a pint of Guinness while I followed the crowd to the wharf and the just-arriving *Nothosaur*, a forty-two-foot research vessel named after a long-necked, sharp-toothed member of the plesiosaur family that had lived during the Triassic Period.

The boat's name alone told me everything I needed to know about its owner.

Michael Hoagland, a well-built, blonde-haired, blue-eyed German in his mid-thirties, waved to the crowd from the bow of his command like a conquering hero while a news reporter waited impatiently for his camera crew to set up.

"Mr. Hoagland, Grady Frame, BBC Scotland. Welcome back tae Loch Ness."

"Thank you."

"You've logged quite a few hours in our little Loch."

"About twelve thousand in my boat, another four thousand hours on land. I know this Loch like the back of my hand."

"Then perhaps ye'd describe the monster ye'll be huntin' for our viewers."

"She's got a head the size of a horse, with a long neck, perhaps three, maybe four meters, and her total length's at least twice that. She probably weighs between twelve and twenty tons."

"Wow. An', in your opinion, she's definitely a plesiosaur?"

"That's what I've been saying, yes. Do the science. Plesiosaur remains have been found all over Britain. Seven thousand years ago the entire north end of Loch Ness was open to the sea. It's easy to see how these ancient monsters could become trapped in our little playground. The Loch is full of wildlife, has an unlimited supply of food, no pollution, and maintains a year-round temperature of four to seven degrees Celsius. Quite ideal for—"

"For an extinct reptile that preferred warmer climates?" It was my voice, strong and sure, but it'd been so long since my ego had donned its Superman tights that I scarcely recognized its return.

The crowd parted, revealing my presence to Hoagland and the BBC cameras.

"And who might you be?" the German adventurer demanded.

"Zachary Wallace, marine biologist, and the man who's going to make you and the rest of these dinosaur hunters look mighty stupid."

A woman's voice crackled over a loudspeaker, "An' how're ye goin' tae dae that, Dr. Know-It-All? By searchin' for a legend ye don't even believe in?"

Two berths down, Brandy stood brazenly atop the *Nessie III*'s wheelhouse. Megaphone in hand, she gestured at me with her bronze, oiled physique, which caught the crowd's attention as much as her verbal challenge. "Why don't ye let the experts see tae their business an' keep yer Americanized opinions tae yersel'."

The crowd cheered, the cameras rolled.

Hoagland fought to take back the spotlight. "Where's your vessel, Mr. Marine Biologist? Where's your sonar equipment? Or do you intend on locating Nessie by hiking through the woods?"

"I don't chase after water creatures, I prefer to find ways to make them chase after me."

The crowd oohed and ahhed.

The BBC reporter recognized me. "That's Zachary Wallace, the man who located a giant squid."

"Well, then," Hoagland said, "let's give him a hand in locating our Nessie."

Before I could react, three of Hoagland's goons jumped down from the deck of the ship. Two grabbed hold of my arms, one my legs, and together they began swinging me.

"*Eins . . . zwei . . . drei!*"

I flailed in mid-air, then plunged backwards into Loch Ness, the freezing waters jolting me as if electrified.

I thrashed and kicked, too terrified to reason, my overloaded backpack filling quickly with water, weighing me down like an anchor. I fought and struggled, but my negative buoyancy was too much, and I slipped below the surface and sank backwards like a dead turtle.

Sound deadened.

My pulse thundered.

The water changed quickly from iced tea to ink, blanketing me within its paralyzing darkness.

I was in serious trouble.

Think! Reason! Get the damn backpack off!

I struggled to unclip the backpack's metal clasp but my numb fingers couldn't budge the stubborn device.

Deeper I fell, twenty feet, thirty . . . my ears ringing, my chest on fire, my body heaving in spasms as the Loch's icy fingers pried their way in.

Where was the crowd? Where they even a bit concerned?

"Awggg!" I inhaled a mouthful of acidic water as a viselike grip clamped down upon my right forearm, dragging me sideways in its teeth.

I fought the beast, lashing at its flesh, until I realized I was being dragged to the surface.

Whoosh! Sound returned with the daylight as my head cleared and True towed me to shore.

Through glassy, half-frozen eyes I looked up and saw the silhouettes of hundreds of amused gawkers standing on the pier. Through water-clogged ears I heard their taunts and laughter.

I felt the muddy bog beneath me and stumbled to shore, my numb fingers still struggling to release the metal catch of my cursed backpack.

True pulled the waterlogged sack off me. "Are ye okay?"

I nodded, then collapsed to my knees, my body shivering from the cold. "Bastards. I'll kill 'em."

"Now ye sound like yer faither. Let them go. Before all's said an' done, we'll get oor revenge."

I nodded, anger once more fueling my resolve.

Evolution usually proceeds by "speciation"—the splitting of one lineage from a parental stock—not by the slow and steady transformation of these large parental stocks. In the allopatric theory, popularized by Ernst Mayr, new species arise in very small populations that become isolated from their parental group at the periphery of the ancestral range. Speciation in these small isolates is very rapid by evolutionary standards—hundreds or thousands of years (a geological microsecond). Major evolutionary change may occur in these small isolated populations. Favorable genetic variation can quickly spread through them. Moreover, natural selection tends to be intense in geographically marginal areas where the species barely maintains a foothold. Small changes occur to meet the requirements of slowly altering climates, but major genetic reorganizations almost always take place in the small, peripherally isolated populations that form new species.

—Stephen Jay Gould "Bushes and Ladders," *Ever Since Darwin: Reflections in Natural History,* 1977

CHAPTER 18

Fort Augustus, Loch Ness

DRIPPING WET, I slung my water-laden backpack over my shoulder and trudged up the banks of Loch Ness, True following me to the public rest rooms. Tourists gawked, and the locals laughed, and it was all I could do to avert my eyes.

Entering the men's room, I stripped down to my boxers, washed the peat from my skin, then squeezed the excess water from my clothes into the sink. With the exception of the specimen containers and vacuum-packed food supplies, everything else in my backpack was ruined, including my sleeping bag and change of clothing.

True opened his own pack and pulled out a few dry shirts and two pairs of wool socks, tossing one of each to me. "Put these on. We'll hitch a ride back tae Drumnadrochit wi' Brandy, then fill our bellies at the Clansman before startin' oot fresh in the mornin'."

"I'm not going back."

"Zack, ye cannae go on wi' nae supplies."

"Then lend me yours and you go back. I need to go on before I lose my nerve, and there's still the entire east bank to cover."

"It's too dangerous alone."

"I'll be fine."

"Yeah, I'm sure that woman who got hersel' killed said the same thing."

"I'll camp out in the Glendoe Forest for the night, keeping a distance from the Loch. We'll rendezvous in Foyers tomorrow around noon."

He thought it over. "A'right, Foyers it is. But promise ye'll keep a guid fire goin'."

"Done. True, before you go, there's one thing I need to ask you. The other day, I woke up early and ran into your father. He was wearing the tunic of a Templar Knight, only his uniform was black."

The expression on True's face changed. "I cannae discuss this wi' ye, Zack."

"Your father's sword was covered in blood."

True turned on me then, bulldozing me against the wall. "Are ye insinuatin' my auld man had somethin' tae dae wi' that woman's murder?"

"No, but I—"

"Now listen tae me, Zachary Wallace. One o' oor faithers might be a killer, but it isnae the auld man who saved yer life seventeen years ago, see?"

"Okay, okay, easy big fella."

He backed away, then slapped me playfully behind my ear. "Sorry, lad. There're things goin' on in the Highlands that ye cannae see, battles between traditionalists like my faither, who aim tae keep the Highlands pure, an' those like *yours*, who wish tae cash in on oor wild lands. Me? I'm a' for progress, but there's a fine line between economic benefits an' environmental ruin. As tae these Templar, from whit I ken, they operate independently ootside the Cooncil, an' the Black Knights, they dinnae like ootsiders lookin' into their business."

"Black Knights?"

"Ne'er ye mind." He handed me his backpack. "Here, take my stuff, I'll meet ye in Foyers. Jist make sure ye keep that fire goin' tonight, I dinnae want tae read yer obituary in the *Courier*."

*   *   *

Barefoot, my wet boots hanging from True's backpack, I headed out of Fort Augustus, following General Wade's Military Road. It was late in the afternoon, but the Glen's summer days were growing longer, and my goal was to make it to the eastern bank of Loch Ness well before dusk.

As I walked, my mind wandered.

Two people were dead, and while their deaths were being blamed on a mythical creature, my mind told me the mystery had more to do with the political undercurrents surrounding the Highland Council than a water beast. Of the two major players involved, I knew I'd get nothing from Alban MacDonald, and only lies and deceit from my father.

But a new clue had emerged, one that had accidently slipped out of my friend's mouth.

The Black Knights of the Templar.

What was this secret sect? What was their mission? And how were they tied to the goings-on at Loch Ness?

An hour passed before I found my way around the southeastern tip of the Loch to its eastern banks. From here, Loch Ness ran north another twenty-three miles, bordered by the Glendoe Forest, which hugged the base of the imposing Monadhliath Mountains.

The east side of the Loch was far less populated than the west, the country wilder, the forests denser, and much of the shoreline was inaccessible.

General Wade's Military Road circled around the forest before turning north along the B862 that led to Foyers. Not wishing to take a long detour, hoping to stay as close to the Loch as possible, I paused to put on True's socks and my damp hiking shoes, then abandoned the single lane tarmac and cut through the forest, remaining parallel to the waterway.

After twenty minutes, I came to a newly paved winding access road that cut through the dense foliage, the sounds of Nature interrupted by the noise of heavy machinery. Following these sounds led me a quarter mile up the road to a massive construction site. A posted sign read:

GLEN DOE HYDROELECTRIC DAM
AUTHORIZED PERSONNEL ONLY

I remembered having read about the new power station, most of which was supposedly being built underground. It was going to be a large plant, its capacity between fifty and one hundred megawatts, with water, collected from seventeen kilometers of underground aqueducts, relocated in a new reservoir located more than six hundred meters above Loch Ness. The reservoir would be situated at the head of Glen Tarff, impounded by a massive dam, thirty-five meters high and one thousand meters long.

Whether Alban MacDonald liked it or not, technology was invading Loch Ness.

Milling about the outside of an imposing chain-link construction fence were more than a dozen protesters, their banners identifying them as the Scottish Wild Land Group.

An auburn-haired woman in her early forties introduced herself by thrusting a picket sign in my hand. "Glad ye could join us, brother, the TV reporters should be arrivin' anytime. I'm Gloria Snodgrass, assistant director o' the SWLG Steering Group, an' you are?"

"Confused. What's all this about?"

"It's aboot savin' oor Glen. The government ministers' decision tae go through wi' this hydroelectric plant will cause irreversible damage tae oor peat bogs and rivers, an' dae ye ken how much forest we're already losin'? The dam alone requires three new access roads, an' ye can add another twenty-two kilometers o' pipeline tae that order. An' that's no' countin' the seventy-five kilometers needed jist tae build the reservoir."

"I understand, but—"

"But nothin'. Grab yer sign an' come join us before the cameras get here."

"I can't. Sorry."

"Sorry? You'll be the one that's sorry when we lose oor upland areas. Hey—"

Waving her off, I circled the construction fence, hoping to get a glimpse inside. Building a large-scale hydroelectric scheme so close to Loch Ness must have required a detailed environmental assessment, but then how does one properly access the ecological impact on an undiscovered water creature?

With no foreman visible and no way in, I headed back down the road toward Loch Ness, not sure what to do with this potentially new piece of the puzzle.

Foyers, Loch Ness

The town of Foyers lies a third of the way up Loch Ness on its eastern shore. While the beginnings of the village can be traced to an inn, built back in 1655 at a time when Cromwell's troops occupied Inverness, it was not until the late 1800s that the North British Aluminum Company put Foyers on the map. For years the aluminum mills dominated the industry, until a drastic drop in the price of the metal, combined with Kinlochleven's easier access to the open sea forced the towns-people to refocus Foyers primary source of commerce. The answer lay in the village's abundant and varied sources of water, which included lochs, streams, and the River Foyers, which plunged a spectacular 140-foot chasm into Loch Ness. In their search for a suitable source of power for a new Highlands hydroelectric plant, British engineers quickly targeted Foyers Falls. Work began in 1969 with the construction of a two-and-a-half-mile-long pressurized tunnel connecting Loch Mhor to Loch Ness . . .

". . . this major undertakin' allowin' the turbines, erected in the auld aluminum plant we're now passin', tae reverse the flow o' water back tae Loch Mhor at night when demand wis easier tae calculate, keepin' the head water supplied at all times."

The tour guide paused as the open-air bus rolled to a stop and belched exhaust in front of the old smelting plant.

Twenty-four-year-old Justin Wagner fought to conceal his yawn from the tour guide, then nudged his childhood friend, Amber Korpela. "We've seen the falls, let's skip the rest of the tour and go boating."

"Not yet. I want to see Boleskin House. The original owner was supposed to be heavy into devil worship. Did you know that after he died, Jimmy Paige bought the house and—"

"Amber, who cares? I didn't fly all the way from Alaska to see some stupid house. Let's grab a few more rolls of film, rent a boat, and do some serious monster sighting."

Taking Amber by the hand, Justin dragged her past the tour guide and off the bus. "Sorry, dude, Nessie calls."

Twenty minutes later, the two Alaskans were hiking down a wooded hillside path through lower Foyers, heading for Loch Ness.

Glen Doe Forest

With the sun beginning to set, I found my way to a small clearing in the thick of the forest, adjacent to a twisting creek that drained into Loch Ness. Whoever had occupied the campsite last had used dead branches to fashioned a lean-to, no doubt to keep out of the rain. Exhausted and hungry, I slid my backpack off, then set off to gather wood for a fire.

After finishing a less-than-appetizing can of green pea soup, I set my tent up beneath the lean-to. A heavy forest separated my campsite from the waters of Loch Ness, which loomed a good hundred yards down sloping woods to the west. With darkness settling on the Great Glen, I began feeling a bit uneasy, my thoughts lingering on True's warning. Like it or not, I was vulnerable, and I seriously considered spending the night in the lower branches of a tree. But the likelihood of being attacked so far from the water's edge was considerably less than falling out of a tree and breaking my neck, so I opted for a weapon.

Using my hunting knife, I fashioned several four-foot-long spears out of tree branches before my eyes grew too weary to focus. Stoking the fire one last time, I crawled into my sleeping bag, and spent the next few hours drifting in and out of a restless sleep.

Foyers, Loch Ness

The motorized raft, commonly known as a *Zodiac*, spewed oily fumes as it cut an erratic course through darkness and mist.

Justin Wagner tried to quell the hot waves of frustration coursing through his blood. Four hours earlier, he and Amber Korpela had rented the watercraft, guiding it across Loch Ness to its western shores. They had journeyed as far south as Cherry Island, enjoying a sun-soaked summer evening exploring the man-made crannog before embarking on the long ride back. But with their reserve tank of gasoline running low and dusk coming quickly, Justin had decided to save time and distance by taking a northeasterly shortcut across the Loch.

That was over an hour ago.

Justin, an accomplished boater back in Alaska, had not counted on the sun disappearing so suddenly behind the mountains, nor had he planned on the bank of fog moving in from the east.

The whine of the Zodiac's single-prop sixty horsepower engine, combined with her companion's constant course changes, had given Amber Korpela a pounding headache. "Okay, Magellan, enough's enough. Where the hell are we?"

"Somewhere in the middle of Loch Ness . . . I think."

"No shit. Don't you have a compass?"

"What makes you think I'd have a compass?"

"I don't know. I guess I didn't expect you to be stupid enough to get us lost on *Loch Ness!*"

"You want to take the tiller, be my guest."

"Instead of zigzagging back and forth, why don't you just keep us pointed in one direction until we hit land?"

"Land? Can you see land in this fog? What if we're pointing north? We could cover twenty miles before we hit—"

"Shh! I think I hear something."

"Yeah, my stomach growling."

"No, I'm serious. It sounds like people's voices. Justin, cut the engine."

Justin turned off the motor. The raft rose and dropped beneath its own swell, then continued drifting forward. "You're crazy, I don't hear a thing."

"Shh. Listen."

Justin listened, then he heard it . . . splashing sounds, followed by strange whimpers, coming toward them from their right. "Sounds almost like a baby crying."

Amber leaned out over the bow. "Oh my God, look! It's a deer . . . no, it's a herd of deer."

Justin moved next to her as the heads and slender necks of a half dozen Sika deer appeared out of the fog. "Excellent. The deer know their way, we'll just follow them in to shore. Told you I'd get us back to Foyers."

"How do you know they're headed to Foyers? They could be swimming towards the western shore."

"At this point, who cares?"

The first two deer paddled past the Zodiac's bow, their hoofs churning water in a frenzy of movement, their nostrils lathered in foam with the effort.

"Justin, do they seemed frightened?"

"They're probably cold."

Another deer appeared from out of the fog. Suddenly the animal let out a high-pitched, "*nehhhh–*" tossed its head back . . . and disappeared in a froth of waves.

Amber clutched Justin's arm. "Did you see that? Oh my God, something huge just dragged that deer underwater!"

Justin searched the surface. "No. It . . . it must've got tired and drowned, that's all."

"It didn't drown! Something ate it!"

"Easy, girl. I was just teasing you before about Nessie. There's no such thing."

"Hey, I'm not stupid. I'm telling you, something big just took that deer. Start the engine!"

They grabbed one another as the Zodiac rocked violently, then spun counterclockwise several quick revolutions before drifting sideways.

"Okay, what the hell was that?"

Now Justin was trembling. "Let's just get out of here."

"Justin, watch out!"

Emerging from the mist, a panicking buck veered for the Zodiac, lunging its front hoofs out of the water and over the edge of the rubber raft.

"Shit!" Grabbing the wild animal by its neck and antlers, Justin fought to shove the two-hundred-pound beast back into the water without being lanced. "Amber, help—"

The buck continued thrashing and kicking, intent on climbing out of the water, when it was seized by its hindquarters by an unseen force and dragged below.

Pulled off-balance, Justin Wagner tumbled overboard after it.

"Justin!" Amber knelt on her bench seat, looking in every direction. "Justin? Justin, where are you?!" She heard splashing sounds behind her and turned to the source. "Justin?"

"Ambhhhhhh—" Justin's head poked free of the freezing waters, his arms slapping frantically at the fog-covered surface. "It's fuuuuckinnng freeeezing!"

"Hold on!" Amber climbed back to the stern. "Okay, you can do this." She pushed the tiller out of her way, then stood behind the outboard and attacked the starter cord with both hands.

It took her several awkward jerks before the engine started. But as the revving propeller caught water, the bent tiller sent the raft lurching sideways, spilling Amber Korpela headfirst into the Loch.

The bone-chilling water, combined with his soaked clothing, were zapping Justin's strength. Through blurred vision he saw Amber fall overboard, the now-empty Zodiac left to cut wide circles across the surface.

Pathetic. Okay, boat first, then Amber . . .

He kicked for the vessel, never hearing the whines and yelps from the deer, his heart skipping a beat at Amber's bloodcurdling scream.

"Amber?" Justin stopped swimming and spun to his left. Through the fog-laced surface he saw something dark and massive breach a half dozen boat lengths away, rolling and twisting in a frenzy of movement that whipped icy water and warm fleshy shrapnel at his face.

A column of deer swam past him, whimpering and gasping with their exertion.

Justin tried to move, but couldn't, not until the attack ended with one final heavy splash.

The silence that followed was petrifying.

With trembling hand, Justin touched his forehead, smearing away gobs of blood and bone fragments.

"Amber . . ."

The whine of the approaching Zodiac grew louder, snapping him into action. Justin swam as hard as he could, then lunged for the passing water craft, his chest bouncing off the inflatable's side, his fingers managing to catch the raft's trim line.

Too weak to pull himself on board, Justin managed to loop his wrists around the rope, his weight counterbalancing the Zodiac's trajectory.

The motorized raft raced away, towing its semiconscious passenger along with it.

I'm fifty-nine years old, lived here all my life. When I was fourteen, we had a local farm, down here at Drumnadrochit. My late brother and late mother were in the car with me, and we were headed to Inverness. I was looking out at the Loch, its surface flat and calm, when I yelled, "Stop the car!" My brother stopped, and we all saw this huge commotion right in the center of the Loch, just opposite Aldourie Castle. The monster was gray-brown, and massive, the size of a bus. It flipped over, just flipped right over like that, crashing down. You could see it, and the waves from that point were about three feet high and ebbed to each side of the Loch.

—Ronald Mackintosh, retired salesman

I was making a routine road report call to my office using the AA box at Brackla when I turned and saw, across the water and a few hundred yards out, a head and neck and broad humped body moving from side to side. It was something out of this world, as if a dinosaur had reared up out of the Loch. After seeing it, I swore never again to venture out on Loch Ness in a small boat.

—Hamish Mackintosh, Automobile Association Patrolman, 2 February 1959

I AM SOARING THROUGH DARKNESS, *the world deaf and silent. I am underwater . . . entering a cave. I am floating. Free.*

Below me lies the body of a man, stretched out on jagged rock. Naked and broken. A lifeless soul. I hover closer.

It is me.

"No! No!"

Entangled in the sleeping bag, I kicked my way out and half crawled, half stumbled from the tent into the pre-dawn gray, my racing heart threatening to leap out of my chest.

Calm down! Breathe! You're okay, Wallace . . . just another dream.

I paced the campsite, frantically speaking my thoughts, forcing myself to refocus on the images of this bizarre new night terror. "I was underwater . . . but not as a child, this time as an adult. And I was dead. How did I die? Why was I naked? Was it a vision?"

I stared at my hands, which were still trembling, then suddenly I froze.

Something was moving through the woods!

Like a frightened deer, I looked left to right, right to left, the forest damp and still. Traces of gray mist still cloaked the ground, waiting to be burned away by dawn's first light.

And then my eyes caught movement.

There were three of them, shadowy figures, all cloaked in black, following the stream in the direction of the Loch.

I searched for my hiking boots. Shoving them over my bare feet, I tugged on the laces, then hurried after the three intruders.

They were well ahead of me, their dark tunics the perfect camouflage, though every now and then I caught a glimpse of a flashlight's beam.

The Black Knights?

The mountainside steepened now, the creek widening as it raced to empty into Loch Ness. The leaves were wet, the rocks by the stream covered in heavy moss, making the going treacherous. I rolled my ankle, yelping in pain, then paused, quickly tying my laces for more support.

That's when I noticed the blood.

Patches of crimson streaked the tops of several rocks, as if a bleeding corpse were being dragged along the brook's path.

I hurried on, jogging down the slope, then heard the telltale whine of an outboard motor.

By the time I emerged from the forest, the Zodiac was racing away from shore. In the dim light I made out three men aboard the craft, all dressed in black, a heavy burlap sack between them, soaked in blood.

*   *   *

The eastern bank of Loch Ness is so long and straight that, looking north on a clear day, one can see the surface meet the sky. This view stayed with me over the next three hours as I followed the tree-lined shore, making my way slowly toward the village of Foyers.

In my backpack were several swabs of blood taken from the rocks. The lab in Inverness would tell me if it came from an animal or human, and then I'd confront Alban MacDonald.

In due course, the sun's rays crept over the Monadhliath Mountains, taking the chill off the crisp morning air. From the south, a dull throbbing echo bellowed into thunder as the research vessel, *Nothosaur*, rumbled by, its twin engines sending heavy mud-colored wakes crashing to shore. As the boat passed, I could make out several dozen sonar buoys lined up behind the transom. Hoagland's crew were launching the underwater listening devices every mile or so, creating their own sonar array. I knew they were not alone, that at least two other expeditions were completing similar tasks.

By nightfall, Loch Ness would be "Loch Mess," pinging like an amusement park video game gallery, distorting every underwater contact for miles.

I arrived at a boathouse around eight-thirty that morning, already feeling exhausted from lack of sleep. With Foyers still several miles ahead, I decided to stop for breakfast. As I sat on the edge of a pier, munching on processed cheese and crackers, a small fishing boat approached from the north, two local women on board.

The craft made a wide turn toward shore, then docked along the boathouse pier.

"Morning, ladies. How's the fishing?"

"Fish are no' bitin'," replied the shoulder length-blonde. "They havenae been bitin' a' season."

"Hey, Marti, is he no' that scientist? Ye ken, the one in the paper."

The blonde perked up. "Oh aye, ye're right! Pleased tae meet ye, Dr. Wallace. I'm Marti Evans, an' this is my friend, Tina. Ye headin' tae Foyers then?"

"Yes."

"We've jist been. Best be hurryin', afore the Polis remove the body."

My skin crawled. "Body? What body?"

*   *   *

I could see the crowd a quarter mile away as I neared the Foyers River Inlet, and it took me several minutes to pick my way through the throng of locals. Reaching the police barrier, I waved at Sheriff Holmstrom to get his attention.

Holmstrom lifted the police tape to allow me through. "Dr. Wallace. Can't say I'm surprised. Seems every time we meet, someone's been butchered."

"What happened?"

He led me toward the water's edge to where a beached Zodiac was surrounded by crime scene investigators. The bow had been tied off, a gray tarpaulin tossed over the left side of the raft. The soaked ends of the tarp floated in the water, revealing a slowly spreading scarlet stain, pooling in the shallows.

"Yesterday, at approximately 4:45 P.M., two Alaskan tourists, Amber Joy Korpela, age twenty-four, and her companion, Justin Thomas Wagner, age twenty-five, rented this watercraft from a boathouse in Lower Foyers. The couple were last seen circlin' Cherry Island, sometime around nine. Accordin' tae witnesses, the Zodiac beached itsel' between six an' seven this mornin'. Prepare yoursel'. This one's gruesome, even worse than the last, but I think ye'll want tae see."

The sheriff lifted the edge of the tarp.

"Oh, Jesus . . . "

Unable to pull himself from the frigid water, Justin Wagner had managed to loop both his wrists around the Zodiac's guide rope. His upper torso had dangled alongside the raft as it motored, pilotless, across the Loch, his lower torso dragging through the water. There was no telling how long the victim had been in the water, but the exposed flesh on his arms, neck, and face appeared bluish, bordering on translucent.

What was frightening was Wagner's facial expression, a frozen mask, revealing both pain and terror. The glazed eyes were open and bulging, the purplish mouth grimacing, the teeth bared.

The rest of the victim's body was covered by the raft.

Holmstrom nodded to one of his men, who, with gloved hands, pushed aside the raft while carefully lifting the remains of Wagner's shirt, exposing his waistline.

The sight caused me to gag.

There was no lower torso. Whatever had bitten Justin Wagner had consumed his hips, buttocks, and legs in one devastating bite, its teeth leaving behind puncture marks along the circumference of the jagged wound. A trail of unraveled waterlogged intestines drifted back and forth in the wash, the rest of the victim's internal organs having fallen away long ago from the void where Wagner's waist had once been.

I staggered back, the scene sending the blood rushing from my face.

Holmstrom signaled for the tarp to be lowered, then followed me up the embankment. "Are ye okay?"

I shook my head. "I'm about a million miles from okay."

"Those teeth marks?"

I nodded, feeling nauseous. "Yes, Sheriff, the pattern's identical to the scars around my waist. And no, I have no clue why I'm still alive."

"Ye'll help us find it then?"

I nodded, sucking in several deep breaths, fighting to keep my breakfast down. "I'll help you, only let's keep it between us for now. Folklore's one thing, but you've got an apex predator that's gone on a rampage."

"Agreed."

Waves pounded the shoreline, causing us to turn. Another research vessel was slowly rumbling by, three tourist boats following in its wake.

Holmstrom spit. "This place is turnin' intae a bloody zoo. The A82's backed up from Drumnadrochit tae Inverness wi' campers, an' God knows whit it'll be like when word of this latest killin' spreads."

I nodded. "Worse, the Loch's becoming jammed with sonar buoys."

"The judge gave ye the opportunity tae run things. It's no' too late."

"It's not my style."

"Whit's yer plan then?"

"First, I need to finish my own investigation of the Loch. You can help by giving me access to your crime lab."

"Crime lab? Whit for?"

I reached into my backpack, handing him the plastic bags holding the swabs of blood. "Have these analyzed. I need to know if they're animal or human."

"Done. How can I reach ye?"

"I'll reach you. Give me your cell number.

He handed me a business card. "My mobile phone's on the back, it's always on." He gazed out at the Loch, then looked me in the eye. "Guess I wis one o' those that laughed . . . ye know, after hearin' you were afraid tae get near the water an' all. But after seein' that body, well . . . I can't say I blame ye."

"Analyze those samples, Sheriff. I'll be in touch."

*   *   *

True showed up thirty minutes later, cursing up a storm about all the traffic around Loch Ness. The good news was the lodge was booked solid, the bad being his father now needed him back in Drumnadrochit by early evening. He agreed to accompany me along the eastern bank until his sister picked him up later by boat.

Things were looking up for Brandy as well. She had doubled her tours and tripled her prices, and still the *Nessie III* was sold out for the remainder of the week.

The monster craze was alive and well, and the Highland locals were cashing in on what was shaping up to be a record-setting tourist season.

By noon, word of the latest attack had spread across Great Britain like wildfire. By then, True and I had arrived in Inverfarigaig, a village of homes scattered among managed forests of spruce and Douglas fir. As in Foyers, the rocky embankments of Inverfarigaig were clogged with thrill-seekers, their cameras and zoom lenses mounted on tripods, their camcorders and binoculars scanning every wave and shadow that skirted the surface of Loch Ness. Vans and campers, parked along General Wade's Military Road, lined the single lane tarmac clear to Dores, and many a tourist could be seen standing on their car roofs to gain a better vantage.

It was a "braw day" on the Loch, the sky high and blue, free of cloud cover, and the approaching summer beat down upon us unmercifully.

Seeking a break from the sun, we followed a footpath into the Farigaig Forest, its heavy canopy embracing us in cooler temperatures. Diverting from the path, we followed the twisting banks of a brook as it trickled down the mountain side. A carpet of moss was spotted with bluebells, foxgloves, and other wildflowers, and the scents and sounds soothed my spent nerves.

I didn't see the squirrel as much as I tripped over it.

The forests of the Great Glen are populated with red squirrels, fast creatures that feed on seeds, chestnuts, and pine nuts. This one was lying on its side by the creek, its tiny chest heaving as it gasped each labored breath.

As we watched, the suffering animal seized and died.

True bent down to give it a nudge. "Poor wee thing—"

"Don't touch it!" Setting down my backpack, I retrieved a pair of rubber gloves, a jar, and a plastic specimen bag. "Remember what I said yesterday about the Loch's food chain? This might be an important clue. Take this jar and fill it with water from the brook, while I bag our little friend here."

We collected the specimens, then continued following the stream as it backtracked up a steep terrain slick with vegetation and heavy in jagged rocks. Along the way we found more dead animals, including a half dozen osprey and a peregrine. True stumbled upon a burrow and was immediately attacked by a fox, the agitated creature circling and growling as it snapped at his boots. We managed to chase it away, but only after resorting to striking it several times with a stick.

"I've never seen a fox act like that before. Dae ye think it wis rabid?"

"Maybe. But I suspect there's something else going on, something that's affecting this whole ecosystem. Come on, let's keep climbing."

Another half mile's ascent and the forest opened up below us, revealing a breathtaking view of Loch Ness. We climbed up to the summit, then took a well-earned respite on a public bench.

"Zack, can I ask ye a question?"

"Ask."

"Whit made ye change yer mind aboot goin' after the creature?"

Reaching down, I picked a wildflower, absentmindedly pulling apart its petals. "When Brandy was hurting herself, why do you think she was doing it?"

"Doctor said it wis 'cause she wis angry."

"Maybe I'm angry too."

"Angry at whit?"

"For the longest time, I was angry at Angus. It was because of him that I took off in that rowboat. Now I'm more angry at myself, at having to deal with this whole damn thing."

"It's no' *your* fault ye were attacked. That wis fate."

"I don't believe in fate. Fate's like folklore, it's an excuse for an unexplainable circumstance. I believe in science, in dealing with reality. It's why I'm angry with myself. Had I dealt with my own reality seventeen years ago, I wouldn't be in this mess today."

"Ye were only nine, how can ye blame yersel'? Look at whit ye've been through. Two drownings now, an' still ye've survived."

"You call this surviving? I'm afraid of the water, and I wake up every night screaming."

"Dreams or no', ye're still alive, which is mair than that laddie back there can say. It wis fate that saved ye seventeen years ago, jist like it wis fate that led ye tae become a marine biologist."

"Meaning what?"

"Meanin', if anyone's destined tae figure oot whit this ancient creature is, it's you, Zachary Wallace."

"Well, I don't know about fate, but I do know about science, and science tells me this monster's not an ancient creature, at least not a plesiosaur. I think it's something else entirely, most likely a hybrid of a species that's been inhabiting Loch Ness for a long time."

"Like Angus's Guivre?"

"I don't know, but I know someone who does."

"Zack, please, dinnae start in again on my auld man."

"Just listen. This morning I saw three men, all cloaked in dark tunics, and they were carrying something in a burlap sack, something that was bleeding. I collected swaths of the blood, the sheriff's having them analyzed."

"Good. Then we can ease yer suspicions aboot my faither, once an' for a'."

The sound of a boat's horn drifted up to us from below.

"That'll be Brandy. How aboot I talk her intae picking ye up on the return trip. If ye ask me, I think it's yer destiny tae get back intae her guid graces."

"I hope I live that long."

"She usually circles back past Tor Point around dusk. Try tae make it there by then."

He waved, then bounded down the path.

I watched him disappear into the forest, my mind drifting back to the image of Justin Wagner's remains.

Seventeen years ago I had survived a similar attack. Had I done something to lure the creature up from the depths? And what had I done, consciously or unconsciously, to prevent it from devouring me?

Alban MacDonald had rescued me, perhaps he knew. But old Crabbit was concealing his own secrets.

Who were the Black Knights? What were they doing out at night? And what, if anything, did all this have to do with the attacks on the Loch?

I gathered my belongings and headed down the mountain path, determined to find out.

The Diary of Sir Adam Wallace
Translated by Logan W. Wallace

Entry: 25 October 1330
I scrawl these words by ember's glow, as hours pass like days, an' my sanity remains lost in this hellhole.

At some point sleep must have taken me, for when next I opened my eyes, the gate was nearly finished. 'Tis an enormous structure, weighin' no less than fifty stone, its width conformin' tae the size o' the river narrow that allows the Loch tae escape tae the sea. Sir Iain has sharpened the bottom flanges intae fierce points. They are meant tae be driven intae the river's bed, an' once set afore the openin', MacDonald claims the current alone should keep the gate frae movin'.

When the last bolts were tightened, MacDonald gathered us in a circle, then brought me taae its center. "*Ecce quam bonum et quam lucundum habitare fratres in unum*—Behold how good an' how pleasant it is for brethren tae dwell together in unity. Adam Zachary Wallace, dae ye believe in God, who hasnae died an' will never die?"

"Aye."

"Dae ye, through fear o' the flames of Hell, swear total obedience tae oor Master, Jesus Christ?"

"Aye."

"Dae ye gie up yer ain free will as a soldier o' Christ?"

"Aye."

"The soldier o' Christ kills safely; he dies the mair safely. He serves his ain interests in dyin', an' Christ's interests in killin'. The warrior is gentler than lambs an' fiercer than lions, bearin' the mildness o' the monk an' the valor o' the knight. Oor Order adorned the Temple o' Solomon wi' weapons instead o' gems, wi' shields instead o' crowns o' gold. Oors is eager for victory, no' fame, for battle no' pomp. We abhor wasteful speech, unnecessary action, unmeasured laughter, gossip an' chatter.

We despise a' things vain, an' live in one house accordin' tae one rule, wi' one soul an' one heart."

Reachin' oot, he took my hand, then opened my flesh wi' his sword. "Adam Zachary Wallace, wi' this blood oath, dae ye swear allegiance tae the Order o' the Knight?"

"Aye."

"Brethren o' the Templar, are there any objections tae acceptin' this novice intae the Order?"

None responded.

MacDonald reviewed the rules o' the Order, then asked whether J had a wife an' family, debts or disease, or if J owed allegiance tae any other master. "None," J replied.

As prompted, J knelt, askin' tae become a servant an' slave of the Temple, swearin' obedience tae God an' the Virgin Mary.

MacDonald recited Psalm 133, then said, "Arise, Sir Adam, for as o' this day an' forever mair, ye are a Templar Knight. Noo, my bretren, as we stand here by the Gate o' Hell, fashioned by oor ain hands, there is one mair allegiance which a' o' us must make."

MacDonald removed the silver casket frae roond my neck an' held it up in the light. "In the name o' Robert the Bruce, oor one an' true King, we take this blood oath. Like those who came afore us, sworn in secrecy tae protect the Ark o' the Covenant, so too must we keep the contents o' this silver casket safe. Tae dae so, we willfully join leagues wi' the De'il, usin' evil tae stand guard against evil, so that we may preserve the guid. By this heinous coven, the white tunic shall be replaced by the black, the cross o' Sir Galahad wi' the Braveheart, an X symbolizin' oor contract wi' Satan. Oor followers shall be few, o' noble birth an' born only tae oor Clans, an' we shall take oor secrets tae the grave an' beyond."

An' so, in the depths o' the earth, on the threshold o' Hell, oor blood wis shared an' oor coven wis made, the coven o' the Black Knights.
J ken noo that J shall ne'er again see the light o' day . . .

The modern theory of evolution does not require gradual change. A new species can arise when a small segment of the ancestral population is isolated at the periphery of the ancestral range. Large, stable central populations exert a strong homogenizing influence. New and favorable mutations are diluted by the sheer bulk of the population through which they must spread. They may build slowly in frequency, but changing environments usually cancel their selective value long before they reach fixation. But small, peripherally isolated groups are cut off from their parental stock. They live as tiny populations in geographic corners of the ancestral range. Small peripheral isolates are a laboratory of evolutionary change.

—Stephen Jay Gould, *"The Episodic Nature of Evolutionary Change,"*
The Panda's Thumb: Reflections in Natural History, 1980

CHAPTER 20

Urquhart Bay, Loch Ness

THE RESEARCH VESSEL, *Northosaur*, drifted in 730 feet of water, adding to the picturesque backdrop of Urquhart Castle. The banks of the ruins were lined with tourists, the scene recorded by a half dozen TV camera crews, the footage destined to be used in news reports around the globe as B-role.

Michael Hoagland remained on deck to shout imaginary orders to his crew until the last camera was finally lowered, then he hurried inside to the control room and the ship's sonar system.

*   *   *

Sonar systems function by emitting ultrasonic pulses from an acoustic projector. Hydrophones then analyze these reflected signals to determine if an obstacle or object is present within the field.

There are two basic types of sonar: passive and active. Passive sonar, used aboard submarines, analyzes incoming noises without creating its own sounds so as not to give away the vessel's location. Active sonar emits loud "pings" that can be set at different frequencies, bearings, or angles. Pings travel at a speed of approximately fifteen hundred meters per second. If an object lies in the beam's path, it will be detected on echo-ranging sonar.

While more aggressive, the limitation of active sonar is that it takes time to adjust the projector, emit a ping, and listen for an echo. To combat this challenge, engineers developed the sonar buoy, a free-floating unit that emits its own system of pings, allowing operators to detect objects moving through its acoustical field.

The Portable Acoustic Measurement System, known as PAMS, consists of an array of sonar buoys, distributed along the surface in a preset pattern. PAMS signals are linked to an acoustic data acquisition system, a GPS receiver, and a radio telemetry sub system. Positional data is then transmitted by way of a UHF radio link to the analysis station where signals are evaluated.

*　　　*　　　*

Over the last nine hours, the *Nothosaur*'s crew had deployed sonar buoys every two kilometers, beginning in the waters off Fort Augustus. Consisting of two parallel rows, the array ran north to Tor Point, where the Loch's width narrowed and the field was reduced to a single row of buoys which concluded at Lochend and the Bona Narrows.

Now it was time to reap the fruits of their labor.

Hoagland stalked the control room while his sonar expert, Victor Cellers, finished checking the *Nothosaur*'s buoy field. Victor was Hoagland's brother-in-law and the Nessie Hunter felt fortunate to have him on board. The forty-two-year-old American with cystic fibrosis was strictly "on loan" to him from his sister, Deborah, who expected the former Navy man back at his Seattle-based video company in two weeks . . . and in one piece.

"So, Victor, the field is operational, yes?"

"Operational and reliable are two different things. The buoys are pinging and I'm receiving data, but the signal's loaded with tons of garbage."

"Garbage?"

"Noise interference." Victor pointed to his main monitor, displaying a GPS image of Loch Ness and the *Nothosaur*'s sonar buoys. "Everything from Foyers south to Fort Augustus is congested with pinging sounds. I'm picking up signals from at least two other active sonar buoy fields, and they're positioned too close to ours to allow an undistorted signal analysis. It's the equivalent of trying to peer at the stars using a telescope in the middle of Manhattan. Face it, Michael, we're not the only game in town. There's just too much interference to acquire an accurate reading."

Hoagland muttered a string of curses in German.

"The good news is, if they're interfering with us, then we're interfering with them as well."

"Then all of us are wasting our time and money."

"In a nutshell, yes."

"Victor, contact the other vessel's captains. Organize a sit-down at the Clansman Hotel for later tonight to discuss the situation. Either the Highland Council resolves this matter, or we're all leaving."

Dores

It was a ten-mile hike from Inverfarigaig to Dores, another two if I were to meet Brandy and True at Tor Point. Added to the eight miles I had already logged earlier that day, I was exhausted by the time I reached Dores Beach, a pebbled shoreline that stretched back to grassy, wide-open knolls and General Wade's Military Road.

The area was packed with locals, tourists, and media. Limping up the gravel beach to the grass, I dropped my backpack and collapsed, careful to keep my head low so as not to be recognized. The moment I sat down, I realized the last hour of walking on pebbled beaches had done me in.

The village of Dores sits on the easternmost corner of Loch Ness where the lake suddenly narrows to half its mile width. Follow the shoreline west and you reach Tor Point. From there, the Loch runs north again until it bleeds into the River Ness.

Tourists and locals alike had gathered on Dores Beach to watch two dozen daring windsurfers, their sailboards whipping across the Loch's windblown surface. Powerful gusts were coming in from the southwest and were harshest inland, forcing the daredevils to keep a dangerous distance from shore.

I wondered if they'd be so brave had they seen Justin Wagner's remains.

From Dores Beach, the Loch ran south as far as the eye could see. Mountainous walls bordered her on either side, and the sun was just beginning to dip behind the peaks to the west.

Behind me, a large contingent had gathered by the roadside to listen to the exploits of famed Nessie watcher Steve Feltham. Years earlier, Feltham had sold his home in England to stalk the monster on film. Now he lived in a converted van, his dedication making him a legend of sorts, though his toil, while adding to the monster lore, had proven nothing.

Feeling my back muscles stiffen, I gathered my belongings and left the beach, limping up the hill to the Dores Pub, hoping a quick beer might lessen my pain.

Big mistake.

"Look, there he is!" A petite blonde dressed in a hideous blue blazer ran towards me with her microphone, dragging her inebriated cameraman with her. "Dr. Wallace, hi! Shar Bonanno, for the BBC. Can we get your reaction to today's Highland Council meeting?"

"I wasn't there, so I have no idea what—"

"They're talking about rescinding the law that protects Nessie. You think it's true?"

"Do I think what's true?"

"That the Council wants to capture the monster."

"No comment."

"The Council's also hired an American scientist to organize the search. He's en route as we speak."

"Good for him. Look, I just came in for a quick beer."

"You look like you've hiked quite a ways. Have you been tracking the monster?"

I pushed her microphone out of my face and entered the bar. "A Guinness, cold as you've got."

An older, inebriated Scot who looked like he'd been sitting on his bar stool all day looked me up and down, then smelled the air. "Heh, neebr, goat a deid an'mal in yer bac'pac, or iz it ye tha' bloody stinks?"

My brain took a moment to translate. "Actually, yes, there is a dead animal in my backpack, but I probably stink, too."

He waved at the air, then moved aside for two police officers. "Dr. Wallace?"

"I know, I know, I'm dropping them off at the lab."

They looked at one another, momentarily confused. "Sir, Sheriff Holmstrom sent us. We're tae escort ye back tae Inverness Castle."

"Now what for? Is the judge locking me up again?"

"No, sir. It's yer faither. Seems there's been an accident."

*   *   *

The dungeon had been transformed into a Hollywood movie set, portable lighting lining the back corner of the ancient cellblock, removing every "annoying" shadow from Angus's chamber. Two film crews were packing up their equipment as I arrived, along with what remained of an Emergency Medical Team.

The star of the show was propped up in bed in his T-shirt. An IV dripped into his left arm, a cardiac monitor hooked to his right. At his side was a doting nurse, an Asian woman with dark brown wavy hair and infatuation in her eyes, though she was no more than half his age.

"Ah, there's my laddie! Zachary, say hello to Nurse Kosa."

"Kasa. Francesca Kasa."

"Whit's the diff'rence? Me Kasa is su Kasa, eh, son."

"And why do you need a private nurse?"

"Your father had heart problems earlier this afternoon."

"Heart problems?"

"Aye, son. Had trouble breathin'. Felt like an elephant wis squattin' on my chest. Barely dodged the Grim Reaper, I did. Imagine Johnny C. wis lookin' doon at me an' smilin'. But I pulled through, so no tears, lad."

"I'll try not to get too emotional. By the way, nurse, what's his EKG say?"

"It's normal now, but we're still doing blood tests. The guard found him slumped over, unconscious."

"Uh-huh. So why isn't he in a hospital?"

Angus winked. "Since it wis jist a mild attack, the judge, bein' the wise man that he is, felt it better I stay here, oot o' sight of the media, though I think Maxie might have accidentally invited them a' in."

"Right. Well, I've got work to do. Try not to die on us while I'm gone."

"Wait, lad. Guard, I need tae talk in private wi' my son. Wid ye mind escortin' everyone oot?" He turned to his nurse, patting her lightly on her derriere. "You too, darlin'. Jist make sure yer back here in an hour for my sponge bath."

She blushed, checked his IV drip, then followed the others out, the guard locking Angus's cell door behind her.

We were alone.

"Son, wid ye mind fetchin' me another pillow?"

"Fetch it yourself. You pulled that old heart attack stunt on mom when I was seven."

He grinned sheepishly. "Did I? Lord knows, it still gets them every time."

"Where'd all this food come from?"

"Local hotels sent it ower. Business is soarin', an' they're grateful, as they should be. Even got yer room comp'ed. Order whatever ye like, rent some dirty movies, it's a' on yer auld man." He took a deep breath, then made a face. "Whit's that foul stench? Smells worse than an anchovy's twat."

"They're *specimens*, collected from around the Loch. A few dead birds and a squirrel."

"Birds an' squirrels? Christ, lad, why dae they no' jist hang me now an' get it ower wi'." He tore the IV drip from his arm. "Listen, Nature Boy, I need ye oot on the water, no' strollin' the woods like some pixie."

"That's what scientists do, Angus. We look for real clues, not the ones published in the *World Weekly News*. The animal that bit me is obviously a predator, and it's overcome its fear of man, assuming it ever had one."

"Well now, I see ye finally admit tae bein' bitten. Thought ye looked mair focused. Danger'll dae that tae the mind. So then, how dae ye plan on findin' it?"

"First, I have to know what it is I'm looking for. Then—"

"Then ye'll need a boat, equipment too. I can get ye a' ye need."

"How?"

"Go see Theresa. She'll be in her summer hoose, in the hills above Foyers."

"And why would Johnny C.'s widow want to help me?"

"She'd be helpin' me."

"God, you're pathetic." I shook my head and left, wondering why I was wasting my time with him.

*　　　　　*　　　　　*

It was almost midnight by the time I tracked down Sheriff Holmstrom in his office. "Sheriff, I need your lab to perform some blood work on these animal specimens. Any word yet about the swatches I gave you earlier?"

"We're workin' on it." He looked through my backpack. "Dead birds . . . a squirrel? Is this really necessary? Looks tae me like ye're shootin' in the dark."

"Maybe. But we have to . . . " I paused, as speakers squawked to life from outside his window. "What's going on?"

"Highland Council hired an American scientist tae organize things at Loch Ness. They're bringin' him straight from the airport, press conference's scheduled tae take place on the castle lawn the moment he arrives. Leave the specimens wi' me, I'll see the crime lab gets them."

"Thanks." I shook his hand, then headed outside, curious.

A small sound stage had been set up for the cameras, with Inverness Castle lit majestically in the background. Everywhere I looked were reporters and film crews, the whole catered affair organized by the Highland Council's Division of Tourism.

A buzz rose from the crowd, which squeezed in tighter to the stage as Owen Hollifield stepped to the podium.

"Good evenin', an' welcome tae Inverness, gateway tae the Scottish Highlands. My name is Owen Hollifield an' I am Provost o' the Highland Council, the governin' body that presides over Loch Ness. Over the last forty-eight hours, the Council's been reviewin' progress in our ongoin' investigation tae resolve the mystery o' Loch Ness an' how it relates tae the tragic deaths o' several tourists. Wi' three research teams now combin' the Loch an' several dozen smaller parties staked out on land, the Council felt it imperative that we appoint an expert tae organize our search an' resolve disputes among the, uh . . . monster hunters, if ye will. We searched worldwide, and while there were at least a dozen candidates we considered, one name stuck out among the rest."

Hollifield paused to read from a three-by-five card. "The scientist of whom I speak has earned a reputation for organizin' research teams an' locatin' their objective. In January o' this year, his team succeeded in doin' somethin' no other research group had ever done, track down and film a giant squid."

"Huh?" I pushed through the crowd to take a closer look.

"Ladies an' gentlemen, it gives me great pleasure tae introduce tae ye, Dr. David Caldwell o' Boca Raton, Florida."

Had I been hooked to Angus's EKG monitor, my thundering heart would have exploded the graph. There was David, waving from behind the podium like some conquering hero, using my accomplishments as his proverbial pedestal.

"Thank you, thank you . . . my God, what a nice welcome. It's truly an honor to be here in Scotland, working with the Highland Council, and . . . well, what can I say, I'll do everything in my power to resolve this mystery, once and for all."

"We'll take a few questions, an' then Dr. Caldwell's off tae his hotel."

"Dr. Caldwell, wasn't it, in fact, Dr. Zachary Wallace who caught the giant squid on film?"

"Damn straight," I mumbled, pumping my fists.

David grinned his Cheshire cat smile. "Certainly my former colleague played a role on our team, but I was head of the mission, the one responsible for its success. Dr. Wallace, unfortunately, was more responsible for sinking our submersible."

You son of a—

"Yes, the young lady in that attractive blue blazer."

"Dr. Caldwell, have ye ever even been tae Loch Ness?"

"Not per se, but hey, water's water. If we can find a giant squid in the Sargasso Sea, then we should have no problem finding your plesiosaur."

Idiot . . .

"How do you know it's a plesiosaur?"

"Well, I—"

"What proof do you have?"

The provost took over before David could shove his other foot in his mouth. "We'll, ah, hold yer questions there. Dr. Caldwell's had a long flight an' needs his rest. Tomorrow mornin', Council will be meetin' tae discuss what we'll do wi' Nessie once we—"

"Hey, David!" My body trembled as I pushed toward the front of the stage.

The crowd encircled me, their cameras still rolling.

David looked down from the podium. "Zack? Jesus, what, uh, what're you doing here? Ladies and gentlemen, my, uh, my colleague and good friend, Dr. Zachary Wallace."

I leaped onto the stage in one adrenaline-enhanced bound. "You mean former colleague, don't you, asshole?" Before he could respond, my right cross smashed him squarely in the face, dropping him like a sack of potatoes.

Camera strobes lit the night as I stood over him, my teeth grinding my father's grin. "Welcome tae the Highlands, ye bastard."

It was about 7:30 in the evening and my son, Jim, and I were working
in a loch-side field about two kilometers south of Dores when we noticed
something moving about halfway across Loch Ness. It was big and black,
and I realized after fifteen years of farming I was finally seeing the monster.
The Loch was calm and everything was quiet, not a noise anywhere,
just this thing moving steadily forward. It was quite eerie.

We decided to get the boat out and try to intercept it. Four of us got
in and set off. As we got closer we could see more details. There was
a long head and neck coming about two meters out of the water, and
the body had humps. Its color was dark and it had to be at least fourteen
meters [45.9 feet] long. As we moved closer it rose up a bit, put up a great
disturbance so that our boat spun around, then was gone.

The one thing I'll always remember is that eye.
It was oval-shaped and jaundice and it looked right at us.

—Hugh Ayton, Balachladaich, August 1963

CHAPTER 21

Inverness

I AWOKE TO AN INCESSANT POUNDING on my door. Fearing I had been screaming again in my sleep, I rolled out of bed with a groan, every muscle in my body raw and aching.

"Who the hell is it?"

"Maxie. Open up!"

I unbolted the door and opened it, then staggered to the bathroom sink, and downed several aspirin.

Max followed me in, carrying a rolled-up newspaper. "Still sleeping? It's two-thirty in the affie."

"I was up late, poisoning my body."

"And behaving like our father, yeah?" He held open the newspaper.

The black-and-white photo captured me standing over David, fists balled, face contorted in a wild leer. The caption read: "*Wallace Welcomes Colleague to Loch Ness.*"

"At least they got my good side."

"Caldwell threatened to press charges. Don't worry, he backed off when I threatened a countersuit of slander."

"Let him sue, I've got nothing to lose." I turned over the paper, my eye catching another article.

Council Amends Laws

In the wake of the gruesome attack on Alaskan resident Justin Wagner and the suspected deaths of at least two other tourists, the Highland Council voted unanimously to amend the "Protection of Animals Act of 1912" and the subsequent "Veterinary Surgeons Act of 1966." The 1912 Law prevented the water creature, known as "Nessie," from being netted by researchers and monster hunters, while the 1966 Act outlawed attempts to take tissue samples from any Loch Ness water beast. Fisheries Protection Board bailiff Theron Turman agreed with the changes, but was quick to point out that the

amendments refer only to large water creatures and that it was still illegal to net trout or salmon in Loch Ness.

"Yeah, I read that article, too. What's it all mean?"

I shook my head in disbelief. "It means they want to capture the creature."

Observation Lounge
Clansman Hotel

With an extensive boat dock located directly on Loch Ness, the Clansman Hotel has always been the favorite convening spot for Nessie hunters, and the Highland Council wasted no time in securing it for their own proceedings.

Provost Owen Hollifield checked his watch, then knocked again on David Caldwell's suite. "Afternoon, doctor. Ye ready?"

David opened the door, his eyes red from jet lag. "Born ready. I take it Council did everything they were supposed to?"

"Aye. The laws were amended, an' we've a'ready begun talks wi' two construction firms. As for the monster hunters, we've selected the three most qualified captains an' vessels as ye requested, an' if ye don't like these, we've applications from forty tae fifty more. Everyone from local fishermen tae computer geeks tae ex-Royal Navy wants tae be here."

"Three's plenty. Anymore and they start tripping over one another."

"That's already happenin', I'm afraid. Many have dropped sonar buoys, an' the signals are crossin', foulin' one another up."

"I'll handle them. I've dealt with their types before."

Hollifield led him down a carpeted hallway to the adjoining banquet room. "Be fair warned, there're also a few curators here who insisted on bein' at this meetin'. One's from the Smithsonian, the other two work at the British Museum of Natural History. Treat them kindly, they can make waves."

"Understood."

They entered the Observation Lounge, a banquet room offering panoramic views of Loch Ness and the pier where several large research vessels were now docked. A portable corkboard on wheels was positioned near the head of the conference table, a map of Loch Ness pinned to its surface.

Five men and two women milled about the buffet tables, helping themselves to an early dinner.

Hollifield took his place before the head of the table, David on his right. "Gentlemen and ladies, if ye please."

The expedition leaders and museum curators took their seats.

"This is Dr. Caldwell, the gentleman whom Council has appointed tae organize our search. Dr. Caldwell, our Nessie hunters; Michael Hoagland from the German research vessel, *Nothosaur*, Scott an' Debbie Sloan, American cryptozoologists wi' the *Galon*, an' Bill Plager, a marine biologist serving aboard the fifty-seven-foot ship, *Great White North.*"

"A pleasure. Now I know you have some grievances you want to discuss, but before we get into that, let's talk about our objective. You, and dozens of Nessie hunters before you have spent several decades and untold thousands of dollars chasing after underwater photos and sonar recordings. Now all that's changed. With the monster's sudden thirst for blood, I think it's safe to say something large inhabits Loch Ness. In other words, we've got the proof, it's lying in the morgue, what we want now is to capture the beast."

Scott Sloan scoffed. "Capture it? Aren't you being rather presumptuous, and more than a bit melodramatic? For one, who said anything about a thirst for blood?" He looked at his wife, who nodded.

"Scott's right. And besides, how do you capture something that's so elusive, we've yet to get a decent photo of it in over seventy years?"

David winked at the provost. "My skeptics said the same thing about the Giant Squid. The game's changed, folks, deal with it. For whatever reason, Nessie's no longer satisfied with feeding in the deep. She's become a real meat eater."

Bill Plager ran a callused palm over his bald spot. "Meat eater or no', ye'll no' capture anythin' until ye get these amateurs tae stop droppin' their damn sonar buoys all over the Loch."

"Us?" Hoagland stood. "It's your buoys jamming our grid!"

"Easy, boys," David warned, "there's no unions here. Either you fellas play nice or we'll boot your asses off the Loch."

Dr. Saumil Shah, Associate Curator at the Smithsonian, raised his hand. "A question, please. Assuming you can even locate this water creature, where do you think you're going to keep it?"

"Right here." David stood, then circled Urquhart Bay on the map with his pencil.

Meghan Talley rolled her eyes.

"Okay, I can see a few *doubting Thomases*, but think about this. The bay provides us with a natural habitat, with three shorelines we can use to pen the creature in. Council's already negotiating with engineers and construction companies who said they can drop steel fencing from a pre-fab bridge spanning the entire mouth of the bay, in effect, cordoning it off from the rest of the Loch. The fencing'll be secured to the bottom using concrete anchors and supported along the surface by a series of buoys. Naturally, the shoreline surrounding the bay will have to be fenced in as well. It'll be the largest animal pen in the world, and I guarantee, the most popular."

"Plus," added the Provost, "it'd allow us tae study the creature while still protectin' the legend . . . an' our tourists."

David offered a cocky smile. "Now I'll answer your questions. Yes, ma'am, and you are?"

"Meghan Talley. My husband, Mark, and I are curators at the British Museum of Natural History. We were at your press conference last night when you publicly identified the predator as a plesiosaur. Exactly what did you base your analysis on?"

"Decades of sightings. Photos. The usual stuff."

"I see." Meghan's blue eyes blazed. "And is this the type of scientific protocol we can come to expect?"

"Look, lady, what difference does it make what I say it is? Once we capture it, we'll look under its skirt and know for sure, right?"

"It's ass-backwards, *doctor*. This is still supposed to be a scientific expedition."

"Says who?" David paced around the table, chest out. "I've been hired to organize a hunt, plain and simple. You want to call it a scientific expedition, knock your socks off. Me? I say we capture the thing, then sort the science out later."

"My wife's right," Mark Talley said. "If you don't know what you're hunting, you can't even be certain it's one creature. You're also basing your assumptions on Nessie lore. Chances are, it's not something anywhere as romantic as a plesiosaur. What if it's just a giant sturgeon?"

"A sturgeon?"

"Yes, Dr. Caldwell, a sturgeon. Look it up. It's an anadromous species, over 200 million years old, that proliferates in Loch Ness. The Baltic sturgeon looks almost like a Thresher shark, and it can grow over twenty feet in length. You think the public's going to pay good money to see a sturgeon?"

David glanced back at the provost. "It's not a sturgeon. Sturgeons don't have teeth big enough, sharp enough to do the kind of damage that happened to that Alaskan kid."

"Our point, doctor, is that you're jumping the gun with all these announcements and expenses. Why not slow down, figure out what it is first, then go after it."

David shook his head. "No. See, all you curators and monster hunters have been doing it the same way for decades. It's high time for a more aggressive approach. Isn't that right, Mr. Provost?"

Hollifield nodded. "Council's puttin' up £50,000 sterlin' for the capture o' the beast, an' *National Geographic*, who won the bid tae film everythin', jist added another £100,000 tae sweeten the pot. This money . . . an' credit for the capture, will be split by Dr. Caldwell, the Council, an' only those vessels participating in the search."

David returned to the map. "I'm dividing the Loch into three sections. The *Nothosaur* will cover the northern end of Loch Ness, from the Abban Water Fishery south to Urquhart Bay. The Sloans and the *Galon*'s crew will patrol Urquhart Bay south to Foyers. Since Bill Plager has the largest and fastest of the three vessels, he'll take Foyers south to Fort Augustus. As a necessary first step, I'm asking each of you to commit to the mission by immediately collecting your own sonar buoys. You'll then redistribute them, following my technician's instructions, in a specified pattern in your assigned areas. In addition to keeping an eye on your own grid, your signals will be uploaded to a master signature management system aboard my boat, which I'll be selecting tomorrow morning from a list of local applicants."

David circled the group again like a young Patton. "In a few days, we'll be supplying your vessels with extra-heavy fishing nets, which should arrive in Inverness later this week. By then, we expect to have most of the mouth of Urquhart Bay cordoned off. Once the monster is targeted by our sonar grid, all boats will converge upon its location and we'll net it."

Meghan Talley shook her head. "Simple as that, huh?"

"Look, lady, we're dealing with a big predator living in a big lake, but it's still just a lake. I mean, where else is this thing gonna go? We locate it, we net it, we pen it. It's cut-and-dried."

"What about the museum?" Dr. Shah asked.

"Once we capture the monster, we'll begin fielding applications from curators and other scientists to study Nessie."

"Applications? You expect us to apply?"

"This is business, Mrs. Talley. And let's get a few things clear. When it comes to the press, all interviews go through me. And I don't want to hear any talk about Nessie being a sturgeon, or your application may just find its way to the bottom of our pile. *Capiche*?"

Meghan Talley started to say something, but her husband grabbed her arm.

"No more questions? Good. Redistribute your sonar buoys, boys and girls, Nessie hunting season just began."

Aldourie Castle
Northeastern Bank of Loch Ness

Gray skies cast a pall over the Great Glen. The dark water was as smooth as glass, blemished by occasional wisps of fog that rolled across the surface like tumbleweed.

I hiked north along the eastern bank of Loch Ness, continuing my search for clues, my T-shirt soaked from a late afternoon downpour that had scattered many of the tourists. By five-thirty I found myself along the banks of Aldourie Pier and a galley-stance that had once supplied a British garrison more than a century ago. A battered aluminum canoe was beached in the tall grass, its exposed bottom covered in algae. There was no one else around.

I continued on, approaching the grounds of Aldourie Castle. The ancient baronial mansion was set several hundred yards back from the Loch, surrounded by open acres of land. Four-story spires topped the abandoned estate, its silhouette dwarfed by a backdrop of emerald green forested slopes carpeted in pine and larch.

Aldourie Castle had been reconstructed several times since its main tower had been built in 1626. The most recent work completed a cement pad that separated the foundation from the first floor. At the time, its owner, Colonel William Fraser-Tytler, claimed it was done to fireproof the estate. According to locals, the colonel was more concerned about "finally putting to rest the ghost of the lady in gray," a spirit said to be haunting the castle grounds.

If childhood memories were the spirits that haunted me, then Castle Aldourie was certainly a part of them, for this was the site where Angus had seeded in me his superstitions about devils and dragons.

I moved to the edge of the bank where my father had dangled his young son. Had the drunken bastard been clairvoyant, or was he just playing me as he'd always done?

Perhaps as he was doing now . . .

Staring below into those dark waters, I seriously began to wonder.

And then I looked up and saw the object.

It was a pale figure, bobbing along the surface several hundred yards away. Had the water not been so smooth, I'd have never seen it, but its movement was causing ripples along the Loch's otherwise tranquil surface.

Was it a deer?

With visibility poor and the fog thickening, I couldn't be certain, but it looked to me . . . like a body!

There was no one else around, no boats in sight.

What to do?

I looked back at the canoe, my heart pounding.

Okay, Wallace, you swore you'd take action when the time came, well, the clock's ticking.

I jogged back to the canoe, my muscles moving like liquid lead, my bladder tingling with fear. Reaching down, I flipped the algae-infested boat over, exposing a rotted wooden paddle and a dozen or so angry bullfrogs.

"Sorry, boys."

The inside of the canoe reeked of standing water. Using the waterlogged paddle, I pushed away curtains of cobwebs, then dragged the vessel over the grass toward the small pier.

Underwater . . . lungs on fire, the shadow rising with me . . . get to the light!

"Whoa!" I shook my head, fighting to clear the subliminal image. "Stay calm. Better to face your fear in daylight."

The Great Glen rumbled with thunder, its placid waters challenging me to violate their serenity.

Lowering the canoe into the water, I tried to imagine what William Wallace and his band of followers must have felt while they waited at Stirling to confront Longshanks's army. Outnumbered, they had confronted their fear head-on and, in doing so, won a decisive battle.

"Fear? Maybe the dragon represented fear? Maybe that's what Angus was trying to tell me. Everyone must face their own personal dragon at some point."

Idiot. Since when did Angus Wallace ever speak philosophically?

I checked the canoe, verified there were no leaks, then, leaving my backpack on the dock, climbed down a small wooded ladder and eased myself into the boat. Balancing myself, I gripped the rotted oar and began paddling away from shore in water deeper than the North Sea.

So far so good. You can do this.

With the fog rolling in, it took me a long moment before I could relocate the bobbing object. My shoulder muscles knotted as I paddled, ending each stroke by tracing a *J* in the water to keep the canoe moving along a straight course.

Two hundred yards away, the ripples increased in intensity.

Within minutes, the chill of Loch Ness began filtering through the bottom of the aluminum boat, numbing my feet. Ignoring the cold, I switched sides and continued paddling, the canoe's bow pushing through the thickening veils of fog.

I was close now, maybe twenty boat lengths away, when I heard splashing noises up ahead.

Something was struggling in the water . . . whatever was out there was still alive!

"Hello?"

I paddled harder, my imagination racing. *Was it a capsized boater? How long could someone stay afloat in these frigid waters?*

I thought I saw a head go under then rise again, perhaps arms slapping at the fog-strewn surface. "Hang on, I'm almost there!"

Reaching the body, I executed a wide *C* stroke, spun the bow around and leaned over.

"Oh, geez."

It wasn't a person and it wasn't alive. It was a massive fish, a sturgeon, seventeen feet long, only it was covered in dozens of gushing bite marks, each bloody divot measuring eight to ten inches around, four inches deep.

As I watched and stared, the carcass was dragged under again and attacked, as if by a school of piranha.

"Christ, what the hell's happening?"

Whomp!

My heart leaped as something heavy struck the bottom of the canoe, its impact reverberating through my bones.

Whomp . . . whomp-whomp!

More strikes, in staggered succession. I was being attacked!

I regripped the paddle and was about to stroke when the canoe was walloped again from below with such force the aluminum plates by my feet dented upward and separated, releasing a stream of icy water.

Jesus, Wallace, haul ass!

I stroked like a madman, driving the sinking boat forward, my heart nearly stopping as the bow skidded atop the remains of the resurfacing sturgeon.

"Dammit!" I veered the canoe to one side, my shattered nerves tingling as my plunging oar struck something solid swimming below.

Whomp . . . whomp!

The canoe rocked as it was bludgeoned again, the water at my feet three inches deep and rising.

This isn't happening!

Somewhere in the back of my mind, I heard my inner voice remind me, *Easy, Wallace. It's just a loch. It can't hurt you if you don't go in.*

"Shut up!"

Lowering my shoulder, I paddled like an Olympian, aiming for a distant shoreline now mired in fog. The frigid water in the canoe was now was up to my ankles.

A giant shadow, rising to meet me!

Subliminal images blinded me. "A hundred yards . . . just keep paddling!"

Mouth opening around my lower torso . . .

"Eighty yards . . . come on, Wallace!"

Water up to my calf, the canoe growing noticeably heavier.

Something jagged, tearing into my flesh!

"Sixty yards . . . where's the damn pier?"

Get to the light, Zachary, get to the light!

Whomp!

"Get the hell away from me!"

My blistered hands and forearms burned, my entire body straining now to move the water-laden canoe.

I was getting closer. I could see Aldourie Castle. I could see its green pastures of lawn.

And then the rising water wet my buttocks, and I knew I was going in.

Fifty yards . . .

The canoe wobbled with every stroke, only it scarcely moved.

Forty yards. Stay in the boat as long as possible!

The bow rose, the stern bobbed, then sank beneath me.

Oh, hell.

Releasing the paddle, I stood, then launched myself into the Loch, its all-too familiar embrace blasting my breath away as my churning legs leveled out into an awkward crawl stroke. My hiking shoes were concrete blocks, my clothing binding me, my fear preventing me from ducking my head underwater as I swam.

Twenty yards, Wallace . . . twenty damn yards! Two first down markers . . .

An image flashed in my mind's eye. *The body of a man. Naked. Dead.*

"Awffff!"

Distracted, my forehead smashed painfully against a wood piling, striking it so hard I actually saw purple stars.

Get out of the damn water!

Reaching out blindly, I groped for the ladder, then dragged myself up its splintering rungs. Dizzy from the cold and exertion, I reached the summit and collapsed to my knees upon the pier, then lay back and closed my eyes, rubbing the aching knot on my head.

Eyes shut, I watched flashes of light skate past my eyelids as I listened to the waves lapping quietly below.

"You're okay. Breathe."

Calming my breaths, I allowed my weight to sink as I forced my mind to return to the subliminal images.

Something seemed different this time . . . clearer than the images from my previous night terrors. What was it?

Underwater . . . the light!

This time I had seen the light more clearly. It wasn't the sun's rays penetrating the deep, and it wasn't some heavenly glow, it was a brilliant artificial lance . . . an underwater lamp, penetrating my watery tomb like a lighthouse beacon.

I opened my eyes, my thoughts racing with the revelation. "That's what saved me seventeen years ago! It was an underwater light! It must have chased the creature into the deep."

I regained my feet, staring at the Loch in defiance. "I know your weakness now, Nessie, whatever the hell you are. Your eyes, they're sensitive to bright light. The next time we meet, I'll be ready."

My thoughts returned to my adventure in the canoe, and now I was confused, for it was not Justin Wagner's killer that had attacked that sturgeon. No, these water creatures, whatever they were, had been smaller, yet quite ferocious.

Was it Nessie's young, or another species?

"There's something bizarre happening here, something that's affecting the entire ecosystem." Remembering the lab, I searched my backpack for my cell phone and Sheriff Holmstrom's number.

"Sheriff, it's Zachary Wallace. What's the story with those blood samples and specimens I asked you to have analyzed? Hello?"

"I'm sorry, Dr. Wallace, I don't know how tae say this . . . but, well, it seems one o' our technicians misplaced yer samples."

"Misplaced?" My gut twisted in knots. "Exactly what was misplaced?"

"Everythin' ye gave us, I'm afraid. We're still searchin' the lab, an' rest assured, the man responsible's been disciplined, but—"

I hung up, cutting him off.

Angus was right, I was wasting my time.

Cursing aloud, I grabbed my backpack, then found cover beneath a larch. Stripping off my wet clothing, I changed into dry shorts and jeans.

And then another thought hit me. *Crabbit MacDonald! He was the one who had the underwater light. How did he know to carry it when he rescued me?*

"That old bastard . . . he knows exactly what's down there."

Returning the pack to my back, I continued hiking, double-timing it north, wondering what scared me more, the creatures inhabiting Loch Ness, or the thought of confronting the old man.

... there is the familiar, and I have to say rather irritating confusion of Natural Selection with "randomness". Mutation is random; Natural Selection is the very opposite of random. In true Natural Selection, if a body has what it takes to survive, its genes automatically survive because they are inside it. So the genes that survive tend to be, automatically, those genes that confer on bodies the qualities that assist them to survive.

—Richard Dawkins *The Blind Watchmaker: Why the Evidence of Evolution Reveals a Universe Without Design,* 1986

A feasible explanation is that the "Monster" may be some type of deep water animal which only rarely comes to the surface. It is possible these animals were cut off in Loch Ness from the ocean many ages ago by earth movements, and their descendants managed to survive.

—C. Eric Palmer, Curator of Natural History, Glasgow Museum, 1951

CHAPTER 22

Bona Narrows, Loch Ness

WITHIN THE HOUR, I found myself on the northeastern-most point of Loch Ness. From here, I could either find a means to cross the channel known as the Bona Narrows, bringing me again to Loch Ness's western shoreline, or I could continue on following the eastern bank another twelve twisting miles, passing Loch Dochfour and the River Ness—a winding route that would eventually lead to Inverness and the Moray Firth.

The thought of being back on the Loch in a boat unnerved me, so I continued trudging along the eastern shoreline in my wet hiking boots, prepared to walk all the way to Inverness if I had to.

The powers-that-be were about to intercede.

As I approached the Bona lighthouse, I saw the water bailiff's motorboat suddenly race across the channel, then veer sharply towards me.

Calum Forrest waved at me from the pilothouse. "Michty aye, Dr. Wallace. Ye do get a'roond, dae ye no'?"

"So they tell me. Is there something I can do for you?"

"Perhaps there's somethin' I can dae for *you*. Come aboard, I'll ta' ye across."

"No thanks. I, uh, I think I'll walk."

"What? A' the way tae Dochfour Weir? Dinnae be daft."

Before I could respond, he drove the bow of his vessel onto the gravel shoreline.

I hesitated, my pulse racing.

"C'mon, there's nae need tae worry aboot you-know-who."

His conviction, combined with the size of his boat, gave me the comfort I needed. Pushing the craft's bow away from the shallows, I climbed aboard.

"Just for the record, how can you be so sure our friend won't show up?"

"Gie me a wee bit o' credit. I may no' have yer degrees, doctor, but I've been on these waters since afore ye were in nappies. The big 'uns, they dinnae like the shallows, 'cept lately, 'course, but only after dark."

"Big ones? Then you've seen them?"

"Nah." Calum aimed the boat for the western shoreline, keeping the motor at a low idle so we could speak. "A' I've seen wis the imprint that big female left on Invermoriston beach. Same as you, yeah?"

Female? How did he know it was a female? My eyes darted back and forth between the old man and the water's surface. "But how—"

"I'm the water bailiff, Doc. 'Tis my job tae ken whit goes on in Loch Ness."

"And how do you know it was a female?"

"A guid guess, that's all."

I didn't believe him. "Why didn't you mention any of this in court?"

"Well then, naebody asked me, did they, so stuff them, says I. As for bein' there in the first place, yer faither's bastard barrister sup'ineed me. I said what I had tae, but far as I'm concerned, he can burn in Hell if he thinks any o' us wearin' the tartan'll support Angus's nonsense."

"Then I take it you don't believe my father's story?"

"Nor dae ye, but no' 'cause o' whit I said. So keep at it, young Wallace, yer daein' fine. An' ye're right in focusin' on the Loch as a whole, for the answers tae a' ye seek lie here, no' in chasin' ghosts. But be fair warned, when it comes tae Loch Ness trust nae one, for there's far mair at stake than ye can possibly imagine."

"If you know so much then help me."

He shook his head. "I cannae dae that, laddie. I've taken a blood oath, dae ye ken whit I mean?"

"No, I don't ken . . . I don't understand. If there's so much at stake—"

"My grandfaither, God rest his soul, wis John Reid Forrest. His mother wis Clan Stewart, his wife, my mum, Clan MacDonald."

Message received. The Forrests were descendants from two of the largest clans in the Highlands. I'd sooner budge a mountain than move Calum Forrest. "And the Black Knights? Were they also part of your heritage?"

"Black Knights? Never heard o' them." He accelerated across the Bona Narrows, barely avoiding a tree stump.

"What separates the Black Knights from the rest of the Templar, Mr. Forrest? What's their mission?"

Calum yanked back on the throttle, then pushed his face in mine, so close I could taste his last meal under his breath. "I dinnae ken nothin' aboot no Black Knights, see, an' dinnae ask me that again."

We rode in silence until we reached the western shore. The old man wiped spray from his brow, then thought for a long moment. "Tell me, lad, have ye been salmon fishin' since ye've been back?"

"Salmon fishing? No. Why? Catch any big ones lately?"

"Naw. I've been too busy wi' a' this trial nonsense. One o' these days, I'll have tae get ower tae their spawnin' grounds an' have a wee look. Or maybe ye should have a look, aye?"

His eyes held mine, ensuring the message was delivered, then he guided us closer to shore, throttling back as the hull scrapped against the shallows.

"Go wi' God, young Wallace. May Sir William's courage flourish in yer heart."

I jumped down to the beach, then watched him speed away without so much as a nod.

I was back in Lochend, the tranquillity of the Great Glen lost amidst the heavy traffic of the A82 at my back. To the south, Loch Ness's waters reached across the valley like the shadow of a giant serpent. Her black waves lapped at my feet, and her distant thunder rumbled above her mountains, threatening an evening shower.

At that moment, I felt like Dorothy, lost in the land of Oz. Calum Forrest was my Scarecrow, pointing me toward the yellow brick road, warning me to ignore the wicked witch and stay focused on the path that lay ahead. Yet what he wasn't saying seemed more important than what he was. Surrounded by clues, I was homing in on the truth, but still couldn't see the forest for the trees.

Calum Forrest. Blood of the MacDonald and Stewart clans, and no doubt a member of the Black Knights. He knows what Nessie is, but as a Black Knight, he can't say. Still, as water bailiff, it's his sworn duty to protect the Loch, but that's causing a conflict with his blood oath to the Black Knights.

"So he's reaching out to me, hoping I'll resolve the problem for him."

As if in response, the heavens growled, unleashing a flash of white lightning that disappeared over Aldourie Castle.

"Okay, Dorothy, time to find the wizard."

Wait . . . what was it Calum said about salmon? The spawning grounds . . . he wanted me to take a look.

Tightening the straps of my backpack, I jogged south, hoping to make it to Brackla and the Clansman Hotel before being struck by lightning.

Clansman Hotel
Brackla
7:45 P.M.

Vietnam veteran Pete Lindner sat on the transom of his seventeen-meter cruise ship, *Wiley*, keeping an eye on the weather as he finished off the last of his prawns and white wine. Two years earlier, the former billing manager at Verizon had taken an early retirement when Jonathan Deval, an old war buddy in the Royal Navy, had offered him a partnership in his Great Glen touring business. Since then, Lindner had spent his winters in New York with the grandkids and his summers in the Highlands, ferrying passengers up and down the Caledonian Canal from Fort William to Inverness.

But recent events had forced a change in plans. The business was clearly in Loch Ness, and the profits were too high to be wasting time and fuel trekking back and forth all the way to Fort William. So Lindner told his partner he'd stay put in the Loch, riding the tourism wave as long as he could, even if it meant mooring off Cherry Island.

Locating an open berth at the Clansman was sheer luck, tougher than finding a parking space in Manhattan.

Lindner finished off another prawn as a rental car screeched to a halt in the adjacent parking lot. Three men exited the vehicle, all in their early thirties, their laughter egged on by the alcohol moving through their bloodstream.

The leader and oldest of the three was an American named Chuck Jones, a talented musician who had once toured with Lynyrd Skynyrd. Jones was on hiatus from his job in law enforcement, forced to the sidelines because of a severe neck injury. The man who had planned the vacation was his cousin, Ron Casey, who also worked for the police, but as a crime scene photographer. The youngest of the trio, Chad Brager, was a former USC ice hockey defenseman and Ron Casey's best friend. The three had been on holiday in London when word of the Nessie attacks had broken. A road accident, a brainstorming session, and a quick shopping spree provided them with equipment and a plan.

Chuck Jones popped the trunk of the rental car, stepping aside to allow his more adept buddies to struggle with a heavy burlap bag and what looked like the carrying case for a trumpet.

Amused, Lindner watched as the three made their way onto the pier, stopping at berth after berth to negotiate with the local boat captains. In succession, each shook his head no, forcing the Americans to continue their search.

Eventually they came to the *Wiley*.

"Evenin'," said Jones. "That's a fine boat you've got there. Twin diesels. Hydraulic stabilizers. Classic displacement. Bet she's a steady ride."

"Think you know your boats, do you?"

Chad Brager smiled. "A fellow American, thank God. I swear, I can't understand half the things these Highlanders say."

Lindner nodded. "So boys, what're you up to?"

"Actually," said Jones, "we were hoping to do some night fishing."

"I'm a cruise ship, not a charter. What's in the burlap bag?"

"Bait." The Americans laughed.

Jones leaned in closer. "We don't really need a charter, what we want is to do a little night trolling. You know, maybe catch Nessie on film."

Lindner sipped his wine, half-concealing his grin. "Show me what's in the burlap bag."

Jones nodded to Brager, who untied the canvass, revealing a dead sheep, its hindquarters broken and disfigured. "Local farmer sold it to us. Said a tourist backed over it this morning as he pulled out of a lay-by."

Jones pointed to the transom. "We've brought plenty of cable. Be easy to rig to your boat."

Lindner chuckled. "Boys, there's thousands of people lining the banks of Loch Ness trying to photograph this creature. What makes you think you're gonna capture it on film, and at night, no less?"

"I'm a professional photographer," Ron Casey said, patting his carrying case. "Do most of my work at night. Even with the cloud cover, we'll have a nice full moon in a few hours, with plenty of light to do some long exposures."

"We've got the bait, that's half the battle." Jones said, growing serious. "We're willing to pay a little extra . . . if you can handle the pressure."

"Save the psychology, I'm immune." Lindner looked them over, estimating their worth. "Four hundred for the night, and that's pounds, not dollars. Plus I get 10 percent of anything you make from these photos, assuming you get lucky."

"Ten percent?" Chad shook his head. "No sale."

Jones checked his wallet for cash. "Tell you what, we'll bump it to four-fifty, but you'll get nothing from the photos."

Lindner drained the rest of his wine, casually glancing at the weather. Though the Loch was still smooth, the wind was picking up. With any luck, the rain would come, and it'd be an early night.

"Okay, gentlemen, but I wanna see cash up front. And keep that dead animal in its bag until after we hit deep water. I don't need the water bailiff hassling me."

Clansman Hotel
10:45 P.M.

The full moon was just peaking over the eastern mountains by the time I staggered up the tarmac leading into the Clansman Hotel. I called True on my cell phone, leaving him a message to meet me in the lobby as soon as he could. I was tired and sore and hungry, and I smelled something awful, plus my skin itched from dried peat. Heading inside, I figured I'd use the public rest room, clean myself up a bit, then get some take-out food while I waited.

Bad move.

The banquet room was cordoned off for a private party, packed with celebrities and media and local officials.

I approached the maitre d', who looked at me like I had just crawled out of a sewer. "Sorry, sir, this is invitation only."

"That's okay, I just want to order some takeout. Where can I—"

"This is the Clansman Hotel, sir, no' a McDonald's. Why don't ye try a local farmhouse."

"Zachary Wallace!"

It was David Caldwell, dressed in a tuxedo, surrounded by reporters. He approached with his entourage, wasting no time in baiting me. "Jesus, Zack, you smell like something the cow just shit. What've you been doing for work since the University fired you? Cleaning outhouses?"

My mind screamed at me to walk away, but my ego, ignoring the left side of my brain, instead chose to step in the proffered dung. "David, how's your face?"

"Bruises heal, Zack. Too bad the same doesn't apply to damaged reputations."

"Don't worry. It won't be long before the locals see you for the phony you are."

"Days, Zack. In a few days I'll have captured a legend, and you'll be nothing more than a speed bump on my road to fame and fortune."

He turned to his right and waved. "Over here, babe."

My eyes widened as Brandy approached. She was wearing an ebony cocktail dress with a plunging neckline that revealed the swell of her deeply tanned breasts. She moved like she knew she belonged.

"Brandy, you've met my former colleague, Zachary Wallace."

"Aye, though I've smelled him in better days. Did ye get lost on the moors then, Zack?"

My mind searched for a witty retort.

"Maybe."

Brilliant.

Brandy slipped her arm around David's waist, her accent straining to be more American than Scottish. "So, have you heard? David's selected the *Nessie III* to be the lead vessel in his quest to capture the monster. We'll be spending quite a lot of time together."

The Gael in my blood boiled. "Yeah? Well this time, I hope you're heavily insured."

That one put the fury of the Highlands back in her. "At least I willnae be havin' tae worry about bunkin' down alone at night."

David smirked. "Brandy told me about that whole impotence thing. Geez, Zack, tough break. I can only thank God I don't have that kind of problem." He winked, patting Brandy's buttocks. "If you see the *Nessie III* rockin', don't come a-knockin.'"

I leaped for him, fingers splayed, aiming to crush his birdlike windpipe—only I forgot about that cursed velvet rope.

My knees caught and, unable to right my balance beneath the weight of my backpack, I fell face-first to the floor.

David stepped back and laughed. Patrons circled, a few photographers even snapping pictures. Before I could react, I was lifted off the floor by two large security guards and physically escorted out the rear exit.

Loch Ness
12:02 A.M.

The moon was high in the midnight sky, its rays filtered behind a thin veil of cirrus clouds.

Ron Casey stood behind the *Wiley's* transom, his camera poised atop the Bogen Manfrotto wilderness-style tripod. He rubbed at his eyes, tired after four hours of peering through the Nikon F3HP. Through the 300mm f4.5 telephoto lens, he could still see the dead sheep as it bounded along the surface, several hundred feet off the stern. One end of the heavy-steel cable had been rigged to a cleat located behind the twin engines' mount, the other was attached to their bait. Chuck had slit the animal's belly open just before he'd released it, and in the near-perfect nocturnal light and powerful zoom lens, Casey could just make out what remained of the sheep's floating entrails.

What Chuck and Ron had failed to mention to the *Wiley's* captain was that the cable was attached to the carcass by a seven-inch steel hook, its barbed end threaded between the sheep's rib cage and out its mouth.

Chad Brager drained the rest of his beer and belched. "So? Still floating?"

"Barely. I'll wait a few more minutes before I shoot another series of 30-second exposures."

"You sure this high-speed film'll work?"

"I'm not using it, I told you that three hours ago. Faster speeds aren't better for long exposures, the images come out too grainy. Drink your beer, I know what I'm doing."

Chuck Jones leaned in to whisper. "Forget that nonsense, I'm out to hook that sum'bitch. You guys can take all the photos you want after we haul its dead ass back to port."

"Yeah, well I'd settle for one blurred shot at this point. You sure this captain knows what he's doing?"

"Let's find out."

Jones stumbled forward, entering the pilothouse. "So what's the story, skipper? Been four frickin' hours and we still haven't seen a goldfish on that fish finder of yours. You sure that thing's working?"

"It's working fine. Maybe that full-proof bait of yours is scaring the fish away."

"Or maybe we should try another spot?"

"It's your money, I just figured you'd want to create a nice scent trail." Lindner pointed to the ship's navigational console and a real-time GPS chart representing Loch Ness. "We've been cruising back and forth between Brackla and Urquhart Bay. The area's a hot spot for Nessie sightings. Better to keep the scent strong in one locale . . . unless you think otherwise."

"No, guess that makes sense. Hey, what're all these bright objects on your screen?"

"Sonar buoys. Power pack gives off thermal radiation. The Loch's lined with 'em now, but I don't think they've become active yet. Just as well. All that pinging scares away the big fish."

Clansman Wharf
12:20 A.M.

Dr. Michael Newman, associate director at the National Institute of Standards and Technology, waited impatiently on the dock as two local delivery men stacked the last of the seven aluminum crates into the

Nessie III's pilothouse. Newman scrawled his name in triplicate on the offered invoice, then turned as David Caldwell and the local woman made their way, arm in arm, toward the berth.

"Ah, there's Dr. Newman now. So, Doctor, is everything hooked up and ready to go?"

"No, everything's not hooked up and ready to go. The equipment just arrived, it took six hours just to get it out of customs, and another two hours to find a delivery company, all of which *you* were supposed to handle. We need to speak."

"Speak."

"In private."

"It's okay," Brandy said, "I'll see ye on board." As the two men watched, she removed her spiked heels, hitched up her dress, then climbed over the rail.

David watched her climb aboard the *Nessie III*. "God, what a package. So Newman, what's up?"

"I can see what's up. Look, Caldwell, when you came to the NIST seeking help, we agreed to lend you our equipment, not risk it."

"How are you risking it?"

"Are you kidding? This boat's older than dirt and about as buoyant. The engine's on its last legs, the interior's way too small for our needs, the electrical system's been hot-wired and it's totally inadequate, the bilge pump's shot, and I've seen logs with better stability."

"Yes, but you're forgetting the importance of keeping the locals involved. It's good PR, plus it opens doors."

"I know what door it's opening. I've also seen plenty of local fishing boats that would easily meet our needs."

"Maybe, but I'm dealing with television and the global media, and the *Nessie III*'s owner's got a body on her that can boil water."

Newman slammed his clipboard against a piling. "Listen here, Caldwell, I will not risk tens of thousands of dollars worth of state-of-the-art sonar equipment just so you can get laid."

"Shh, geez, calm down. Look, first thing in the morning, I'll get the Inverness Council guy to requisition a new generator. That'll solve your power needs, the rest we'll figure out as we go."

"This is ridiculous."

"It'll all work out, trust me. Meanwhile, go check in. Order some room service and a movie or something, then get some sleep. I'll see you in the morning."

12:25 A.M.

I remained hidden beneath a grove of pine trees, watching David converse with his obviously agitated companion.

He was not the only one who was seething.

First, David had used me as a scapegoat, costing me my job with FAU. Then my so-called colleague had taken credit for my *Architeuthis* lure at his press conference.

Now he was stealing my girl!

Okay, maybe Brandy wasn't exactly my girl, but she certainly didn't belong with that scumbag.

I ground my teeth, watching as the man David had been talking to left Brandy's boat and headed down the dock to the hotel. David waved half-heartedly, then climbed aboard the *Nessie III.*

"Look at that cocky bastard. Now he thinks he's gonna sleep with her."

I pulled out my cell phone and tried calling True again, but there was still no answer at the lodge. *Probably getting hammered at Sniddles.*

Or maybe it's a sign, the right side of my brain whispered to me. *Don't just sit around and let this candy-ass move in on your girl. Get off your butt and do something about it!*

Leaving my backpack beneath the trees, I hurried down the hill, then crept quietly onto the pier.

Loch Ness
12:32 A.M.

Pete Lindner's heart jumped a few beats as the red blip materialized on his fish finder. "Hey . . . hey!" He banged on the back window of his pilothouse, getting Chad Brager's attention. "We've got company."

Brager hurried into the pilothouse. "What is it?"

"Hard to tell. Look for yourself." He pointed to the screen where a red blip was shadowing the *Wiley*. "It's pretty deep, two, maybe three hundred feet down and still a ways back, but we've got its attention."

"Jesus. How big's this thing?"

"Big, too big, which is why you shouldn't get too excited yet. It's probably just a school of char, they like it about those depths. Just the same, tell your photographer buddy to keep shooting, maybe he'll get lucky."

Chad hurried from the pilothouse and returned to the stern. "Captain says there's something big following the bait. It's either a school of fish, or . . . "

"Yeah!" Jones pumped his fists. "A hundred and fifty thousand pounds. What's that in dollars, Casey?"

"Who cares? Will you quit jumping!" Casey hunched over his camera, his right thumb pressed against the free end of the cable lock, keeping the telephoto lens open. "Damn it, we're starting to bounce again. Chad, go tell the captain to cut his speed."

"What am I, your errand boy?"

"Just do it."

Ron Casey returned his right eye to the telephoto lens. As he watched, the bait suddenly disappeared.

"Whoa."

"Whoa what?"

"Either our bait sank, or it was just snatched."

"Look!" Jones pointed to the length of steel cable as it strained against the cleat. "We hooked it, baby!"

Fiberglass moaned, then began cracking along the edges of the cleat.

Casey looked at Jones, a lump in his throat. "I thought you said this boat could handle a big load?"

"It can, I mean it should. The monster must've gone deep. Maybe the—"

Captain Lindner bounded from the pilothouse. "What the hell's going on back here?"

Casey pointed to the line. "We think we hooked Nessie."

"Hooked? You never said anything about catching it!"

The boat lurched, causing the tripod to tip.

Casey caught the camera as the stern dipped hard to starboard.

The captain fell sideways against one of the outboards, then held on tightly as he examined the cleat. "Are you assholes crazy? The transom's not made to drag this kind of weight."

The boat rolled back to port, the steel cable catching the starboard engine's propeller, sheering off two of its blades.

"Son of a bitch! I just had that prop rebuilt!" The captain hurried back to the pilothouse, Chuck Jones trailing.

"Skipper, relax, you're about to be famous. All we have to do is haul this monster in, and we'll have enough money to buy you a dozen new props."

Lindner shut down the starboard engine, then pushed down on the port throttle, his vessel straining to move against the ungodly force. "Haul it, Mr. Jones? Haul it where?"

"Into the shallows. The Bona Narrows."

"By the time we reach the narrows, this boat'll be kindling."

The vessel rolled hard to starboard again, sending both men caroming across the navigational console.

The captain grabbed hold of the wheel, yanking it hard to port. Pushing down on the throttle, he accelerated, his lone engine fighting to achieve six knots. "Your plan's got a few holes in it, hotshot. For one, whatever you hooked weighs more than my whole damn boat. For another, it ain't too crazy about having a hook in its mouth."

A *screech* of wrenching steel pierced the night as the cleat and part of the transom wall behind the outboard motors began peeling away from the hull's mainframe.

"Christ, it's tearing my vessel apart!" The captain grabbed the radio. "Mayday, Mayday, this is the *Wiley!* Mayday . . ."

Clansman Wharf
12:57 A.M.

Having made it to the *Nessie III's* berth, I hid behind a piling to listen. I could hear voices belowdecks, but they were muffled.

Seeking a better vantage, I climbed over the rail, creeping forward into the pilothouse.

The tiny cabin was crammed with aluminum equipment cases, stacked high along the back wall, partially covered by a gray tarp. Curious, I pulled back the covering, reading one of the invoice tags in the dim light.

UHF Master Radio Link. Property of NIST.

It was equipment for the sonar arrays' master analysis station.
". . . David, stop!"

Hearing Brandy's voice, I dropped to my knees and pressed my ear to the deck.

*   *   *

"What's wrong?" David cooed.

"Slow down a wee bit, I'm no' yer whore!"

"Whore? Brandy, you and me, we're a team, partners on a great adventure. When viewers see me, they'll see you. That's the association I'm going for . . . unless you aren't up to it? I mean, if that's the case, tell me now, because there must've been a hundred applicants dying to be my partner on this gig, but I picked you."

"Why? So ye could get intae my knickers?"

"Of course not. You and me, we have a chemistry. I know you feel it, too, don't you, babe?"

I clenched my fists, ready to storm her cabin.

"Maybe if ye'd slow down a bit, I'd feel it more, yeah?"

"Okay, I'll slow down, but this is the fast track to stardom. You and me, we're gonna be famous. We'll be Hollywood's next power couple. You, uh, do want that, don't you?"

My veins burned as I heard them moaning and kissing.

And then I heard something else—a mob of people, running down the pier.

It was the captains and crew of the three research vessels, all hurrying to make way. A dozen more civilians were heading for the *Nessie III*, led by the Highland provost.

I was trapped.

Wedging myself into the far back corner of the pilothouse, I dragged the metal cases around me to form a blind, then draped the gray tarp over the top of the stacks.

"Dr. Caldwell! Dr. Caldwell, are ye aboard?"

I heard David stumble up the stairs. "This really isn't a good time, Owen."

"We jist received a Mayday call from a local cruise ship. They claim they've hooked Nessie!"

From a slit between the stacks I saw Brandy dart inside the pilothouse, her shapely legs exposed clear up to the tail of David's dress shirt, which barely covered her buttocks.

The engine sputtered twice, belched a cloud of noxious fumes, then chortled, rattling my skull against the back wall. David entered the pilothouse, shirtless, followed by Owen Hollifield, who barked out orders to Brandy. "Head south, their last reported position wis jist north of Urquhart Bay."

Loch Ness
1:09 A.M.

The notion that maybe they'd made a big mistake was firmly planted in Ron Casey's mind as he watched sections of plank tear away from the transom, the rotting fibers disguised behind a fresh coat of paint.

"Chad, hit it again!"

Exhaust billowed from the port outboard as Chad Brager took another whack at the steel cable with the hand axe. "No good, I can't get any leverage, it just keeps bouncing off. If we can . . ."

Chad paused, he and Ron staring at the cable, which had suddenly gone slack. "What happened?"

"Don't know. Either the cable snapped underwater, or . . ."

Free of its biological anchor, the *Wiley* leaped forward and accelerated.

Chad and Ron looked at one another, unsure, then backed away from the transom, their eyes searching the water.

*   *   *

Chuck Jones leaned over the captain's shoulder, staring at the red blip chasing after them on the fish finder. "What do you mean it's rising?"

"Look for yourself, hotshot. It can't free itself by going deep, so now it's coming after us."

The captain stared at the fish finder's depth gauge as its numbers rapidly spun backwards . . . 43 meters . . . 29 meters . . . 14 meters . . .

"Sweet Jesus . . . hold on!"

Captain Lindner veered hard to port.

Wha-boom! The starboard flank exploded out of the water as if struck by a tank, the blow driving the already listing boat beyond its center of gravity.

The vessel rolled, sending its captain falling sideways as a wall of frigid black water burst through the pilothouse windows. He tumbled in blindness, unable to right himself as the *Wiley* continued to roll hard to port, seeking its new equilibrium.

Wood and steel groaned in his ears, was muffled, and then the pilothouse settled underwater beneath its breached hull.

The captain pulled himself to his feet, stunned to see the inverted pilothouse filling rapidly with water. Heart pounding, his hands and arms burning from the cold, he pressed his face to the floorboards above his head and sucked in several desperate breaths of air, his mind racing.

Sparks of light sizzled in protest along the navigational consoles. Cans of beer free-floated past his face, startling him in the darkening cabin. The water level continued rising, forcing him to swim in order to breathe. Somewhere below his kicking feet was the ceiling and the sound of a creaking door—his escape route.

Below and to the right.

Captain Lindner ducked his head and kicked for the cabin door. Feeling for the knob, he managed to push it open, then froze.

It was passing beneath the boat, its form revealed in the moonlight. The thickly muscled back was chocolate brown in color, adorned with a horsehair dorsal fin that tapered back to a finless rounded tail. As long and wide as two tour buses connected end to end, the creature moved left, then right, left, then right as it swam, twisting with snakelike undulations.

It passed quickly, and though he had just missed seeing its head, Pete Lindner knew he had seen a sea serpent, as cold as the devil, as ancient as time itself.

His heart thundered in his chest and his lungs threatened to burst, but still the captain refused to venture out, intent on giving the dreadful animal another twenty seconds to vacate the area.

Instead, the cabin, along with his exit, spun counterclockwise and out from under him, and then the capsized boat lurched forward, dragged stern-first through the water by the powerful creature still leashed to its transom.

Trapped underwater, enveloped in darkness, Lindner groped at the suddenly alien walls, desperate to relocate an air pocket that no longer existed. His palms banged awkwardly against the inverted forward windshield, and then he gagged, belching bubbles as he fought blindly to untangle himself from the languid remains of Chuck Jones.

Unable to reason, unable to see, he clawed in ever-tightening circles, fumbling through the suffocating blackness for an exit.

Spent lungs expelled primal gurgles.

Arms stopped moving, eyes ceased seeing.

Silence took the *Wiley* as the Loch's icy claws reached out once more to claim its dead.

*   *   *

Chad Brager surfaced fifty feet from the capsized boat. Years of playing ice hockey on frozen lakes had acclimated him to the sudden cold, and his lifeguard training at USC kept him from panicking. Treading water, he called out for his companions.

"Chucky! Ron!"

Steam dissipated from his head, his body losing heat rapidly.

Gotta get out of this cold water before hypothermia sets in.

He turned to swim back to the boat, then realized the capsized hull was spinning, the boat moving towards him!

"Oh shit . . ."

Brager turned and swam, his arms and legs barely moving through the layers of clothing. Pausing, he forcibly yanked off his shoes, allowing himself a quick glance back.

The boat's hull was coming at him stern first now, the fractured transom and its cursed steel cable just visible above the waterline.

Brager tore off his windbreaker jacket, then launched himself into a rapid crawl stroke.

Two hundred feet . . . it's got two hundred feet of goddam cable!

His heart jumped as he registered the gunshot *twang* of snapping steel line––its echo as clear as the opening trapdoor of a gallows.

A dam-bursting wave of adrenaline ignited Brager's muscles, propelling him through the water—even as searing pain ignited his half-frozen nerve cells as he was jolted forward . . . then mercifully released from consciousness, his spine crushed and severed, his torso savagely ripped apart and swallowed.

*   *   *

The *Nessie III* slowed.

I stood quietly, nudging the tarp away so I could see.

The *Nothosaur* had arrived first, judging by its proximity to the capsized boat. The other two vessels circled close by, their spotlights aimed at the black water.

David fumbled with the radio, Brandy finally grabbing it from him. "*Nothosaur*, this is the *Nessie III*. Come in."

"This is Hoagland. We were too late. Three bodies went into the water, the *Galon's* recovered the lone survivor. He's babbling, but in shock. A chopper's flying in to transport him to Inverness."

David took the microphone. "Hoagland, this is Caldwell. Did he say what happened to the others?"

"Negative, but we found the remains of a forearm floating in a jacket sleeve. I think we can assume the rest of him's warming the belly of our friend."

I slumped to the deck, bile rising towards the lump in my throat. *And there, but for the grace of God, go I . . .*

"As an M.I.T. trained scientist and inventor, I had always been intrigued about the possibilities of using modern technology to resolve the mystery of Loch Ness.

Dr. Charlie Wyckoff and I began our search back in 1970, but a full two years would pass before our first sighting. We were standing on shore, above Urquhart's Castle, when a hump surfaced in Urquhart Bay. Through my telescope, I saw something that resembled the back of an elephant. I could make out its crest and estimated the hump was at least twenty-five-feet long and four feet out of the water. I managed to get some footage of what looked like a blob on the water, but the photos all turned out blurry."

—Dr. Robert Rines, Academy of Applied Sciences Member: American Inventor's Hall of Fame

CHAPTER 23

Loch Ness

THE *NESSIE III* REMAINED in the area another two hours until the sun rose, by which time my bladder had inflated like a hot-water bottle.

Brandy docked. David kissed her good-bye, he and the provost heading off to prepare for yet another press conference. I waited until she went below, then climbed from my makeshift hiding place and crept out of the pilothouse onto the main deck.

"I was wonderin' when ye'd be leavin'?"

Startled, I turned, Brandy now dressed in a lavender bathrobe.

"You knew?"

She leaned back casually against the stern rail, arms folded against her chest. "I smelled ye the moment we stopped movin'."

"Why didn't you say anything?"

"I figured ye'd a'ready made enough o' an arse out o' yersel' for one evenin'. Still afraid o' the water, are ye?"

"Your brother has a big mouth."

"An' *you* should've said somethin'. Ye think ye're the only one stricken by a phobia?" She parted her robe, showing me an exquisitely tanned leg, the inner thigh blemished by a series of zig-zagging white scars. "When depression hit, I turned tae hurtin' mysel'. Sort o' gives all new meanin' to the term, shavin' yer legs."

"But you got over it?"

"I control it, that's all. Pills take the edge away, but the fear's always there. It sort o' lurks on the periphery, waitin' for me tae let my guard down."

I nodded. "I think I'm more angry now than scared. Guess that's an improvement."

"No' necessarily. Anger's a double-edged sword. While it gives ye the strength tae hunt one monster, it can turn ye intae another."

"Meaning?"

"Now's no' the time."

"No, go on. Finish."

"Okay then. The Zachary Wallace I knew never resorted tae usin' his fists tae make a point. Angus Wallace, on the other hand . . ."

"David's way out of line."

"That's Angus's ego talkin'."

"Brandy, I'm not about to let David destroy my life."

"Seems yer life was sufferin' long before David Caldwell ever came along."

"And you put it in my face. Why him, Brandy? Of all people, why get involved with him?"

"Look at me, Zachary. My boat's fallin' apart, I'm barely survivin', an' I've no money nor savings nor rich parents to borrow from. Bad enough I'm alone, but tae face the coming winter wi' no means tae live? David's job, it pays more in one day than I can earn in a good week."

"And in exchange, you're sleeping with him."

Her eyes angered. Stepping closer, she struck me hard in the chest with the heel of her palms. "First off, mister, I am no' a whore. Second, I'll sleep wi' who I please, when I please, an' it's none o' yer damn business!"

Glancing over my shoulder, she spotted David, Owen Hollifeld, and the engineer from NIST approaching along the pier.

"Ye need tae leave."

"Look, I'm sorry—"

"Did ye no' hear me? Get off my boat. Go on!" She pushed me toward the rail.

I climbed down just as David reached the berth. "What's all this?"

"He was lookin' for ye," Brandy lied. "Had tae threaten tae arrest him for trespassin' before he'd leave."

The NIST engineer hurried on board to check his equipment. The provost got in my face. "We're no' gonnae have any trouble from ye, are we Dr. Wallace?"

"I was just leaving."

"Good," David chirped. "I hear there's a nice vacant cell next to your father's."

I raised my hands, slowly backing away. "I was just making conversation with the lady. Do whatever you have to do to catch your monster, but you'd better think twice before you hurt Brandy, that's all I've got to say."

I walked away, the veins in my neck throbbing, my inflated ego shunting off any remaining whispers coming from the left side of my brain—

"Hey, *Angus!*"

—my psyche deflating once more as Brandy buried her open mouth against David's.

Inverness Castle

"Well, whit did ye expect?" said Angus, finishing his Scotch broth soup and chips. "Ne'er mess wi' a Scots livelihood, especially a woman's. Brandy kens whit she's doin', believe you me."

"I love her."

"Love? Ah, that's jist yer knob talkin'. B'sides, there's plenty o' fish in the sea. Last thing ye need is tae be hitchin' up wi' a MacDonald."

I shook my head, wondering how I'd sunk so low as to be asking advice about women from my father.

"So, lad, tell me again about this latest attack."

"I told you all I know. According to the papers, the American photographer's still in a coma."

"But he lost the camera?"

"Yes."

"Bollocks. My trial restarts next week. While every Nessie encounter pushes me that much closer tae freedom, Maxie says it's still no' enough. I need yer help here, son."

"Son? Not Alice or Deirdre? Why am I your son when you need something?"

"Point taken. Now when will ye go after this thing?"

"Not until I know more about it."

"Ugh . . . ye're wastin' valuable time. Whit else is there tae ken aboot it?"

"For starters, why did a benign fish-eating creature suddenly add red meat to its diet?"

"An' how dae ye expect tae learn that oot?"

"I don't know, seeing as how the Sheriff's lab conveniently managed to lose all the specimens I collected. Guess I'll just have to get more." I stood, heading down the corridor. "We'll talk in a few days. I wanna check out the salmon-spawning grounds."

"The spawnin' grounds? Zachary, wait! Forget the spawnin' grounds, laddie, ye're jist wastin' whit little time I've got left. Zack, are ye listenin' tae me? We need proof, real proof that this thing is oot there an' that it's killed folk. Call Theresa, she'll—"

"For the last time, I'm not interested in speaking with Johnny C.'s widow, or for that matter, any other woman you've shared bodily fluids with."

Pushing past the guards, I left the holding area and trudged up the dungeon's winding stone stairwell, the echoes of my father's rants following me until I reached the castle's ground floor.

Aboard the *Nessie III*:

An exhausted Michael Newman limped out of the *Nessie III*'s cramped pilothouse, desperate to stretch his aching back. For the last six hours he had sat behind the makeshift wooden desk bolted to the pilothouse decking, attempting to patch together a working sonar grid. Each of the thirty-four sonar buoys floating in Loch Ness had to be recalibrated so that data transmissions could be received and analyzed, and in many cases, Newman had to order a less-than-pleased boat captain back out to reposition his vessel's buoys. Just when it finally seemed the NIST engineer had his grid up and working, the *Nessie III*'s new generator had conked out, shutting down his GPS receiver, sending his blood pressure soaring.

It had taken him the rest of the afternoon to fix the problem, and now Newman's lower vertebrae felt as if someone had been twisting them with a monkey wrench. "Caldwell! Wake up and get in here."

David, asleep on a chaise lounge chair, opened his eyes. "We up and running?"

"We're up. Come in and I'll show you how it works, then I'm done. My back can't handle another minute of this."

David followed him inside.

"Now pay attention . . . and don't drip suntan oil on my equipment! See this monitor on the left? Hit Control-M and it displays your grid."

Newman typed in the command, displaying a GPS satellite view of Loch Ness, divided by grid lines. "The Loch's so long that I had to divide the screen into three sonar zones." Newman clicked on an area with his mouse. "There's your north display, central . . . and south. Use the mouse to zoom in and out."

"The grid's active?"

"All sonar buoys are active and pinging as of ten minutes ago. I set the target strength to report and record any objects larger than a sea turtle. If something large crosses the array's acoustical beam, an alarm will sound, and the targeted info will appear on this second screen."

"Good, great . . . so where's the monster? If the array's active—"

"It's active, but that doesn't mean there aren't dead zones. We're dealing with a cold-water trowel that's over eight-hundred feet deep. Even pinging the hell out of it, you'll still have geological anomalies and pockets around the shoreline that'll remain cloaked."

"Okay. So how much isn't cloaked?"

"Best guess? Between 85 and 90 percent, and that's about as good as it gets without one signal interfering with another. It took me all day and evening to get the array set, so you tell those boat captains of yours they'd better not move or add another buoy to the field, or I'll personally feed them to the monster. And another thing, warn your girlfriend I'd better not find that new generator being used for anything but the sonar control station. If she so much as plugs a hair dryer into that machine, I'm leaving and taking my equipment with me."

"Know what, dude, you need to lighten up."

"What I need is a chiropractor and bed. So good hunting and good night. If you need me, don't call until morning."

Newman exited the pilothouse, then limped off toward the Clansman Hotel.

Invermoriston

It was late in the day by the time I arrived along the banks of the River Moriston.

The rivers of the Great Glen that feed Loch Ness also serve as autumn spawning grounds for the Atlantic salmon. As the waters warm toward the end of April, the salmon begin their seasonal run from the Moray Firth south through the River Ness into Loch Ness, eventually making their way up the rivers and streams to lay their eggs.

The River Moriston had a well-earned reputation as a popular salmon area. Each spring and summer, visitors watched from lookout posts as the big females leaped out of the water, struggling to make their way up the Falls of Invermoristion, leading into the calmer breeding pools.

Salmon lay eggs by the tens of thousands, producing young fish, known as parr. Once hatched, the parr consume their egg sacs, beginning what will be an annual eight-inch growth spurt. It takes about two years for the fish to become smolts, a time when bodily changes prepare them for their eventual return to the sea. Salmon grow even more rapidly in salt water, and by the time they reenter Loch Ness as adults, they may weigh as much as forty pounds.

After a steady hour of hiking parallel to the river, I came to a rocky area where the Moriston climbed steeply. Setting down my backpack, I situated myself atop a nice-sized boulder and took in the beauty of the falls, my mind wandering.

Angus had testified that John Cialino had been swarmed by a school of salmon just before he'd been attacked by the monster. While it was not unusual to see salmon along the surface, I still remained skeptical, especially when it came to the creature's diet. For one thing, salmon were epilimnion, meaning they preferred to inhabit the upper regions of Loch Ness. If the creature fed solely on salmon, there'd have been far more surface sightings over the years.

Then again, it had been a school of salmon that surrounded yours truly when I'd been bitten seventeen years ago.

Still, I reasoned the predator I was after preferred charr or pike or even Anguilla eels. Charr were migratory fish, smaller than salmon but far more numerous, and they inhabited the deeper regions of the Loch. Pike were also deep-water fish and grew as large as three feet in length, but did not exist in vast numbers in Loch Ness. Anguilla, on the other hand, not only grew in excess of eight feet and several hundred pounds, but were known to prefer the depths, suspending themselves vertically off the bottom of the Loch. Anguilla had poor eyesight and hunted by smell, but only frequented Loch Ness during the spring and summer months when the water warmed.

And yet Calum Forrest had specifically directed me to the salmon-spawning grounds.

I checked my watch. An hour had passed, and yet I still hadn't seen a single salmon leap the falls.

My cell phone rang. It was True.

"Zack? I stopped by Inverness Castle, but ye'd a'ready left. Angus . . . he says ye're headin' for the salmon burns?"

"I'm already here."

"An' where's here?"

"The forest, just west of Glenmoriston."

"Okay, I'll come and fetch ye."

"Don't bother. It's kind of nice here, peaceful. Besides, I still want to do some exploring, maybe take a few specimens. I'll probably just camp here for the night."

"Zack, have ye lost yer mind? The monster killed no' far frae there only last week."

"I'm much farther inland, in high ground. I'll be fine."

"Zack—"

"We'll meet tomorrow morning back at the lodge. See you then."

I powered off the cell phone, then left the boulder and headed farther upstream, looking for a suitable place to make camp.

Inverness

As chief prosecutor in the Angus Wallace murder trial, Mitchell Obrecht had been feeling pressure from his superiors ever since the defendant had dropped his "Nessie bomb" in court. Experience alone told Obrecht that Angus was lying, but with each subsequent attack, the chances of winning a conviction—and salvaging his career—appeared to be a diminishing prospect.

It was Obrecht who had persuaded the judge to take a two-week continuance, knowing he needed more time to prove Angus Wallace had planned his entire over-the-top defense. The good news was that Wallace's defense opened the door for the prosecution to prove John Cialiano's murder had been premeditated. The bad news, the sudden difficulty in separating the monster's unprecedented rampage with Johnny C.'s murder.

Obrecht looked up as his assistant, Jennifer Shaw, entered the office, carrying a thick brief.

"I hope that's your PI's report."

The blonde smiled. "It is, and he found all sorts of new goodies on Johnny C. and his merry widow. For instance, did you know Cialino suspected his wife was having an affair with Angus?"

"I'm listening."

"He hired his own private investigator two months after he bought Wallace's land. Apparently, Theresa and Angus were doing a little rendezvousing in a bed and breakfast in Dores."

"Is that so?" Obrecht sat up, intrigued. "And what do you have to back this up?"

She opened the brief and removed a manila folder. Inside were separate photos of Angus and Theresa Cialino, both entering the same bed and breakfast.

"What good is this? There's not a single photo of them together."

"I'm working on it. Meanwhile, the Cialinos' resort opens in three weeks and they're booked solid. Even the flats sold out, and they were asking twice the appraised value. This whole Nessie thing's made Theresa Cialino a very wealthy widow."

"She was wealthy before. You're grasping at straws, Jennifer. All you have are rumors wrapped around innuendo, nothing solid I can use to charge Theresa as an accomplice, or even to confront her with on the witness stand. No, forget money and forget the affair. The real key is to prove this monster, or whatever it is, had nothing to do with Johnny C.'s death. If we can do that, then everything else falls into place."

"What about the water bailiff? That guy definitely knows more than he's saying. I think we should recall him. Let's find out why all these mysterious Loch Ness drownings never made the papers? Maybe the bailiff knew exactly what they were and told Angus?"

"Again, how do you prove it? Calum Forrest is old Clan. He'd sooner die than speak out against his own." Obrecht paused, absorbed in thought. "Wait a second . . . "

"What?"

"The weak link . . . it isn't Angus or Theresa or this water bailiff, it's the son . . . Zachary."

"What do you mean?"

"The kid's no dummy. He's still out there searching."

"If you call walking around the Loch searching."

"Don't underestimate him. If something's really happening out there, my bet is he'll find it. And when he does, he won't hide the truth, not even to save his old man."

"Okay, so what do you want me to do?"

"Contact your private investigator. Tell him to shadow Zachary Wallace. Whatever the good doctor learns, I want to know, too."

Glenmoriston
1:45 A.M.

"Huh!"

I shot up in my sleeping bag in pitch blackness, my T-shirt soaked in perspiration, my flesh covered in goose bumps. My muscles trembled with fear, but it was not from the night terror.

There's something outside the tent!

I stifled my breathing and listened to the forest, the sound of my pounding heart throbbing in my ears.

Sounds . . . on my left! Something's leaving the river, moving along the rocks—moving toward me!

Get the light!

I grabbed my flashlight, a sixty-five-thousand candlepower waterproof lantern I had purchased the previous morning in Inverness. Clicking on the beacon, I slipped on my hiking boots and peered outside the tent.

The boulders? Nothing.

The tent grounds? Nothing.

Had I dreamed it? The hairs standing along the back of my neck assured me no.

"Ahhh . . . shiiiiiit!"

I hurled backwards into the tent in searing pain, the light flailing from my grip, my body sent writhing in spasms, an immense beast upon me, its stiletto-sharp teeth tearing into my left boot and ankle as if I'd stepped into a bear trap!

I thrashed about on my back in the darkness, kicking the unseen, gnashing brute with my free leg, while my right hand strained to reach my light.

Grabbing it, I turned the beacon upon the source of pain.

The beast released me and froze, its round, opaque eyes turning luminescent silver in the light, its chocolate brown head poised to strike again, its mouth, filled with bared fangs, dripping with my blood.

My brain churned data, even as my body remained paralyzed in fear.

Anguilla eel.

Seven footer.

Hundred and fifty pounds.

A high-pitched growl emanated from its open mouth, caused by its gurgling bloody spittle. It was a Mexican standoff, the animal held at bay, mesmerized by my light, me by its jaws and their proximity to my more vital organs.

And then I heard something else . . . something bigger, and it was approaching quickly through the woods.

The eel heard it, too, its growls intensifying as it grew more agitated.

The second beast was right outside the tent, circling!

I blinked back sweat, coiling my injured body to move, when the canvass was suddenly lifted away as if caught in a tornado's updraft, my light glinting off a gold-plated sword as the ancient weapon lashed across the flashlight's beam, its deadly blade lopping off the head of the startled eel.

"Jesus Christ!"

I was up on my haunches, my entire leg throbbing in pain, my free hand shielding my eyes from the three lights that cloaked the identities of my rescuers.

"He's been bitten."

"Aye, looks bad. He'll need medical attention."

Their voices muffled by hoods.

"Can ye walk, lad?"

I stood, trying my weight on my injured ankle. "Ahh. It's too sore, it might be broken."

"You two take him, I'll grab the Anguilla."

The beams lowered, revealing the three Templar Knights, all cloaked in black tunics from hood to boots. Two of the men, one on each side, shouldered my weight while the third collected the gushing remains of the Anguilla eel, stuffing it into a heavy burlap sack.

We hurried through darkness along an unseen path, the Knights' flashlights continuously searching the brush.

"The eel . . . why did it attack me?"

No reply.

"How did you know I was out here?"

No reply.

I saw lights up ahead. We were approaching a village.

"Why are the Black Knights guarding Loch Ness? What's their mission?"

The three Templars stopped dead in their tracks.

The leader turned and approached, raising his bloodied sword to my face. "Ye think ye ken somethin', Dr. Wallace?"

"I . . . I know there's something affecting the wildlife inhabiting the Glen. I also know the Templar care deeply about the land. But what you're doing . . . patrolling the forests . . . it's not going to change anything."

"Whit's done is done. We'll dae whit we must."

"It may not be too late. Maybe I can help."

"How?"

"Leave the remains of the eel with me. I'll take it to a lab, I'll do an autopsy myself. Whatever caused that eel to attack might be affecting the monster in the same way."

"No."

"Let him try," urged the Knight on my left.

"I said no. If word got oot—"

"I'll tell no one, I promise."

"I dinnae trust him," spat the Knight on my right. "Remember, he's Angus's kin."

"Aye. Enough said."

We continued on.

"Forget my father," I called out. "Do you think I trust him? Don't you remember what happened to me when I was nine? Believe me, I'm nothing like him."

The leader slowed, coming to the edge of the woods, but I could tell he was listening.

"One bad egg shouldn't destroy an entire clan. I swear, on the soul of my kin, Sir William Wallace, that I won't speak of what I find. Ever!"

We left the woods and hurried down a cobbled path, eventually coming to the Glenmoriston Arms Hotel.

My escorts left me on the porch stoop. One of them banged on the front door, then they disappeared into the night.

A yellow porch light flicked on. The front door creaked open, revealing an elderly man wearing a bathrobe. "We're filled beyond capacity, go away."

"Wait, I'm injured. Could you phone a doctor?"

The old man stepped out onto the porch and inspected my bleeding foot. "Whit happened tae ye?"

"A wild dog . . . it came out of nowhere."

"Hmm. There's a doctor stayin' wi' us. Wait here, an' dinnae bleed a' ower my porch."

He went back inside, leaving the outside light on.

That's when I noticed the burlap sack.

The Diary of Sir Adam Wallace
Translated by Logan W. Wallace

Entry: 25 October 1330

For hours the Knights hammered away at the cavern walls, fittin' an iron framework meant tae support the gate intae the timeless rock. At first I thought the noise wid bring another beast, but the sounds apparently kept them at bay.

MacDonald had designed the gate so that it could be raised an' lowered within its framework by chain. We are close tae finishin', an' for that, I am relieved. Still, I've had time tae ponder the repercussions o' oor actions against Nature, an' have pushed MacDonald for answers.

"We arenae violatin' Nature, Sir Adam, as much as usin' her. Since the time o' Saint Columba the monsters' numbers have diminished. Noo, at each summer's end, the gate shall be lowered intae the river's path, preventin' the ripe females frae escapin' tae the sea tae spawn. At the start o' each spring, we shall again return, this time tae raise the gate, allowin' the young Guivre entry. In this way, the beasts' numbers shall multiply again at Loch Ness, while keepin' Scotland's Grail safe for all time."

"An' whit if the females refuse tae spawn in Loch Ness?" I asked.

"Dinnae be sae stupid. A ripe female has tae lay her eggs somewhere. Better it be here, where they shall serve oor purpose than oot at sea."

"An' whit if Loch Ness cannae handle sae many of the creatures? Perhaps God intended their numbers tae dwindle? Perhaps the food supply cannae—"

"Enough! Ye think it wis God who created these monsters? 'Twis Satan for sure, an' noo they shall dae oor biddin'. Hand me the Bruce's casket."

MacDonald had widened a fissure in the rock face jist above the entry that had brought us tae this hellhole. Gently, he placed the silver container ontae the newly-crafted shelf, then covered it wi' Templar Cloth. "May the Bruce's divine spirit keep Satan at bay, and may his Holy Grail be returned to the light when God so determines Scotland shall again be free."

I pause noo frae writin' this entry. Sir Keef has announced the gate is ready tae be lowered intae its frame, a task that will require oor combined strength.

God willin', my next entry shall be made by light o' day.

My friend, James Cameron, and I were fishing in a small boat about two hundred meters off Tor Point, close to Aldourie Castle. It was about 10:00 P.M. when the boat started rocking on calm water. Suddenly, the head and neck of a large animal reared from the Loch, not more than 30 meters from us. A moment later it descended, leaving much commotion in the water. The head I saw was wide and ugly and continuous with the curve of the neck, and it looked like it had a brown-black mane.

—Dan McIntosh, Dores, July 1963

My brother-in-law, James, and I went our from Inverness that evening, our intention—to walk from Dores to Tor Point. And then we saw it! Paddling across the Loch was this black creature. There was almost no commotion in the water and it made great speed.

—Miss E.M. J. Keith, Headmistress, Rothienorman School, Aberdeenshire, 30 March 1965

The head was similar to that of a python, the neck was elongated and thickened as it tapered back. I could not see the body, but whatever moved it through the water was a strong method of propulsion. I was fascinated and thrilled . . . and, at the same time, frightened.

—James Ballantyne (brother-in-law) 30 March 1965

MY LEFT ANKLE ACHED as I rode the Harley-Davidson north on the A82, heading for Inverness. X-rays had revealed no broken bones, but the ankle was badly bruised and swollen, and required more than forty stitches to close wounds inflicted by the Anguilla's barbed vomerine teeth. My bandaged foot was now immobilized in a walking boot, a contraption consisting of sacs filled with compressed air and a series of Velcro straps.

True had left a half dozen messages on my cell phone, but I was avoiding his calls. The Black Knights had found me too easily the night before, and while I was grateful for being rescued, I felt sure it had been True who had tipped them off to look for me.

I thought of Calum Forrest's words: *Be fair warned, Young Wallace, when it comes tae Loch Ness trust nae one, for there's far mair at stake than ye can possibly imagine.*

I trusted True with my life, but decided to keep him in the dark about my new plans, beginning with the autopsy and toxicology report on the eel's remains.

Bypassing the sheriff's department left me few choices in regards to locating a lab. Forensic pathology in Scotland is usually contracted out through universities. The Northern Constabulary used Aberdeen University's toxicology department, while the Grampian Police sent samples to their lab in Aberdeen. In both cases, results still had to cross the sheriff's desk. Raigmore Hospital had a lab, but the chances of gaining access without calling attention to myself were slim to none.

That left me one last option.

Tidwell Animal Center was a small redbrick building located on Perth Road, not far from Raigmore Hospital. Earlier that morning I had phoned the proprietor and head veterinarian, a woman named Mary Tidwell. I described myself as visiting pathologist, hired by my cousin, a local farmer, to investigate the slaughter of one of his prized sheep. As it was a Sunday, she agreed to rent me use of her lab for a few hours, then send out for blood work on Monday.

Parking the Harley around back, I removed the bloodied burlap sack and my cane from the motorcycle's boot, tucked my baseball cap over my head, and hobbled to the side entrance.

Mary Tidwell greeted me at the door. A transplanted American in her late forties, her accent revealed a Midwestern upbringing.

"Dr. Botchin?"

"Yes, ma'am," I said, nearly forgetting my alias. "Really appreciate this. And please, call me Spencer."

"Anything for a fellow American, Spencer. My, what happened to your foot?"

"Dog bite. Damn pit bulls. Once they get hold of you . . . well, you know."

"The sheep remains are in that bag?"

"Yes, ma'am."

"It seems rather heavy and quite bloody. May I see it?"

"Wish I could, because personally, I'd love your opinion, but I gave my cousin my word about keeping things quiet."

"I respect that. Come in."

She led me through a linoleum-floored hallway reeking of animal feces, then to a green-tiled surgical chamber. "That'll be forty pounds for use of the lab and another thirty for the blood toxicology report."

I dug through my pocket, handing her a wad of bills.

"Of course, Spencer, if there's any chance the sheep has contracted anthrax—"

"No, ma'am, I assure you, it's nothing like that."

"Still, Dr. Wallace, I'm afraid I'm going to have to insist on examining whatever's in the bag."

"Dr. Wallace?"

She gave me a disarming smile. "Come now, Zachary, surely you don't think that cap's a suitable disguise. Your face has been on every telecast and newspaper for weeks. Now level with me, what's in the bag?"

I decided Mary Tidwell was someone I could trust, mostly because I had little choice, but being American, I knew she held no ties to any clans. I told her about my investigation and how I'd been attacked, leaving out all references to the Black Knights. She agreed to help me, and within minutes, we had donned surgical gloves, masks, eye shields, and gowns and were extracting vials of blood from the lower torso of the decapitated Anguilla eel's remains.

"I'll have to send these samples out to the lab for analysis," she told me, "but I'll keep everything under my name. They'll do an initial test using an immunoassay kit, isolating negative specimens from potentially positive ones. If toxins are present, a second test, using a gas chromatograph-mass spectrometer should tell us what's present."

"If it's okay, I want to examine the Anguilla's brain," I said, removing the football-sized head from the sac.

Dr. Tidwell handed me a scalpel, and I began cutting through the thick, rubbery flesh, peeling it away until I reached the skull. She took over with an electric saw, making several transverse cuts through the dense bone. Prying open the incisions, she was able to remove the cross sections, exposing the eel's brain.

The small organ, about as narrow as the spinal cord to which it was connected, resembled six hen eggs, set in two rows of three.

Dr. Tidwell pointed to the numerous pustulant brown lesions that covered the creature's brain. "This animal's definitely been exposed to toxins, and judging by the extent of these lesions, it's been over a prolonged period of time."

"How could it have survived?"

"Oh, these Anguilla are hardy animals, able to inhabit fresh and salt water, even in heavily polluted areas. When it comes to injuries of the central nervous system, they have the ability to effect repairs by regenerating axons from cell bodies located in the brain. What concerns me are these lesions here, in the forebrain. They'll have destroyed the eel's traits of initiative and caution."

"Resulting in overly aggressive behavior?"

"Definitely. Considering how nasty this fish is to begin with, I'd say you were lucky to only sustain minor injuries."

"Then, assuming Loch Ness's largest inhabitant was affected by these same lesions—"

"Yes, that might explain why it's been on a rampage of late . . . assuming, of course, the monster, whatever it is, has a similar nervous systems and was exposed to the same sort of toxins."

She collected a few samples of brain tissue, then bagged the skull. "I have a friend who's a technician at the lab. I'll give her a call, maybe she can get the results back to me within the next few days. Where can I reach you?"

I gave her my hotel and cell phone number. "Mary, I'd appreciate it if you said nothing about this to anyone. There's a political under-current that seems to control things in the Highlands, and—"

She nodded. "I won't say a word."

*   *   *

Twenty minutes later, I was weaving in and out of traffic again, this time racing the Harley south on the A82, heading back to Drumnad-rochit. Pieces of the Loch Nessie puzzle whirled in my mind like a centrifuge. A solution was forming, but there were still a few impor-tant clues missing, and to acquire the next one meant confronting a ghost from my past.

Entering the village, I pulled off the side of the road leading up to Glen Urquhart and the Drumnadrochit Lodge, then phoned True.

"Zack, geezus, lad, where've ye been?"

"I had a little accident last night, but I'm all right. Can you meet me at the Clansman Wharf as soon as possible? I need to speak with your sister."

"Sure, sure, be there in twenty."

Several minutes later, True's pickup truck drove by, accelerating past my hiding place and onto the main highway.

Maybe it was the anxiety of confronting the Crabbit, maybe it was the fact that I was getting closer to learning the truth, but as I waited until the dust settled, subliminal images splayed across my mind's eye like a photographer's flash—strange, shattered memories from the first time I had drowned.

Dark water, as cold as death. My scrawny limbs, heavy as lead, unable to move. A nightmarish presence . . . rising beneath me to finish its meal, then something else . . . a second boat and a light.

I closed my eyes and tried to remain calm, willing the shunted memories to come, hoping to catch a glimpse of a past that continued to elude me.

And then the long-sought image came into focus.

It was a light, appearing next to an approaching boat, far above my head and just below the surface, and it cast its heavenly glow into the depths, parting the curtains of blackness—revealing the monster! It was dark and frightening and as large as any whale, and its terrible jaw was open, poised around my waist, The points of its teeth pressed against my frail body, tasting my flesh, unsure if I was edible prey. But the light was now passing directly overhead, the brightness of its blessed beacon burning into those freakish jaundice-yellow eyes. The hideous creature darted away, releasing me to another light . . .

A warm feeling came over me then, as I vaguely recalled seeing old man MacDonald in his rowboat as my spirit hovered over him. He was drenched in my blood, his bearded mouth pumping my purple lips with his life-giving breaths, until I gagged and wretched at the sudden, agonizing pain and opened my eyes, staring up into his shaggy, pit bull face.

I had cried as I bled in his arms, then passed out as he carried me through the woods to the nearest doctor.

He had saved my life, but did I ever thank him? The only thing I could recall was waking in my own bed days later, feverish and sore from having been stitched back together.

In the weeks to come, my body would heal, my mind choosing to bury the truth of my near-death experience with my childhood.

*   *   *

I found Alban MacDonald in his private room behind the lobby desk. He was whittling a piece of hickory with his Sgian Dubh. The dangerous–looking blade of the stainless steel knife was capped with a staghorn handle.

The sight of the weapon let a bit of air out of my ballooning confidence. Gripping my cane, I entered his domain.

"Mr. MacDonald, do you have a minute?"

"No."

"The Anguilla's brain was filled with lesions."

"Dinnae ken nothin' aboot any eel."

"The lesions are affecting their behavior, sir, making them unnaturally aggressive. But you already knew that, didn't you?"

"Go away. I dinnae have time for yer blethers."

"Whatever's causing the lesions in the eel population is probably affecting the monster's behavior, too."

He ignored me, continuing his whittling.

"We need to talk." I hobbled toward him, refusing to cower, even as he rose to his feet, brandishing the knife.

"I said go away!"

"You want to stab me? Go ahead. I already owe you my life, it's yours to take back if you want it. But I'm not leaving until I get some answers."

He stared at me for a god-awful minute, then lowered the blade, slipping it back into its leather sheath as he fell slowly back into his rocking chair. "Whit is it ye want?"

"Seventeen years ago, when you saved my life, you knew the creature that attacked me was afraid of bright light. How did you know?"

"I served as water bailiff a long time. I ken whit I ken."

"What else can you tell me about the creature?"

"Nothin'."

"It's trapped in Loch Ness, isn't it?"

The old man looked up at me then, his expression of concern confirming my suspicions. "Go ask yer rabbittin' faither, seein' as he's the one that's been fillin' yer heid."

"You're wrong about Angus. He refuses to tell me anything, and it's his life that's at stake."

MacDonald scoffed.

"What was the sworn mission of the Black Knights, Mr. MacDonald? How does it relate to the creature?"

He stood, his patience shot. "I think it's high time ye were gone."

"I'll go, but those monster hunters won't be leaving. This time they'll stay until they've captured the creature, or are forced to kill it. Either way, it'll be on your head."

I hobbled out of his chamber, then out the lodge to the Harley. I climbed on the bike and was about to gun the engine when I saw the old man emerge.

For a moment, I wondered if he meant to talk or stab me.

"I have yer word as kin o' Sir William Wallace that ye'll no' speak o' this tae anyone?"

"Yes, sir."

He fidgeted, still contemplating his decision. "Dinnae ask me again aboot the Black Knights, that I take wi' me tae the grave. As tae the monster, I dinnae ken whit she is, I've only caught glimpses o' her twice, a' I ken is she's the last o' her kind, though whit kind, again, I cannae say. She's big, though, bigger'n any afore her, an' that's 'cause she's been trapped a long time, unable tae leave the Loch Ness tae spawn. Nature took ower an' jist let her grow. Born in blackness, she'll aye prefer the deep, at least she aye did 'til jist this past winter. At first I thought it wis a' the blastin' at that damn resort that sent her topside, jist like it did when she attacked ye seventeen years ago. But I wis wrong. Somethin' isnae right wi' the Loch, an' it's affected her mind an' her appetite, jist as it's affected the eels. Lesions, ye say?"

"Caused by some kind of toxin in the water. I don't know where it's originating from or why it hasn't been detected up until now, but it's definitely affecting the wildlife."

"Aye, but there's a more immediate problem. The creature's tasted human flesh again, an' that makes her very dangerous. Same sort o' thing happened long ago with another o' her kind, back when I was a lad. Still, I dinnae want tae see her put doon, she's served us well."

Served who well? The Black Knights?

"Dae ye think ye can free her to the sea?"

"I don't know. Where's the Loch's underwater access route into the Moray Firth?"

He shook his head. "Off wi' ye now, laddie. Godspeed."

I started the engine, then shut it off. "Mr. MacDonald, thank you for saving my life."

He hesitated, then shook my offered hand. "Make it a life worth savin'. One mair thing. Her eyes may be weak frae aye livin' in the dark, but her sense o' smell's unequaled. That's how she hunts. It's said she can sense a man by smellin' the terror in his blood. So take heed."

I nodded, then gunned the engine and drove off, feeling as if an old scar had finally been picked clean to heal.

Clansman Hotel

True was waiting for me in the parking lot when I rolled in ten minutes later. "Ye're late. Sweet Jesus, whit happened tae yer foot?"

"I fed it to an Anguilla eel." I glanced over his shoulder to the wharf and a hub of activity. "What's going on down there?"

"Trucks arrived this mornin' wi' some steel nettin'. A' the boats are bein' fitted wi' them. Urquhart Bay's been cordoned off intae a giant pen. Now whit's this aboot an eel?"

"Later. Is Caldwell down there?"

"Aye. Playin' head honcho for the cameras."

"Playing's the word. Can you call Brandy on her cell phone? Ask her to join us up here, I need to speak with her away from Caldwell."

*   *   *

Leaning back against a pine tree, I could see Brandy as she swaggered down the wharf in all her glory, waving to television crews and journalists. True waited for her at the end of the pier, and I watched as brother and sister spoke.

*   *   *

"So, Brandy, then it's true?"

"What're ye talkin' about?"

"Zack says ye're sleepin' wi' this Caldwell fella."

"Is this what ye called me out for? Tae discuss who I'm buckin'?"

"I'm concerned, that's a'. Wi' a' ye've been through—"

"Listen here, bro, there isnae anythin' between David an' me 'cept some heavy flirtin', an' most o' that's for the cameras."

"An' one Zachary Wallace as well, aye? I heard whit happened at the Clansman. Ye're rubbin' it in his face, are ye no'?"

"Aye. An' if ye let on about it, I'll smack ye so hard, it'll kill the fuc'in' Crabbitt!"

*   *   *

They started up the hill together, then broke into a footrace, Brandy taking the lead, giggling as True tackled her from behind. The sight of them wrestling in the grass brought a smile to my face, and I tried to recall the last time I'd actually laughed out loud.

For the life of me, I couldn't remember.

When I looked up. Brandy was standing over me, hands on hips like some Greek goddess. She motioned to my walking boot. "Looks like ye stuck yer foot in yer mouth one too many times."

"And it looks like you've got every camera in the Highlands focused on your ass."

"No' yet, but be sure I'm workin' on it. So Mr. Zachary Wallace, what is it then? Be brief, us lowlife whores need our rest."

"Look, I . . . I'm sorry if I insinuated anything."

"An' whit did ye insinuate?" demanded True, joining Brandy. "I hope for *your* sake ye didnae call my wee sister a whore?"

"No, I—"

"He claimed I was sleepin' wi' David Caldwell just so he'd rent my boat."

"An' are ye?"

"'Course not. I'm shaggin' David 'cause he's cute an' macho an' he's got a nice package."

"Well, that's a whole lot different then." Satisfied, True lay down in the grass, covering his head with a big, hairy forearm.

My blood pressure soared.

"So, Zachary Wallace, what was it ye wanted then?"

"Your sonar array . . . it won't find the monster."

"An' how dae ye know that?"

"There's a basic flaw in 'Mr. Big Package's' strategy. It's the same reason none of the other sonar expeditions ever found a thing. But I'll tell you what will work . . . in exchange for your sharing with me the array's password and security codes."

"Ye've got tae be jokin', Zack? Ye want me tae help ye hack into our sonar's central control station?"

"You have my word I won't touch the programming. My intentions are only to access certain information concerning the fish population and the Loch's geology. As soon as I'm finished, you can change the security codes."

"Forget it. If David ever found out, he'd fire me for sure."

"Come on, Brandy," said True. "Caldwell'll never ken anythin' aboot it. Ye've got his balls in the palm o' yer hand."

The image set my teeth to grinding. "Forget it then," I growled. "I wouldn't want you to compromise your position."

"Good."

"Good!"

"Was that it then, Mr. Wallace, 'cause I'm quite busy these days."

The right side of my brain urged me to say something, to tell her to leave David, to confess that I loved her, but instead I was only able to muster, "I guess that's it then."

Hydrophobia was not the only fear I'd yet to overcome.

I was working at the Academy of Applied Sciences when
Dr. Rines contacted me about joining him in Scotland. His mission:
To obtain underwater photos of the large animal he believed occupied
Loch Ness. Using a strobe light invented by our colleague, Dr. Harold
Edgerton, our team set up an underwater camera and lights rigged to
our boat's sonar, so that contact with a large moving object would trigger
the strobe camera to snap pictures once every fifty-five seconds. With our
camera loaded with rolls of high-resolution photographic film I'd
created for NASA, we set out to find the monster.

On August 8, 1972, our sonar detected a large underwater
animate object. We changed course, passing over the object,
which was moving very fast. Within seconds, it was gone.

All was not lost. Our camera managed to capture a photo of
an appendage, perhaps a flipper or possibly a fin or pectoral limb.
Whatever it is that is down there, it's very large, and resembles
no species I had ever come across before.

—Dr. Charles Wyckoff, Academy of Applied Sciences, August 1972

CHAPTER 25

Inverness

TWO DAYS PASSED. I spent most of that time alone in my hotel room, icing my foot and researching eels on my laptop.

What I learned about the creatures was eye-opening.

There were eight known species of conger, with *Anguilla anguilla*, the European version, considered the largest and most fearsome of the lot. Females could reach ten feet and weigh more than 250 pounds. Unlike common eels, the Anguilla could use its pectoral fins to venture on land. Their muscular bodies were enveloped in sheets of slime and their broad heads had protruding lower jaws and long needlelike teeth which, as I could attest, made for a devastating bite. Shy unless provoked, the Anguilla preferred deep water, burrowing in the muddy bottom, which would make them undetectable to sonar. Living in darkness, it would venture on land almost exclusively at night.

But it was their migration pattern that sent my mind reeling.

Anguilla eels that inhabited Loch Ness were notoriously slow to mature, taking fifteen years or more before they were old enough to spawn. When ready, the adult females abandoned the Loch, traveling up the River Ness under cover of darkness for the North Sea. Upon leaving Britain's coast, the eels followed scent trails, swimming thousands of miles west against the currents to reach the deeper waters of the mid-Atlantic. This amazing journey triggered some dramatic physiological changes in the animals' bodies. Upon descending to depths beyond 10,000 feet, the serpents suddenly stopped feeding and began losing their teeth. Their guts quickly degenerated, and their gonads became greatly enlarged. Upon finally reaching their ancient breeding site, the adults would spawn, then die almost immediately, each female leaving behind some 8 million eggs. The eggs that were fertilized developed into clear-colored larvae, called elvers. Over time, the young then rode the Gulf Stream thousands of miles east back to Europe, continuing the conger eels' bizarre circle of life.

And where did the adult Anguilla eels of Loch Ness journey to spawn?

The Sargasso Sea.

*   *   *

With no monster sightings in days, and nothing significant appearing on David's sonar array, the Highland Council was beginning to get concerned. They had invested a lot of money in penning off Urquhart Bay, and the entire world was watching and waiting . . . and forming opinions.

Despite the deaths of five people, there was still no real proof directly linking any of the killings to a lake monster. No creature had been sighted and no bodies recovered, save for Justin Wagners, and there were rumors spreading that in fact, his injuries had been a result of being run over by the Zodiac's propeller. Ron Casey was recovering in Raigmore Hospital, but the crime scene photographer could remember nothing about the boating incident that had led to the drownings of his two friends and the vessel's captain, and never claimed having seen a water beast.

The pressure was mounting, and most of it was on David Caldwell and my father, whose trial was set to reconvene in the next twenty-four hours.

*   *   *

My hotel phone rang on the eve of Angus's continuance, chasing me from a catnap. "Hello?"

"Zachary? Mary Tidwell. I just got the results back from the lab."

I sat up in bed. "Go on."

"Two things. First, traces of beta blocking chemicals were found in the eel's blood."

"Beta blockers? As in heart medication?"

"Yes. Most likely ingested from feeding on Ferox trout, which come in contact with the chemicals near industrial areas before entering Loch Ness."

"And the brain lesions?"

"Those were caused by PCB's . . . hydrocarbon poisoning. Somewhere out there, oil's leaking into the Great Glen."

Sniddles Club, Drumnadrochit

True and I waited until the waitress set down our drinks and left before continuing our conversation.

"So," I pressed, "do you think there's a pipeline leak or not?"

"Shh, lower yer voice. There's a million bloody reporters snoopin' roond the Highlands these days." He drained half his beer, then belched. "Jist 'cause ye find an eel wi' lesions, disnae mean it wis exposed tae oil in Loch Ness. First off, they're aye doin' water tests. Second, crude floats, people wouldae seen it."

"And what if it's not even getting into Loch Ness? What if it's coming through the remains of an underwater passage that connects the Loch with the North Sea?"

"Whit passage? That's a' theory."

"Just humor me, True. Where are the closest oil fields to Loch Ness?"

"There's two o' them, baith located jist offshore in the Moray Firth. The Beatrice Field's twenty kilometers off the coast in the inner firth. Big field, wi' three platforms. The Cialino Field's smaller, belongin' tae you know who. Johnny C. bought it for pennies on the pound frae Talisman Energy."

"Talisman Energy? Now why does that name sound familiar?"

"They've been in the news. A few years back, Talisman wis implicated in a lawsuit that accused the company o' collaboratin' wi' the Sudanese government, jist after yer President Bush declared it a terrorist state. The country wis run by mair o' thae Islamic extremists who used profits frae Talisman's oil wells tae buy weapons . . . weapons they used tae commit genocide against their Christian population. Word is, close tae two million people died."

"Lovely. No wonder Johnny C. got himself such a bargain."

"Aye."

"These fields in the Moray Firth, what happens to the oil after it's pumped?"

"The crude's stabilized, then sent through export pipes to the Nigg Oil terminal for processin' an' export. Niggs wis also owned by Talisman, an' it's had its share o' problems, too. No' long ago the EPA found leaks in the pipelines at the tanker terminal carryin' supplies frae Beatrice. Pipes are aye corrodin'. Problem is, companies like Talisman an' Cialino drill closer an' closer tae shore every year."

"Any supply lines feeding into the Great Glen?"

"A few, but they're heavily monitored."

"Any chance of getting hold of a map that shows the buried distribution lines?"

"Hmm . . . maybe. Got a few muckers at Niggs who might help. If no', I can aye hitch a ride back oot tae my last rig an' borrow a few things, if ye ken whit I mean."

True's cell phone rang. "MacDonald. Hey, sweets. Jings, no shyte! Sure, he's right here. Okay, I'll tell him."

He hung up. "That wis Brandy. David Caldwell wants tae meet wi' ye right now, doon at Urquhart Castle. Alone."

Urquhart Castle

The steel-gray modular bridge stretched end to end across the mouth of Urquhart Bay, each of its free-floating prefabricated platforms twenty-eight feet long and fourteen feet wide. Lightweight and portable, the newly completed expanse had been designed to support army and commercial vehicles, though its use on Loch Ness would be limited to pedestrian traffic only.

A construction pontoon stood a quarter mile offshore, the boom of its three-hundred-ton capacity Shearleg Derrick rising 250 feet into the mouse gray sky. The crane was supporting a spool that fed fourteen foot wide, 750-foot long lengths of chain-link fencing down through the modular's precut slots. Each length was weighed down by a five-ton concrete weight, which served to anchor the steel barrier to the bottom.

David Caldwell, wearing a yellow hard hat and mirrored sunglasses, stood on the southern shoreline of the bay, the ruins of Urquhart Castle at his back. The area was fenced off, preventing the public from accessing the bridge. Still, the tourists and media were out in droves, snapping pictures of "Nessie's new habitat" and David Caldwell, too, as if he were the monster hunter, Carl Denham, about to capture King Kong.

I gave my name to a security guard, who allowed me to enter. "David?"

He signaled me to approach.

"David, why're you wearing a hard hat?"

"Hello? We're standing in a construction site."

"Construction's in the bay. The only thing that hat'll protect you from are birds as they shit on your head."

"More sarcasm. What happened to us, Zack? I thought you and I were a team?"

"Some team. My brains and your mouth."

"Say what you will but it worked. We were the first to catch a giant squid on film."

"We? You took all the credit and blamed me for losing a sub."

He turned to me, feigning sincerity. "I was wrong in doing that. I'm sorry."

I ignored his offered hand. "What is it you want?"

"Brandy told me about your offer. You still interested in gaining access to our sonar array?"

"Go on."

"I can't allow you access into the system, but I am willing to let you monitor the array from your laptop . . . in exchange for telling us why we still can't track the monster."

"I want it in writing, authorized by Provost Hollifield."

"Whatever." He reached into his pants pocket, handing me a folded piece of paper. "That's a Web link my engineer just set up for you. It'll connect you to the array.'

"Fax the agreement to my hotel. Meanwhile, I'll check out the link. If it suits my needs, I'll call you on your cell phone and tell you everything you need to know."

"Do it soon. That provost guy's getting on my nerves."

"What'd you expect? You're spending their money, they want results."

"Results? The creature's been around for fifteen hundred years. All of a sudden they're in a rush?"

"They certainly rushed getting that bridge pieced together. How much they end up spending?"

"About a million dollars or pounds, I forget which. Either way, it's nothing. They'll make that back in crossing fees alone during the first few months."

"You're not actually going to allow people out there?"

"Damn straight. We'll have guardrails up, separating the tourists from the plesiosaur. It'll be safe."

I could have spouted off then, lecturing him about dinosaurs and timelines and how a deepwater feeder, whatever was out there, wasn't about to surface during the day just to please a bunch of humans with cameras.

Instead I only shook my head and walked away.

I believe the Loch contains Zeuglodons, also known as Basilosaurus, which means "King of Reptiles." Basilosaurus was a prehistoric ancestor of modern-day whales, though it actually looked more like a sea serpent. It was 55–75 feet long and very narrow, had a five foot skull and a blowhole on its snout, and was prevalent all over the world some 37–53 million years ago. These beasts could have swum into Loch Ness in search of food when there was ample access from the sea.

A long, thin whale is closer to eye-witnesses descriptions than a plesiosaur.

—Dr. Roy Mackall, Cryptozoologist

I WAS BACK IN MY HOTEL ROOM an hour later, my laptop set to the sonar array's Web link. Using my touchpad, I could zoom in on each section of the Loch, obtaining real-time data on any biologics passing by the pinging buoys.

Before I could begin, however, I was interrupted by a knock on my door. *Not another reporter . . .*

I peeked through the peephole, then opened the door for a stocky waiter with short, dirty blond hair and matching beard. "You must have the wrong room, bud. I didn't order room service."

"Compliments of your father, sir." He handed me a card.

Dearest Zachary:
Tomorrow's a big day for both of us.
Keep up your strength, my faith's in you.
—Your loving father.

Now what was Angus up to?
"Set it by the desk, please."

He pushed the cart of food inside, then noticed the laptop screen. "Hey, is this some sort o' sonar array? We're studyin' these things in university. My professor, he writes for the *Fish an' Fisheries* journal, the one put out by Edinburgh, St. Andrews, an' Leeds."

"I've read it. They do nice work."

"Yeah, they're pretty intense. I helped compile information used in one o' their special issues, it wis about how fish are smarter than scientists once thought. Ye know, steeped in social intelligence, cooperatin' wi' each other when it comes tae spottin' predators an' catchin' food. Stuff like that."

"So you're a marine biologist posing as a waiter?"

"Jist an undergrad tryin' tae pay my way through university." He extended his hand. "Ed Homa. It's a real pleasure tae meet ye, Dr. Wallace."

I shook his hand. "I was just about to take a peek in on Loch Ness. Want to watch?"

"Aye, that'd be amazin'."

I sat down at the desk and clicked on the northern third of the Loch, focusing my search from Lochend south to Urquhart Bay.

"So, Doc, where do ye think Nessie might be hidin'?"

"I'm not searching for Nessie. It's schools of fish I'm after, beginning with the salmon population. As I'm sure you know, they prefer the surface waters."

"Aye, sure."

Finding nothing, I clicked to another section of grid, then continued, one after the next, unable to find any fish.

"Uh, so where are they?"

I ignored him and moved on, focusing my search south toward Invermoristion.

Still nothing.

I shut the laptop fifteen minutes later, having failed to locate a single school of salmon. "Bizarre."

"Whit's bizarre?"

"They're not out there . . . or maybe they never arrived."

"Whit never arrived? Ye mean the salmon?"

"Yes. It's as if they're avoiding Loch Ness."

"Whit about the other species?"

"I can't be sure about the deepwater species. The array still has blind spots along the bottom. Still I—"

The phone's ring cut me off. "Wallace. Oh, sorry, David, guess I forgot about you. Uh, yeah, hold on."

I turned to the waiter. "Sorry, do you mind?"

"Oh, sure. Hey, Doc, thanks."

"Good luck in school." I waited until he left before speaking. "Okay, David, you wanted to know why the array's not working, let's see how well informed you are."

"Zack, I don't have time for your games."

"Pay attention. A few years back, a federal court ruled the Navy could no longer use its high-intensity LFA sonar system. Do you remember the reason the system was shut down?"

"Who cares?"

"LFA is low frequency active sonar, David, the optimal word being *active*. The Navy's signal would have blasted hundreds of thousands of square miles of ocean with enough sound to deafen, maim, and even kill whales."

"And this has what to do with Loch Ness?"

"Jesus, David, wake up! Loch Ness is essentially a long, giant trough. Everything reflects off her walls, every wake, every sound, every ping. And every monster hunter before you has made the same mistake in hunting the beast with sonar."

"Which is?"

I shook my head in disbelief. "Active sonar, David! The creature's sensitive to sound. The pinging from your buoys is scaring it off. It's hiding along the bottom somewhere, or in its lair, wherever that might be. And it won't come out again until you—"

"Switch the array from active to passive! Gotta go!"

I lay back, listening to the dial tone, wondering what wheels of fate I had just set in motion.

Dr. Wyckoff and I returned to Loch Ness in 1975, this time armed with both sonar and a time-lapse strobe system, the latter capable of taking underwater photographs every 35–40 seconds. Even with our new technology, I was still worried about getting good shots. Because of the high saturation of peat in the water, the range of an underwater camera is very short, due to reflection and scatter of light.

Our breakthrough came on a late overcast afternoon on June 20th. Without warning, our boat's sonar detected a large object crossing our starboard beam—one minute it was there, the next . . . gone. It was just enough contact to set off the camera. Most of the photographs were too obscured in silt to see, but in one shot, you can clearly make out a long-necked creature that resembles an extinct plesiosaur or elasmosaur! We sold the pictures to *Nature Magazine*, then, with the help of Sir Peter Scott, applied to both Houses of Parliament to get this elusive creature protected under the conservation act. Unfortunately, I had to return to Boston (to defend and protect the American patent system) but with the photos, I felt certain other scientists would join the battle, continuing our work. To my dismay, the scientific body remained skeptical, and for the most part, stayed away.

—Dr. Robert Rines, Academy of Applied Sciences Member: National Inventor's Hall of Fame

CHAPTER 27

Inverness Castle, Scottish Highlands

"**THE HIGH COURT OF JUSTICIARY,** case number C93-04, is now back in session, Lord Neil Hannam presiding. All rise."

I stood as the judge took his place at the bench and addressed the jury. "Ladies and gentlemen, as you are well aware, there are extraordinary circumstances surrounding this case, and you are to be commended for your patience and understanding. Mr. Rael, is the defense prepared to continue its case?"

"We are, my lord."

"Lord Advocate?"

Mitchell Obrecht nodded. "Her Majesty's Advocate is ready, my lord."

"Very well. Mr. Rael, when last in session, you were questioning your witness, Dr. Zachary Wallace. Do you have any further questions of the witness at this time?"

"No, my lord."

"Lord Advocate, would you like to cross-examine the witness?"

"Indeed we would, my lord."

I was recalled to the witness box and sworn in. Angus seemed almost amused as he watched from his seat behind the prosecutor's table.

"Welcome back, Dr. Wallace. What happened to your foot?"

"Camping accident."

"Camping. Yes, I understand you've spent the better part of the last two weeks camping and exploring Loch Ness."

"Yes."

"When court was last in session, Mr. Rael asked you, and I quote, 'hypothetically speaking, if a large water creature did prey in Loch Ness, is it possible it could have developed a taste for human flesh?' To which you responded, 'Hypothetically, yes, but only if this creature was a predator and not a vegetarian, and only if the creature's diet had been substantially altered by some unusual break in the food chain,' end quote. My question then, Dr. Wallace, is if, in the last two weeks, your investigation has proven either of these conditions to be true?"

He knows something . . .

"Doctor?"

"Justin Wagner's injuries indicated he'd been attacked by a predatory animal. None of the other deaths could positively be linked to a water creature."

"Thank you, but that wasn't my question. What I asked was whether there was anything in *your* investigation that's shown either of your two previously mentioned conditions to be true."

I hesitated. "It seems certain populations of fish that normally frequent Loch Ness at this time of year may not be present."

Murmurs filled the chamber, quieting quickly.

"In other words, a break in the food chain?"

"Yes."

"And which species of fish are missing from Loch Ness?"

"Numbers are significantly down among the larger breeds, specifically among the salmon."

"And how do you know that, Dr. Wallace?"

The waiter! "I've uh, I've been provided with access to the monster hunter's sonar array."

"Ah. So let me be clear here, you found no salmon in Loch Ness?"

"None. At least within the limits of the array."

"Maybe you could quickly walk us through the salmon's spawning routine."

"Salmon are born in the rivers feeding Loch Ness. As they get older, they migrate into the Atlantic, where they grow quite large.

When it's time to spawn, a salmon may travel thousands of miles, using the Earth's magnetic field to direct it back to the freshwater pool where it hatched."

"And when do the salmon usually start arriving in Loch Ness?"

"At the end of each winter when they're large and well fed. The fish must wait until the rivers are swollen, since they often have to leap up waterfalls and beyond strenuous currents. Once a salmon returns to its birth pool it spawns, and it usually won't eat again until it returns to the ocean in the fall."

"According to your testimony, when you fell into Loch Ness seventeen years ago, you were surrounded by a school of salmon. Is that correct?"

"Yes."

"What month was that?"

"August."

"Then summer is the season a school of salmon would be found in Loch Ness?"

"Spring and summer, yes."

"But not this summer?"

"So far . . . no."

"And what might cause the salmon population to avoid Loch Ness this season?"

I hesitated, not wanting to bring up the subject of pollution until I had proof. "When a salmon approaches Loch Ness, a chemical memory enables the fish to literally smell its own river. It's possible something's interfering with that process, but that's just conjecture. For all we know, they may have diverted to another Highland loch or river—"

"But not Loch Ness? At least not this season?"

"No, not this season."

"And if not this season, then certainly not this past winter?"

"No. The water's too cold to spawn."

"I see. Then February is certainly out?"

"Yes."

"Thank you, Dr. Wallace. No further questions."

The judge looked at Max. "Mr. Rael?"

"My lord, the defense has no further witnesses."

"Lord Advocate?"

"Yes, my lord, we'd like to recall Mr. Angus Wallace to the stand."

My father shot Max a worried look, then strutted to the witness box. The clerk of the court verified that Angus knew he was still under oath, while the prosecutor circled like a shark.

"Mr. Wallace, I'm going to read back to you your testimony regarding the death of John Cialino . . . a death that occurred on the fifteenth of February. And I quote, 'so I hit him, square in the nose. It was a good shot, and he stumbled back a few steps, then twisted his ankle on a rock and tumbled over the edge, right into Loch Ness. I dropped to my knees and looked over the slope. John was treading water, in fair shape, though blood was pouring from both nostrils. Suddenly the water came alive with salmon, must have been hundreds of them. Some were leaping straight out of the water, a few smacking John right in the head. Then I saw a huge animal, long and serpent-like, at least fifteen meters, and it was circling John and those salmon like a hungry wolf.' End quote."

Angus looked pale.

"Salmon, Mr. Wallace. In your testimony, you saw hundreds of salmon, yet according to the expert testimony of your own son, there are no salmon in Loch Ness this season, and certainly not in a winter month. So how do you explain seeing so many salmon on February the fifteenth?"

"I'm no' a marine biologist, I jist saw whit I saw."

"Let's return to what you said. In your testimony, you claimed Mr. Cialino owed you a final payment on land you had sold him. How much was the final payment for?"

"Fifteen thousand pounds."

"And he never paid you?"

"Naw."

The prosecutor walked over to his assistant, who handed him two manilla envelopes.

From the first, Obrecht removed a Xeroxed copy of a bank check. "Do you recognize this, Mr. Wallace?"

Angus stared at the note. "Aye. It's a cancelled cheque for my last payment."

"And what's the date on the cheque?"

"February 23."

"Paid a week after Mr. Cialino's death. And upon whose account was the money drawn?"

"Theresa Cialino."

The courtroom buzzed with opinion.

"So Mrs. Cialino paid you a week after you were arrested for her husband's murder? Do you find that a bit suspicious, Mr. Wallace?"

"Since when is honesty suspicious? Theresa kent whit happened tae her husband wis an accident, an' I needed the money for my heart medicine. They've got my land. A deal's a deal."

"Yes. The question, of course, is what deal you're referring to. The real estate transaction . . . or something else." The prosecutor opened the second folder, removing a set of color photographs. "Mr. Wallace, do you recognize these?"

Angus leafed through the set. "It's a bed 'n' breakfast in Dores. One photie's o' me, another's o' Theresa Cialino. Whit' yer point?"

"How often did the two of you rendezvous at this particular bed and breakfast?"

"Rendezvous? Ye make it sound as if we were sneakin' around."

"Just answer the question," Judge Hannam said.

"Dinnae really ken. Maybe half a dozen times. The chef's an auld pal o' mine. Makes the best oatcake an' haggis, neeps an' tattie this side o' Fort William. Been there wi' Johnny an' a'."

"And how long have you known Mrs. Cialino?"

"We met seven or eight years ago."

"Did her husband know the two of you had been meeting at a bed and breakfast in Dores?"

Another murmur rose, but quickly died.

"I widnae ken. Ye'd need tae ask him."

Obrecht returned to his desk, his assistant Jennifer, exchanging the photos for a thick file. "Mr. Wallace, would it surprise you to learn that John Cialino had hired a private investigator to follow his wife?"

"No' at a'. Theresa's awfy bonnie, as ye can see, an' Johnny wis awfy paranoid."

"Yes or no, Mr. Wallace, were you and Mrs. Cialino having an affair?"

I glanced from Angus to the widow, as did most of the courtroom. She sat stoically, staring straight ahead, but her jaw muscles were clenched.

"There wis no affair, Mr. Obrecht. Sorry tae disappoint ye."

"You never slept with Mrs. Cialino?"

"Objection." Max was on his feet. "My lord, I'd say Mr. Wallace has answered the question, yes?"

"Overruled. The defendant will answer the question."

Angus averted his eyes, mulling over his reply. "Aye, once, but it wis quite a while ago."

"Had the two of you ever discussed problems in her marriage at these bed and breakfast rendezvouses?"

"We discussed many things ower breakfast, Mr. Obrecht."

"Including her husband's murder?"

"Objection!"

"Sustained."

The courtroom held its collective breath while Mitchell Obrecht gazed at the jury, confirming his message had been delivered. "No further questions for this witness, my lord."

Court adjourned for the day, releasing dozens of reporters to file their stories in time to hit the evening news. Feeling bad about my testimony, I waited around, hoping to speak with my father.

*   *   *

When the crowds had thinned, I signed in at the security check point, then limped down the stone stairwell into the bowels of Inverness Castle, pausing at the bottom step when I heard a woman's voice.

Quietly, I peeked around the corner.

It was Theresa Cialino, and she was speaking to Angus, her tone quite anxious.

"They won't make me testify, will they?"

"Theresa, calm doon."

"I don't want to testify, Angus. What if he asks me directly?"

"Darlin', relax. Obrecht disnae ken enough tae ask."

"He knew enough to ask about the salmon. And he found the cheque."

"A' o' which is circumstantial, though I telt ye no' tae pay me after whit happened."

"I'm sorry, I'm sorry . . . you know I was a lunatic that week. I had to run the company, I just started paying stacks of bills . . . I never knew what you'd told the police."

"Shh, calm doon. In the end, none o' it'll matter anyway."

"Angus . . . maybe we should just come forward, I mean, it's not too late. Maxie could recall Calum. He could question him about everything that happened last winter. His testimony alone might—"

"No, no, an' no! Bad enough I wis kicked oot o' the Order. Damn if I'll be subjectin' my best friend tae Alban MacDonald's fury. No, Theresa, we stick tae the plan, that's the best bet. You watch, Zachary'll soon find the monster, then a' this'll be behind us."

"I wouldn't get your hopes up. Your son's no closer to locating the creature than he was when he first arrived. And despite your prodding, he still hasn't approached me about borrowing our boat."

"He will."

"What if he doesn't? Face it, Angus, your son's still afraid."

"No he isnae! Zachary's got Wallace blood runnin' through him, an' he'll come through, jist as I predicted. Where's yer trawler?"

"Docked in Fort Augustus."

"Contact the captain. Have him bring her up tae the Clansman's Wharf. Be easier tae get Zack tae board her an'—"

"And what?" Revealing myself, I stomped over to his cell, fists balled, my veins boiling. *I'm no' a murderer, Zachary, I didnae dae it, son.* Liar!"

Angus looked deathly pale. "Son, it's . . . it's no' whit ye think."

"Shut up! You used me in court, then you prodded and pushed me, baiting me to go after the creature just so I could solidify your alibi . . . your lie. Well it's over. I've testified, now I'm going home, and you and the merry widow here can rot in hell for all I care."

"Zack, wait! Dinnae leave, son, ye cannae go now!"

Ignoring the pain in my foot, I hurried down the corridor and back up the stairwell, covering my ears against his rants and wails.

In the summer of 1986 we ran sonar tests in preparation for Operation Deepscan, the most extensive search of Loch Ness ever conceived. Laurence Electronics agreed to supply us with Simpson-Lowrance X-16 sonar units, selected because they'd record anything seen in the Loch's depths onto a paper chart. Each unit had a range of thirteen hundred feet and could target objects as small as twelve inches and one inch apart.

On October 9th, 1987, Operation Deepscan began - the largest sonar sweep of a freshwater body ever attempted. Over 250 news reporters and 20 television crews attended the event, more than showed up for the Gorbachev-Reagan summit in Reykjavik, Iceland, in '86. We began our search in the waters off the Clansman Hotel. Nineteen boats formed a line across the width of Loch Ness, each outfitted with an X-16 sonar unit. Following the flotilla was the New Atlantis, a faster boat fitted with a Simrad Scanning sonar, designed to home in on any identified contacts. On the first day, three strong sonar contacts were recorded between 78 meters (256 feet) and 180 meters (590 feet). The best of the three was recorded over 140 seconds at 174 meters just off Whitefield, opposite Urquhart Bay. After a thorough analysis, David Steensland of Laurence Electronics stated that the three targets were larger than a shark, but smaller than a whale.

–Adrian Shine, Director: Operation Deepscan, Royal Geographic Society

CHAPTER 28

Urquhart Bay

"**IT'LL BE THE MOST EXTENSIVE** search and capture ever undertaken, and when it's done, the monster will be locked safely in her pen."

David Caldwell stood at the podium of the outdoor sound stage, Brandy at his side, as he addressed members of the Highland Council. Upward of a thousand locals and tourists listened, along with scores of reporters, news personalities, and their camera crews.

"Would you break down this plan for us, Dr. Caldwell?"

"That's why we're here. As you can see, the pontoon bridge has been completed in record time. What you can't see is below the waterline, where two-thirds of the steel fencing is now in place. The remaining third, located close to the northern shore, is purposely being left open."

David pointed to the *Nessie III* and the *Nothosaur*, both vessels now positioned inside the perimeter of the arcing pontoon bridge. "The first phase of our plan was to ready the pen while using our active sonar to keep Nessie within her lair. Lives saved, mission accomplished. Now it's time for phase two, actually capturing the monster. Now that she's good and hungry, we'll set our trap. Once it gets dark, we'll be lowering one more buoy into the water—only this one will be located in the middle of Urquhart Bay, well inside the pen. Attached to it will be loads of juicy bait. Once the monster enters, the crew of the *Nothosaur* will net the creature while our construction team lowers the remaining fence into position, sealing off the pen."

I stood near the back of the grandstand and listened as dozens of reporters yelled out their questions over one another, David focusing on the few he hoped he could answer.

"Dr. Caldwell, assuming you do capture the monster, what's going to prevent it from simply escaping by land?"

"Eventually we'll be adding perimeter fencing. For now, we're in the process of lining the shoreline with underwater speakers. I've discovered Nessie avoids loud sounds. Once the monster's captured, we'll turn up the volume along the shoreline's speakers and that'll be that."

"Won't that aggravate the creature?"

"Nah. We'll play Mozart or something mellow, like 'Auld Lang Syne.'"

The crowd laughed, David basking in their adoration.

"Dr. Caldwell, once she's inside, how long will it take to seal off the pen?"

"According to the crane operator and his team, they'll be able to complete the job in less than fifteen minutes."

"What happens after you capture her?"

"First we'll make sure her pen's good and tight, then we'll use remotely operated submersibles to get a good look at her. Once she gets used to her new habitat, we'll open it up to the public."

"Don't you mean the paying public?"

"Hey, you pay to get into the zoo, don't you? That's what this'll be, only like no other zoo in the world."

There were a hundred questions I wanted to shout, but what was the point? Besides, I had no stomach for it; the revelation of my father's crime eating me up inside.

Mentally, I felt fried, and if I hadn't sent True on an errand to his oil rig in the North Sea, I'd have probably been on the next flight back to Miami.

But before I could leave with a clear conscience, there was one last thing I had to do.

Grabbing my cane, I limped away from the fairgrounds, making my way through the growing throng. The hillsides surrounding Urquhart Bay were already packed with hundreds of people staking out their vantage for the evening's spectacle-to-come. There were blankets and chairs, sleeping bags and tents, barbecues and spits, and folding tables covered with food. Vendors hocked their wares, and musicians dressed in minstrel costumes played, their tunes in sharp contrast to the heavy metal music coming from boom boxes and CD players across the main lawn.

It was the event of the year, perhaps of the century if the guest of honor chose tonight to make her appearance, but I had other plans.

Climbing aboard my motorcycle, I gunned the engine, heading south toward Invermoriston.

*   *   *

Despite my father's "confession," there was still an undercurrent of lies, deceit, and secrecy surrounding the Loch Ness predator that prevented me from just walking away. And when it came to keeping secrets in the Highlands, one need look no farther than the Clans.

While the ancient Scottish lowlands were ruled by its border chiefs and lords, the Highland geography, with its mountains and glens, lochs and islands, forced populations to congregate in smaller clusters, known as Clans. Clan is a Gaelic word that translates to "children" or more appropriately, "family." Each Highland "family" was run by a chief, whose name his followers took. The chief served as supreme leader and lawgiver and all clansmen swore their allegiance as "kin." Each clan had a coat of arms and tartan, which distinguished rank, not by the plaid, but by the number of colors in the weave. In the harsh environment of the Highlands, the clan represented solidarity, a form of government, and protection against enemies.

Over the centuries, the size of the clan chief's estate grew, and he'd often sublet the land to his clansmen for farming, a practice later known as crofting.

The clans' rule came to an abrupt end in 1746 with the last Jacobite uprising and the defeat of Bonnie Prince Charlie at the Battle of Culloden. King George's "Disarming Act" outlawed the tartan and the clans' system of government, paving the way for a Highland central authority. Crofters, tenants of the land, lost their stability, although subsequent crofting acts were eventually established to protect the rights of rural farmers. Still, the once-powerful clans and their centuries-old ways gradually faded into the shadows.

The Black Knights of the Templar were operating in these shadows, and from what I surmised, their members had come from the most established of the old clans.

The question I needed answered: What was their objective?

*   *   *

Calum Forrest was kin to both Clan Stewart and Clan MacDonald, two of Scotland's most powerful families, a fact further made evident by the location of the water bailiff's croft. The nearest crofting community was in Grotaig, set high above the Loch through dense Scots pine, but Calum's scenic ten hectares, like the land my father had sold to John Cialino, were located right on the Ness's banks, just south of Invermoristion.

It took me twenty minutes before I finally found the single lane dirt access road that led me to Calum's lakeside croft. Barbed-wire fencing marked the property, and its one-story farmhouse and barn were set far back from the water's edge. Six hundred sheep, all congregating close to the dwellings, dotted the fenced-off grassland.

As I rode closer, I noticed a small wooden pier jutting out into the Loch. The water bailiff's boat was nowhere in sight.

Following the unpaved road into the Forrest's driveway, I parked next to an old tractor re-painted lime green, which had seen better days, and walked over to the farmhouse.

I knocked on the door. No answer. I walked around back and peeked in the kitchen door window, but it was dark inside, no one home.

Wind blew off the Loch, whistling through the farm's fence. The wooden posts that supported the barbed wire were gray and rotting, in desperate need of repair.

Most crofters were poor, the land never intended to provide locals with a living. Crofters had to find additional employment in order to support their families, in Calum Forrest's case, it meant working as water bailiff. Still, it helped that he was raising sheep. Highland sheep farms were subsidized by the government. Without these monies most farmers would go bankrupt, a reality blamed on poor soil conditions, harsh weather, and the distance to major markets.

Leaving the farmhouse, I walked to the nearest gate of the grazing fence, staring out at the magnificent view. A late-afternoon storm was brewing, kicking lather off the surface, and even at this distance, I could feel its spray on my face. It must have bothered the sheep, for the animals remained huddled in the near corner of the acreage.

And then I noticed something bizarre.

All the grass nearest the farmhouse had been heavily grazed upon, much of it exposing bare earth, yet the grass closest to the Loch remained high and untouched.

And yet the herd refused to venture away from the farmhouse.

Curious, I unbolted the gate and entered the grazing area. The heavy scent of farm animals filled my nostrils as I moved past the sheep and across the untouched grassland, heading for the far fence that bordered Loch Ness's shoreline.

Arriving at the opposite gate, I immediately noticed several things.

Unlike the fencing near the farmhouse, the wood and wire along the Loch side was brand-new and far sturdier, its gate heavily chained. More curious were coils of barbed wire set along the outside of the fence, creating a barrier that separated the grazing area from the Loch's fifteen-foot drop-off.

But the mental alarm bells truly sounded when I spotted the aluminum shed housing a portable generator and the half dozen bundles of wire that fed *into* Loch Ness!

Desiring a better vantage, I scaled the bolted fence, then maneuvered down a tight, twisting foot path bordered by barbed wire which led to the boating dock. Walking out on the pier, I lay down on my belly and scanned the water's edge.

There were eight underwater floodlights, set in pairs and all facing out toward the Loch.

Now I knew why the sheep were huddled away from the water—they were afraid! Calum was afraid, too, but he'd chosen to adopt new defenses rather than expose the creature to the rest of the world.

Why?

Wind whipped at my face, the once-clear sky growing overcast and gray. Feeling more than a bit uneasy on the dock, I walked back to the gate, scaled it, then returned to my motorcycle just as it began to rain. The barn door was unlocked, so I pushed the Harley inside, then lay back against a bale of hay while I awaited the return of Calum Forrest.

Aboard the *Nessie III*
Urquhart Bay
9:45 P.M.

Wind whipped across Loch Ness, rattling the pilothouse windshield while churning the dark surface into three-foot swells.

Brandy Townson stood steady at the wheel, her mind preoccupied with keeping the *Nessie III* clear of Urquhart Bay's unforgiving shoreline.

Michael Newman sat behind her at the sonar array, his head in his hands, his stomach queasy from the constant rocking. Being stuck inside the pilothouse was only compounding the engineer's seasickness, and he desperately needed to get off the water and back into his dry, warm hotel room.

"I can't take this anymore, I'm going to be sick!"

"No' in here," Brandy yelled. "Use the head."

Hand over mouth, Newman took off down the steps, barely making it to the bathroom in time.

David emerged from below, not bothered by the motion. Slipping behind Brandy, he nuzzled her neck.

"David, stop. That tickles."

"David stop, David stop. That's all I've been hearing from you over the last week. What's the problem?"

"If ye don't mind, I'm tryin' tae keep us off the rocks."

"You know what I mean. That first night in the bar, you were all over me. Now you act like I have a disease."

"I'm just feelin' a wee bit vulnerable. I'm comin' out o' a bad marriage, ye know."

"That's not it. If you remember, you came onto me, obviously so I'd choose your boat to lead this hunt. You used me."

"Oh, please! Like *you're* so innocent. I needed the job, an' ye've never hesitated paradin' me around in skimpy outfits, usin' me as Highland arm candy. Business is business."

"If that's the way you want to play it, fine. Just so you know, I met with a very wealthy woman earlier today who offered me use of her boat. It's about three times the size of this piece of driftwood, and the press'll eat her up just as much as they do you."

"Ye're lyin'."

"Her name's Theresa Cialino."

"Johnny C.'s widow?"

"You got it. So you'd better start making nice again or . . ."

Michael Newman stumbled back into the pilothouse, his face pale. "Caldwell, I can't handle much more of this. We either do this now, or you drop me off somewhere."

"Relax, I just spoke with Hoagland. The buoy with the bait's in the water. You can reset the array from active to passive."

"Thank Christ." Using the mouse, Newman clicked on a command, then typed in PASSIVE.

Across Loch Ness, thirty-four pinging sonar buoys went silent.

Calum Forrest's Croft

I opened my eyes, enveloped by darkness. Thunder echoed in the distance, and for a frightening moment, I'd forgotten where I was.

The barn.

I must've dozed off, but something had woken me.

The storm?

The wind?

No, it was a beeping sound, coming from my laptop.

I fumbled for the machine and opened the monitor, its luminescent screen bathing my surroundings in blue light. The GPS real-time image of Loch Ness gradually came into focus, highlighted by thirty-four green dots representing the sonar buoys.

The word ACTIVE had changed to PASSIVE in the upper-right corner of the screen.

The beeping sound was coming from a sonar alert. Heart pounding, I typed in a command, isolating the object's location.

The screen changed, focusing in on the middle third of the array. A tiny red blip was moving south, following Loch Ness's eastern shoreline.

I typed in IDENTIFY OBJECT and pressed ENTER.

BIOLOGIC. Length: 15.75 meters.

        Speed: 13 knots.

        Direction: South by southwest.

        Location: 2.48 kilometers south of Foyers.

Almost sixteen meters? That made it over fifty feet long!

As I watched the screen, the red blip suddenly altered its course and crossed the Loch, heading toward the opposite shore.

Jesus . . . It's moving in this direction.

I pushed open the barn door, shocked at what I was now seeing.

It was night, a nasty one, the dark shoreline directly behind the perimeter fence bathed in an artificial white light. Calum's boat was docked at the pier. Two sheep were *baaing* in a small clearing outside of the fence, the animals tied off to stakes located close to the water. The patch of grass was made visible in the darkness by a red light coming from a lamp post situated atop the perimeter fencing.

Then I saw Calum. The water bailiff was dragging a third sheep to the clearing. The petrified animal was on a short leash, and it was bucking against him furiously.

Calum knelt in the grass and attached the free end of the leash to something unseen on the ground. Reentering the grazing area, he secured the gate, then hurried toward a corner post and pulled a lever on an electrical box.

The shoreline's lights were extinguished, leaving the land and Loch enveloped in blackness save for the red patch of light where the three sheep huddled together, bawling into the night.

I glanced at the laptop. The red blip had crossed over to our western shoreline and was continuing its approach, the object now less than a mile from Invermoriston.

This is insane. He's . . . he's actually feeding it!

Patches of lightning flashed overhead, revealing storm clouds, mountains, and Calum, still at his post. Sweat poured from my body. My flesh tingled.

The blip grew nearer.

Trembling, yet needing to get closer, I slipped out of the barn and crept toward the fence.

The three sheep fought their collars, their cries becoming more desperate.

I crept along the outside of the fence, close to where the rest of the herd huddled and snorted.

The blip passed Invermoriston, erasing any doubts.

I continued along the perimeter until I was within forty yards of the water's edge. Deciding I was close enough, I knelt in the mud and waited.

The sheep continued mounting and gnawing at one another in fear.

And then they froze.

I never saw the monster as it approached the shoreline, I only saw a dark mass, its upper torso as large as a school bus, as it emerged like a shadow, and then its wide, serpentlike head became bathed in the red pool of light, and its immense jaws snapped, lightning-quick, upon two of the sheep. One disappeared into the night, the other flipped up into the air, then landed awkwardly on its back, its hind legs fractured, yet still kicking. While the injured animal flopped on the ground, its surviving companion wrenched and twisted its head, finally freeing itself of the leash's collar.

The sheep darted away.

The heavens ignited in a blaze of white and navy, revealing the silhouette of a towering head and neck which lashed sideways across the patch of red light with impossible, heart-stopping quickness.

The open jowls snatched the fleeing sheep, the monster flinging its head back, engulfing the farm animal in one whole, sickening motion.

It was brutal and frightening and startling to behold, yet I looked on, paralyzed, my eyes as wide as saucers as the heavens darkened again and the monster morphed once more into the shadows.

Before the creature could advance, the shoreline suddenly reappeared, bathed in its brilliant white light, driving the devil back into its watery domain.

Shaking, I forced myself to take deep breaths. The creature I had just witnessed was as cold and cruel as the Loch itself, as violent as nature could be. It was pure animal, pure evolution, existing solely on instinct. It was magnificent in its primal beauty, and frightening in the ruthlessness of its attack.

I needed to see more. I needed to *know* more.

Regaining my feet, I grabbed my laptop and hurried around to the front of the gate, quietly letting myself in the grazing area.

Calum stood over the remaining sheep, then shot the injured beast with a revolver. Dragging the dead animal to the water, he pushed the bleeding carcass over the edge. He reentered the grazing area, then saw me as he approached the back of the farmhouse, stopping dead in his tracks. "Ye saw?"

"Everything." Lightning flashed overhead. "Let's talk inside."

He thought for a long moment, then I followed him up the stoop of his back porch and into the farmhouse.

Urquhart Bay
11:25 P.M.

Michael Newman pointed at the screen, too excited to remain seasick. "We lost it after it passed Invermoriston, then it reappeared. See? It's staying deep, hanging out in the middle of the Loch, just south of Invermoriston."

David peered over the engineer's shoulder, high on adrenaline. "Invermoriston? That's like what? Ten miles south? How do we get it to swim up here?"

"Give it time. Maybe it'll smell the bait?"

"And maybe we'll lose it again. The bait's just sitting in the water. If it wanted it, it would have taken it long ago. This thing's not stupid."

David looked out the starboard window. Though the wind had died down, it was still drizzling, thinning out what had been a capacity crowd of more than three thousand. "Brandy, move us closer to the buoy, I have an idea."

Calum Forrest's Croft
11:37 P.M

I sat at Calum's kitchen table, my pulse beating in rhythm to a grandfather clock ticking somewhere in the darkened living room.

The water bailiff set out two cups of coffee, then added a shot of whisky to each. "Aye takes me a nip or three afore my nerves calm doon. My wife, God rest her soul, often had tae dae it for me."

"How long have you been feeding it?"

"Since afore ye were born, an' long afore that, but only in winters. Come summer, there's plenty o' fish."

"But not this summer?"

He glanced at my injured foot. "I think ye a'ready ken that answer, dae ye no'?"

"This sheep croft, how long has it been in your family?"

"Since the time o' yer kin, Sir Adam Wallace."

"Sir Adam Wallace? Never heard of him."

"Then it's best ye ask yer faither."

"I'm asking you. Was Adam Wallace a Templar Black Knight?"

"He wis the first."

"So the mission of the Black Knights was to feed these creatures?"

"It's a part o' it, an' we call them Guivres. The one they call Nessie's the last."

"Why's she the last?"

"Cannae say."

"Then let me say. From the size of her, there's no way Nature ever intended her or her kind to be permanent inhabitants of a fresh water loch, even one as big as Loch Ness. That means the Black Knights must have cut off her passage to the North Sea . . . am I right?"

Calum said nothing, but the twinkle in his eye encouraged me to continue.

"Now why would the Black Knights want these monsters stuck in Loch Ness?" I thought a moment. "You were using them! You wanted to keep people away. That's it, isn't it?"

"Sort o'."

"Fine. Forget about the Knights' mission for now. I'm more concerned with why this creature's feeding on humans."

"As am I."

"The Anguilla eel that attacked me had lesions in its brain, caused by hydrocarbon poisoning."

"Whit's that?"

"It comes from oil. There's oil leaking somewhere, and it's getting into the Loch. You're the water bailiff, have you—"

"I havenae found any oil."

"Okay. But what if it's coming through the passage that connects the Loch with the North Sea?"

The old man considered this scenario. "Aye, that's possible."

"Then there really is a passage! Tell me where it is."

He shook his head. "I cannae dae that. Besides, the passage collapsed years ago, back when they built the A82. It trapped a few o' the Guivres in Loch Ness, preventin' the rest o' their kind frae enterin'. Nessie's the last o' them. The alpha beast, as Doc Hornsby wid say."

"And now she's gone crazy."

"Aye."

"Those underwater lights . . . when did you install them?"

"No' that long ago."

"Winter? Spring?"

He avoided eye contact. "Maybe winter."

"What happened this winter that you felt a need to install the lights?"

"Ye said it yersel', Nessie went crazy!" He pushed away from the table, obviously agitated. "Whit are ye gonnae dae now that ye ken? Will ye kill her like yer faither wants? Is that why ye're here?"

"My father wants the monster killed?"

"Dinnae play games, I want tae ken whit ye'll dae tae her."

It was Alban MacDonald's words, and I offered the same reply. "I'll free her if I can. Is that what you want?"

I thought that would please him, but instead he turned away, his fists balled, his weathered face turning red.

"Wait a sec . . . you want her dead, too, don't you?"

"It's past her time an' she's dangerous, but I cannae dae it."

"Because of your oath as a Black Knight?"

"Aye."

Suddenly remembering the laptop, I yanked open the lid, checking for the blip. "Oh shit."

The monster was heading north, closing fast on Urquhart Bay.

I was along the south shore of Loch Ness, fishing for brown trout, looking almost directly into Urquhart Bay, when I saw something break the surface, then disappear. I kept watching, keeping an eye out, fishing gently, when a great elephantlike shape rose from the water. It was a large black object . . . a whalelike object. It submerged, then reappeared a matter of seconds later, and I noticed it had rotated, turning before surfacing.

I called to my friend, Willie Frazer, who himself had a sighting a year earlier, almost to the day. He saw it, too, and we realized it was moving toward us, moving against the current. It was two hundred meters away, and people on the other side of the Loch were watching it, too. It remained along the surface for fifty minutes, the longest sighting on record.

—Ian Cameron, former Superintendent of the Northern Police Force, June 1965

Urquhart Bay

DAVID WAVED to the reenergized crowd, then climbed over the starboard rail, his rubber-soled shoes slipping along the wet surface. "Newman, hand me that fishing gaff, then hold on to my belt so I don't fall in."

"I need to check the array."

"You'll check it in a minute. First I want to hook the bait rope."

Michael Newman handed him the reach pole, then grabbed him about the waist. "This is a mistake. The *Nothosaur* should be dragging the bait, not us."

"We need them to cut off the plesiosaur's escape."

"Wake up, Caldwell. Sonar says the creature's fifty-two feet long. That's almost twice the size of this rickety old tub."

"Will you relax. Once it enters the bay, we can always cut the rope. You eggheads worry too much."

"At least we know better than to be playing with an aluminum reach pole out on the water during a lightning storm."

"Chill, *mom*." David leaned out, slapping the hook end of the fishing gaff at the buoy's submerged rope. "Got it, first try, too. Here, grab the pole while I climb back over, and don't lose it, it's a lot heavier than it looks."

Gripping the aluminum pole, Newman pulled the hooked rope toward him. "Geez, it weighs a ton. What's on the end of this?"

"Dead cow. Hoagland sawed off its legs so it would bleed a nice trail. Here, help me guide the rope back toward the stern, then we'll tie it off."

Struggling with the gaff, it took them another five minutes before they gained enough slack to loop the rope around a metal cleat.

Newman wiped his wet hands on David's sweatshirt. "There. You can cut the line to the buoy without me, I'm checking the array." The engineer reentered the pilothouse, searching the sonar grid.

The red blip was gone.

"Not good."

"What's not good?" Brandy asked.

"I lost the monster. It disappeared somewhere along the shore-line."

"So find it." She pushed down on the throttle, feeling the *Nessie III*'s engine strain to drag the dead cow through the water.

"I can't find it!" Newman snapped back. "Must've slipped into a blind spot along the western slope." The engineer's eyes widened as the blip reappeared. "Oh God, there it is! Jesus, it's already in the bay!"

"What?"

"It's in the fucking bay! Caldwell, cut us loose!"

"What?"

"Cut us loose!"

"Are you crazy? I just—"

The *Nessie III* lurched sideways as an immense force snatched the bait and dragged it into deeper water.

The wheel was wrenched from Brandy's hand, the *Nessie III* pulling hard to starboard, its keel half out of the water.

Brandy fell, as did the sonar array, Michael Newman with it. Tumbling on his back, he slid out the open pilothouse door and smack against the submerging starboard rail as the boat continued to roll.

David grabbed for the bait rope, which was all he could do since he had no knife to cut it with. As the starboard rail dipped into the water and the crowd roared somewhere off to his right, he glanced over his shoulder, shocked to see the port side of the *Nessie III* blotting out the storm clouds as it began its surreal topple towards him.

David dove underwater seconds before the capsizing boat completed its 180-degree roll.

Brandy could only curl in a ball and cover her head as the pilothouse went topsy-turvy around her. She somersaulted blindly across her instrument panel, then was struck by a freezing wall of water that burned her skin.

The flooding cabin creaked and groaned, blanketing her in darkness.

* * *

On the banks of Urquhart Bay, thousands of onlookers stood, yelling and gesturing and snapping photos as the *Nessie III* capsized. For several adrenaline-pumping moments, the boat's hull was forcefully dragged sideway through the water, and then the cleat tore free, releasing the vessel.

The metal clasp skimmed across the surface. As it sank, it caught several loops of the heavy fishing net that, moments earlier, had been tied off atop the pilothouse roof, dragging it with it.

* * *

The bow of Calum Forrest's speedboat bounced erratically across the dark surface, spraying me every few seconds with cold water. Ahead, I could see the lights outlining Urquhart Bay while on my laptop, I saw the red blip reappear as it entered David's pen.

Moments later, my heart skipped a beat as the Web link shut down.

* * *

Michael Newman surfaced, wheezing and gagging. The engineer was freezing, the frigid water locking his muscles. His mind in shock, he considered swimming the three hundred yards to shore, then he saw the current created by the circling fishing net and decided maybe it was better to just stay right where he was.

Brandy was still in the submerged pilothouse. Despite being in total darkness, she knew her boat like the back of her hand, and it only took her a few seconds to locate the inverted cabin door and swim free.

David surfaced thirty feet from the capsized hull, his only thought, to prevent the monster from escaping. Looking back, he was excited to see the *Nothosaur* blocking the exit of the pen, while the crane on the construction pontoon lowered the first of the remaining six lengths of fencing into place.

Beautiful.

Satisfied, he turned, swimming back toward the capsized boat, never noticing the partially submerged fishing net closing on his right. Without warning, he was swept away, loops of heavy rope ensnaring his right arm and both ankles.

"Hey! What the fah—"

An intense force, like that of a grade four rapids, dragged David under. Frantic, he twisted and kicked and fought his way back to the surface, his limbs now hopelessly entangled.

The *Nessie III*'s hull was too slick with slime and algae to allow Brandy and Michael Newman to climb out of the water. Instead, they huddled together by the slowly sinking vessel, their breath visible above the chilly waters.

"Ha . . . help!"

They looked around, trying to locate the source of what sounded like a gurgling scream. Newman pointed to their left as David surfaced and was dunked again.

"Ah, gees, he's caught in the net." Brandy felt along the back pockets of her jeans for her Swiss Army knife. "Stay here!"

Kicking away from the hull, she swam out, waiting for David to circle by again.

* * *

Michael Hoagland watched the action through binoculars from the starboard deck of the *Nothosaur*. "Victor, how much longer?"

The sonar tech's eyes were focused on the pontoon behind them. "The last panel's being readied now."

"As soon as it's lowered, get us over to that capsized boat!"

* * *

Brandy treaded water, her heart racing as the circling net approached. Anticipating its path, she avoided it, then grabbed for David as he rushed by.

He went under again and she leaped for him, brandishing her knife.

David felt the disturbance and lunged blindly for her.

Brandy pushed him aside, fighting to keep herself from becoming caught in the entanglement of loops. Remaining spreadeagled atop the netting, she felt her way to David's left leg and began sawing at the thick, wet rope.

And then they stopped moving.

Freed of the current, David thrashed his way back to the surface, gagging in her ear. "Cut me loose!"

"Stop yer squirmin', I'm tryin'!" She continued attacking the rope, unaware that something immense was now rising slowly beneath them.

*   *   *

Calum steered his boat to the edge of the pontoon bridge. "I cannae get inside the bay!"

I saw the *Nothosaur*, and beyond it, the capsized *Nessie III*. I saw David thrashing in the water, caught inside a partially submerged fishing net, and I saw Brandy, trying to free him.

And in my mind's eye, I saw the monster, rising from the depths to take them, just as it had taken me seventeen years earlier.

Tearing off my shoe and walking boot, I grabbed the log-sized plastic case in my right hand and climbed onto the prefabricated bridge.

I hurried across the structure, then dove into the water, swimming as fast as a frightened man could.

My eyes watered, the icy temperatures like a vise on my lungs, each breath a forced gasp, my throat tensing up.

I reached David, "where's Brandy?"

She surfaced next to him. "Zack, we're both caught . . . I lost my knife!"

The light, Zachary, get to the light!

Move!

I ducked my head underwater, aimed the light cannon, and pressed the power switch.

The underwater beacon ignited, blazing a penetrating funnel of light into the depths. The beam illuminated a tea-colored environment swirling with particles of peat. I saw Brandy and David's legs, entangled in the drifting latticework of cocoa brown netting, my heart nearly stopping as I spotted the breaching monster's head!

It was rising directly beneath us, thirty feet and closing, a dark majestic serpent as wide as an SUV. As it moved closer, the light caught its hideous snub-nosed snout and fang-filled outstretched jaws in mid-yawn, the insane creature intent on devouring both Brandy and David.

Fighting through my fear, I maneuvered the angle of the beam, catching the ascending leviathan flush in one of its sensitive yellow eyes.

The monster spasmed as if hit by a laser, then whirled about in a sudden 180-degree retreat. I caught a blurred glimpse of an enormous brown tail before I was literally driven free of the surface by its retreating wake.

I grabbed a quick breath and ducked my head again, the light cannon's beacon catching the tip of the beast's tail as it disappeared into the darkness in a flurry of peat and bubbles. My right ankle jerked free of the net, a reflex, as it suddenly went taut and submerged, dragging Brandy and David with it!

Kicking hard, I lunged for the edge of the net with my free hand and held on, allowing it to tow me into the depths as I struggled to reach Brandy.

She grabbed onto my arm and held tight, using my body as leverage as she struggled to free herself from the heavy bonds entangling her left knee.

We were submerging at a frightening speed, dropping an atmosphere every few seconds. The pain in my ear passages tore into my brain as we jettisoned beyond eighty feet, when Brandy slipped out of her jeans and pulled her leg free.

We floated away, no longer encumbered, while the net continued below into darkness, dragging the hopelessly encumbered David along for the ride.

I hovered there in the blackness and silence of watery space, searching for him with the light. The edge of the beam caught his pale face, his expression—frozen in horror—as he disappeared into the frigid depths of Loch Ness.

Brandy tugged at my elbow and we kicked toward the surface. I kept the beam aimed below as long as I could, hoping David would see it.

Get to the light, David. Get to the light.

We surfaced and exhaled, gasping for air, our extremities no longer functioning in the cold. Desperate moments passed, until we were finally hauled out of the water by the *Nothosaur*'s crew, and dropped on the deck.

Crewmen draped wool blankets over the two of us and we held on to one another, panting and dripping and shivering. Brandy threw an arm around my neck and hugged me, her purple lips cold against my face.

"Thh . . . thought ye were afraid o' the water?"

I pressed my mouth to her ear. "More afraid of losing you."

She hugged me tighter, saying nothing.

Michael Newman, wrapped in his own blanket, flopped down next to us. "Caldwell?"

I shook my head.

Captain Hoagland tapped Brandy's shoulder, pointing at the construction pontoon and derrick. "Look, the pen's sealed. We've got the monster trapped."

It was true, the pen had been sealed. And then I heard the crowd cheer amidst a strange sound. It filled my ears like rolling thunder, only it wasn't thunder, it was David's underwater speakers, pumping out a familiar cadence from my childhood.

It was bagpipes, the recorded sounds originating around the shoreline, the bizarre tune muffled behind layers of water.

David was right, the acoustics were keeping the creature from accessing land, but they were also tormenting the beast, enraging it.

Without warning, the incensed creature struck the perimeter fencing. Metal screeched and connecting hinges snapped as sections of the floating bridge expanded and buckled under the ungodly force. A dozen of the prefabricated platforms broke free from one another, held together only by the interconnected lengths of chain link fence.

The crowd gasped. The *Nothosaur*'s crew looked stunned.

Four hundred feet below, the monster whirled about in the darkness, then struck again.

This time it pounded the just-completed northern end of the barricade, its head bulldozing the underwater barrier. The strike severed the cables connecting the last platform to its concrete land anchor, collapsing the entire expanse.

Protesting metal rent the night as twenty-eight-foot sections of bridge buckled and broke free from one another like a derailed locomotive.

The monster kept at it, driving its enormous head through two wobbling sections of fence until it managed to thrash itself free.

As the animal escaped into open water, the bait line snapped, leaving behind an entanglement of fishing net and the lifeless body of David James Caldwell II.

I'm guessing it was around 4:15 in the afternoon on July 30 that Sue and I noticed a dark shape appear and disappear three times very quickly. Whatever it was, it was about 150 meters from shore, moving into Urquhart Bay. The object then appeared to churn about in a left turn and surface a little farther away.

—Alastair Boyd, Art Teacher

It looked like the top of a huge tire inner tube, at least six meters (approximately twenty feet) long. It was only visible about five seconds, but it was definitely an animal of some sort.

—Sue Boyd, Art Teacher

CHAPTER 30

Inverness

BRANDY MOVED IN WITH ME that night. Having lost her home, all her worldly possessions, and her livelihood, she had nothing left.

She said it didn't matter, as long as she had me.

It was nearly 3:00 A.M., the summer sun already gray in the eastern horizon by the time we squirmed together between the crisp hotel sheets, our entwined naked bodies creating all the heat we'd need. Too exhausted to make love, I simply held her until she fell asleep, then I slipped out of bed and sat at the desk with my laptop.

I was exhausted. Sleep tugged at my brain, but I was too afraid to doze. The intensity of my night terrors had been increasing, and after what had just happened on Urquhart Bay, I was simply too exhausted to face them again. Images of my childhood drowning had now been replaced by something else, and this vision was even more terrifying because it was not of my past. In truth, I feared it was my destiny.

Stay awake until dawn. You'll rest easier in the daylight.

I forced myself to focus through the fatigue.

The last forty-eight hours had revealed new pieces of the Loch Ness puzzle, but they were swirling in my head, and I was too tired to think.

Organize your thoughts. Write them out so you can see them.

Activating the laptop, I began typing.

Angus and Theresa.
Anguilla eels and the Sargasso Sea.
Calum Forrest feeding the monster every winter.
The mission of the Black Knights.
Adam Wallace.

> **The collapse of the North Sea aquifer in the early 1930s.**
> **Calum Forrest erecting underwater lights last winter.**
> **Oil seeping into Loch Ness.**
> **Beta blockers found in eel's bloodstream.**
> **John Cialino's death.**
> **Angus deliberately lying about the salmon.**

I stared at the screen, then cut and pasted, reorganizing my notes in what I surmised to be a chronological order.

Adam Wallace.

Calum had said Adam Wallace was the first Black Knight. Strange that my father had never mentioned him. Whatever the Knights' primary mission, it had obviously included feeding the species referred to by both Calum and my father as Guivres.

Fast-forward to the construction of the A82 in the early 1930s. According to Calum and my own unpublished theories, dynamiting the basin had collapsed an underground river that served as a North Sea access way, trapping a few of the creatures within Loch Ness. Both Alban and Calum confirmed Nessie was the last of her kind in the Loch. Calum said he and his late wife fed the beast during winters. That made sense, since the fish population of Loch Ness in winter would not be enough to sustain such a large predator. Of course, it was also possible that the beast had adapted to Loch Ness winters by hibernating.

Since Loch Ness was not teeming with 60-foot creatures, the animal my father had called a Guivre was most likely a mutant. Under normal conditions, mutations can occur in one of every 100,000 creatures. Beta-blockers in the eel's bloodstream would decrease the animal's sex drive. If the Guivre was a mutant, it was most likely sterile, explaining why there was not a breeding population of its kind in the Loch.

Whatever Nessie was, she obviously preferred to inhabit the Loch's deepest waters—

—until last winter.

Somewhere in the Great Glen, oil was leaking, and it was finding its way into Loch Ness. Though still undiscovered by the water bailiff and Scotland's EPA, it had nevertheless altered an entire season's migration of fish. Since the spawning fish could only enter Loch Ness from the River Ness, that meant the oil was most likely deterring them before they reached the Bona Narrows.

The oil had also altered the disposition of the eel population and the Loch's last Guivre. The Black Knights were patrolling the shorelines at night, trying to keep the tourists safe from the agitated Anguilla—and Nessie? Was that their mission?

No, it had to be more than that.

Last winter, as a precaution, Calum Forrest had reinforced his croft's fencing and installed underwater lights, along with . . .

Stop!

I stared at the computer screen, reworking the last assumption in my head.

Yes, Calum's lights were designed to scare off the creature, but that fence was still kindling to something as huge as Nessie. I had assumed the fence had been reinforced, but maybe . . . maybe it was just newer than the rest of the perimeter.

Maybe Calum had been *forced* to replace the rear fence last winter after the creature had attacked his herd of sheep?

But Calum was filled with rage. He not only wanted to keep Nessie away, he wanted it dead.

"My wife, God rest her soul, often had tae feed it for me."

His wife? Had the monster killed his wife?

A shiver ran down my spine as I typed out: **Investigate Mrs. Forrest's cause of death.**

Calum could have killed Nessie himself. He could have poisoned one of the sheep offerings, or lured the beast in close to shoot it, but he hadn't. The oath of the Black Knights had kept him from seeking revenge.

What mission could be so important?

And what had my father done to remove himself from the Order?

So it was possible Tiani Brueggart wasn't Nessie's first victim, there was a good chance the monster had killed last winter. Angus was close friends with Calum Forrest. Fiercely loyal, the death of his friend's wife, if true, must have surely upset him. Was that the reason he'd been banished from the Templar? Had Angus attempted to kill Nessie against Alban MacDonald's orders?

Angus and Theresa.

I stared at the clue, and then, suddenly, everything hit me at once.

Johnny C.'s death was no accident, Angus had killed him to be with Theresa! But instead of pleading guilty to involuntary manslaughter, my wily father had gone for broke. Knowing the creature was out there, knowing it would probably kill again, Angus had created his "Nessie defense," making himself a local legend while forcing the Black Knights to destroy the creature that had killed his best friend's wife.

It was a clever plan in its own sordid way, filled with risk and rewards. If Angus could prove the monster was out there, then he'd be found innocent and have Theresa Cialino, sharing in her inheritance. The two lovers would live happily ever after, while Angus still maintained his blood oath as a Black Knight.

All my father needed was to make sure a jury would find him innocent. To do that, he needed an expert on the case, one who not only could convince a jury that the monster really did exist, but someone who could even track it down.

And so, after seventeen years of silence, my father had reached out . . . and used me again!

Anger surged in my veins, tempered only by the fact that it had been my testimony that had exposed his lie.

I stared at my notes, still seething.

Anguilla eels and the Sargasso Sea.

One monster was on the loose, the other was sitting in an Inverness jail cell, waiting to be released so he could spend the rest of his days with his mistress.

Anguilla eels and the Sargasso Sea.

Angus had counted on using the scars of my childhood to play out his charade, but it had been my research, *my* testimony that might end up burying him!

Anguilla eels and the Sargasso Sea.

And what would my role be in the rest of this unholy mess? With David dead, the Highland Council would most likely approach me again for help, but I had no interest in capturing the beast. As far as I was concerned, it was already captured, in a lake twenty-three miles long. The key was to find the oil leak, shut it down, and return the biology of the Loch to its normal state.

Anguilla eels and the Sargasso Sea.

I kept staring at the words.

Anguilla eels and the Sargasso Sea.

Anguilla eels and the Sargasso Sea.

The left side of my brain finally took over, allowing the mental gear to tumble into place.

"Jesus, how could I have been so fucking blind!"

I clicked on the sonar array program, rewinding to the system's passive sonar recordings. The computer must have captured the monster's sonar signature earlier that evening, but I'd been too preoccupied to listen.

Locating the recording, I turned up the volume.

Blee-bloop . . . Blee-bloop . . . Blee-bloop . . . Blee-bloop . . .

My heart raced, my head swimming with the implications.

Blee-bloop . . . Blee-bloop . . . Blee-bloop . . . Blee-bloop . . .

"It is . . . it's the Bloop! How could I not see it? It was there, it was right there in front of me the whole time!"

Brandy stirred. "Zack? What's wrong?"

I leaped onto the bed. "I know, Brandy! I know what Nessie is! She's not a plesiosaur, she's not a dinosaur, she's not a sturgeon or a myth or even an ancestor of modern-day whales, but she is a precursor!"

"A precursor?" Brandy sat up in bed. "A precursor of what?"

"The Anguilla eel!"

"An Anguilla? Nah . . . how can that be? She's so big."

"It's Nature's way. The ancestors are always larger. Then evolution takes over, it adapts, it makes adjustments, based on environment and competition, and the availability of prey. Anguillas and these . . . these

Guivres, for lack of a better name—they're both born in the Sargasso Sea."

"How dae ye know that?"

"Because Nessie's not the last Guivre, and she's not a mutant, her kind's not extinct! Her species still inhabits the Sargasso. The Navy tracked them on sonar, called them *bloops*, but no one knew what they were. It was the bloops, I mean the Guivres, that attacked the giant squid. Like Anguilla, they spawn in the Sargasso Sea, then the young drift on ocean currents back to Britain and the rest of Europe. Being smaller, Anguilla could follow the Ness River into the Loch every spring. The larger females leave in autumn when they're old enough to spawn, but their big cousins, these Guivres, they were always too large to access the Loch through the river, instead they followed the Ness Aquifer—an undiscovered, underground river that flows from Loch Ness into the North Sea. But the passage collapsed seventy years ago when the A82 was dynamited—"

"Trappin' Nessie?"

"Yes!" I paced the room, my mind on fire. "She must be a female. Female Anguilla grow really big, much bigger than the males, so the same probably holds true for Guivres. They leave Loch Ness when they're ready to spawn, returning to the Sargasso Sea. But Nessie's trapped, it's screwed up her biological clock. She can't spawn in freshwater, her DNA won't allow that, so instead, she just kept growing, getting larger and larger. She's a mutant, Brandy, and now she's become dangerous, her brain filled with lesions caused by an oil leak."

"Oil? I dinnae understand?"

"There's oil leaking somewhere into Loch Ness. My guess is it's seeping into the aquifer, which is why no one's discovered it. The eel that attacked me had lesions on its brain. It's not lethal, but it affects the animal's disposition. The oil's also preventing salmon and other fish from entering the Loch. It's affected the food chain, altering Nessie's diet!"

"Sweet Mary. Zack, how long will she live? How much bigger will she get?"

"I don't know. Anguilla die after they spawn, it's sort of a biological termination device. Who knows with these Guivres?"

"Geez, Zachary, ye really did it! Ye solved the mystery, everyone said ye would. But calm down, ye're makin' me crazy. Come an' sit by me."

I took several deep breaths, then crawled into bed with her, cuddling under the sheets.

"What are ye gonnae do then? Call a press conference?"

"I don't know. I'm not sure what good it would do at this point. Science is one thing, but we've got a berserk animal on the loose. And it's . . . complicated."

"What do ye mean?"

"Angus lied. Nessie never killed Johnny C. Angus knew about the creature and used it as an alibi."

"Then he *did* murder Cialino?"

"Yes, and it was premeditated. If I don't produce this evidence, Angus walks away, Scot-free, as they say."

"But if ye tell the truth, yer father'll be found guilty."

"And most likely hanged."

She pulled me closer. "We're both exhausted. Get some sleep before ye decide anythin', a tired mind cannae think straight."

"I'm too pumped up to sleep."

She rolled over, her eyes seducing me as she climbed on top of me, pulling me into her warmth.

Our lovemaking soothed my brain fever, at least for the moment. When we were through, Brandy curled her back and buttocks against my chest and fell asleep. I put my arm around her and closed my eyes, comforted by her warmth and the arriving dawn.

*   *   *

Soaring through a watery graveyard. A flash of light. I am in a cavern. Alone. Enveloped by darkness. Not alone! Death whispers at me, growling in my brain. Stop! Stop! Stop!

I shot up in bed, bathed in sweat.

Brandy stood over me, trying to shake me awake.

"Zack! Zachary, look at me! Look at me, Zack, it was just another nightmare."

I turned and looked at her, consumed by fear, unable to find my voice.

"What was it then? What did ye dream?"

"I was in the monster's lair. It was dark and cold . . . cold like death. It seeped into my bones. It surrounded me, whispering into my brain. I couldn't see them, but something was out there, creeping in on me, and my flesh and my mind crawled in their presence. They encircled me . . . no escape—"

"Gees, yer whole body's tremblin'." She pulled me next to her and held me. "It was just a bad dream, Zack. It was just a nightmare."

She was wrong, of course, for I knew what it was.

As True would say, it was my destiny.

It was in mid-March and I was working on the banks of Loch Ness. I'm the area manager for an insurance company, and I cover a large part of the Highlands. Anyway, I was finishing some paperwork when, out of the corner of my eye, I saw this black hump come out of the water. I thought, "heavens" and looked at it again, and sure enough, it went back into the water and came back out again, and then back down. I thought, "I've seen it . . . after all these years, I've actually seen it!"

It's just typical of these things that I didn't have a camera with me and no one else to corroborate. But on the hump, I would say it was black, sort of a dark black color, and it had water coursing off of it, and it was just big . . . I think that's the best way to put it. It certainly wasn't a seal, it certainly wasn't a fish. All I can say is that, looking at the Loch, that somewhere in there is the Loch Ness monster. And as far as I'm concerned, I've seen it."

—Gary Campbell, Inverness resident, 14 March, 1996

CHAPTER 31

Upper Foyers, Loch Ness

HAVING BARELY SLEPT, I found myself racing the Harley-Davidson south on General Wade's Military Road, climbing the hills toward Upper Foyers with the rising sun.

I had called Max earlier, requesting a private meeting with Theresa Cialino at Inverness Castle. He told me the prosecution had decided not to call her as a witness, believing her testimony might dissuade the jury from seeking the death penalty, in the likely event they found Angus guilty. Max told me I could reach her at her summer estate in Upper Foyers, but asked that I return to Inverness in time for the barristers' closing remarks.

I turned onto the B852, a single-track road with sharp twists and turns, following the highway to Upper Foyers.

The Cialino's summer home was an estate that had once belonged to John Charles Cuninghame, the seventeenth and last Laird of Craigends, a powerful family dating back to the fourteenth century. The residence had horse stables and acreage for grazing, along with a spectacular view of Loch Ness and Foyers Falls.

I parked the Harley, then knocked on the huge double doors. Expecting a servant, I was a bit surprised when Theresa Cialino answered her own door. "Hello, Zachary. Do you want to come inside?"

"Not really."

"You don't like me, do you? I can understand why. I don't blame your father for what happened, I blame my husband. Money changes a person. It changed John. He became a control freak."

"Lady, I really don't—"

"When he drank, he became a bully. I know you can't relate to these things, but—"

"I can relate. More than you know. It still doesn't make things right."

"Zachary, I only slept with your father the one time. Back when John and I had briefly separated. I know what we did was wrong, but—"

"I'm not here to judge you."

"I love your father. His friendship . . . it got me through a difficult time."

"Great. Look, Angus said you had a boat you could lend me."

"Your father didn't kill Johnny. What happened out there was an accident."

"Tell it to the judge."

"Zachary, Angus is your father, and he loves you."

"Our definition of love probably differs. Angus tosses around the word to use people."

"You're wrong. Yes, he needed you in court, but there were other motives. He's been worried about you."

"He'd better worry about himself. Now can I borrow the boat or not?"

She shook her head, exasperated. "It's the *Brooklyn-224*, you'll find it docked at the Clansman Wharf. Keys are in the master suite, under the pillow. Take it, take whatever the hell you need, I don't care anymore."

It was the first thing she said we agreed on.

Inverness Castle

I was late getting back. Having missed Max's closing remarks, I managed to slip inside the courthouse, finding my seat next to Brandy just as Mitchell Obrecht was concluding his final speech to the jury.

"Remember, ladies and gentlemen, it is not the Loch Ness monster that is on trial here, but the man who used the monster as an excuse to commit premeditated murder . . . murder in the first degree. What is happening in Loch Ness today has no bearing on the heinous events that took place on February 15. More than a dozen eyewitnesses testified that Angus Wallace struck John Cialino, Jr. on the bluff overlooking Loch Ness. The defendant's own son testified that Angus Wallace was lying when he said a school of salmon lured a water creature to the surface.

"Facts, ladies and gentlemen, not folklore. There was no monster attacking John Cialino on February 15, there was only Angus Wallace and his lust for Theresa Cialino. Premeditated murder . . . murder in the first degree. Your verdict will do more than send this monster away, it will send a message throughout Great Britain and the world that Scotland will not accept such unscrupulous behavior in our society, that we are a nation of law, not an unwitting sideshow. Now is the time of reckoning. Now justice must be served."

The judge gave his final thanks and instructions to the jury, then they were led out of the courtroom.

I turned to Brandy. "I need to speak with my father."

"Go on. I'll meet ye back at the hotel.

       *   *   *

By the time the guards let me pass, Angus had changed back into his prison uniform and was back in his cell.

"Ye missed yer brother's speech. It wis quite movin'."

"I met with Theresa."

"So I heard. Whit're yer intentions then?"

"Who was Adam Wallace?"

He sat on the edge of his bed and rubbed his face, which seemed to have aged ten years in the last two weeks. "I see ye've been talkin' tae my guid pal, Calum, aye?"

"Answer the question."

"Adam wis first cousin tae Sir William Wallace, an' he wis jist as brave a soul. In Spring o' the year 1330, he accompanied Sir James the Good, commonly kent as the Black Douglas, on a mission o' great importance, tae take Robert the Bruce's heart tae the Holy Land."

"Yeah, yeah, I know the story of the Braveheart. What I don't know is the story of the Black Knights."

"Dae ye ken whit a blood oath is?"

"Does that mean you won't tell me?"

"No' unless ye wish tae become a Knight."

"I don't have time for this nonsense."

"Nor dae I. Now whit are yer intentions wi' the monster?"

"Why do you want it dead?"

"Why? Because it's dangerous."

"It killed Calum's wife, didn't it?"

"That, I cannae say. But it went after *you*. An' that's enough for me."

"That was an accident. It was lured up by the salmon, real salmon, not the kind you used in your alibi."

"My guilt or innocence has no bearin' on this. Whit's important now is that this monster is dealt wi', once an' for a', afore it kills again."

"Interesting how the jury's deliberating upon the same thing."

I turned and left, knowing that might well be the last time I'd see him alive.

Clansman Wharf

True met me an hour later in the Clansman parking lot. I was surprised to see the media had vacated the wharf.

"A'right, Zack, I got yer message an' brought ye a' that ye wanted an' mair," True said, pointing to a rental truck. "But I'll expect an explanation afore we make way."

"I told you, there's crude oil leaking into Loch Ness. You and I are going to find it."

"Ye want tae find an oil leak, call the EPA. This deep divin' suit ye had me fetch is for somethin' else entirely."

"The oil will guide us to the monster's lair. I mean to descend into the passage and reopen it, releasing the Guivre to the North Sea."

"Free the Guivre? Dae ye work for bloody PETA then? Bloody hell, Zachary, first ye're too feart o' even gettin' on a docked boat, now ye want tae go swimmin' wi' Nessie? An' whit makes ye think I'll help ye wi' this crazy plan?"

"If you won't help me, I'll find someone who will. I'm sure those monster hunters are game."

"Thae arseholes?" True shook his head. "Why dae ye want tae dae this, Zack? My sister loves ye. Take her away frae this dreary place an' live oot yer lives. Ye dinnae need this tae be happy."

"It's not like I have a choice. You said so yourself, it's my destiny to deal with this animal."

"Dinnae listen tae whit I said, listen tae whit I'm sayin' now! Fuck this destiny crap."

"Destiny aside, I can't live anymore with these night terrors."

"An' ye think by doin' this crazy stunt, the dreams'll go away?"

"I don't know. Maybe. All I know is I keep waking up every night, screaming like a lunatic."

"Better than the monster chewin' on yer bones."

"The underwater lights will keep it away, at least long enough for me to reopen the passageway and release it."

"Ye're still crazy."

"Not yet, pal, but I'm getting there. Think about it. If I do nothing and these night terrors continue to worsen, how long do you think it'll be before I really end up in a padded cell? Think that'll help my relationship with your sister? No, I've thought long and hard about this, and it's better I face the devil now, than deal with it in a mental ward."

True mulled it over. "I see yer point. Guess ye cannae keep livin' like this."

"Anymore than you and the rest of the Black Knights can spend all your nights patrolling the Loch."

"Black Knights? Whit're ye talkin' aboot?"

I slapped him on his rock-hard shoulder. "Come on, big guy, did you really think I wouldn't recognize that physique of yours bulging beneath that black tunic? Or that bilge water you call cologne? You're the one who killed that Anguilla eel and saved my life, and I'm grateful. You did what you had to do, now let me do the same."

He shook his shaggy head. "Shouldae let that eel eat its way up tae yer bollocks, that's whit I shouldae done. Come on then, help me wheel this gear tae yer boat."

True unlocked the back of the rental truck and pulled up the aluminum slide door. Secured inside were a half dozen wooden crates and what looked like an oversized bright orange space suit, supported on a heavy steel frame.

"There she is, the Newt Suit. Best damn atmospheric divin' suit we got."

"How'd you manage to borrow it?"

"Told the boss I wanted tae service it afore I dive the rig next week. These things need lots o' attention, the better they build them, the mair complicated they get. Still, it beats a' hell oot o' the auld JIM suits."

I pointed to the crates. "And the detector and demolitions?"

True winked. "Them I stole."

*   *   *

With the Newt Suit's rig on wheels, it took us less than twenty minutes to secure everything onboard the Cialino's yacht.

The *Brooklyn-224* was a fifty-seven-foot twin-screw diesel trawler, with an eighteen-foot beam and wide-open bow and stern decks. Its interior was tastefully decorated, its lavish furnishings done in maroons and creams, its woods polished teak and mahogany. The aft saloon's master quarters was luxurious to a fault, complete with a king-size bed, plasma screen television, steam room, and black onyx marble whirlpool.

I paused to gaze at a framed photo in the master suite. The image was of a young John Cialino in his early twenties standing with a group of firefighters in a New York City firehouse, a sign reading *Brooklyn Heights Engine 224.*

"This guy was a fireman?"

"Guess that explains the boat's name." True looked around and whistled. "Ye ken whit, Zack? I say screw the monster. Let's you an' me get Brandy an' a few o' her friends an' take this barge oot on the Moray Firth. A week or three an' ye'll forget a' aboot thae nightmares, that I promise."

"No." I reached under the bed's silk pillows, found the yacht's keys, then headed for the wheelhouse.

True followed me up to the main deck, then peered out the open venetian blinds. "Ye sure aboot no' wantin' tae take that cruise?"

I looked out the window.

Brandy had just exited a cab and was heading for our berth. "Damn. Wait here."

I hurried outside, meeting her halfway up the dock. "Hey. What're you doing here?"

"I've been lookin' all over for ye. The jury came back, they delivered their verdict less than an hour ago."

"Already?" *No wonder the media had vacated the wharf.* "What did they rule?"

"Guilty. Murder one." She looked up at me, tears in her eyes. "I'm sorry, Zack."

She hugged me and I held her close, not sure how to react.

"Murder one? Jesus, I guess I was hoping they'd give him involuntary manslaughter."

"Angus needs tae see ye right away. He sent me tae fetch ye."

"He'll have to wait."

"Zack, there's talk o' the judge renderin' the death penalty. Ye need tae go see yer father. Ye need tae tell the judge what ye know."

"I will. Later."

"What're ye up tae then?" She pushed past me, heading for the trawler yacht. "This is Johnny C.'s yacht, isn't it? Come out, True

MacDonald, I see ye in there!" She climbed aboard before I could stop her, then she pulled back the gray tarp that covered the Dive Suit.

"Bloody hell. Finlay True MacDonald, I hope ye're no' plannin' on goin' down in this thing."

"Not me."

"Zachary? Oh no . . . no way."

"I'll be fine."

"Fine? Against that monster? How will ye be fine?"

"Its eyes are sensitive to bright lights. I'll be surrounded by them."

"An' what are ye intendin' tae do down there? Fit it for glasses?"

"He wants tae free it tae the sea," blurted out True. "I telt him he wis crazy."

"Crazy? He should be committed."

"I'll be okay."

"I'll say, 'cause ye're no' goin', an' that's final!"

I turned to True. "Start the boat."

"Don't ye dare."

True looked at us, then ducked inside the wheelhouse.

"Damn ye, Zack—"

"Brandy, I love you, and I want to be with you forever, which is exactly why I have to do this. That night terror I had this morning, I've been having them almost every night since the Sargasso thing, and they're getting worse. I know it sounds crazy, but going down into the Loch and freeing this creature is the only way to end the nightmares."

"It'll end yer nightmares . . . an' yer life. Dinnae do this, Zack. Please dinnae put us both through this pain."

The twin engines growled to life.

"I love you, Brandy. Forgive me." In one motion I picked her up over my shoulder—

"Let me go!"

—and tossed her over the starboard rail.

I released the stern line, yelling, "True, get us out of here!"

Brandy surfaced, gasping from the cold water. "Bastard!"

The boat lurched forward, its tea-colored wake washing over Brandy's head.

The Diary of Sir Adam Wallace
Translated by Logan W. Wallace

Entry: 8 November 1330

Ten days. Ten long days have passed since I wis carried, half-deid, back tae Inverness. I am far frae whole, yet I am alive, spared by God, cursed by fate ... my mind still lost in the bowels o' Hell. But finish this entry I must, if only for those that must one day carry on my anointed task.

When last I wrote, Sir Keef had announced his work on the iron framework an' pulley system had been completed. Sure enough, the slides that wid support the massive gate were mounted in place along the tunnel's narrowest point, along wi' two single pulleys and ropes.

Noo 'twis time tae set the iron gate intae position within the frame.

Like the gate o' a drawbridge, oor iron barrier wis designed tae slide up an' doon within its housin', lowered an' raised by the two ropes looped on pulleys. The task afore us required we raise the gate above the mooth o' the river by its ropes, so it could be fed, bottom end first, intae its slide, then lowered within its frame.

Bein' the maist nimble, Sir Keef an' his brother, Alex mounted the frame so as tae thread the gate's heavy ropes through their pulleys first. Three o' oor rank then joined Sir Keef along the opposite bank wi' his rope, while MacDonald, mysel', an' Sir Alex worked the rope on the near shore.

Gruntin' an' groanin', the seven o' us managed tae raise an' swing the gate over the surface o' that dark roarin' river. As it neared the arched ceilin', the two brothers reached oot an' guided it intae position within its heavy frame.

Sir Keef had used oil tae lubricate the sides o' the metal, an' we let oot a great cheer as the gate slid easily an' straight doon through the framework an' intae the stream, the iron grid preventin' anythin' larger than a weel dug frae passin' through its borders.

An' then Sir Keef lost his footin' an' he tumbled intae the ragin' water.

The current drove him intae the lowered gate, but oor barrier stood the test. Wi' Sir Keef holdin' on, we pulled on the ropes an' raised baith gate an' Knight frae the torrent. I reached oot for him, helpin' him tae the rocky embankment an' safety while MacDonald secured the ends o' baith ropes tae a metal spike anchored along the base o' the tunnel's arch.

It wis then that the Guivre struck.

Never have I seen a creature sae large move sae fast. Its first attack tore Sir Keef frae my grip, its horrible jaws strippin' flesh frae his bones afore releasin' him—deid an' bloodied—intae the river.

Lookin' doon, I saw the Guivre's young circlin' in the current, attackin' Sir Keef's remains, an' I realized we were greatly ootnumbered. As I ran tae retrieve my sword, the adult creature struck again, this time takin' Sir Alex.

The two Knights on the opposite bank were trapped. MacDonald could only watch as they were snatched, shaken nearly tae death, then released, one after the next, the monster's tactic— tae render its prey defenseless for its young.

The two wounded Knights screamed as the juvenile serpents attacked, feastin' and quarrelin' amongst themselves as they gnashed through oor comrades flesh an' limbs like rabid dugs.

MacDonald drew me back against the far wall, raspin' intae my ear. "Go! Return tae Inverness! Carry the Knight's mission!"

"I'm no' goin' wi'oot ye!"

"I'll follow, but first I must re-lower the gate. Take this torch. Distract the demon." Afore I could object, MacDonald ran for the anchored ropes.

But the adult Guivre wis too fast, snatchin' MacDonald, shakin' him within its terrible jaws until the life gushed frae his mooth.

I wis the last one left. Torch in one hand, William's sword in the other, I crept in the shadows toward the gate's set o' ropes, intent on trappin'g the cursed beast.

The adult Guivre rose oot o' the river ontae the embankment, revealin' its entire girth tae me. Its terrible stench burned in my nostrils, an' the flame frae my torch danced in its rounded eyes, yet it didnae attack . . . wary o' either my light or my cousin's deadly sword.

I crept backward, keepin' my eyes on the monster. The ropes were close now, beckonin' me tae reach doon an' release them frae their anchor. Choosin' tae preserve the sword, I lowered the torch an' untied them wi' my freed hand.

The iron gate dropped, its sharp ends impalin' several o' the Guivre young circlin' in the river.

A'fore I kent whit happened, I wis taken frae my feet by the adult, my metal battle dress an' torso crushed within its jowls as I lashed at it blindly wi' my sword. I felt the return o' a heavy blow, an' I must have struck deep, for it flung me loose an' I flew through the dimly lit cavern, landin' hard in the darkness.

The remainin' torch flickered and died. I lay on my side, breathin' heavy an' in great pain, unable tae see my hand afore my face. My sword wis gone, lost somewhere along the rocks. An' then I heard the Guivre young snarlin' an' I got mair terrified as they advanced.

God came tae me then in the form o' a wisp o' cool air. I wis close tae the tunnel entrance!

Blind an' on hands an' knees I crawled, feelin' my way until I reached the mooth o' the narrow access tunnel. Movin' on a' fours in the pitch black, I smashed my heid over an' again, yet continued on through that suffocatin' darkness, each precious second distancin' me frae thae demons.

In time the sounds o' the roarin' underground river faded an' the tunnel opened tae the great chasm we had descended a lifetime ago. Somewhere, high above me, wis my escape, yet how could J ascend such a dangerous mountain in darkness blacker than night?

Still, J had tae try, for if J wis tae die, J'd rather it wis frae a fall than the fangs o' the De'il.

Feelin' my way tae the chasm wall, J climbed, each handhold threatenin' tae cast me intae oblivion, each reach intae the darkness flirtin' wi' unseen ledges. How long J ascended J cannae say. At times J paused tae catch a few precious moments o' sleep, at times J wondered if J wis still risin', so confused were my senses.

J never saw the daylight, but J heard the rush o' the wind. It led me tae the mooth o' the cave where the night's stars greeted me like a long-lost friend. Exhausted as J wis, J continued on, refusin' tae stop until the dawn.

Even wi' the light, J stayed far frae LochNess's bank.

At some point J must've passed oot, for when J awoke, J wis being carried by William Calder's men. His daughter, Helen, cares for me noo, an' soon J will ask for her hand.

Meanwhile, J am haunted by frightful dreams . . . dreams o' death. Each dawn J awaken, screamin' frae my bed, my mind trapped in that hellhole where my eight comrades perished. The priest claims the dreams will pass, but J ken better, for the journey has scarred me for life.

Yet return J must, at the beginnin' o' each autumn an' again at the end o' winter, for J have taken a blood oath . . . the oath o' the Black Knights. Salvation has blessed me wi' life, fate cursin' me an' mine wi' its task . . . tae return again—tae raise an' lower the gate.

Tae protect the freedom o' Scotland.

—Sir Adam Wallace, 1330

I was on the A82, traveling north out of Fort Augustus. Glancing to my right, I saw a dark, slick animal rise out of the waters of Loch Ness, trailing what had to be a ten meter [thirty-three foot] wake. When I realized what I was looking at, I nearly went off the side of the road.

—Mr. Bill Kinder, Lancashire, 9 April 1996, approximately 10:00 A.M.

My brother, James, and I were on our fishing boat, which was fitted with a Koden CVS886 Mk II Color Sounder, its 28kHz transducer directing a 31.6 degree beam vertically downward. The CRO screen displays different strengths of echo in different colors. We were testing the device when we detected a weird shape in fifty-five meters of water. The object was eighteen meters [59 feet] long, about nine meters [29.5 feet] wide.

—Robert West, Fraserburgh, April 1981

CHAPTER 32

Loch Ness

TRUE SHOOK HIS GREAT VIKING HEAD as he accelerated the trawler yacht away from the dock and into deep water.

"Brandy's gonna kill ye, assumin' ye ever survive this lunacy."

"I'll make it up to her."

"That, I doubt. So, Captain Ahab, exactly where we headed?"

"North. Follow the western bank until we reach the Bona Narrows. It's where the fish must enter the Loch, the oil's got to be seeping somewhere close by."

He gave me a weary look, then turned the wheel, guiding us toward the northern entrance of Loch Ness.

Inverness Castle

"Ye say he means tae go underwater tae battle this demon?" Angus squeezed his eyes closed, rubbing his face. "This isnae whit I wanted, no' at a'."

"What did ye want then?" Brandy spat back. "Ye've been pushin' an' pushin' him ever since he returned, hell, ever since he was born."

"Same as my auld man aye did tae me! Life's tough, ye ken. Ye got tae have a thick skin tae—"

"Don't *you* lecture *me* on life, Angus Wallace! An' don't *you* talk tae me about tough love. My mum died when I was seven an' my arsehole father kicked me out when I was sixteen. What *you* call tough love, I call no love at all. Yer son came all the way back tae Scotland because he sought yer approval, an' all ye've done since he arrived was lie tae him an' push him tae find that monster. Well, congratulations, ye've got what ye wanted. Guess some things'll never change, eh?"

She turned to leave, but he grabbed her arm through the cell bars.

"Let go, or I'll break it off."

"It's no' whit I ever wanted, lass, it's whit had tae be. It's the only way I kent tae help Zachary."

"Bollocks."

"Zack's sufferin' inside, has been ever since that night he first drooned. I ken whit he's gone through. My ain childhood demons made me a bitter auld man on my best days an' a nae-guid drunk on my worst. A restless man cannae be a guid family man, Brandy, 'cause he's aye seekin' pleasure frae somewhere else. That wis me, still is. I never wanted that for Zack."

"So you pushed him intae locatin' the creature?"

"Aye. 'Twis the only way he could conquer his fear."

"An' get ye out o' prison, I suppose."

"Aye, that's true enough, but see, if anyone could locate Nessie, I kent Zachary could. After a', he did it back when he wis only nine years auld."

Brandy's eyes narrowed. "What are ye talkin' about? 'Twas the salmon that led the monster topside when Zack was attacked. Purely an accident."

"That's 'cause Zachary cannae remember, at least his mind willnae let him. Trust me, Brandy, that wisnae an accident. My laddie wis a clever sort, even back then. Figurin' Nessie fed in the deep, he rigged underwater microphones tae his fishing lines an' recorded the sounds o' the bottom-dwellin' schools. Took him months tae perfect it, but on the day o' his ninth birthday he wis ready, intent on impressin' me wi' his wee invention. 'Course me, bein' the restless arsehole that I am, wis mair interested in dippin' my wicket than bein' wi' my son."

"So Zack set out with his Nessie lure alone in that rowboat? Gees, Angus. An' now he's doin' it all over again."

"Aye, but we cannae let him, can we? I need yer help lass, so come closer an' listen carefully, there's no' much time, an' an awfy lot tae be done."

Loch Ness

Locating oil and gas reserves buried beneath the bottom of the ocean, as well as leaks from crude oil pipelines, relies on a variety of technology designed to detect anomalous concentrations of dissolved gases and emulsions in water. When oil is present, its surface film can be measured using the intensity of its reflected light. The interface detector True had "borrowed" was an antenna-shaped device that used a small laser beam to detect oil along the surface, along with a second probe that measured the energy absorption of insoluble liquids in the water itself.

The device was now rigged to our port-side bow, its data sent through my laptop.

As we crept north along the western shoreline, the needle twitched, the levels increasing as we approached the Bona Narrows.

"Have ye got somethin', Zack?"

"It's just a trace. Let's follow the narrows downstream a bit and see what happens."

We left Loch Ness and followed its river, True keeping us close to the northeastern shoreline. As we passed the Bona Narrows Lighthouse, hydrocarbon gas levels jumped, increasing again as we approached man-made Loch Dochfour.

The farther north we ventured, the greater the hydrocarbon levels. "The northern current's moving the oil," I said, "keeping it from being noticed."

"Aye, an' it's a nineteen kilometer journey frae the Moray Firth intae Loch Ness. Nae wonder the fish're turnin' back. But we still dinnae ken where the oil's originatin' frae."

"Take us back into Loch Ness, True, I want to explore the eastern shoreline."

*   *   *

"My faither, yer grandfaither, Logan Wallace, he died in these very waters when I wis aboot yer age. An awfy gale hit the Glen an' his boat flipped. Everyone says he drooned, but I ken better, see. 'Twis the monster that got him, a' part o' the Wallace curse."

"Are ye talkin' aboot Nessie?"

"Nessie? Nessie's folklore. I'm speakin' o' a curse wrought by nature, a curse that's haunted the Wallace men since the passin' of Robert the Bruce."

"Zack! Hey, wake up!"

My eyes snapped open. "Sorry."

"Yer damn monitor's twitchin' like a polecat's tail."

I checked the laptop, then glanced out the port side window. We were nearing Aldourie Castle.

"Shut her down, True. We're here."

"Aye? Whit makes ye sae sure?"

"Just a hunch."

"A hunch, aye? Ye expect me tae believe that? Yer faither telt ye this, didn't he?"

"Long ago, through the wisdom of whisky. He claimed the dragon's lair was down there. Said us Wallaces were cursed, and that the devil himself lurked in the shadow of our souls."

"A drunk disnae offer any wisdom, Zack, jist ignorance. Ye dinnae need tae dae this. There's better ways tae die."

"And better ways to live."

"At least let me go wi' ye then. I can have a second suit brought within eight hours."

"Sorry, big guy, but this is strictly a solo act. Now show me how to use that dive suit."

*   *   *

Man has been searching for better ways to explore the depths since humans first learned they could hold their breath. The challenge lies in transporting an adequate supply of air, while handling the complexities associated with water pressure. In seawater, the weight of water increases by one atmosphere for each thirty-three feet, meaning, at thirty-three feet, the water pressure doubles, at sixty-six feet it triples, and so on. As pressure increases, air volume within a contained space decreases by the same ratio, and the density of the air is likewise compressed. For human beings, this means the deeper a diver goes, the greater the "squeeze" on air spaces within the body, including the lungs and sinus cavities. Prolonged activity underwater can also lead to dangerous increases in nitrogen in the bloodstream, maxing out normal scuba dives at 130 feet.

To access deeper depths required shielding a diver against these enormous pressures, leading to the invention of the first atmospheric dive suit, or ADS. An ADS is an underwater suit and helmet, its internal pressures maintained at one atmosphere. With an ADS, there is no need for compression or decompression. Special gas mixtures are not required, and dive times can be extended by many hours, with divers able to comfortably attain depths exceeding twenty-five hundred feet.

The first atmospheric dive suits originated in the seventeenth century. They resembled bulky suits of armor with long air hoses, and were created so that treasure hunters could explore sunken ships. Advances continued through the 1900s, leading up to the development of the JIM suit, named after its chief test diver, Jim Jarrett. The JIM suit allowed greater freedom of movement in deeper, colder water, and quickly attracted the attention of the oil and gas industry, who needed a means to effect deep water repairs to pipelines.

With new oil monies invested in the technology, the JIM suit soon evolved into WASP suits, which used thrusters in place of articulated legs. While bulkier and requiring more deck space, the WASP gave divers greater range and mobility underwater and became the workhorse in pipeline repair.

The Newt Suit combined the best of both worlds. Like the JIM, the Newt resembled a space suit, with a backpack added that housed air tanks, a life-support system, propeller, and thrusters, which the diver operated using controls within his boots. The headpiece was made of a clear, heavy acrylic, allowing for unobstructed vision, and two-pronged claws extended out of the suit's "mittens" for grasping.

True explained all this to me while he rigged the Newt Suit's support frame and built-in winch to the starboard rail.

"The suit's got twenty joints, makin' it easy tae maneuver, an' the aluminum surface is a breeze compared tae the auld JIMs. The problem a novice like yersel's gonnae have is dealin' wi' the turbidity an' currents. The suit's got a large surface area, which means it'll catch a lot o' water. Get caught in a nasty current, an' ye become a human underwater kite. If that happens, and it will, ye'll need yer thrusters an' propeller. They're controlled usin' pedals in yer boots. Right boot's the thrusters, propeller's in yer left. The air tanks on yer back'll give ye three hours of air, but yer umbilical adds another forty hours, no' that ye'll need it."

"Umbilical?"

"Aye. One end connects tae yer backpack, the other tae this free-floatin' life-support system." True pointed to a five-foot aluminum barrel. "That unit holds yer backup power source, plus an independent oxygen re-breather an' surface communication system. I had tae add a wee generator tae get enough juice tae feed a' these underwater lights. Two lights are rigged tae yer backpack, one rear-facin', the other forward. The third light'll be hooked up front along yer waistband, allowin' ye tae maneuver it usin' yer claw. It can be turned off an' on independently of the two bigger lights, jist in case ye want tae reserve yer batteries."

"Three lights should be fine."

"Aye, well if it wis me, I'd want a bloody lighthoose beacon comin' oot o' my arse. Now pay attention, we need tae go ower these demolitions."

True pried open a wooden crate and removed a small metal tube about the size of a Cuban cigar, along with a red plastic cap.

"We call this a G-SHOK. On the rig, we use them tae clear away rock an' debris. Comes in two parts. This long piece's the cartridge. It's filled wi' highly compressed liquid gas, at the end of which is a primer. The red cap's an electrical fuse. Pop the cap ower the primer an' it sends a small charge intae the liquid, causin' a chain reaction. Within ten seconds, the gas expands tae 800 times its volume, an' boom."

"How big a boom we talking?"

"Big enough tae split rock. If ye need mair than ten seconds, the fuse igniter can be detonated usin' its timer option. Set the timer on the outside o' the cap frae one tae three minutes, then snap it ower the cartridge, same as before."

"And how am I supposed to carry all this stuff?"

"After we get ye intae the Newt, I'll snap a utility belt roond yer waist. The belt contains compartments for a dozen G-SHOKs an' caps."

"Anything else?"

"There's an auld wool sweater in that box. Better put it on. Suit's heated, but the water gets even colder along the bottom."

I grabbed the garment, then noticed a man walking out along Aldourie Pier.

True stared at the Newt Suit, debating. "Zack . . . whit if I said there might be another means o' gettin' doon there . . . ye ken, intae the monster's lair?"

"Hey, isn't that your father?" I pointed to where old man MacDonald was standing, watching us.

"Shyte, it's him a' right."

"What's he doing?"

"Keepin' vigil, nae doubt. Damn Templar."

"What were you saying about accessing the lair?"

"Uh . . . nothin'. Come on, if ye're gonnae dae this, then let's dae it."

I climbed into the lower torso of the Newt Suit while True connected the umbilical cord to the aluminum barrel and backpack.

"Ye ready then?"

I nodded, sliding my arms and head into the upper half of the dive suit as True lifted it over me. With a twist, the waistline clicked down upon the lower torso. True snapped the hinges shut along both sides of the waist.

Sweat poured down my face, my faceplate fogging with steam. Retracting my hand from its sleeve, I wiped my forehead clean, while True opened the tank valves on my back.

A cool stream of air blew into the helmet, lifting the fog.

I raised my arms, amazed at how flexible the appendages were.

True fixed the utility belt around my waist, then lowered the bulky pack supporting the underwater lights and air tanks onto my back. I would have toppled over the side had my suit not been attached by cable to its support frame.

"Easy, Zack. Ye'll feel steadier once ye're underwater."

True activated the winch, raising me off of the deck. Looking down, I watched as my boots passed over the rail, and then I was slowly lowered into the water up to my chest.

For a long moment I hung there, my feet in the water, my upper body still tethered to the winch. The thought of what awaited me below sent shivers down my spine.

I focused upon the noise from my own shallow breaths until static crackled in my right ear. "Zack, can ye hear me?"

"Loud and clear."

"Let's go through yer checklist. Activate yer thrusters by pressin' doon on the ball o' yer right foot. Use it like the accelerator o' a car."

I pressed down, too hard, as the powerful twin thrusters' shot me clear out of the water, smashing my head piece against the winch.

"Easy!"

"Sorry." I eased back, the Newt Suit bobbing like a cork. "That was cool."

"It's no' a carnival ride. The propeller's the pedal in yer left boot, designed tae move ye horizontally. Dinnae use it until ye're close tae the bottom."

"Understood."

"Feel for the toggle switch in yer left glove. That's the master switch tae yer underwater lights."

I flicked the switch, my forward-mounted beam glancing off the dark surface. "Works fine."

"Usin' yer pincers, reach for one o' the G-SHOKs at yer waist. Make sure ye can grip baith the cartridge an' fuse . . . but dinnae put them together!"

It took a few tries until I could get a feel for the pincer mechanisms in each mitten. "No sweat. I think I'm ready."

"An' I think ye're aff yer heid," True muttered, as he climbed over the rail. He gave me a quick 'thumbs-up,' then disconnected my support cable, and down I went.

It was a frightening sensation, falling like an anchor into the darkness, and I panicked, forgetting everything I'd just learned.

"Thrusters, Zack! Right boot!"

I pressed down with my foot, breathing easier as the thrusters slowed my descent.

The beam from my forward light cut through the darkness. I was dropping through a brown tea-colored world, but everything seemed to be spinning. I squeezed my eyes shut, feeling sick."

"Speak tae me, Zachary."

"Dizzy, I'm just a little dizzy."

"Ye're spinning. Look inside yer headpiece. Jist below yer lower jaw, ye'll see a set o' gauges."

I opened my eyes, focusing on the digital display.

"Check yer compass, it's in orange. It shows direction an' course, sort o' like a submarine. Press on yer thrusters again an' come tae a complete stop."

I did as told. "Okay."

"Call oot yer depth tae me."

"Two hundred thirty feet."

"Have ye stopped spinnin'?"

"Yes."

"Good. Now ease off the thrusters an' continue descendin' while callin' oot yer depth."

"Two-sixty. Three hundred. Three-thirty . . ."

"Still droppin' too fast. Press doon on yer thrusters gently, let's slow ye up a bit."

"Three-fifty. Three-seventy."

"That's better. Now, the light on yer waist is tethered. Take a moment an' lock it intae the pincers of yer right glove so it'll be there when ye get closer tae the bottom."

"Got it." Securing the light in my right pincer, I aimed the beam into the darkness, feeling more in control. "Four-sixty. Five hundred feet. Five-forty—"

"Dinnae get cocky, Zack. Keep it slow an' steady. Whit dae ye see?"

"Not much. Even with the light, visibility's still less than fifteen feet. Outside the beam, the water's pitch-black."

"Like swimmin' in ink. I want ye relyin' on yer digital display. Which way are ye pointed?"

"South, at one-five-two degrees."

"Keep an eye on yer position, or ye'll be walkin' in circles. By the way, yer backup system's ower the side, the umbilical cord's feedin' fine. How deep are ye now?"

"Oops, I just passed seven hundred feet."

"Hit yer thrusters, afore ye bury yersel' in the bottom!"

I pressed down again, slowing my descent until I regained neutral buoyancy. "I'm good . . . I'm good."

"Good? Ye're turnin' my hair good an' grey. Check yer gauges again."

I was in 723 feet of water, the pressure outside of my artificial skin over twenty atmospheres, the temperature a chilly thirty-eight degrees.

Inside, I was dry and cool.

I felt a current at my back and allowed it to push me ahead as I looked down, aiming my handheld beam.

The bottom passed twenty feet below my boots. It was a murky desert of mud, its flat expanse desecrated here and there by petrified clumps of Scots Pine. The massive trees were embedded in the soot, belching tiny streams of gas, their plankton-covered branches reaching out for me like the rotting arms of Loch Ness's dead.

Jesus . . . what am I doing down here?

"Zack, ye still alive?"

"Sorry. I'm drifting, guess I'm about twenty feet off the bottom."

"Ye see oor friend?"

I'd been so preoccupied with surviving the descent I'd completely forgotten about the monster!

I looked around nervously, my anchored shoulder beams revolving back and forth like a lighthouse. "I don't see anything."

"Whit aboot a cave?"

"Nothing."

"By the direction o' yer umbilical I can see ye're headin' south. Did ye want ta head south then?"

I checked the digital compass. *One-seven-two . . . he's right, I am drifting south.* "Standby." I pressed down with my left foot, activating my propeller for the first time.

The powerful motor blasted me through the alien underworld, my arms reaching out awkwardly for balance as I soared through the abyss doing eight knots.

Easing back on the propeller, I slowed, then used my thrusters to execute a turn. After a few tries, I was able to steady my heading at zero-nine-zero, moving due east, aiming for the eastern bank and Aldourie Castle.

Through the brown-black darkness I flew, the intensity of my beating heart causing the arteries in my neck to throb. I looked left then right, feeling like a lone antelope on a lion-infested plain.

And then my eyes caught movement, a brief shimmer along the bottom.

I slowed, circling back as I searched the gray-brown void.

And then I saw it.

It was an Anguilla eel, a big one, maybe ten feet long, only it wasn't slithering like a sea snake, it was hanging vertically off the bottom, the tip of its tail buried in the sediment, its head aimed at the surface.

As I drifted slowly over the eel, my light reflecting off the opaque eyes of another and another, then dozens more, all frozen in the same vertical holding pattern, like a ballet of cobras, caught in a trance.

"Zack, whit dae ye see?"

"Eels. Must be hundreds of them. They're just hanging off the bottom, as if standing on end. It's eerie."

"An' dangerous. Steer clear."

"Wait . . . I see something else."

I eased forward using my propeller, aiming my light along the bottom. The beacon caught the jagged edge of a dark shadow. Moving closer, I saw that it was not a shadow, but a chasm, cutting across the Loch's bottom like a miniature version of the Grand Canyon.

"It's a narrow trench, and it looks pretty deep. The eels are positioned around it, almost as if they're sentries standing guard."

"Stay downcurrent if ye can. Anguilla have poor eyesight, but if they smell ye—"

"The chasm's about sixty feet wide. If I hover over it, I think I can drop down nice and easy without disturbing the eels."

I pressed gently on my thrusters, ascending higher over the rift before engaging the propeller again. Slowly I circled, the handheld beacon shining down upon a hole so deep it seemed to absorb my light.

I never noticed the elongated tract of sediment, piled eighteen feet high, that wound more than fifty feet along one edge of the crevice. Nor did I see the two luminescent-yellow eyes that gleamed up from it as I circled by.

"Stand by, True, here I go."

I pulled my feet away from both boot controls, allowing the weight of the Newt Suit to sink me—too fast . . . way too fast!

Sensing the sudden disturbance, the once-sedate eels broke from their ranks. They whirled about in a chaotic frenzy, then swarmed in on me, snapping at my arms and legs from all angles, bashing my face mask and backpack with their powerful bodies. I tried to fend them off, but there were too many of them, and I was moving two speeds too slow. My lights kept most of them from my face, but they attacked my legs without mercy, their sharp needle teeth clawing my metal skin, their muscular torsos whipping at my gear, and I was petrified of losing pressure within the ADS.

Then, as suddenly as it began, the assault ceased.

"Jesus . . ." I sucked in deep breaths, then retracted my left arm from its sleeve and mopped the sweat from my face.

"Zack? Are ye okay?"

"The eels . . . they came at me, all of 'em at once. Then they just disappeared. Holy shit . . . and now I know why."

"Why? Whit is it?"

Looking around, I realized I had dropped into the chasm . . . and I was still falling.

"True, I'm descending within the canyon. Standby."

Pressing down on my right foot, I engaged my thrusters and slowed my descent. Raising my right arm, I aimed the hand-held light and looked around as a blizzard of brown sediment fell into the trench from above, obliterating my view.

And then something immense plowed sideways into me with the force of a locomotive and an immense pressure squeezed my brain, bashing me into unconsciousness.

Well, the day that I saw the monster, it was the end of September and
I was driving back from Inverness. I came up the hill where we came
in sight of the bay, glanced out across it, and saw this large lump.
The nearest I can tell you is it looked like a boat that had turned
upside down. It was about ten meters [thirty-three feet] in length, and
nearly three meters [ten feet] in height from the water to the top of the
back. It was a mixture of browns, greens, sludgy sort of colors. I looked at it
on and off for a few seconds, because I was driving. Must have seen it three
or four times, and the last time I looked, it was gone! I thought to myself,
"Oh, there's Nessie. 'Bout time I saw it, I've been living here a year." And
then something in the back of my head sort of said, "That's not just Nessie,
that's got to be the Loch Ness Monster that everybody has spent
thousands of pounds searching for, and you're looking at the darn thing."
I nearly drove off the road, but luckily I didn't because we had a fairly
new car. Can you imagine what the insurance claim would have been like?

When I got home I thought, "I need a strong drink." But there was
none in the house, so I thought, "Right. Strong coffee will do."

—Val Moffat, Loch Ness resident, September 1990

CHAPTER 33

Inverness Castle

THERE WERE NO MEMBERS of the media present, only two shell-shocked guards and Francesca Kasa, my father's private nurse, who hovered over Angus as he lay slumped on the floor of his cell.

"Angus, listen to me! You're having a heart attack! Hang on, I've called the hospital, an ambulance is on the way."

The nurse turned to the two guards as Angus lay there groaning. "They'll never get a gurney down that circular stairwell. We need to carry him up. Now! Come on, move!"

The two guards hurried into the cell.

*   *   *

Sirens blaring, the ambulance roared up the driveway behind Inverness Castle, then backed up to the police barracks just as the guards emerged carrying Angus.

A female EMT jumped down from the back of the van, her long, raven-colored hair tucked beneath her cap. With one of the guards help, she removed the gurney, "Lay him down, quickly!"

The guards complied, just as their superior, Captain Douglas Galliac, hurried over from his post. "Whit's a' this?"

Nurse Kasa secured Angus to the gurney as the female paramedic hovered over him, listening to his heart with her stethoscope. "Myocardial infarction . . . it's a massive heart attack."

"Probably a blood clot in one or more of his coronary arteries," called out the EMT. "I'm startin' him on Retavase."

The paramedic hooked up a clear IV bag to the gurney, passing the needle end to the nurse, who jabbed Angus in the arm.

"Ahh!"

Captain Galliac went pale. "Is he gonnae make it? Where are ye takin' him?"

"Where dae ye think?" the nurse yelled back.

"Well, I cannae jist let him go, he's been convicted o' murder!"

"An' he could die if ye keep us here. Then *you* can explain tae the media how the sheriff's office executed their prisoner without him ever bein' sentenced."

"What's the holdup, people?" the female driver yelled from the front seat of the ambulance. "We've got a surgical team standing by for an emergency angiogram and stent."

"Oh Bloody Hell . . . Mastramico, Edwards, load him aboard, then follow them tae the hospital. I've got tae find the sheriff. An' no media!"

The paramedic and nurse climbed in the back of the van as the two guards lifted Angus and his gurney to them. The double doors were slammed closed, and the ambulance accelerated away.

The emergency vehicle raced down the winding path of Castle Street, its blasting siren alerting a second ambulance, identical to the first, that had been waiting at the bottom of the hill for the last ten minutes.

The first ambulance, driven by Theresa Cialino, turned right onto the main road, forcing traffic to one side while the second emergency vehicle, driven by her cousin, James Fox, hesitated just long enough for the trailing sheriff's car to appear in his rear view mirror. When it did, he accelerated into traffic, turning left.

Brandy watched the scene from the back of the first van as she removed her EMT's garb. "That was fun. I've never been a fugitive before."

"Accomplice, lass, I'm the fugitive." Angus winced as he removed the IV from his arm. "Theresa, how much farther?"

"Two minutes, hang on." Theresa cut the siren, then pulled off the main road into an industrial park. Slowing to traverse the speed bumps, she followed an alleyway back to a row of self-store garages.

Reaching into her jacket pocket, she removed a garage door opener and activated it.

The second to the last garage door rolled open, revealing a silver 2004 Audi TT Roadster.

Angus, now dressed in a black Nike sweat suit and sunglasses, climbed down from the back of the ambulance. "Well done, team. Brandy, ye're wi' me. Theresa an' Francesca, ye ken whit tae dae."

The nurse reached up and kissed Angus passionately on the lips. "Don't worry about us, we'll be fine."

Angus swatted her playfully on the behind. "Indeed ye will, but another kiss like that, an' I'll really end up in the hospital."

Loch Ness

True MacDonald's eyes grew wide as a thousand feet of umbilical cord quickly disappeared below the surface. "Zachary, can ye hear me? Zachary, come in!"

As the last of the slack was taken up, the floating aluminum barrel suddenly shot across the surface, moving at fifteen knots as it sped toward the eastern shore.

"Shyte!" True hurried into the wheelhouse and started the twin engines, racing the trawler yacht after the barrel.

The aluminum tank struck the embankment with a resounding, *bong*, spun around three times, then was forcibly yanked underwater.

"Gee–zus!" True cut the engines and waited for the barrel to reappear. When it didn't, he gunned the motor, heading south toward Aldourie Pier. "I warned him an' warned him, but did he bloody listen? 'Course not!"

True reversed the engines and drifted in to the pier, tossing the bow-line to his father. "Tie that off, will ye, Pop?"

Alban complied. "Whit happened?"

"Ye ken whit happened. The monster took him."

"Then he's deid."

"He's no' deid!" True rummaged through a wooden crate, grabbing a flashlight and the two remaining underwater charges. Climbing over the starboard rail, he jumped down to the pier and double-timed it toward shore, his father in tow.

"Whit are ye gonnae dae now then, laddie?"

"Rescue Zack."

"Ye cannae! The lair's off-limits, ye ken that."

"I dinnae care aboot breakin' the blood oath," he said, hurrying up the grassy acreage to Aldourie Castle. "Zachary's my best friend."

"Son, listen tae me . . . if the creature took him, ye ken it's a'ready too late."

"He's wearin' a dive suit. He could still be alive."

"No' likely." Alban ran ahead of him, blocking him as he reached a castle drive overrun by weeds. "Finley, wait!"

True paused.

"I didnae stop ye when ye went after him in Invermoriston. But this is different. I cannae stand by an' allow ye tae violate yer blood oath."

"It's ower, Pop. Angus wis right. This creature's got taebe dealt wi', an' Zack cannae dae it alone. Now ye either help me or get oot o' my way, but ye willnae be stoppin' me. No' today."

True pushed past his father and walked around to the side of the baroque dwelling. Rust-stained concrete walls were overwhelmed by a growth of vines, concealing an open, first floor passage.

True pushed the foliage aside and climbed through.

It may be doubted whether sudden and considerable deviations of structure are ever permanently propagated in a state of nature. Monstrosities sometimes occur which resemble normal structures in widely different animals. If monstrous forms of nature are capable of reproduction (which is not always the case), as they occur rarely and singly, their preservation would depend on unusually favorable circumstances. They would, also, during the first and succeeding generations cross with the ordinary form, and thus their abnormal character would almost inevitably be lost.

—Charles Darwin, *The Origin of Species*, 1859

If we had believed the Loch Ness monster did not exist, we would have certainly said it loud and clear. Instead, the totality of the evidence, the eyewitnesses and the sonar led me to say, after thirty days on the Loch, that there is definitely something here that has to be resolved.

—Kirk Wolfinger, Producer 1998 NOVA Expedition at Loch Ness

CHAPTER 34

Loch Ness Aquifer

THE COLD WATER shocked me awake. I could feel it seeping into my Newt Suit, soaking through my clothing.

I opened my eyes.

I was horizontal, suspended on my left side, my mechanical arms pinned awkwardly behind me. My head throbbed, my mind still in a fog, yet it seemed as if I was moving . . . pushing left then right, left then right, traveling very fast through the darkness.

It was a bizarre sensation.

Only then did I realize I was in the monster's mouth!

The creature must've have taken me as I dropped into the crevice, snatching me sideways to avoid my lights.

A wave of fear shot through my body like electricity. I struggled to move then quickly stopped as I felt the creature compensate by clenching its mammoth jaws tighter upon my already breached dive suit.

If it wanted to, the Guivre could crush me in seconds.

I whispered into my headpiece, "True? True!"

No response.

Carefully, I retracted my arms from the aluminum sleeves and ran my hands along the inside of my suit. Just below my right quadriceps I felt water trickling in . . . originating from the razor-sharp tip of a dense, daggerlike tooth! Another fang had punctured one of the joint capsules above my shoulder, this one drawing blood, and two more had pierced my left leg and were pressing against my flesh.

Looking back over my shoulder, I could see the roof of the creature's mouth. A single row of curved, barbed teeth ran down the center of the throat, attached to the eel's mandibular bone. These were Nature's "hooks," preventing the eel's prey from escaping.

A shiver ran down my spine as I checked my depth gauge—812 feet. Since the Loch's depth near Aldourie Castle was only 725 feet, we had to be moving through the crevice. Before I could deal with this unfathomable predicament, another smacked me square in the face.

When the monster had bitten me, I had instantly blacked out, due to the sudden change in pressure when the creature's teeth pierced my suit. The Guivre's teeth were now sealing the holes. If and when it opened its mouth, its fangs would retract, and the sudden increase in pressure would crush me faster than I could drown!

My body went rigid. I began hyperventilating.

Stay calm, Zachary, you're not dead yet! Breathe.

Opening my eyes, I looked out the helmet's clear bubble, realizing my lights were no longer working. Feeling inside the left glove, I verified that the master toggle switch had been turned off, probably a reflex action just before I had passed out.

I contemplated switching them on, but feared startling the monster. I couldn't do that, not this deep.

Looking below my chin, I focused on my instruments.

The heading was zero-six-zero. We were moving east by northeast . . . only now our depth was rising.

725 feet . . . 680 feet . . . 630—

Where were we? In Loch Ness, or the underwater passage, heading for the North Sea?

I had to know.

Reaching my right hand back into its sleeve, I felt for the pincers, still gripping the handheld light. Holding my breath, I gently squeezed the device like the trigger of a gun, activating the smaller beacon.

"Oh God . . ."

The hair on the back of my neck tingled, my mind drowning in new waves of panic.

My beam was illuminating the inside of the monster's mouth—a hideous orifice filled with rows of barbed, stiletto-sharp teeth. The upper and lower fangs were easily eight inches, the smaller incisors flatter and as broad as my hand.

That I had survived this monster's initial attack seemed beyond any miracle. The question now—where was it taking me?

Turning my forearm slightly, I adjusted the light's beam so it shone out the side of the creature's open mouth.

The circle of light pierced the blackness, revealing steep rock walls.

I was right! We had traveled beyond Loch Ness's eastern wall and were now moving through an underground passage that would lead us into the North Sea.

I knew we'd never get there, the tunnel blocked somewhere up ahead.

My muscles trembled, my life, once more it seemed, dwindling down to its final precious moments.

The depth gauge continued to rise . . . 570 . . . 545 . . . 520 . . .

And suddenly we leveled out and my ears popped, and I squeezed my eyes shut, waiting to die.

Waiting . . .

Waiting . . .

I reopened my eyes, and was flung from the monster's mouth through the air and into the dizzying darkness.

A sudden painful jolt drove the wind from my lungs as I landed backpack first against what had to be solid rock.

I flopped within my cracked suit, unable to draw a breath, as my mind screamed at me to ignite my lights.

Wheezing for air, I managed to flick the toggle switch in my left glove, powering on all three lights.

The forward beam caught the advancing monster flush in its horrid yellow eyes, sending it ducking back into the underground river whence we came.

My mind fought to recall the gruesome image as my spasming chest struggled to catch air.

The monster's head was colossal, its face a combination of a giant eel and a vampire bat. Snub-nose nostrils were upturned and pronounced, revealing a mouth filled with an assortment of elongated teeth that would put a Tyrannosaurus rex to shame. Most were fixed within the jawline, but several of the larger fangs jutted outside the mouth at bizarre angles like an angler fish, and I wondered if the creature could even close its jowls without impaling itself. A thick, horsehair mane began along the top of the skull, which was covered in pus-secreting lesions, and the eyes were a jaundiced version of those that had gazed at me a lifetime ago in the Sargasso Sea.

I stared down the forward shaft of light that ended at the pool of dark, stagnant water, knowing the monster was waiting just below its gurgling surface.

Everything ached, each breath a painful reminder of my crash-landing. Where was I? No longer underwater, that was for sure. Yet my gauges still reported I was 512 feet below the surface.

I tried to shift within the enormous weight of the dive suit, but only managed to achieve an awkward sitting position. Maintaining the forward beam on the river's surface, I moved my right arm, aiming the pincer-held light at my new surroundings.

I was in a vast underground cavern, no doubt carved into the Great Glen's geology during the last ice age. Above my head, stalactites dripped moisture from an arched ceiling that spanned forty feet above the dark pool of water. The long-dormant aquifer was sixty feet wide, and ran west to east through the tunnel-like chamber of rock, dead-ending at a collapsed wall of rubble to my far left. Across the waterway was a larger jagged shoreline that seemed to run parallel to the river along the length of the passage for as far as my light's beam could penetrate.

I was on the northern shore that seemed more a small outcropping of rock. Rotating the pincers of my right mitten, I aimed my handheld light upon my perch.

"Oh God . . ."

I was lying in piles of rubble composed of decomposed flesh and bone! Some were the skeletal remains of animals, but others were clearly human.

The dragon's lair. The vision from my night terrors!

Waves of panic threatened to drown me in a sea of insanity.

This isn't happening! Six months ago I was in sunny South Florida, working at a university! Six hours ago I was making love to Brandy MacDonald in my hotel room!

"No . . . no . . . no!" It startled me to hear my own muffled voice. "I'm not really here . . . I'm asleep. Wake up Zachary! Wake the fuck up!"

But I *was* here, surrounded by my worst imagined horrors, and now I needed the left side of my brain to take over before the right side sent me cartwheeling over the mental brink.

"Stop! Stay calm! Listen to me, Wallace, you're alive. You're alive inside a cavern, inside an aquifer. You're out of the water, lying on an outcropping of rock. There's air all around you, which means the pressure's fine. Use your lights, use your wits, and find a fucking way out of here!"

The pep talk returned reason to my thoughts.

"Okay, Zack, we'll take this one step at a time. Step one, you have to get out of this Newt Suit, it's the only way you can move. Step two, you've got to get to that dam. Step three, you're going to set the explosives in the rubble and—"

My lights flickered and dimmed.

My heart pounded.

And then I heard them . . . whispers in the darkness, advancing on me from the shadows.

Step four, you're going to panic . . .

Aldourie Castle

Gray daylight bled through smudged ancient glass, casting gothic shadows through the halls of the deserted manor.

True and his father pushed through decades of cobwebs and dust until they reached the study, surprised to find the door ajar.

True signaled to his father, then he yanked open the oak door and burst into the chamber, shocked to find his sister, standing by an immense stone and mortar fireplace.

"Brandy?"

"Whit's she daein' here?" Alban demanded.

Before True could respond, a voice from within the fireplace yelled, "it's bloody stuck!"

Angus ducked under the mantel and stepped out of the shadows, his face and hands covered in soot. "Well well, looks like a dysfunctional family reunion."

"Ye've no business bringin' Brandy here, Wallace," Alban said. "Ye took an oath!"

"Ah, fuck the Black Knights an' fuck yersel', Crabbit. My son's life's worth mair than any oath." He turned to True. "Glad ye're here, big fella. Be a sport an' lend us yer girth, the passageway's stuck."

True glanced at his father, then joined Angus inside the fireplace. The two of them pushed against the back wall until the masonry swivelled on its ancient pivot, revealing a dark hole resembling a vertical mine shaft.

The pit descended straight into the earth, as did a length of heavy rope looped around a pulley, secured to a steel beam high above their heads.

Angus tugged on one end of the rope, drawing up a small wooden platform from the shadows below. "True, are thae charges? I might be needin' them tae clear rubble blockin' the access tunnel."

"I only have two, but they should dae the job. Anyway, I'm comin' wi' ye."

"Me too," Brandy said, squeezing in between them.

"She's no' goin' anywhere," Alban growled. "She's no' a Black Knight—"

"Nor am I a MacDonald," she spat back, "at least no' anymore! Yer blood may run through my veins but ye treat that monster better than ye do yer own daughter."

"I'm yer faither, an' ye'll listen—"

"Father? Ye haven't been a father tae me since . . . since my mother passed away, so don't try pullin' rank on me now!"

Alban started to say something, then stopped, staring at the anger on Brandy's face, seeing her as if for the first time.

"My God, lookin' at ye . . . it's like I'm lookin' at her. Ye've aged intae a bonnie woman, have ye no'. Ye've got yer mum's eyes an' cheekbones, but my temper, God help ye."

"God help us all," mumbled True.

"Ye're right, Brandy. I'm certainly no' deservin' of callin' mysel' yer parent." Alban wiped back tears. "I'm sorry for whit I've done tae ye. I dinnae expect ye'll ever forgive me, but I'll never forgive mysel' if I let ye go in harm's way now."

Brandy's anger subsided, her throat constricting. "Why are ye sayin' this now, ye auld coot?"

"Yer mum . . . she aye calmed me tae reason. I'm a stubborn auld fool, aye have been, but maybe I can change. If ye let me, maybe I can even right a few wrongs afore they bury me, aye?"

Angus nodded. "Well said, brother Knight."

Brandy moved to her father, but Alban, not sure how to react, cut her off with a half hug, half pat on the head. "Okay, listen now, the two o' ye are stayin' here, only I'll be accompanyin' Angus below."

True started to object, but his father's scowl ended the discussion.

Entering the fireplace, Alban reached into the shaft. Securing the two ends of the rope, he stepped carefully out onto the platform. "Been a while since I've done this. Come on then, brother Wallace, yer laddie needs oor help."

"Wait, Angus, take these." True handed him the two G-SHOKs, quickly showing him how to set the fuses.

Angus pocketed the explosives, checked his flashlights, then eased himself into the shaft next to Alban, grabbing the right side of the rope.

The two Black Knights of the Templar released the cable, allowing the counterweight balancing the lift to lower them slowly into the darkness.

Inside the Guivre Lair

They were everywhere, circling in the stagnant waters of the aquifer, crawling behind me along the rocks, creeping out from the shadows. Anguilla eels . . . dozens, perhaps hundreds of them. Saliva gurgled in the back of their throats, the high-pitched sounds received in my headpiece as whispers.

I yelled as loud as I could, hoping to scare them off, but the helmet muted my sounds, and the lesions in their brains made them immune.

I needed to do something and fast.

My lights flickered again and then sparks sizzled behind me. The eels were chewing at the connecting wires of my backpack!

With a grunt, I lashed my mechanical arms at them, the limited range of motion rendering the gestures useless.

Should have listened to Brandy . . . should've listened to True. But noooo, you had to be a tough guy, had to face your fears like brave fucking Sir William. Idiot! Did the thought ever occur to you that maybe the dreams were a warning not to come down here?

My eyes caught movement. Quickly, I adjusted the angle of my dimming forward beam.

In the fading light I could see the milky gray surface of the river and a pair of yellow eyes as they slid back into the water like those of a stalking crocodile.

The Guivre was biding its time, waiting for my lights to fail.

Okay, Wallace, think! The eels probably chewed through the umbilical cord, so it's just a matter of minutes before the entire backpack fails.

The thought of being cast into total darkness with these predators was even more frightening to me than dying. I still had the explosives, but the weight of the Newt Suit made it impossible to toss the mini-bombs.

I realized I had to climb out of my protective armor.

Releasing the smaller hand-held light, I felt along my aluminum skin's waistline with both sets of pincers and removed the utility belt holding the charges. After a great struggle I managed to release the backpack's harness.

The heavy propeller assembly fell away from my shoulders and crashed behind me, the noise sending several of the Anguilla wriggling across the rocks.

Now I was down to one dull light.

With trembling hands, I forced open the snaps on the latches securing the two sections of the Newt Suit together.

Retracting my arms from the metal sleeves, I pushed up on the inside of my headgear. With a *hiss*, the upper torso of the dive suit gave way, separating from the lower half.

Sucking in a few breaths, I stood in the suit, shoulder-pressing the weight of the ADS's upper torso off my shoulders, then carefully laying it on the ground next to me in case I chose a hasty retreat.

Inhaling a dank breath of air, I climbed out of the lower half of the ADS, then snatched up my handheld light, scanning the perimeter.

The eels gurgled at me from the shadows, their bright eyes luminescent in my beam.

I was terrified and totally exposed. The air in the chamber was stale and acrid, making it almost impossible to breathe without coughing.

The light flickered and dimmed to half its remaining candlepower.

My blood seemed to chill within my veins.

The eels slithered toward me from the shadows.

I started choking uncontrollably, the chamber spinning in my head. Shining my handheld light on the broken backpack, I tore away a canister of air, holding it up to my face to breathe.

The Anguilla eels close to the water's edge scrambled for cover as the Guivre emerged from the river, its gruesome collection of teeth dripping lengths of saliva.

A thick coat of slime coated its head, mane, and serpent's neck, and in the dimming circle of light I saw the colors of the spectrum briefly shimmer.

Colors?

I inhaled deeply, confirming the heavy scent.

It was oil! And it was everywhere, dripping down from the ceiling, coating the river.

I searched the ground for the utility belt . . . *where the hell was it? There, beneath the upper portion of the Newt Suit!*

My light blinked off, and I desperately banged it, momentarily resuscitating the beam.

The monster's head rose higher, the creature using its forward pectoral fins to glide its snakelike torso from out of the stagnant waters, while the eels slithered out from the crags of rocks behind me!

I kicked bones and rock at one hissing eel as I tore a G-SHOK cylinder and cap from the belt. Snapping them together, I tossed the armed explosive at the stagnant pool of water, then ducked.

Wa-boosh!

A flash of white light, and then a wave of searing heat scorched my face as I was slammed backward against the rock face.

For a long moment I remained curled in a ball, my throbbing head ringing like a bell.

Get up, dipshit! Open your eyes!

I shook the cobwebs from my brain and sat up, choking on the thick air. Anguilla eels were darting this way and that, and through my blurred vision, I could see a few of their dark hides blazing in flames.

The pool of water was on fire, as was the ceiling, and the fissure above the collapsed section of tunnel on my far left belched blue flames.

The Guivre was gone, but I could see its telltale air bubbles and current as it glided underwater, moving toward the opposite shore.

The blaze began to extinguish, all but that one precious blue flame that burned along the ceiling above the dam of rubble. Somewhere high above the fractured geology was a broken pipeline, and it was leaking crude down into the aquifer, poisoning the lifeblood of the Great Glen and her largest inhabitant.

So much oil had poured into the aquifer that it was now seeping out of the passage and into Loch Ness. It had to be flushed out.

I knew what I had to do.

Tying the belt of explosives around my waist, I began climbing over piles of rocks, making my way quickly toward the eastern end of the chamber. There were animal bones everywhere, some of them fossilized, others still covered by clumps of meat and fur. I stumbled upon a rotting pile of rags and flesh, wedged between two large rocks, and I gagged at its stench.

"Oh, Jesus—"

The victim's face was ashen gray and purple, the remains of the body—twisted and broken. Massive teeth marks riddled the corpse, resembling black tarry holes the size of my fist. Both arms were gone, chewed down to the bone, and the legs had been taken just above the knees. The lower vertebrae of the spinal column protruded hideously out the back of the ebony-colored Italian silk shirt and matching Armani sports jacket, the corpse's cream-colored tie still knotted.

The stitched red monogram was clearly visible along the left hand sleeve: **J. S. C.**

John Cialino.

The remains of Johnny C.'s flesh was not bloated like a drowning victim; he had clearly died as a result of his attack.

The revelation that Angus had been telling the truth seemed to both sicken and invigorate me. I was the guilty party, not he. If there was a way out of this hellhole, then I had to find it, if only to prove my father's innocence.

I inhaled deeply, coughed, then dragged Cialino's corpse out from between the rocks.

The stench was overwhelming.

I hurried over the outcropping to the dam, my body trembling with adrenaline and fear. With Cialino's ghastly corpse tucked under my left arm, I reached out with my right, felt for a secure handhold, then stepped carefully out along the pile of boulders and debris that were blocking the underground river.

The going was treacherous, the rock slick with oil. Step by careful step, I made my way across the obstruction, praying the dying flames above my head would burn just a little bit longer. Hugging a boulder, I inched my right leg around some debris, searching for a foothold, when I slipped, my right hand grabbing blindly overhead, finding a cold, flat piece of metal.

I held on, then pulled myself to a more secure position. I had grabbed onto an iron bar, rusted and ancient, part of what looked like an immense gate buried beneath the rubble.

What was it doing here?

The cavern darkened. Looking over my shoulder, I caught sight of the last pockets of fire, simmering into smoke along the water.

Only the blue flame above my head illuminated the chamber.

Come on, Wallace, finish the job before you end up like Johnny C.

Reaching the dam's halfway point, I quickly set the remaining eleven explosives with three-minute fuses, then dropped each of the ticking cylinders into crevices of rubble and rock.

In my haste, I realized that I should have kept at least a few.

Too late . . . keep moving!

Continuing on, I half-slid, half-climbed over the remaining boulders with Johnny C.'s remains until I found myself looking down upon the opposite shoreline.

"Oh, hell . . ."

By the ceiling's flickering flame I could see two immense shadows. Conger eels, the saltwater relative of the Anguilla. The insane beasts, each well over two hundred pounds, hissed at me like cobras.

Another thirty seconds, maybe less. Get off the dam!

"Yah! Get outta here!" I grabbed a few stones and threw them at the predatory fish, chasing them back several feet.

Go!

Tossing Cialino's remains as far onto the shoreline as I could, I jumped down from the rubble, desperate to distance myself from the dam.

Too late.

My brain seemed to spin in my skull as multiple explosions detonated behind me like dominoes, igniting the darkness in brilliant orange flames. Shrapnel struck my back and head, and a concussion wave blasted me off my feet and into the black river.

The *booms* deadened underwater. For a moment I remained in this near-freezing environment, allowing the pain to subside, then remembering the Guivre, I kicked to the surface, gasping for air in the smoke-filled, flaming cavern, desperate to climb ashore.

As I tried to drag myself out of the water, all hell broke loose.

Rolling thunder roared through the chamber as seventy years and two hundred tons of debris collapsed upon itself in an avalanche of rock and water and flame. The aquifer's long-stagnant waters became a slowly moving river, and then the remains of the dam flushed free, and an ungodly current grabbed me, dragging me backwards into the raging abyss.

Helpless, I was swept away, tumbling underwater in the darkness, my arms thrashing, groping blindly for anything to grab hold of . . . when something grabbed *me*, impaling the left side of my body, and I dangled from its teeth like a kitten taken by the nape of its neck.

The Guivre!

I spun around against the blackness and lashed out at the beast, my right hand slipping between the iron bars of the ancient gate.

The current had pinned me against the grillwork, one of its bent spikes lancing my left hip and thigh. Though my right arm was free of the water, my left knee and arm were pinched between two iron slats. Try as I might, I could not gain enough leverage with my free hand to raise my head above the swiftly moving current.

Metal screeched underwater—I could feel the gate bending with the torrent, but still I could not release myself from its embrace.

Hold on, Zachary.

My chest was on fire now, my inflamed lungs demanding relief. Experience urged me to remain calm while my right foot and knee fought against the current, searching for a foothold to gain leverage . . . something . . . anything to lift myself higher.

But the river was timeless, and my muscles were lead.

I was drowning.

Again!

The mere thought was so humiliating . . . so exasperating—yet it filled me with a strange sense of relief, for I knew the monster could smell me and was closing in, and drowning was a far better way to die . . . better than Sir William Wallace, who had been drawn and quartered, better than Johnny C.

And so I opened my mouth and inhaled the acidic, bitter waters of Loch Ness, letting it take me.

My body convulsed as my mind shattered, my thoughts poisoned with dark, desperate images from my first drowning, intertwined with subliminal flashes of my second death in the Sargasso Sea.

My life was a Greek tragedy, and I laughed at the Grim Reaper as he circled me, for what was I to be scared of.

And then the pain and cold were shunted, and the visions washed away, replaced by my lifeless body, lying on a rocky shelf.

The image from my dreams.

Hold on, Zachary. Hold on . . . Zachary. Zachary. Zachary . . .

*   *   *

"Zachary!"

I opened my eyes. Belched up water. Gagged. Then heaved a breath of life.

I was staring into my father's face.

"Are ye a' right, son?"

I tried to speak but instead ejected a bellyful of icy water tainted with oil. Rolling over, I gagged and wretched some more.

"That's it, son, let it a' come oot o' ye. Ye're gonnae be fine. Christ knows ye've got mair lives than a cat. Still, if I were ye, I'd take up somethin' safer. Like skydiving. Or maybe alligator wrestlin'."

I sat up, my left side bleeding and sore from where the iron gate's spike had caught me. Above our heads, flames rolled along the ceiling like wisps of orange fog, casting the cavern in a surreal hellish glow.

I coughed and spit until I could speak. "How? How'd you find me? How'd you get out of jail?"

"All guid questions, but first . . . where's the monster?"

I shook my head and pointed. "The passage opened. It was in the water. Probably in the North Sea by now."

"No' this one." He aimed the powerful beam of his flashlight at the swiftly flowing river. "Where are ye, demon? Come oot an' show me yer yellow eyes. I want tae see them once mair afore I blast ye back tae hell."

"Dad, what are you doing?"

He smiled. "Dad? Ye never call me that."

"You never liked it."

"Now I do. I see ye found Johnny's remains."

"You were right. I'm sorry . . . I should have believed you."

"Save it." He turned and yelled, "Alban MacDonald, where are ye, auld man?"

"Back here!"

I looked behind my father, surprised to find the Crabbit, preoccupied with digging through piles of rubble along the southern wall.

"Alban, my son's hurt. Take him back through the access tunnel, I've business tae tend tae."

"So dae I. Take him yersel'."

"Damn ye, Crabbit . . . come on, laddie." Angus helped me to my feet, then pointed to a small hole set among debris along the far wall. "Crawl through that tunnel, it'll lead back tae a chasm an' a manual lift. Be quick aboot it, the air here's no' fit tae breathe."

"I'm not going without you."

The dark river belched, the ten-ton Guivre circling somewhere below, readying its next attack.

"Ha! I see ye, de'il, I kent ye couldnae leave!"

"It's an animal, dad, let it be. It's brain's been poisoned, can't you smell the oil? It's everywhere, seeping in from some busted pipeline above our heads."

"Aye. It's originatin' frae one o' Johnny's auld wells."

"You knew?"

"'Course. Bastard's been pollutin' the Great Glen for years. Been payin' off officials in Glasgow in order tae keep things quiet."

"And that's why you hit him?"

"Nah. I hit him 'cause he struck Theresa, an' that's no' acceptable, no' tae me. Didnae ken the dragon wis close by at the time, though I shouldae suspected it, wi' a' the dynamitin' they were daen' that day. Anyway, Johnny got his, now this freak o' nature'll get hers."

"Why?"

"Call it revenge. Now go, afore it surfaces."

Alban hurried over. "I need help, I've no' found it yet!"

"Probably buried among the rubble," Angus spat back.

"I need a' oor eyes tae find it."

"Take the lad, I'm no' movin'."

Alban grabbed my arm, dragging me back toward the southern wall as he mumbled incoherently. "It wis here, laddie, set within a crevice by this wall. Help me find it!"

"Find what? What're we looking for?"

"A casket . . . a silver casket, aboot the size o' a grapefruit. It wis set here, within this wall."

"What's so special about this casket?"

"It's no' the casket, lad, it's whit's inside . . . oor past an' future, a symbol that many have died for, a treasure that shall one day herald Scotland's freedom."

I was weak and in pain, and still quite frightened, yet the old fart was speaking to me in riddles. "A symbol? What symbol? What's down here that's so damn precious your secret society had to protect it with a monster?"

"It's the heart, laddie. The heart o' oor king, Robert the Bruce. It's the Braveheart!"

"The Braveheart?" I shook my head, then stopped, the pain causing me to suspect a concussion. "The Black Douglas tossed the Bruce's heart into battle long ago."

"Folklore," Angus called out. "The Black Douglas died in battle, but oor ain kinsman, Sir Adam, secreted the Braveheart back tae the Highlands. The Templar brought it doon here, so that any English who sought Scotland's Holiest o' Grails wid have tae face Satan's ain demons tae claim it."

MacDonald handed me his spare flashlight. "Search quickly, afore the Guivre returns tae feed upon yer faither!"

"She'll no' feed again, no' on my clan," Angus bellowed, moving to the edge of the river. Reaching into his pocket, he removed a shard of glass he'd found in Aldourie Castle. Steadying the light in his left hand, he sliced open his wrist, allowing the blood to drip into the water.

"I ken ye can smell that, dragon. Why no' come up for a wee taste, eh?"

Angus removed the two G-SHOK charges and fuses from his pocket, readying them in his free hand. "Come on up, Nessie. Come up an' taste this."

The bad air and dense smoke were getting to me, keeping me in fits of coughs. The fires had died out, the chamber dark, save for our lights, and I knew I had to leave soon.

Something burst forth from the river, jump-starting my pulse.

Angus wheeled around, shining his flashlight a hundred paces to the west. "Whit wis that?"

I left the wall, staggering back toward the river and the large object now floating slowly down stream. "It's okay," I called out, "it's just the life-support barrel from—

"—Angus!"

The river erupted behind my father, the wave washing him backwards as the monster's jaws snapped upon the air where he'd stood not a second earlier.

Through whiffs of smoke I saw Angus crawl toward his fallen light as the Guivre's entire eel-like form shot out of the water, its forward pectoral fins propelling its slime-covered girth along the rocky shoreline after my father.

From his back, Angus tossed his explosives just as the creature lashed out at him like a striking python. The twin concussion blasts missed the monster but reignited the ceiling, causing the creature to shirk away.

But only for the moment.

Angus tried to run, but the Guivre cut him off, encircling him with its enormous fifty-two-foot serpent's body. Yellow eyes, blinded from my own detonations, reflected orange flames as the demented creature inhaled the air, searching for her quarry.

Seconds counted and I had nothing, not a weapon, not a—

Whomp!

The heavy steel canister carrying the ADS generator smashed against the iron gate, drawing the monster's attention—

And mine.

Stuffing the flashlight into my back pocket, I dived into the bone-chilling water, allowing the current to sweep me toward the remains of the hanging iron gate and barrel. Kicking hard, I grabbed for the barrier, using its rusted metal bars as a ladder to pull myself out of the river.

I never saw the creature's head as it launched through the smoke and darkness, but I felt its impact as it glanced off the gate and bashed against rock.

The blow seemed to stun the beast, but it also knocked the barrel free, which was swept behind me into the darknes, followed by two-thousand-feet of umbilical cord.

Reaching down from my wobbly perch, I grabbed the line and began pulling it from the water like a madman, trying to locate its severed end before the barrel dragged the rest of the cord away.

My hands registered the decreased weight of the line, and I knew I was close.

"Son, look oot!"

I glanced up as the monster sprang blindly at me again—greeting its dagger-filled mouth with the sizzling end of the live wire, accompanied by several thousand volts of electricity.

Blue veins of current riddled the serpent's head, igniting its slimy oil-covered face. Injured and enraged, it reeled back and shook its head like a wet dog, unleashing gobs of putrid mucus.

The ancient gate groaned and I felt it give way beneath me. As it broke free from its rusted frame, I leaped to the rocky shoreline, the sparking end of the cord still clenched in my right hand.

"Zack!"

The umbilical suddenly went taut, its weight dragging me back toward the river.

I released the cord and looked up as the monster's tail swatted me through the thick air and into oblivion.

CHAPTER 35

I OPENED MY EYES, enveloped in blackness. Intense pain riddled my body. Blood oozed from my head and broken nose, dripping into my mouth. I spat out the warm liquid and struggled to sit up.

From the blue flames that still licked at the oil-drenched ceiling, I saw that I was lying in rubble, close to the tunnel's exit. Through heavy smoke and my dizziness I could just make out a pair of lights by the river's edge, the beams oscillating, then disappearing behind an enormous shadow.

It was the creature, its immense tail lashing to and fro, continuously blocking my view.

And then I saw my father and Alban. The beast had them cornered, their backs to the river.

I felt for the flashlight in my back pocket, then saw it lying in the rubble, its beam reflecting upon something shiny.

The Braveheart?

Reaching into the pile of rubble, I felt for the silver casket, extracting instead the hilt of a massive steel sword.

I focused my light upon the length of its rust-streaked blade and read my destiny.

*   *   *

The blinded Guivre snapped its jaws and inhaled the air, strings of thick ooze glistening from its fangs.

Angus pulled his older comrade to his feet. Whispered, "Alban, it cannae see, an' the smoke's ower thick for it tae pinpoint us. I'll distract it while ye find Zachary. Then the two of ye—"

"A Priest-Knight disnae leave his companion. I'll distract it, you find yer son."

The Guivre continued snapping at the dense air, its gargantuan body all the while slithering forward, driving them closer to the river.

"Bloody Crabbit . . . we're baith gonnae die."

"Willnae be the first time a MacDonald an' Wallace fell in combat."

They backed to the very edge of the river, its rushing waters licking at their heels.

I hurried through the darkness, my scent cloaked by the stench of the burning crude.

Angus turned to his left and saw me coming. Standing, he waved defiantly at the creature, trying to distract it. "Go on then, Nessie, ye dinnae frighten me! Finish me off if ye dare!"

The monster's jaws opened to strike, and so did I, plunging the ancient sword deep into the Guivre's soulless blind left eye, penetrating its diseased brain with my steel.

The creature seized, its body writhing in tight coils, its colossal head whipping upward hard against the ceiling. The impact shattered its skull and unleashed an avalanche of stalactites, while the ceiling's blue flame ignited the monster's oil-soaked hide into a bright orange conflagration.

The ceiling crumbled, the insane beast snapping blindly in every direction. Oil dripped into the Guivre's nostrils and the dragon snorted flames, while Angus and Alban and I huddled together behind a boulder.

The enraged beast's tail whipped over our heads, and the three of us took off running, heading for the chamber's exit. I pushed my father and Alban ahead of me, then paused to look back as the Guivre shrieked its final death cry and collapsed, belly-up, upon the rocky shoreline. The lifeless left eye was gushing dark blood, the sword still positioned deep in the wound. For a moment I thought about retrieving it, but the monster's tail was still flailing from side to side in convulsions.

And then I remembered Johnny's remains.

Hurrying to the river, I searched the bank, then spotted it near the aquifer's opening. As I grabbed the mutilated body by its jacket collar, the monster's convulsing tail flew over my head and landed in the river. Caught within the current, the Guivre's carcass fed slowly into the raging aquifer, nearly dragging me out to sea with it.

"Zachary!"

"Yeah, coming."

Hurrying back to the exit, I dropped on all fours and crawled through the tunnel, dragging John Cialino's remains behind me.

For fifteen minutes, the three of us crept forward on hands and knees, coughing and grunting until we reached the exit and fresh air. Silent moments passed as we lay back and breathed, our faces covered in sweat and carbon soot, my own in blood.

Angus finally reached over and slapped my knee, his piercing blue eyes now soft, glistening with tears of pride. "Dragonslayer, that's whit ye are. Never seen anythin' like it. Sir William an' Sir Adam, they'd baith be proud."

"Was it Adam's sword then?"

"Actually, it wis William's, at least accordin' tae my faither's translations o' Adam's diary. Maybe we should go back for it. Be worth its weight in gold."

"It's gone. Washed out to sea with the monster." I turned to Alban. "I tried to save her—"

He held up his hand, caught between coughs. "I'm indebted."

"We'll call it even," I whispered. Then I remembered. "Alban, the Braveheart?"

"Gone, too. Perhaps it's best. These days, we'd only commercialize it, chargin' people tae gaze upon it frae behind layers o' glass. Let it die wi' Nessie."

"Others may come searching."

"No' likely. The Templar own Aldourie Castle. We'll seal the shaft off soon enough."

Angus motioned to the lift. "Go on, the two o' ye, the weight's balanced for thirty stone. True can use yer help draggin' me an' Johnny's remains up after ye."

I helped Alban to his feet. We stepped onto the platform and tugged on the rope, which raised us easily up the shaft to the distant pinpoint of daylight.

My father watched us ascend, then crawled back into the tunnel.

CHAPTER 36

Raigmore Hospital,
Inverness

NEWS OF MY FATHER'S DARING ESCAPE had gone worldwide by the time the five of us emerged from Aldourie Castle into glorious daylight. Judge Hannam was furious, and many predicted Angus would be the first murderer to swing from a Scottish gallows since twenty-one-year-old Henry Burnett was hanged in Craiginches Prison on August 15, 1963, for shooting his lover's husband.

The irony was lost on no one.

*   *   *

The "announcement" that Angus would be arriving via ambulance at Raigmore Hospital within the hour to "prove his innocence" sent the press and sheriff's headquarters scurrying. By the time we turned onto the A9 highway, seven police cars and two helicopters had joined us. People were waving and honking their horns . . . the whole thing reminded me of O. J. Simpson's escapade in the white Ford Bronco.

Theresa Cialino was at the hospital, surrounded by reporters, when her cousin, James, drove our ambulance through the hospital entrance. We were immediately surrounded by a dozen heavily armed police officers and hordes of media, everyone moving into position as the ambulance's back doors were swung open.

I was the first one out, my head heavily bandaged, my nostrils filled with soot. Nurse Kasa helped my father down from the van, the police immediately shackling his wrists and ankles, as if he were going to escape from this throng.

And then, as the flashes flashed and the cameras whirled, the remains of John Cialino were removed from the ambulance on a gurney, and the lore of the Loch Ness Monster suddenly took on a whole new meaning.

The *Inverness Courier* would later pen the moment as the press conference of "the dead, a dead man walking, and the thrice dead man."

Theresa fainted and had to be carried into the hospital. Angus demanded to be released, threatening to sue the High Court. The judge ordered him to the cardiac unit and sent Johnny C.'s remains to the lab for a forensics evaluation.

It was a bizarre ending to a bizarre trial, one I would have enjoyed more had I not collapsed.

Rushed into the Emergency Room, I was placed on a ventilator and spent the next twenty-four hours in Intensive Care, suffering from carbon dioxide poisoning and a concussion.

*   *   *

I awoke with an all-too-familiar tube down my throat as Brandy entered my private room.

"Gosh, Zack, you look awful."

It was like bad déjà vu.

"Rar roo reaking rup rith ree?"

Brandy smacked me hard on top of my bandaged head.

"Oww."

"That's for tossin' me overboard, ye bastard. An' no, I'm no' breakin' up wi' ye, though I should, after all ye put me through."

"Rarry ree?"

"Marry ye? Is that how ye want tae ask me, wi' a bloody pipe shoved down yer throat? No, we'll wait 'til ye get out o' here, then ye can buy me a nice ring, get down on yer knees, an' ask me properly."

Brandy talked, and I listened. The ambulance driver, James Fox, had released a statement explaining that he had diverted from taking Angus to the hospital only because "the old man convinced me his son was in serious trouble." Both Fox and Nurse Kasa swore that they had found me unconscious on the eastern banks of Loch Ness with Johnny C.'s remains.

For my part, I claimed a loss of memory as to where the Guivre's cave actually was.

Forensics confirmed John Cialino's identity and his cause of death. The High Court of the Justiciary wasted little time in reversing its jury's decision, and Angus was now a free man . . . and a local hero. There was even talk about the Council hiring him as their official "Ambassador of Tourism."

I imagined Angus, dressed in his kilt, eating haggis. "Come tae Loch Ness, where the haggis is aye fresh, an' oor fish bite back."

That one brought a smile to my face.

A brush fire in the forest adjacent to Aldourie Castle had been traced to a broken pipeline owned by Cialino Oil. Scotland's EPA had shut down the leak, and a full investigation was under way.

Through tears of happiness, Brandy described how she and Alban had reconciled. She was staying with him at the lodge, and it was the first time she felt whole again since her childhood.

In truth, it was the first time I had felt whole again, too.

*   *   *

My father came by later the next day with copies of the *Inverness Courier*. His photo was featured on the front page, under the headlines:
VINDICATED!

"So, how're ye feelin', Dragonslayer?"

"My ribs and hip are still sore, otherwise not bad considering."

"Any mair o' thee awfy night terrors?"

"None so far."

"Good, I'm glad for that, son. As ye can read, I'm a free man, an' I've *you* tae thank." He extended his hand, but I refused to shake it. "Whit's wrong?"

"Lying here in bed, I've been doing a lot of thinking."

"Tyin' up a few loose ends, eh?"

"You might say that. Calum Forrest, for instance. Guess you were pretty upset when your best-friend's wife drowned last December. I searched through old issues of the *Inverness Courier* on my laptop, but there weren't any details."

Angus shrugged. "'Twis a terrible thing."

"Interesting that there were so many similar so-called drownings last winter. You'd think Sheriff Holmstrom might have done a better job investigating them, but then how could he, being a Black Knight and all. Guess I can thank him for misplacing all my samples, huh?"

"An interestin' theory."

"I'm still a bit confused about the Black Knights' mission, but it's obvious, despite your blood oath, that you wanted the monster dead, and I don't think it had anything to do with Calum's wife. When we were in the cavern, you claimed the Guivre had tasted human blood again. By *again*, who were you referring to?"

Angus made eye contact, his expression quite serious. "Yer grand-faither."

I sat up in bed. "Your father, Logan? Then he didn't drown?"

"No. He wis a Black Knight, jist like his faither an' aulder brother, an' jist like me, and he died in that hellhole on September 25, 1934. My uncle Liam wis wi' him, an' so wis I. I wis jist a wee laddie, six years auld, yet I can remember whit happened as if it were yesterday."

"What were you doing down here?"

"Lowerin' the iron gate, as we did the start o' each autumn. The gate wis set in place by Sir Adam an' the first Order o' the Black Knights, who were intent on usin' the demons tae guard the Bruce's heart, their sacred keepsake. I imagine these Guivres were a lot like their smaller Anguilla cousins, aye leavin' Loch Ness for the open sea when it got cold. Tae keep the big ones roond an' scare off the English, the Knights wid lower the gate at the end o' the summer, then raise it again each spring."

"And you continued the mission until the tunnel collapsed?"

"Aye. Happened in the winter o' '34, caused by the dynamitin' o' the A82, just as ye suspected . . . only my faiher an' uncle didnae ken it at the time. Whilst I waited in the mooth o' the cave, they went on tae raise the gate, an act they'd done dozens o' times wi'oot incident, their bright lights aye keepin' the creatures at a safe distance. Only this time, a young an' feisty female wis waitin'."

"Nessie."

"Aye. She wis queen of the Loch even then, an' irritated as all hell by the blastin' goin' on along the western bank. As I watched, she snatched yer grandfaither in her terrible jowls an' tore him to pieces, feedin' upon his flesh.

"My uncle dragged me away, but I wis shocked an' scared an' went through a' that *you* went through when ye were bitten, the night terrors, the fear. There were nae heid doctors tae see back then, so I swallowed my anger an' swore revenge. But I'd a'ready taken the blood oath o' the Black Knights, an' Uncle Liam made me swear on my faither's soul that I'd no' forsake the Order. A Wallace aye keeps his word, an' I kept my word, even after the demon tasted ye seventeen years ago."

"And then Calum's wife was killed."

"She wisnae the first, but after she wis taken, I went tae Alban, demandin' we kill the creature. He refused, an' threatened tae kick me oot o' the Order if I ever went public."

"Which you did, during the trial."

"I had tae. No' for my ain sake, but because I kent things wid get worse. Somethin' wis wrong in Loch Ness, that wis obvious, we jist didnae ken whit it wis. An' once that monster tasted human flesh again, I kent it wid continue its attacks, jist like it had after it feasted upon my faither. Mysterious drownin's durin' winter an' its eighteen hours o' night are a lot easier tae keep fraem public scrutiny than attacks durin' oor tourist season."

"And Theresa?"

"She's a close friend, nothin' mair. Her an' Johnny were havin' problems. He got a bit violent wi' her earlier that day, an' she turned tae me for help. So I went tae see him at the construction site. We had words, an' ye ken the rest. 'Course, I couldnae tell a' that in court, that widdae implicated Theresa, an' the poor lass's been through enough. So I claimed he owed me money, only Theresa sent me a payment after I'd been arrested."

"And I was your insurance policy, just in case the monster didn't reappear. You lied to me to get me here, then used me to prove Nessie really existed."

"A' that's true, but it's no' the real reason I brought ye hame." He looked away, facing the window. "God kens I've been a lousy faither tae ye, Zachary, but ye're still my son, an' I've missed ye terribly. An' I kent ye were sufferin' inside, too, jist like I had as a lad. After I received a call frae yer mum—"

"My mother called you?"

"Aye. Back in January. She telt me whit happened tae ye in the Sargasso Sea, an' everythin' yer psychiatrist had tae say aboot yer night terrors an' ye bein' feart o' the water, a' stemmin' frae whit happened back when ye was nine.

"Well, I blamed mysel' for that mess, as did you. But I also kent that the only way for ye ever tae be whole again was tae face yer inner demons. That meant comin' hame tae Loch Ness, but no way in hell were ye doin' that, no' wi'oot a fight anyway. When I wis arrested for Johnny's death, I kent the trial could entice ye hame, an' I kent if I goaded ye enough, the Wallace in ye wid come oot fightin'. An' boy wis I ever right. Ye went after that creature like Sherlock Holmes huntin' Moriarty. But I never intended ye tae face the monster alone, only tae prove it wis oot there."

"So you're saying the real reason you spoke up about the monster and left the Templar was to force me to conquer my fears?"

"As I live an' breathe."

"I don't believe you."

"No? Think aboot it, son. Yer mind wis hidin' the truth aboot the Loch frae ye for seventeen years. Puttin' ye up on the witness stand, revealin' yer battle scars tae the world . . . I had tae jolt that brain o' yers but good. Hell, ye've spent the last seventeen years deceivin' yerself."

I lay back on my pillows, struggling with the revelation.

"Put yer mind tae it, it'll come." Angus bent and kissed me on the forehead. "I've got tae go, I've an interview wi' a Hollywood agent in an hour, but we'll see each other soon enough. Oh, I almost forgot."

He reached into his jacket pocket, then tossed me a folded document. "That's your share o' oor land. You and Maxie each own thirty-three percent. Ye get the rest o' whit's mine after I croak."

"Land? I thought you sold the land to Johnny C.?"

"Leased it. I'd never sell. That land's been in oor family since William Wallace wis jist a lad. At least now we'll start makin' some money frae it, eh?"

"But Dad!"

"Butts are for crappin', son." Angus waved from the hall, his back to me as he paused to eye a pretty blond nurse. "See ye later, Dragonslayer."

CHAPTER 37

Inverness

TWO MORE DAYS PASSED before I was released. The nurse wheeled me out a side exit, just in case any more reporters were still staking out Raigmore Hospital. Brandy was waiting there for me, seated on a new Harley-Davidson, a gift from the local dealership. She was now doing their television commercials.

"You look pretty sexy sitting on that hog."

"Accordin' tae the ads, the vibrations make me horny. Get oot o' that wheelchair and climb on, I'm drivin."

I slid behind her and we kissed, then she gunned the engine and accelerated down the driveway.

*   *   *

The Great Glen was aglow in a burnt-orange sunset by the time we arrived at Aldourie Castle.

"Brandy, what're we doing back here?"

"Loose ends, as ye say." She climbed off the motorcycle, and I followed her into the ancient mansion.

The study had been swept clean, and there were lit candles everywhere.

"This is where you wanted to make love? You're a spooky chick, you know that."

She kissed me, then led me to the fireplace. "There'll be plenty o' time for lovemakin', Zachary Wallace. First, there's some family business tae attend tae."

The back wall of the fireplace pivoted quietly upon its recently oiled hinges, revealing the dumbwaiter.

"Brandy—"

"Go on. I'll be here when ye're through."

I looked at her, uneasy, then stepped onto the platform and lowered myself down the dark shaft.

*   *   *

It wasn't until I reached bottom that I could see the torches. They'd been fixed to the cavern walls, illuminating a corridor that led away from the aquifer's access tunnel, down a different section of the cave.

I followed the lights, then rounded a corner and entered a torch-lit chamber.

There were two dozen Templar present, maybe more, all cloaked in Black hoods and tunics. In silence, they encircled me, and then the leader stepped forward, brandishing his gold sword.

"Zachary Adam Wallace," Alban MacDonald said, his voice muffled behind his hood, "are ye here of your own free will?"

"I am."

"Wi' this blood oath, dae ye swear allegiance tae the Order o' the Knight?"

"I do."

"Brethren o' the Templar, are there any objections tae acceptin' this novice intae the Order?"

None responded.

Reaching out, he took my right hand, then opened my flesh with a brush of his blade.

Alban signaled me to kneel, then recited Psalm 133. "Arise, Sir Zachary, for as o' this day an' forever mair, ye are a Templar Knight. Sir Angus?"

My father stepped forward, his face remaining cloaked. From his tunic he removed a silver casket, set on a braided gold chain. Holding it up to the light, he translated the Latin inscription aloud.

"The Bruce is Scotland, an' Scotland the Bruce. Protect the Braveheart, for freedom's sake . . . the coven o' the Black Knights made."

Angus placed the casket's necklace around my neck, and then I followed the procession to a small alcove.

Alban pressed on a section of rock, which pivoted, revealing a two-by-three-foot hiding place, its walls made of new brick and mortar, lined in silk.

Removing the Braveheart from around my neck, I placed it in its new resting place.

Alban muttered a prayer in Latin, then sealed the camouflaged coffin.

And then, one by one, the Black Knights revealed themselves to me as they shook my still-bleeding hand.

There was Calum Forest and Sheriff Holmstrom, and old man Stewart, my history teacher in Grammar School. True gave me a hearty bear-hug, and I was shocked to see Judge Hannam, who said, "Welcome hame, lad. Now dae us both a favor an' keep yer auld man oot o' my courtroom."

The Crabbit was last in line. He shook my hand in both of his, then inspected my bleeding palm. "I've learned that time can heal a' wounds, Zachary, even history's bloodiest affairs. One day soon, Scotland will achieve her true independence, an' on that day, yours an' mine will present the Braveheart tae her people. Until then, guard its secret well."

"Yes, sir."

"So, then, I understand ye asked my daughter for her hand."

"Stop pressurin' the boy, Crabbit," Angus bellowed, bulldozing his way into our conversation. "It's no' like he knocked her up!"

It took both True and I to separate them.

I guess some wounds take longer to heal than others.

*   *   *

Angus and I were the last pair to ascend.

"I take it Alban decided to reinstate you after you located the Braveheart?"

"I'm sure it influenced his decision. But it wis his idea tae welcome ye intae the Order, one I embraced."

As we approached the top of the shaft, the light from the study shone on my face.

Angus noticed my perturbed expression. "Wis there another loose end ye needed tyin'?"

"Just one. You knew Johnny C. had been bribing the local EPA officials, just like you knew it was the dynamiting at his resort that was driving the creature mad."

"So?"

"So, the Sargasso Sea incident happened back in January, which means you knew about my night terrors a good month before you confronted Cialino at Urquhart Castle."

"Whit's yer point?"

"Was it really an accident, or did you condition the monster with bait so it would be in the bay the evening you struck Johnny C.?"

"Condition the monster? Whit a clever idea. Wish I'd thought o' that." He gave me a wink, then stepped off the dumbwaiter into the fireplace where Brandy was waiting. "He's a' yours, lass. See if ye can get him tae relax a bit an' start enjoyin' his life. The laddie thinks way too much."

He waved, then strolled out the front door to the castle driveway, where Theresa Cialino was waiting for him in her Porsche.

It follows that any being, if it vary however slightly in any manner profitable to itself, under the complex and sometimes varying conditions of life, will have a better chance of surviving, and thus be Naturally Selected.

—Charles Darwin, *The Origin of Species,* 1859

Evolution is not "of a very mystical nature." It depends on accidents. In numerous species these accidents happen often enough to give rise to statistical certainty.

—J. B. S. Haldane, *A Dialectical Account of Evolution,* 1937

Science is not "show and tell." As researchers, we should never base our conclusions on the iceberg's visible tip, nor on man's limited ability to access Nature. If an undiscovered species exists and we have yet to see it, it still exists. For her part, Nature has done her best to keep us away from her depths, be this the cold, peat-infested abyss of Loch Ness or the uncharted waters of the Mariana Trench. Only after we create the means of access shall the mysteries be unraveled. Until then, any conclusions we draw remain unproven.

—Zachary Wallace, Marine Biologist
Loch Ness: A New Theory, Scripps, 1999 (unpublished)

**Sargasso Sea
Five months later**

AND SO MY TALE ENDS, only now I've come full circle, returning once more to this dreadful Sargasso Sea. Brandy's with me this time, and yes, we're married, with a child on the way.

The night terrors? A distant memory.

Brandy and I stood together on deck, hand in hand, as the crew of the research vessel, *Manhattanville,* lowered our remotely operated vehicle over the side. On-board the unmanned submersible were cameras, sonar, and my latest lure, one inspired by a long-forgotten childhood memory.

National Geographic's cameras were rolling, documenting what we hoped would be the first live shots of a species I had dubbed, *Anguilla giganticusnessensis.*

Never shy around a camera, Brandy flashed them her swollen belly, causing me to laugh.

I laugh a lot these days.

An hour later, the last purple blemish of sun crept below the western horizon, just as the ROV arrived at its preprogrammed depth of ten thousand feet. From my master controls I switched the robot's lights from white to red before engaging my "Nessie lure."

The sounds of feeding schools of salmon pumped throughout the deep.

Twenty-seven minutes later, sonar registered our first incoming signal.

"It's a biologic," called out John Beardon, our master technician. "Range just over two kilometers. Speed at seventeen knots. Whatever they are, they're closing fast."

"Put 'em on speaker," I said.

Blee-bloop . . . Blee-bloop . . . Blee-bloop . . . Blee-bloop . . .

Moments later they arrived—five of them in all, juveniles, each still over twenty feet. Their yellow eyes appeared orange and luminescent in the ROV's red lights as they circled the robot, their serpentlike bodies moving gracefully and in sync with one another.

"Standing by with the transmitter dart," I said for the sake of the camera crew.

Brandy pointed out one of the larger animals on the monitor, probably a female. I waited until she circled closer, took aim, then, using the control stick in my right hand, shot her with the homing dart.

The big female barely noticed.

The creatures circled the robot for several more minutes, then left. None ever attacked the lure.

Cody Saults, the documentary director from our first adventure, approached to hound me with more of his questions. "Congratulations, Dr. Wallace, you've done it again. How soon before we know if these creatures will migrate back into Loch Ness?"

"Could be next spring, could be never. Just because the passage's been reopened guarantees nothing. Our hope is that the homing device will allow us to track the creatures and learn more about their species."

"And the monster you faced last August? How big did you say she—"

"I think that's enough left-brain thinkin' for one day," interrupted Brandy. "The good doctor's promised tae rub my achin' back. Did ye know babies are born wi'out kneecaps?"

"Uh, right. Just one last question! Do you ever see a day when the paying public will be able to descend in cages and observe these magnificent monsters in the wild?"

"You know," I said, allowing Brandy to lead me below, "that's a question you really ought to ask my dad."

For updates about ongoing research at Loch Ness, educational links and tours, movie previews, and to enter a Reader Contest to win an all-expense paid vacation to Scotland go to: www.TheLoch.com

To learn more about the Scottish Highlands, see photos, or to plan a vacation, we recommend these sites: www.VisitScotland.com and www.ToScotland.com

CairnGorm Mountain Railway, by Aviemore
Web: www.cairngormmountain.com
Email: info@cairngormmountain.com

Speyside Wildlife, by Aviemore
Web: www.speysidewildlife.co.uk
Email: enquiries@speysidewildlife.co.uk

Highland Wildlife Park, Kincraig
Web: www.highlandwildlifepark.org
Email: info@highlandwildlifepark.org

Loch Ness 2000 Exhibition Centre, Drumnadrochit
Web: www.loch-ness-scotland.com
Email: info@loch-ness-scotland.com

National Trust for Scotland (Culloden Battlefield and Inverewe Garden)
Web: www.nts.org.uk
Email: information@nts.org.uk

Jacobite Cruises, Inverness
Web: www.jacobite.co.uk
Email: info@jacobite.co.uk

Discover Loch Ness, Inverness & Loch Ness
Web: www.discoverlochness.com
Email: tony@harmsworth.com

Scottish Clans and Castles Ltd, Nairn
Web: www.clansandcastles.com
Email: alastair@clansandcastles.com

The Castle & Gardens of Mey, nr Thurso
Web: www.castleofmey.org.uk
Email: castleofmey@totalise.co.uk

Hotels

Drumnadrochit Hotel, Drumnadrochit
Web: www.loch-ness-scotland.com
Email: info@loch-ness-scotland.com

Loch Ness Lodge Hotels Ltd, Drumnadrochit
Web: www.lochness-hotel.com
Email: info@lochness-hotel.com

The Boat Hotel, Boat of Garten
Web: www.boathotel.co.uk
Email: holidays@boathotel.co.uk

The Waterside, Inverness
Web: www.thewatersideinverness.com
Email: info@thewatersideinverness.com

Muckrach Lodge, Dulnain Bridge
Web: www.muckrach.co.uk
Email: info@muckrach.co.uk

Claymore House Hotel, Nairn
Web: www.claymorehousehotel.com
Email: claymorehousehotel.com

The Columba Hotel, Inverness
Web: www.crerarhotels.com
Email: thecolumba@crerarhotels.com

Rental Car

Sharps Reliable Wrecks, Inverness
Web: www.sharpsreliablewrecks.co.uk
Email: enquiries@sharpsreliablewrecks.co.uk

THE SHELL GAME

The following work of fiction becomes
nonfiction in the year 2012.

BY THEN, IT WILL BE TOO LATE . . .

Change is avalanching upon our heads, and most people are
grotesquely unprepared to cope with it.

—Alvin Toffler, *Future Shock*

FRANKLY, I HOPE this scares the hell out of you.

It frightens me and I've researched it, consulted experts, and
prayed about it. I've denied it, tried to ignore it, dreamt about it, then
forced myself to review it over and again until finally I accepted it to
be true.

That's what you do with a death sentence.

The first moments when mortality hits you like a ton of bricks are
the hardest to swallow. "How bad is it? Can you operate? What about
chemo? Well, Jesus, doc, what the hell *can* you do?"

At some point, through tears and the tightness in your chest you
expel the words you never imagined having to ask: "How long?"

The doctor's answer is hard to hear, maybe harder than the death
sentence itself, because even if he's wrong, even if he's off by a week
or a month or even a year, it doesn't really matter—you know your
clock is ticking.

Of course it's always been ticking; it's been ticking backwards ever
since birth. We're born in an instant and die in an instant, our life
those precious moments in between, and no one gets out alive.

When it comes to mortality, being human is both a blessing and
curse. Aware of death, we're forced to try to process something we
can never really comprehend. The first stage of coping with death is
denial, a stage you'll be entering into momentarily. This will progress
to blame, then anger. You'll punch the walls, kick the dog, and curse
God, asking, "why me?"

Eventually you'll make peace with God, because you'll need him
now more than ever. If you're a fighter, you'll fight for every moment.

And that's what I want you to do—fight, because the clock is
ticking backwards and the bells are tolling, only they're tolling for you!

And for your children, your parents and friends, and every loved one and acquaintance . . . every human being you know and might know, and those you will never get to know. There are six billion of us on this planet, and soon—very soon—every one of us save an unknown few are going to die.

To most of you, it will appear to happen without warning, as sudden as the tsunami that struck Indonesia the day after Christmas, 2004. One big wave, a "big rollover." At first you won't know what happened, then slowly. . .slowly and painfully, the realization will kick in that the chaos that surrounds you won't be going away, that the food left in your refrigerator and on your shelves won't last very long, that you and your family are going to starve to death.

Or freeze.

Or be incinerated by a weapon whose impact you'll never hear.

Or succumb to a virus you'll never feel.

Shooting the messenger won't help. Call me a liar, repute my warnings, curse my existence—it won't change a damn thing. Civilization is driving itself off a cliff, and you're just too busy micromanaging your life to see it happening. Open your eyes. It's already begun, the opening moves played out as if upon a great political chessboard:

The 1973 oil crisis—a feint that caught our attention.

The Reagan years—a shift from defense to offense.

Saddam's invasion of Kuwait—the manipulation of a pawn.

Saddam remaining in power—a retreat and reinforcement to control the center board.

The events of 9/11—the sacrifice of a noble knight to expose the queen.

The invasion of Afghanistan . . .

The conquest of Iraq . . .

The attempted coup against Venezuela's leader, Hugo Chavez . . .

The re-election of a President.

The board's in play, and when the final piece falls, everybody loses. I'll be dead before then, and yet the cancer that riddles my body's been a blessing in disguise. Death's cold hand has given me a newfound strength and insight to set in motion my own little series of events that might stave off some of the impending doom, and perhaps save my soul.

What I call the "big rollover" is oil, specifically how the world powers react when supply no longer meets demand.

Doesn't sound like a doomsday scenario?

Look closer.

Oil affects all aspects of our lives. It runs our transportation system: our cars, planes, boats, and trains. Without it we can no longer harvest food for the masses, fertilize our crops, or just as important, bring the goods to market. Oil provides the electricity that heats and cools our homes. It mobilizes our economy—and our military.

Ah . . . the military.

Access to oil on the battlefield often determines the outcome of war. It's been said a drop of oil is worth a drop of blood.

As you read these words, blood is already spilling, and it's going to get a whole lot worse. Oil is society's addiction, and when the lights go out and there's no food to feed Junior, you're not going to care how the cow gets slaughtered, or whether another "insurgent" city got bombed.

I know these things because I was there, working indiscreetly in the backrooms of democracy, where the public is barred and the lies begin. I learned the ropes during the glory days of Reagan, and cut my teeth securing the presidency for George Herbert Walker Bush. I plotted with the neo-cons during the Clinton years, awakening in November of 2000 when we pulled the strings that helped take back the White House. I reveled in the shadows of real power and reaped the rewards I helped sow, never once looking in the rearview mirror, only ahead at the new world we'd convinced ourselves needed creating.

It was cancer that finally opened my eyes, forcing me to look objectively at a future I helped metastasize.

For me it's too late. For my children, my loved ones . . . for you, I toll these warning bells.

The tsunami's coming, it's already on its way!

And you're asleep on the beach.

CHAPTER 1

If it is desirable to alter the life of an entire people,
is there any means more efficient than war . . .

—Carnegie Endowment for International Peace, 1909

December 22, 2010
Tavern on the Green, New York City

THE DINING ROOM IS ALIVE, its heated air recirculating an aroma of lobster bisque and filet mignon, its clothed tables spilling over with patrons bundled in sweaters, feeding among a sea of overcoats and parcels, fine paintings and chandeliers. Frosted windows glitter with holiday lights, everything multiplied in a frenzy of etched glass and mirrors.

Ace Futrell weaves past waiters the way he used to slip 300-pound defensive ends as he makes his way through a twisting hall of mirrors into the Chestnut Room, the paneled dining area one of three looking out onto a central garden.

Kelli Doyle is seated alone at a table for two, staring at her reflection in a large hourglass clock. The remains of her blonde hair, once thick and shoulder length, are tucked beneath a matching wig, set in a tight ponytail.

"Hey, stranger."

No response.

"Kel?"

The frail forty-six-year-old turns, smiles. "Hey, you." She stands, half-falling into her husband's arms. "You were gone too long."

"I know. But I'm home for three weeks. So tell, what did Dr. Eastburn say?"

Her eyes glisten as she beams a smile. "No more chemo. I'm officially in remission."

Ace hugs her again, easing back as he feels her ribs caving beneath his grip. Kelli's three year battle has taken an emotional toll on his psyche, each day lived with uncertainty, every joy hollow.

"Ace, honey, you okay?"

He pulls away, Kelli's thick wool sweater leaving fuzz against his five-o'clock shadow. "Am I okay? You just gave me the best Christmas gift I could ever ask for."

"Sit down, there's more." She reaches into her purse, pulls out an envelope, and places it on the table. "Merry Christmas."

Wiping a stray tear, he removes his overcoat and pulls his chair close to hers. "What's this?"

"Open it."

Ace peels back the flap and stares at the tickets. "A cruise?"

"To the Caymans. Just the two of us. My mother said she'd watch the kids."

"Can we afford this?"

"It was a gift. All expenses paid."

His expression darkens. "Paid by who? Your Swift Boat pals? That lieutenant governor from Alaska; the one always sending flowers?"

"Garry Archer?" She smiles. "Ace Futrell, are you jealous?"

He leans forward, dead-serious. "No games, Kel. Who else in your little circle of conspirators knows about my work?"

"No one. God, what's wrong with you. I've never seen you so paranoid."

"Yeah, well the world's spinning faster these days, and. . . just forget it."

"No, tell me. Maybe I can help."

"I don't. . . I can't accept your help. You'll help me right into an indictment."

She takes his hand. "Tell me."

Momentarily pacified, he steals a quick glance around the room. Lowers his voice. "Senator Groves has his people investigating OPECs latest production numbers. They aren't jiving with petroleum figures he's getting directly from his contacts in Iraq."

"Well, no shit. So how's that affect you?"

He grimaces sarcastically. "Gee, I don't know, I'm only in-charge of compiling data for the World Oil Report, or did you forget how we met?"

She smiles. "We met in college, I seduced you for the last report."

"This isn't a joke. The House Dems are pressuring PetroConsultants for access to my team's raw data. If Groves gets what he wants, he'll put two and two together and—"

"And what? Ace, the trail's a mile long and a decade old and the Dems don't have enough votes to muster legislation for a lunch voucher, let alone make a move against the Department of Energy. The draft's the issue they're circling their wagons around, not oil. But . . ."

"But what?"

"Maybe I should send word to Groves to subpoena me? That'll send the neo-cons shitting in their skivvies."

"You're joking, right?"

"Do I look like I'm joking? I'm sick of these bastards and their take-no-prisoners attitude. They need to be brought down a few pegs."

Ace's face drops. "Who are you, and what did you do with my wife?"

"We both know something has to change. Imagine what would happen if both of us went public."

"Whoa!" He leans forward, his voice a mere whisper. "You survive cancer, now you think you can take on the world?"

"We could do it, Ace. There's still time to galvanize the left before the 2012 primaries. We could help derail these guys, get them out of the White House before the train crashes."

"Stop! Look, I don't know where this is coming from, but it's not going to happen—"

"Ace—"

"Kel, you're not thinking anything through. For starters, IHS Energy runs PetroConsultants, and they'd have me fired within minutes of our first press conference, with ten of their experts refuting my testimony. Second, the moment we come out, we'll get targeted by the machine as 'hostile.' You more than anyone else should know what that means. It'll be a media blitzkrieg, our credibility shot to hell, with the public being told what to think before they can even digest the information."

She squeezes her husband's hand. "And if we do nothing? You and I both know the big rollover's not a matter of if, but when. Imagine the worst-case scenario. Can you live with that? And don't give me some bullshit about chaos theory. We both know how this turns out."

"I'm just the messenger, Kel. Not the hero."

"Situations make heroes." She kisses his hand.

"If you're trying to get laid, you can cut it out. I'm a sure thing."

"I remember the first time I saw you play football. It was in your junior year, against Miami. You were down ten points late in the game, and the Hurricane defense was massacring you. Keller was hurt, the rest of your wideouts couldn't get open to save their lives, and your o-line had nothing left in the tank. Sitting in the stands with my friends, I kept thinking, 'This quarterback might as well forget about winning, he'll be lucky just to survive. Still, every time they sacked you, you kept getting up, trying to rally the troops."

"Kel . . ."

"It was third and long, the pocket was collapsing on you, then suddenly, 'Boom!' You take off running. . . fifty-two yards, first down! Another run and you pick up fifteen more. Then a completion to . . . what was that tight end's name?"

"Tet. Mark Tetreault."

"Right, all the way down to the goal line. Sneak it over, and the crowd's back into the game. Suddenly our defense sees a chance, and they rise to the occasion. Three and out, and you've got the ball again. You brought us back from the dead, Ace. You gave us hope."

"That was twenty years ago."

"Don't underestimate hope, my dear. It's kept me alive."

"Enough with the head games. This isn't football, it's life and death. You start mouthing off about what we know, and there'll be guns aimed at us . . . and those will just be from the American side of the equation! Right now, all I want is for us to be together. Once I submit my report, I'm done with the oil industry."

"You're kidding?"

"Nope. Your disease stole the last three years of our lives, I don't want anything to jeopardize the rest of our time together."

"Which is exactly why—"

"I said no."

They pull away from one another as the waiter interrupts, "Good evening, sir. Something to drink?"

"A vodka, straight up."

"Madam?"

"I'm fine."

Kelli waits until he leaves. "It's okay to be scared, but I'm part of the machine. Don't forget, I know where the bodies are buried. If something happens . . ."

"We're not doing it, Kel, end of story."

"No, I'll tell you how the story ends. Things are going to happen. Bad things. Nine-eleven kind of things, only on a different level. You want some real insider shit? The Pentagon's collecting evidence about OPEC funding terrorists. The House of Saud's already planning their exit strategies, moving money into what they think are untraceable accounts. By next summer Riyadh will fall . . ."

"Jesus."

"Yeah, only Jesus won't be saving us, and he sure as shit won't be greeting us at the pearly gates, not with these neo-cons calling the shots behind the velvet curtain. What we define as democracy our enemies see as hegemony, and our actions are fueling a new band of well-connected, well-funded Islamic extremists. Once we take over the Saudi fields, and we will, Russia and China will give these assholes everything they want, including biological and nuclear weapons. The next 9/11 is the opening volley of World War III. So you tell me, Ace.

Should we stay on the sidelines and get our asses kicked or get in the game while we still have a shot at surviving?"

*   *   *

An hour later they're outside, breathing in the cold winter air. The appetizer of conversation had turned their meal into a chore, and barely a word had been spoken during the main course.

Ace raised his arm to hail a taxi.

"Ace, let's walk. Please?"

They head north, Central Park on their right, the night alive with Manhattan traffic and festival lights.

"Ace, I'm sorry I ruined our evening. It's just . . . I've been thinking about things."

"I can see that."

"It's different for me, you know, being a parent."

"Don't even go there. You were pregnant with Charlie's kids while you were doing Karl's dirty work. And for the record, I've always treated Chandra, Sierra, and Kenny like my own."

"You're right. You've been a great father to them. I only wish I'd given you a son."

"It's not like it didn't come up a million times."

"Hindsight's twenty-twenty. My career took precedence. I should have married you first."

"You're a Republican, Kel. You went for the money."

"Stop." She blocks his way. "No more cheap shots, okay? Let's just be together tonight, we'll sort the rest out in the morning."

Ace sees the urgency in her eyes. "Okay. No more fighting."

She points across the street, to the northwest corner of Seventy-second Street. "The Dakota Building. That's where John Lennon was shot. Let's walk in the park, I want to see the Strawberry Fields Memorial."

Before he can object, she's leading him eastward through Central Park. They follow a narrow path that opens onto a clearing and a garden, made barren by the cold. A mosaic composed of inlaid stones from all over the world lies before them, a tribute to the late musician and peace activist. The word *Imagine* is visible in the moonlight.

Two women are leaving flowers, setting them among others that have accumulated since the last anniversary of Lennon's death, only weeks ago. The women nod to Ace and Kelli, and head back up the path.

Ace stares at the memorial. "I remember the day he died. I was working in Houston. I drove out to the fields and cried like a baby."

Kelli nods. "He had the right idea."

"Just not the right political strategist, huh?"

She ignores the barb. "What do you think Lennon would do if he were alive today? Do you think he'd sit tight? Move to Montana?"

"No. He'd probably throw a concert to make people aware. Organize a political march or something."

"You think it'd make a difference?"

He shakes his head. "Maybe against Nixon, not with these guys. Their roots are too deep. The only way we change course now is with a complete house cleaning. A radical candidate preaching radical change."

"Agreed." She moves closer and whispers, "It's the fourth quarter of the Superbowl and we're losing. You can do it again, Ace. I'll show you how."

He starts to reply when shadows move, catching his eye.

The man is tall, at least six-foot-six. Long and lean. Dressed in a dark raincoat, hands buried deep in his pockets. His eyes and heavy brows are just visible beneath the wool Giants ski cap.

Ace's scalp tingles as he approaches. A whiff of Polo aftershave arrives first, followed by words that glide over a trace of British accent. "Never was much of a Beatles fan. Stones were more my liking."

A spark of light, a double *whooft*, and sound is silenced in the crisp December air.

Time ticks backward as Kelli's cold hand slips from Ace's grip.

He catches her as she goes down, his mind racing to catch up with the moment.

The stranger is gone.

His right hand at Kelli's back is warmed by a pool of blood.

Blood darkens her ivory wool sweater and gurgles in her throat as she fights to form her last words—

—dying in the attempt.

The final heartbeat.

The end of a life lived.

Ace gags. He looks away, then back again, unable to comprehend what has just happened, what is still happening.

His wife—dead in his arms.

His insides rage.

His reality explodes.

Ace shatters the night with a guttural yell, screaming rebuttals to the heavens, refusing to accept God's will, protesting, raging, his soul lost, his existence plunging against his will into a maelstrom of insanity.

For Ace Futrell, the tsunami has struck. The world as he knew it is gone—

—never to be the same again.

A native of Philadelphia, Steve Alten earned a bachelor's degree from Penn State, a master's from the University of Delaware, and a doctorate from Temple University. He is author of the best-selling *MEG* series, *Domain* series, and *Goliath*. Steve now resides in South Florida.